John Masters was born in Calcutta in 1914. Educated at Wellington and Sandhurst, he returned to India in 1934 to join the 4th Prince of Wales's Own Gurkha Rifles. In 1944 he commanded a brigade of General Wingate's Chindits in Burma, and later fought with the 19th Indian Division at the capture of Mandalay.

Masters retired from the Army in 1948 as a lieutenant colonel with the DSO and OBE. He went to America and turned to writing. Several short stories were succeeded by *Nightrunners of Bengal*, the first of an outstanding series of novels set in British India. His most recent books are *Now, God be Thanked*, *Heart of War* and *By the Green of the Spring* which formed his highly acclaimed trilogy of the Great War, *Loss of Eden*, and *Man of War*, also available in Sphere Books. John Masters died in 1983 in New Mexico.

Fandango Rock

JOHN MASTERS

SPHERE BOOKS LIMITED
London and Sydney

First published in Great Britain by Michael Joseph Ltd 1959
Copyright © Bengal Rockland Inc. 1959
Published by Sphere Books Ltd 1976
30–32 Gray's Inn Road, London WC1X 8JL
Reprinted 1976, 1977, 1980, 1981, 1984 (twice)

TRADE
MARK

Set in Linotype Plantin

Printed and bound in Great Britain by
Collins, Glasgow

FANDANGO ROCK

is gratefully dedicated by the Author and the
Typist to their collaborators in the
exacting arts of writing and
friendship

KEITH
and
EMILY JENNISON

FOREWORD

This book is a work of fiction and no reference is intended in it to any person living or dead, except that a few historical characters are mentioned. In the nature of such a book as this, dealing with present problems in a real country, there can be no substitute for such personages as 'The U.S. Ambassador to Madrid', 'the general commanding the Sixteenth U.S. Air Force', etc. It is therefore specially necessary to emphasize that the characters filling such roles in the book are imaginary, and are not remotely based on the actual holders. All U.S.A.F. units in Medina Lejo are of course imaginary, as is Medina itself and the base there. (It might be noted that there are in fact no B-52s stationed at Spanish bases.)

Finally, for their advice, I record here my gratitude to Don Luis Ariño of Zanagoza, and to Kenneth Tynan.

J.M.

CONTENTS

Book One

FANDANGO

CHAPTER 1

Colonel Lindquist's voice was quiet on the intercom, quiet but clear, the way it was on the ground. 'It works. Three minutes and forty-seven seconds that time. We might as well head back now, Dave.'

The B-52 began to wheel slowly against the sun. A few moments later Captain Bill Lockman, in the co-pilot's seat, knew that the colonel had come forward to join them. His voice was suddenly tired – 'Rough mission.'

'They're all hairy,' the pilot said. 'I wouldn't like to do what we've been doing with the bug live.'

The colonel said, 'Nor would I. But someone'll have to before the idea is really checked out.'

'Do you think it's worth it, sir?'

'I don't know. We've got a lot of slide-rule work to do on the ground before I even report it to SAC as a possibility. And even then it will only apply, probably, to the 52s at Medina. It won't work for the 47s and it isn't necessary, yet, for 52s based Stateside. For us . . . well, we're different all the way round . . .'

His voice trailed off into silence. Bill shifted painfully in his seat. Different all the way around. That was about it. A B-52 wing of Strategic Air Command stationed in Spain, when all the rest were B-47s; with a squadron of F-104 fighters on the base under the colonel's command, and all kinds of experiments going on that even the bomber Select Crews didn't know about; and rumours that soon the 104s were going to be replaced by something much, much faster and much, much smaller. And outside all that the sense of difference between the rest of the Air Force and SAC – always ready, always on the front line, each man knowing that the ground on which he stood was zeroed in by a Russian ICBM. And outside that the difference between the Air Force and the other services; and beyond – the civilian world, and children and girls; and then the Span-

11

iards among whom they lived, far, far different again; and then more foreigners ... And there was the loom of the land of Spain, faint and dark across the horizon, at the level of his eyes, and he 55,000 feet above the Atlantic Ocean.

Soon they crossed the coast, just south of San Sebastián, and Bill reached for his descent-before-landing check list.

The colonel spoke again. 'I think I'll take her down, Dave. I've had more rest than you.'

The pilot unbuckled his harness, detached his oxygen line, and climbed wearily out of his seat. The colonel took his place, settled himself, and looked across at Bill. Bill tried to smile, but he knew that his face was tight and his eyes were tired, and he knew that the colonel had noticed.

The colonel said, 'This is a good crew, Dave. Good coordination. I almost forgot to tell you.'

The navigator spoke plaintively from below. 'What do you mean, good? It's the best crew in SAC. And can't you make this flying machine go faster, colonel? I'm altitude-happy. I need some fatter air, and Janie's got a special dinner laid on. It's our anniversary.'

'Congratulations,' the colonel said. 'But what about Salmonson's crew?' Bill could tell that he was grinning.

The navigator's voice became heated. 'They cheat, colonel. Damn it, I believe they pay the Alert officer twenty bucks for every second he gives them prior notice. No one can get to the Cocked line in the time they do . . .'

The colonel said, 'They do, though. Ready, Bill?'

They began the check list. Ten minutes later, as they made the penetration turn on to the final approach, they saw Medina Cathedral straight ahead. The sun was setting behind them, for they were coming out of the west, and the cathedral on its eminence stood out like an ochre fingerpost from the shallow purple sea of twilight. Twin ribbons of light sparkled thinly along the edges of the runway. The bomber came in to land, sliding down from sunlight to twilight, and from twilight to night and earth.

By the time debriefing was over Bill was numb with fatigue. When they left the building and stepped out into the night Colonel Lindquist said, 'If you're going to the BOQ, Bill, I can drop you off.'

'That would be fine, sir,' Bill said. 'I'm bushed.' He climbed into the back seat with the colonel.

'Bachelor Officers' Quarters, corporal,' the colonel said to his driver. He leaned back and ran his hand over his face. After a moment he spoke again. 'You're taking Kit to the bull-fight tomorrow, I hear.'

Bill said, 'Yes, sir. Olmbacher's coming with us to tell us what it's all about.'

The colonel said, 'Olmbacher? Oh, yes, he's a favourite of yours, isn't he?'

'He's the best crew chief on the base,' Bill said. 'He's a favourite of everybody who cares about an aircraft.'

'I hear he's really found a home in Spain,' the colonel said, 'speaks Spanish like a native and all that.'

'Maybe not like a native,' Bill said, 'but very well.'

The colonel was silent for a minute. Then he said, 'How's it going with Kit?'

Bill shook his head and murmured, 'I'm damned if I know. She's a hard girl to pin down.'

The colonel glanced at him with a slight smile on his long face. 'I'm not just being inquisitive. Grace and I got to know her at Westover just after Korea. She's been kept pretty well pinned down by her family, maybe that's part of your trouble.'

'How do you mean?' Bill asked.

'Well,' the colonel said carefully, 'I guess both as people and parents the Fremantles have needed a good deal of reassurance over the years and I've got an idea that Kit has sort of made a career out of supplying it.'

'I've noticed that,' Bill said. The car had stopped outside the Bachelor Officers' Quarters. Colonel Lindquist was leaning back in his seat, apparently in no hurry to go on. He said, 'She's beginning to get a little restive though.'

'I know it,' Bill said. 'A couple of days ago she said the Air Force was nothing but a big prison and this base was just one of the cells in it.'

Lindquist chuckled. 'Life, liberty, and the pursuit of happiness for her. Well, that's our national motto, and I guess marriage looks like just the opposite to all of us sometimes. You do want to marry her, don't you?' The blue eyes were looking directly at Bill of a sudden, and Bill said, 'Yes, sir. Only . . . I don't know how to set about it. Do you think I ought to speak to Ham?'

Colonel Lindquist rubbed his chin thoughtfully with his hand. 'I guess not. At least, I wouldn't. Kit wouldn't take kindly to the idea that it's anyone's business but her own. Well,

13

good luck. You've got a real good girl there, when she's made up her mind where she's going.'

'But I haven't got her,' Bill said ruefully. He climbed out of the car.

A voice from beside him broke in on them. 'Excuse me, captain . . . Colonel, Major Fremantle's been trying to get you.'

The colonel sat slowly upright, his face settling into its compact, wearied lines. His voice was gentle. 'Do you know what it's about?'

'That truck that hit the barn on the Lérida road yesterday, sir. The report in *El Baturro* seems to hint that the driver was drunk.'

'He wasn't,' the colonel snapped. Quiet again, he said, 'Thanks.' The car moved off. Bill saluted and turned away.

What had he been going to say when they were interrupted? About Kit being a hell of a girl, only . . . Only he knew more about 52s than about girls, and Kit was more complicated than any aircraft, and just as beautiful, and more wayward? Also, when he was flying he did the right things from the cold reason of experience and training, but with Kit he often did the wrong thing from the heat of love?

She was coming out of the Officers' Club now, with her mother. The tall lamps around the parking area shone down in her blonde hair and made it paler and more ethereal than it was, and her long thighs and firm breasts rhythmically sprang into prominence and vanished as she walked. That much, at least, those God-awful sack dresses did for women. He found that he was smiling, just watching her; and then she saw him and the level hazel eyes turned.

'Hi,' she said. 'Got the tickets?'

'Olmbacher's got them,' Bill said. 'Good evening, Mrs Fremantle.'

The two women got into their car. Mrs Fremantle said, 'I don't know how you can go to a bullfight. The poor horses.'

Kit smiled faintly up at Bill and then the car rolled off. He stared after it, musingly. She didn't look complicated. She didn't feel complicated; but you have to believe the evidence of your experience, and besides – the Old Man was nobody's fool.

He turned into the BOQ.

CHAPTER 2

For the last two hundred yards they had been moving in jerks, and stops, a few feet at a time. The people surged across the road in front of them, and small boys darted under the wheels, shouting and waving. Bill glanced at the temperature gauge and stopped the car. It was hot, under a lowering grey overcast.

The crowd surged past, so close packed now that the men and women and ragged boys forming it had lost their separate entities. Bill slid out from behind the wheel and struggled around to open the door for Kit. The sound broke over him in waves, and for a moment he felt like getting back into the big American car, where he'd be protected by the tinted safety glass and shiny metal and polished chrome. The Ford looked enormous, jammed in there against the dusty kerb between two little European bugs.

Catherine Fremantle and Master Sergeant Olmbacher got out after him, and the three of them joined the crowd surging slowly down towards the bull-ring. Olmbacher gave Bill the tickets.

Bill looked at them and shouted, 'Sergeant, what does *sombra* mean?'

'Shade,' Kit answered impatiently, before Olmbacher could speak.

The dust floated about them in a yellow haze. The bull-ring loomed ahead over the heads of the shuffling crowd. It seemed to be like a football stadium, but there were two tiers of arches running all the way round, and it was a dusty, ochre colour, like the landscape beyond, and it was made of small bricks. Two flags hung limp on staffs above the main gate, one the national red and yellow of Spain, the other white with the shield of this city of Medina Lejo emblazoned on it.

The shape of the arches was Moorish, Oriental. Bill smelled blood in the dust. The bulls would die under his eyes, blood pouring from their mouths, their backs a bloody pulp of broken skin and torn flesh. He shouldn't have allowed her to persuade him to take her. He shouldn't have given her a carnation to wear on her shoulder. This was not a football game.

But she said she wanted to find out, that she *had* to find out. She said you had to find out about everything.

15

On the left now there was barren earth, and then the Milagro River, and low cliffs on the far bank. On the right – more bare earth, rising to the stark, sun-baked hills, the same colour as the bull-ring. Behind, the street ran back between the dusty maples and the tenement buildings towards the sudden brown cliffs of the cathedral, and the hanging golden dome, all shimmering in the moving haze of the July afternoon. On top of the golden dome the glittering cross of steel was shaped like a sword.

In front of the cathedral was the big Plaza San Marco, and in the middle of the Plaza there was a huge bronze statue group on a high stone platform. The statue showed the saint, San Marco, dressed as a Roman soldier, kneeling, holding up his short sword like a crucifix. Standing beside him with head raised and body tensed was a huge bull. The bull had an enormous pair of testicles, almost twice life-size.

All that was outside the cathedral, and the people were coming from there to here to see the bullfight, and all this was something else that Kit kept saying she had to find out about, for the Spanish were truly devout and the statue was truly indecent; and the Spanish were truly kind, and they were going to the bullfight.

Close to the bull-ring the crowd had become denser than ever as it funnelled slowly towards the high entrance. Sergeant Olmbacher took out his handkerchief and mopped his forehead. He grinned down at Kit – 'Butterflies in the stomach?' She shook her head, and he said seriously, 'It can be pretty unpleasant.'

Bill yelled, 'What got you so interested in bullfighting?'

The sergeant said, 'I don't know, captain. Unless it was to find out what makes the Spanish tick ... since I was going to spend two years here.'

Bill looked curiously at him. He was pale-skinned, blue-eyed, his thick, fair hair crew cut; a master sergeant and a master mechanic. Everyone on the base knew that Pete Olmbacher understood the working of machines. It was vaguely surprising as Colonel Lindquist had hinted yesterday, to find him also delving into the working of people, especially of foreigners as strange to his character as Spaniards.

'Cold water! Lemonade! Eye-shades!' the vendors screamed.

They were at the entrance, the curved brick wall towering up directly over them. The shouting and the calling became hollow as they went in under the great arch. They passed out of

16

the wide tunnel and into the arena. The reverberating sound fell back and Bill stopped involuntarily, wondering, where has it gone, everything, the noise, the crowd, the people? The stone tiers ran round in pale ochre rings, sweeping down in gradual steps to the circle of grey sand. The crowd was shuffling outwards along the stone banks, thinning again into individuals as they went to their places. The cries of the vendors drifted up, thin and dispersed to the low, glaring overcast.

The circle of sand was surrounded by a barrier of thick wood, five feet high. Several narrow openings had been cut in the barrier, each guarded by a small outer barrier, so that a man, but nothing larger, could slip in and out. The front row of seats, in which the three of them sat, was some feet back from the barrier, and also higher, so that they were looking down into a narrow passage that ran the whole way around the ring. Two great arched entrances, guarded by gates, tunnelled under the stands into the arena, and close by to Kit's right there were two lower gates, heavily barred. Today there was no direct sunlight, and so no shade. The heat and the glare fell evenly everywhere.

Sergeant Olmbacher leaned across. '. . . That box up there, with the flags, is allotted to the president of the *corrida*. The wooden fence round the ring is called the *barrera*, and the passage down there is called the *callejón* . . .'

'*Perdóneme.*'

Bill looked around. Olmbacher was already on his feet, his knees pressed back against the stone platform on which they were sitting. Two women were edging past, heading for the vacant seats on Bill's right. The one in front was plump and middle-aged, dressed in black, wearing very high heels, and dark glasses, her smoothed black hair streaked with grey. Behind her was a girl of Kit's age – slight but big-bosomed, dressed in a cool cotton print with white shoes. She carried the inevitable dark glasses in her hand and her eyes were dark, full, and deep. The two women passed, and the proud fine curve of their noses and the straight dark lines of their eyebrows showed unmistakably that they were mother and daughter. They sank on to the stone next to Bill, the younger nearest to him, and the obsequious old attendant passed cushions along to them, cap in hand.

The tempo of preparation increased everywhere. An old high-wheeled wooden cart, drawn by two horses and carrying two huge barrels, ambled around the arena in concentric circles, water dripping unevenly from a steel cross-pipe under the tail-gate. The crowd came in faster, moving steadily down from the arches of the upper tier, streaming in through the entrance tunnels. The band began to play brassy, martial music. Bill lit a cigarette, leaned over the broad wooden rail in front of them, and peered down into the narrow circular passage, the *callejón*. There were men in business suits down there, smoking cigars, and talking to each other with their heads close, like men one saw in the theatre intervals in New York, or outside the little jewellery stores off Fifth Avenue in the lunch break; a big, coarse, blue-jowled policeman in a cheap grey cotton uniform with a red band round his hat, his belt sagging under his paunch from the weight of his pistol in its holster; two men in faded blue, meat hooks hanging from their belts and a motley of black and red and pink stains and splashes all over blouse and trousers.

'My God look at those guys,' Bill said suddenly. 'That's blood on them, caked on. They can't have washed those clothes for a year.'

Kit shook her head impatiently. She was in a sulky mood today, he thought, ready to bite his head off at the slightest provocation, or without any. He returned to his study of the *callejón*.

There were men in white with red sashes, black berets, and white sneakers down there, long switches in their hands; and another Broadway character, a real sharp cat, in a loud suit and pointed blue suède shoes. Olmbacher told him the man was an *apoderado*, a matador's agent.

A sudden stir of movement ran round the arena. The murmuring of the crowd voice checked, and then started again all together, a little louder.

From high in the stands a trumpet blew a slow, high call. The water-cart had gone, the circle of sand was empty. Across the arena three men struggled to open the tall gates of an entrance. The procession of the bullfighters entered the ring, three abreast. Olmbacher said, 'The matadors are in the front row – Manrique on the right, in blue, Muralla on the left, in gold, Aguirre in the centre in black. Their clothes are called suits of lights.'

Bill heard Kit repeating the names under her breath – 'Manrique, Muralla, Aguirre.'

Behind the matadors marched more men in brocade, then mounted men wearing Sancho Panza felt hats with a black

18

bobble on one side, and long spears held upright, and armour on one leg; then the men in the red and white; and a mule team, the empty trace dragging in the sand behind them, red plumes bobbing on their heads, the men with whips walking beside them.

Bill lit another cigarette. Kit held out her hand and he gave her one and lit it for her. The matadors walked in a strange and insolent manner, stiff-legged, with slow and deliberate paces. The band played and the brilliant colours crossed the sand slowly. Under the president's box, they stopped. The matadors bowed slightly, not looking up, and lifted their hands to their heads; but they did not take off their winged black hats, only pressed them down more firmly on theirs heads. Then they all turned, insolent as ever. The horsemen left the ring, and the mule team.

The matadors and the peons came towards where they sat, fanning out a little – Manrique in blue to right, Muralla to the left, and Aguirre straight towards them, in black.

Directly below them Aguirre began to unwind the gorgeous parade cape that had been bound over his shoulder and under his arm. He was a slender, narrow-hipped man, very Spanish-looking, with a long upper lip and a long, dark, sad face, like those Bill had seen in a hundred portraits in the Prado – rather big ears, deep gashes in the skin from the sides of his nose to the corners of his lips. With a hint of a smile and a small bow he threw the dress cape across the *callejón* towards the women on Bill's right. The young one caught it, smiling and began to arrange it over the rail in front of her, spreading it out so that the brilliant colours showed to the fullest advantage. She might be his girl friend, Bill thought, or perhaps his wife – if bull-fighters ever got married. Kit and Olmbacher were watching her with interest.

There were two horses in the arena now, galloping round in opposite directions. The rider's black capes flowed out behind them, the red plumes in their sweeping black hats shook in the wind, and the band played louder.

Aguirre was in the *callejón* directly below them, a pink-and-yellow fighting cape in his hands. Bill watched him walk slowly towards one of the narrow passages that led into the arena. The suits of light were scattered all round the barrier now. The fat policeman was talking to one of the Broadway characters. The horsemen left the ring.

The trumpet blew.

The crowd noise fell slowly away, ebbing out from the arena

through the Moorish arches. Bill found his mouth suddenly dry. The stone circles of the tiered stands wavered and were gone. There was no stone or brick here, only the people, standing on each other rank by rank from the pale sand to the sky. He gripped the railing, his right hand on the edge of Aguirre's dress cloak.

Beyond, a door slammed. Just in his line of vision, a broad black back slid out of the darkness under the stands towards the bright circle of sand. The crowd gave a deep, murmuring gasp, and the black bull was in the ring. For a moment he checked, and turned back so that Bill saw his bright eyes, wide horns, and small hoofs. Then he turned again and galloped wide-legged, heavy as a truck, light as a tiger, towards a trailing cape the other side of the arena. A roar, the cape flashed once, the bull turned like a cat outside the little gap into which the man had disappeared, came at full gallop towards the next cape. The crowd sighed, and sat down.

The minutes passed, in the sweeping of the pink-and-yellow cloaks across the sand, in the sway and stop and fierce turn of the black bull. The hour struck when, finally, the bull stood with his head down, his back slippery and shining dark, ten feet in front of the barrier and directly in front of Kit.

Manrique attacked it messily, with many thrusts. His eyes glittered and the sweat shone on the side of his face, turned to them, as he raised the sword slowly, for the fifth time. Bill saw the bull's flesh open to receive it and the sword slide in to the hilt. Manrique's tight lips exploded outwards in a gasp as he leaned far over and stood away, but the bull did not die. Manrique took another sort of sword, and stabbed down with it at the base of the hanging head, twice.

Whistles and catcalls rose and a cushion sailed past Bill's head into the ring, over the dying, unkillable bull. Bill felt his gorge rising. He muttered to Kit, 'This is worse than a butcher's shop.' He saw that she was holding tight to the wooden rail, and put out his hand to comfort her, but she pushed it away.

Manrique struck down again, and suddenly the bull dropped, suddenly as a light switched off. The crowd was eight thousand separate roars, and eight thousand piercing, angry whistles. All round they were standing on their seats and whistling. A score of cushions hurtled into the ring. Manrique stood in the arena by the dead bull's nose, slowly turning his head to look at every-single person in the crowd. His lips moved once, forcibly spitting out a single word. Then he picked up his black hat, bowed very slowly towards the president, and walked out of the arena.

Bill spoke across Kit to Olmbacher – 'You like *this*?'

The master sergeant said carefully, 'Captain, you like baseball and I guess you have to take the bad games with the good. Manrique's luck ran out.'

Bill said, 'I guess I'd say the bull's was, being tapped for a fight in the first place, and meeting such a clumsy butcher when they got him here.' He turned to Kit. 'Are you sure you want to stay for the rest of this?'

'Oh yes,' she said. 'It's no good running away.'

The mule team dragged the carcass out of the ring with shouts and cries and cracking of the whips. Again the trumpet blew, and again the heavy door thudded, and again the black back slid from the pen into the circle of sand . . . Muralla, gold. The bull stopped, and would not charge the tantalizing, dragging capes, but stood with lowered head and brooding eye, watching.

Bill found that the ugly slaughter of the first bull had aroused a strong emotion of anger in him. He was no longer a disinterested spectator. Now he muttered under his breath, 'Go on, charge. Don't take any notice of the cape.'

For the rest of the playing of that bull he could feel his own hostility flowing out towards the bullfighters, and his sympathy towards the brave, tortured bull. When it died, fairly cleanly and at the far side of the ring, he sat back and mopped his face with his handkerchief. He said, 'There must be things about us that the Spaniards understand as little as we understand this. The only thing to do is leave it that way.'

Olmbacher said, 'If you can.'

Kit was looking at him coldly. After a while, their looks meeting and holding, Bill grinned and said, 'Whatever it is you're feeling, it suits you.' He stretched out the fingers of his hand and slowly she touched them with hers. It was a private sign which she sometimes answered, sometimes didn't. He saw that her anger of a moment before was drifting away from her grasp, and saw that she resented his power to make it go.

He hesitated, but he had to speak. He said, 'Are you sure you don't want to go now, honey? Because, really, I do, I can't enjoy this . . . it's so unfair. And I know you're trying to understand what it's all about, and I'm afraid you'll get mad at me.'

Sergeant Olmbacher said, 'It isn't supposed to be fair, captain. It isn't a contest at all. As far as I can make out it's more

21

like a performance of *Hamlet*. It would be all wrong if the actor playing Hamlet was able to alter the result. We know how it's going to end, and what matters is how it's done.'

Bill said, 'Well, I say it *is* a contest, and an unfair one.' The trumpet blew for the third bull, and Bill raised his voice rebelliously. The trumpet ended in a sudden hush and in the hush Bill heard his own voice loud and clear – 'And I say I'm on the side of the bull.'

The matador Aguirre was standing behind one of the small outer barriers directly below them. He turned slowly and looked at Bill, the hint of an inverted smile pulling down the corners of his long, wide mouth. From somewhere behind an American voice called, 'I'm with you, Bill.'

Bill turned and saw Captain Fisher and his wife, five rows back, Paul's fingers and thumb together in the gesture of approval. Other American faces sprang out at him from the Spanish sea. There seemed to be hundreds of them, all turned in his direction, some nodding, some frowning in disapproval.

'Bill!' Kit said sharply. 'You're making us conspicuous.'

The pink-and-yellow capes began once more to make their swirling patterns in the sand, and the crowd roar rose in a jerky crescendo. Peter Olmbacher muttered, '*Verónica* . . . and another . . . and another . . . *media-verónica,* and *recorte.*' The figure in black turned and strutted away from the bull, coming towards them. He walks like a fairy, Bill thought sourly. All the matadors walked like fairies.

Aguirre was there beneath him now, leaning over the barrier to take a pair of long, paper-ribboned, barbed darts from an assistant. His eyes moved up and he stared briefly at Bill before turning, the darts in his hand, and walking out towards the bull. The swing of his hips seemed more exaggerated now, as he placed one pink-stockinged foot directly in front of the other in his steps, the darts held high with delicately arched hands, arms raised.

The bull charged, Aguirre leaped gracefully in the air, his arms swung down, the darts stuck into the bull's shoulder. Aguirre ran off and the bull turned sharply, the darts hanging down his withers, held in the flesh by the barbs. Aguirre slowed to a walk. 'Christ,' Bill muttered. 'How would *he* like a pair of those in his back.' The matador was at the barrier, his hands outstretched for another pair of darts. Bill thought that this one was the worst of the lot. He seemed to be enjoying the cruelty.

22

Kit whispered, 'Bill, if you're not quiet, I'm going to sit somewhere else.'

Bill said nothing. The bull ran back and forth across the sand in slower, heavier charges. The time came when Aguirre walked to the barrier and the man in blue suéde shoes rested a sword on the barrier on its scabbard, its hilt towards the matador, and Aguirre pulled out the sword and walked towards the president's box. He stood a moment there, looking upward, the winged hat extended in his right hand, his head and pigtail bare, then he dropped the hat to the sand and, turning, walked slowly towards the bull.

'Natural. Another. Another. Another, to the left ... *Pase de pecho.* And again. *Manoletina.* And again. And again. *Recorte* ... This is a lot better, captain. He's building a good *faena.*'

The red cloth moved, the bull charged. The man was on his knees and the bull charging. Bill was quiet. The lonely black figure in the sand, and the black bull joined to him by the red cloth, made a single shape and suddenly, breathlessly, laid hold of all his attention. The skin of his scalp prickled, his hands were wet and the roar of the crowd lifted up in huge steps of sound, rhythmic as slow breakers on the shore – '*Olé!*' one, two, three, four, '*Olé!*' a single crashing shout, '*Olé!*'

The bull stood still, head down, feet together. Aguirre sighted along the raised blade. His left leg bent at the knee, toe pointed as in the step of a minuet. He flowed into action, forward. The bull tossed its head, the sword-hilt sticking out of its shoulders. Aguirre watched it for a moment. The bull charged him, and the helpers ran forward, capes swirling.

All the magic was gone, as quickly as it had come. 'Not again,' Bill muttered. But it was, again, and again.

Kit said, 'What bad luck!'

Olmbacher agreed. 'He would have got an ear, at least. Now he'll be lucky if he gets anything.'

Bill muttered, 'Do it right, for God's sake.'

And again, when the sword failed to kill that time, he whispered savagely, 'I bet it would make a better job on you, if it had the chance.' The attempts to kill went on and on, and Bill grew more angry.

The failing, gallant bull, its back in shreds, tottered half a pace forward after another downward stroke with the long cross-pieced sword. Aguirre's face was clenched in a furious horror,

Bill cried in agony. 'The goddamned fairy couldn't pop a paper bag.'

Kit's elbow jerked savagely into his ribs and she was saying furiously, 'What do you think he feels like?' Olmbacher leaned across and muttered in a low voice, 'The ladies on your right are Aguirre's sister and mother. The sister speaks very good English.'

Bill looked at the Spanish ladies quickly from the corner of his eye. What had he said, while those wretched women sat and suffered?

The crowd sighed and he knew that the bull had died at last. The shouting became confused and contradictory, but slowly the applause overcame the whistling. The matador began to make a circuit of the ring, followed by his brocaded peons. Bill watched him glumly, feeling that Fate had once more trapped him into doing the wrong thing. The man was a public performer, and getting paid for it, and it was sheer bad luck that he had to be sitting next to his sister.

Kit was on her feet, clapping hard. Bill thought, I should do that too, if I want to make up to her; but I can't. The matador and his peons were coming closer, running a few paces, then walking. A leather wine bottle sailed down. Aguirre caught it dexterously, drank, and swung it back into the stands. Flowers flew out in single blossoms and small bouquets ... Now he was here, directly below them on the sand, his hand raised.

Kit tore the big red carnation from her shoulder, wrenched it free of the pin and threw it towards him.

Aguirre caught it neatly, and held it up. Looking towards her, and slowly, with the exaggerated motion he had used when raising the darts, he bowed, the red flower held out at arm's length to her. Slowly he brought it to his lips, and kissed it. Cheers and laughter from all around. A man's voice shouted, '*Que guapa es, y rubia!*' Something about pretty. Aguirre left the arena, carrying the flower in his hand, and Kit sat down. She stared at Bill and said, 'Well?'

Bill said, 'It was your flower.'

How did Olmbacher know who the women in the next seats were, and if he knew why didn't he say so earlier? The women were looking into the ring, where the fourth bull had just entered. The girl half-turned and, as she did, Kit leaned across Bill and spoke to her. 'He had bad luck at the end, didn't he?'

The girl smiled shyly and answered, 'Yes. The bull was made

of rubber. It is so painful then ... the poor bull, the poor matador. Everyone is unhappy.' She made a small unhappy gesture with her hands, but still smiling shyly. She spoke a pure, accurate English of England, a little halting, some of the accents dragged out so that she said *thee* bull instead of *th' bull*. Beyond, the older woman turned, and smiled, and made a small nodding motion of acknowledgement. Bill, pressed back into his seat between the smiling women, tried to smile in a neutral manner.

The girl said, 'He is my brother, César. That matador.'

Kit said, 'Oh,' and then, 'I didn't know . . .'

Looking at the Spanish girl Bill thought he could now see the family resemblance. She had the same mouth and eyes as the matador, only there was nothing cruel about them in her.

Manrique, in blue. Bill supposed it must be good, because the crowd was again in that rhythm of shouting, and the band played and the red cloth swirled. At the end Manrique too walked round the arena in triumph, holding an ear of the dead bull in his hand. The crowd had forgiven him for the earlier butchery, but he had not forgiven them. He held the bull's ear and shook it at them as though he wished it were theirs, singly and collectively. The leather bottles arched through the air and Manrique took no notice, but only shook the ear and stalked on round the arena, never once breaking into a run.

Trumpets again; gold, Muralla. He began to see the pattern of the spectacle, and once or twice, as the cape swirled long and low and arabesque across the sand, he almost found himself on his feet shouting, as the people roared and the band played.

The sixth and last bull entered the arena, and he didn't need Olmbacher's confirmation to know that this was a 'good' one. The sigh of the crowd said it, and the way the bull ran hard and straight, lifting its forelegs off the ground when it struck, letting out a short grunt of fury and effort each time, turning fast, striking again. One, two, three; the swirl to a count of two; and three – '*Olé*' like a thunderclap; and begin the silent count again. Now the sad horse and the bull, locked into a single heaving shape right below him. Now the horse down, the rider down, his leg pinned under the horse and the white horns plunging down at him. Bill was on his feet . . . but a pink cape swirled the bull away. The horse struggled up, the bull trotted back, paused, rammed in against the lance point.

The horses left, other men ran out with darts.

25

Aguirre strode out alone with the sword and the red cloth, took off his black hat and held it out to his mother. The crowd cheered thunderously, and Aguirre threw the hat towards her. It went wide, so that it was Olmbacher who leapt up and caught it. Bill held out his hand for it, but Olmbacher leaned across and, smiling, gave it to the Spanish girl.

Aguirre passed the bull six times, closer and slower each time, and the band began to play. His sister turned shyly across Bill to Kit. 'They're playing *"El Rondeño de Aragon"*. It is his own pasodoble.'

Kit said, 'His own? Composed in his honour?'

The girl said, 'He composed it himself, and it is his own. *El Rondeño de Aragon* is one of his nicknames.'

Aguirre passed the bull behind his back, three times, then turned it short so that it stopped, head down. The crowd sound died and the music stopped. Aguirre moved the red cloth slowly down, a little sideways, the sword extending it. Olmbacher was muttering, 'Watch this. He has to get the bull's fore-feet level with each other, or the shoulder-blades close the gap he has to put the sword through . . . And the head down. Ah, he's moved again.'

A low thunderous roar filled the arena . . . louder, louder. Who was shouting, where was that sound coming from? Was it the bulls in the pens? No, they were dead. Or the crowd booming so? Was this what they did at the moment of the killing of the last bull? Señorita de Aguirre was staring at him, and her mother too, their faces full of fear. *They* didn't know. The crowd was silent, everyone staring at his neighbour and the roar growing louder. On the sand the motion was frozen, the splashes of gold and scarlet and yellow and green, frozen all in their places, the trodden sand violet in the lateness of the afternoon, Aguirre himself frozen, the red cloth down and the bull's nose glued to it, the long sword out from shelter now, ready in his hand.

Bill jumped to his feet. Of course he knew! Anywhere but in the bull-ring, in a medieval century, he would have recognised it long since. The sound burst directly overhead and all round, simultaneously the whining scream in the sky and the moan of the crowd. An enormous silver bulk blacked out the sky, flashed light into his eyes.

'The 52s!' Bill shouted.

The bull jerked up its head, bellowed, and ran twenty paces

towards the centre of the arena. The crowd was on its feet, everyone staring up.

Slowly the near-panic subsided. The crowd sank back with a long sigh – all except the American airmen among them, who continued to stare upwards. The huge swept-back wings sliced across the sky and vanished. The first was gone and another behind it, wheels down, flaps down, nose up, engine intakes and turbines screaming, and high overhead the thunder of a fourth and fifth, dragging vapour trails from their engines as they circled for the landing. Mission Coconut Three, Bill thought; must be a wind coming up, to use this approach.

The Americans sat down. Aguirre walked to the bull, lowered his cape, and plunged in over the horn in a single savage thrust. The bull's head jerked up and Aguire spun round, red sword and red cloth flying away. He fell on his knees in the sand. The weary bull watched as he struggled to his feet almost beneath its nose.

Backing away from the bull, Aguire looked at his left hand, and shook his arm. The hand flopped loose at the end of it. Turning his back on the bull he walked to the barrier, and everyone in the arena heard him call curtly, 'José! Bandage!' His face was tightly pulled together in rage. The man in blue suède shoes expostulated in whispers. Aguirre pushed his arm over the barrier, and a doctor from the pen below hurried forward. More argument, but in the end the man called José slit the red cloth a little, pushed it into Aguirre's left hand, closed his fingers tight round it, and held them there while the doctor bandaged the fingers into that position, so that the cloth and the stick to which it was fastened could not fall out of his hand. The bull watched, standing alone in the ring.

The dulled sword in his right hand, Aguirre walked towards the bull. Reaching it, he paused, lowered his left arm with the cloth dangling inertly from it, and ran in with the sword. The sword went in, and sprang out. Again; and all the time the crowd was silent. Again; this time the sword stayed in; but the bull did not die. Aguirre jerked his head, and a peon ran out to him with the other sword, with the crosspiece. Once, twice, three times Aguirre struck down. A trumpet sounded, and at the fourth attempt the bull fell.

His sister threw him his hat. He caught it, bowed curtly towards his mother, and strode quickly out of the ring and out of sight. The frozen silence of the crowd began to dissolve. Shouts

27

rose, and hankerchiefs waved. A voice cried in Spanish and Bill turned to Kit. 'What was that?'

She said ' "The Rich One has no luck but by God he's got guts." That must be another nickname . . . Now they're saying, "Give him an ear." . . . "He's gone." . . . "Give the ear to the Americans, then ." '

'Are they saying that?'

'One man did. Because of the 52s. We certainly know how to make ourselves popular.'

Olmbacher said, 'That was just bad luck. They only have three *corridas* a year here.'

Everyone was standing up now, and the arena was empty. They began to shuffle towards the exits. When they reached the aisle Kit hung back until the Aguirre ladies came up. Smiling at them, she said, 'I hope he's not badly hurt.'

The girl said, 'A broken wrist, I think. It has almost made him popular . . . but he will not be able to fight for some time.' She broke off to smile at a woman still standing in her place. The woman said something in Spanish and Miss Aguirre answered, 'Yes, a pity,' and moved past. The woman took off her dark glasses and for a moment Bill thought she was looking at him, before he saw that it was Kit, beside him, who interested her. Bill noticed that she was chic, like a Frenchwoman and about thirty. Her black hair was loosely waved round a high forehead – and then they were past, and Kit was muttering in his ear – 'Did you see that woman in black? That's about the first one I've seen in Spain who isn't wearing a dress too tight for her.'

Miss Aguirre overheard, and said, 'That is Señora Arocha. She is a dressmaker, a modiste.' Bill nodded and smiled. The girl seemed to want to be friendly. Kit recognized it too, and said, 'I'm Catherine Fremantle. And this is Captain Lockman . . . and Master-Sergeant Olmbacher.' The Spanish girl smiled from one to the other of them, all still shuffling forward down the passage, and Bill and Olmbacher shook hands with her and with her mother, as the girl made the introductions. 'I am Isabel de Aguirre, and this is my mother, Doña Teresa de Aguirre.'

Kit said, 'My father's the Information Services officer at the base.'

The girl said, 'I know. I have seen you in the city with your parents in your car, the De Soto station wagon. It is beautiful. We shall perhaps meet again tomorrow, Miss Fremantle. We

28

have been invited to the cocktail party at Colonel Lindquist's.'

Kit said, 'Wonderful! Bill and I will be there. Won't that be nice, Bill?'

'Sure. Wonderful,' Bill said heartily. He had nothing against this girl. Kit had spoken as though he hated all Spaniards.

Isabel de Aguirre said, 'It is possible César will be there. He has a contract to fight in Teruel tomorrow, but now . . .' She shrugged. 'Please excuse us now? We will go to the hospital to see him.'

She smiled, her mother smiled, and the three of them smiled, and they parted. A moment later they reached the open air. It was cooler now, the light was flat and blue in the dust. Bill drew a deep breath and raised his arms in a luxurious stretch. 'Phew!' He shook his head. 'What a thing that *corrida* is. It's like going back a few centuries, to trial by ordeal, or something.'

Olmbacher said, 'That's right, captain. Trial is a good word.'

Bill said, 'O.K., but I guess I just don't have a strong enough stomach for it, any more than I have for eating these squid in ink and you-know-whats . . .'

'Bull's testicles,' Kit said shortly. *'Criadillas.'*

'Yeah, those.'

'How do you know?' she said. 'You've never tried.'

Bill said nothing. She was mad at him and he knew enough to keep his mouth shut.

They came to the car, almost alone now against the kerb, deserted by the school of Fiats, Renaults, S.E.A.T.S, and Citroëns that had surrounded it. A blue-and-black Ford sedan, a 'little' Ford. There in front was the city, and the cathedral, and the cross which was also a sword. Here were the people, walking back together in the flat evening light towards the city, but the three of them were alone because they were Americans. She had something, in wanting so passionately to understand all this. That was what made her special. He would have liked to go along with her, but he had a job to do, and that took so much time, so much attention.

He unlocked the door of the car and they got in. It was like a furnace inside and they quickly rolled down all the windows. Bill started the motor, thinking glumly that it had been an experience all right, but one which he would not willingly repeat. Then Kit's hand came over seeking his and he took it, relaxing. Nothing worth while came all at once, and on a platter.

CHAPTER 3

The fence was in the way. Kit moved her shoulders impatiently and walked a few paces farther forward. Now she was out of the shade of the tree, but the fence was still in the way. The sun had lost its power and the tree shadow slanted long beside her across the last few feet of the yard, up the wire fence, down the other side, to die in the cracked earth beyond.

The fence was a tight mesh ten feet high, bent outward for the last two feet, and barbed. Beyond it, the shadow of the tree lay on Spain. Inside it, whatever the treaty said about sovereignty, the shadow lay on the United States. A mile farther along the wire it was different; that was the Spanish half of the joint base. But here in Medina East, it was the 94th Bombardment Wing, Heavy Jet, of the Sixteenth Air Force, Strategic Air Command, United States Air Force. Commander – Colonel John G. Lindquist, U.S.A.F.; Information Services Officer – Major J. Hamilton Fremantle, U.S.A.F. Here all the men and aircraft were American; here there was an Officer's Club and an Enlisted Men's Club and an Air Force Exchange, two swimming pools, three baseball diamonds, one football field, several tennis courts, and all the uniforms, trucks and specialized jargon that had formed a backdrop to her life since her father went back to the Air Force in 1950; and here there was Bill Lockman, six feet one of brown-haired all-American young man, tanned and good-looking – and good – who was in love with her.

She walked slowly forward again, and locked her fingers in the wire. The plain stretched east, a pale ochre in colour, towards the hill and houses and domed cathedral of Medina Lejo. To her right the fence bent sharply back in a right-angle, and beside it the main road from Zaragoza and Huesca ran straight to the city. Three big trucks were coming towards the base, light wind lazily dragging the dust south from under their wheels. A man striding slowly in the opposite direction moved his donkeys across the road to be out of the dust, and went steadily on towards the distant dome. Behind her, behind the row of semi-detached officer's houses, they were running a jet engine on the test-bed in the maintenance section across the runways. It was a mile away, but its whine filled the air under the other sounds – the truck motors, the sough of the wind, the raised voices from the house behind her – 'Kit! it's nearly six o'clock.'

She knew it was nearly six o'clock; but the low sun shone on the dome there, four miles to the east, and the city below hung in dark shadow. Slowly the edged cross took fire and for a minute the steel sword glittered above the dome. The plain that stretched from here to there, and across all this part of Aragon, was called the Llano Triste, the Mournful Plain. Mournful because of the eternal drought. Some years the people of the villages would exchange one litre of wine for one litre of water; the young teacher of the Spanish class had told them.

This was America, and that was Spain ... The ruined camp of a Roman legion. The hill itself, now crowned by the cathedral where Marco, Roman soldier and secret Christian, had gone alone to pray. In the year A.D. 112. They'd come for him and found, guarding him as he prayed, a wild black bull. Hence the grotesquely equipped statue in the Plaza. Later, they crucified Marco on the hilltop, and his last words were *I defy thee, Trajan!* The motto of the city and province. Perhaps of Spain. She didn't know, couldn't find out. Golden domes and silver swords, and *criadillas* and strong red wine – all these beyond the fence; inside it, peanut butter, and Bill on the point of asking her to marry him.

'Kit! Where are you? It's almost time to go.'

She sighed, and turned, and walked towards the house. Her mother was standing in the hall, staring at herself in the mirror, her hands in her black hair. She is here, but not here, Kit thought. She must have weighed herself again, and found that she was up a pound from lunch-time. Her footsteps made her mother turn. 'Where *have* you been, Kit? There's dust on your dress.' She advanced and patted the dust off. 'There. Spain's so dirty ... Hamilton's in the living-room.' She picked up her hat and turned again to the mirror. Dismissed, Catherine wandered through into the living-room. Hamilton was her father, and Dad, but her mother was Peggy.

Her father was slumped on the sofa, an extra-dry Martini in his hand, shoulders stooped, long legs stuck out, the light glittering from the lenses of his horn-rimmed spectacles. The glass in them had no prescription. Her father's eyes were twenty-twenty. The spectacles were protective coloration, Madison Avenue, 1937.

'Hi there, Kit,' he said. 'How do you feel? These affairs al-

31

ways take a year off my life. I had a nightmare last night, that the gate guards refused to let in the mayor.'

'The Spanish Air Policeman would know,' she said.

'He might, and then he might not,' her father said, taking a deep gulp from his glass. 'Anyway, I don't need nightmares. The drought's within ten days of breaking the local record. That's our fault . . . the last series of A-bomb tests.'

'They don't really believe that, do they?' she interjected. 'Señor Damas said that no one did, except the illiterate – and superstitious.'

Her father shrugged. 'Then the world's full of illiterate and superstitious people. Actually, it's a Red whispering campaign. If anything goes wrong, the Yanks are responsible. The Russians let off bombs all the time, but does anyone blame them for hurricanes, cloudbursts, and droughts? By God, Kit, if I could ferret out the people who *start* these whispers . . . !'

He drank again. Kit sat down. Mother would be ten minutes yet with her hat and face. Whenever Dad had a bad day he got like this, brooding on failure, and how he could find a spectacular short-cut to success – like his younger brother Glenn, founder and president of Fremantle & Harrington, Public Relations Engineers. That was about the time that Dad, getting along with B.B.D.O., but nothing spectacular, had joined the Air Corps in '41. At the end of the war, he'd gone back to Madison Avenue; and by 1950 realized that he wasn't going to make the grade, ever, not like Glenn; and then the Korean War, coming as a godsend, gave him an excuse to get back into the Air Force and stay there.

He finished his Martini and stood up. 'Good news all round. There was an increase of seven per cent in the number of illegitimate births recorded for May and June, in Medina, compared with the same months last year. *El Baturro* duly reported it. There has been an increase of twenty-four per cent in the number of unmarried men in the city area, counting the base – but that doesn't interest the mothers of the girls . . .' He raised his voice, 'Peggy, it's time to go.'

Her mother's voice answered, 'Just a minute. There!'

Soon they were in the car, and rolling the five hundred feet to the Lindquist's house. When they got inside Kit thought that most of the guests must have already arrived, for they were spread all over the living-room, glasses in hand, and had over-flowed into the hall. The colonel's hi-fi layout was carpeting the conversation with music. The colonel himself greeted her with a half-formal hug, and a smile. She called him Lindy, and had often wished, since the Westover Base days, that he were her father; there wouldn't be the same permanent weight of responsibility on her then. He was quite tall, quite thin, and until you got to his hair you would think he was hardly thirty, for his face was smooth, clean shaven, and unlined, and his blue eyes young and wide in the long face; then the hair – a shock standing up *en brosse* like a thick crew cut, and almost dead white. He was over forty, had been a great bomber pilot in the war, and had many decorations.

She accepted a Martini from one of the white-jacketed Spanish waiters hired from the Officer's Club for the occasion. She saw that she knew all the Americans well, and had met most of the Spaniards at least once. That was Señor Carvallo, the president of the Provincial Diputación, which seemed to be a kind of local legislature. The man with the bald head was Señor Núñez, the Civil Governor; he was talking to Major Jack Nagel and General Guzmán, the Military Area Commander and representative of the Captain-General, and hence of Franco, and probably the most important man in Medina. And the short plump one with the thick glasses and the peering head-pushed-forward manner was Señor Macías, the Alcalde, the Mayor of the Most Ancient, Most Loyal, Most Indomitable City of Medina Lejo (it said all that in the full coat of arms carved in the stone above the great gates of the Ayuntamiento) . . . and here was Colonel Portuodono, the commander of the Spanish base, moving his small frame gracefully through the crowd, looking at her with a little satirical nod.

'Good evening, Kit. Tonight you pretend the party is in "21", eh? You make a mistake. This sophistication is too much for a plain man like Bill. You will frighten him. Why can't you look like an honest vanilla American? That dress!'

'Shhh,' she whispered, smiling. 'You like it?'

The little colonel rolled his eyes with an exaggerated gesture. 'Like it? You don't know what it does to us Latins to see that smooth, sun-bronzed skin and blonde hair rising from the plain, smart black . . .'

'Oh, Ramos, be quiet,' she said again. He was a dear, and his little black eyes missed nothing.

He said, 'I do not like cocktail parties. I would rather talk to you alone. Or look at you. People are nice singly, or in pairs. In large groups, they are terrible. The cocktail party is not to get to know people, but to avoid doing so.'

33

She nodded agreement. Her mother loved cocktail parties.

Colonel Portuondo said, 'And how did you like the *corrida?*'

She said, 'I don't know. I'm still confused. Wasn't it awful about the 52s coming over though, just at that moment? Were you there?'

'Me? No. I was schooling my horses at the Club Hípica . . . But, my dear girl, you must not be upset about the B-52s. Yes, I heard what happened. Your poor father spoke to me this morning, greatly concerned about the effect it might have on Spanish-American relations. He is too sensitive about it . . . like so many of you. The base brings much money into Medina and these people know perfectly well they have to pay for it with a little inconvenience occasionally. Never, never forget their motto here – I defy thee, Trajan! They will defy their mother, their father – the Church itself, if there is no one else to defy. That is in the character of any Spaniard, but above all of these, *baturros*, these people of Aragon.'

Her father joined them. 'Good evening, colonel. Have you heard the latest? About San Marco's Armlet? . . . It's supposed to have turned up in Dallas, Texas – in the art collection of one of our oil billionaires. The mayor just told me.'

Colonel Portuondo said, 'But that's ridiculous. It is far too well known for the thief to ever to be able to show it.'

Her father said, 'Sure, but don't you see – here's the whispering campaign again that I was telling you about. It's the Commies. It's got to be.'

The colonel said, 'It is possible.'

'I'm sure of it,' her father said. He wandered off. Colonel Portuondo looked at her quizzically. 'You see? Your unwilling country has taken on the role of Atlas, and your poor father is Atlas's big toe . . . and it is being bitten by ants. Red ants.'

Kit said seriously, 'But don't you think it probably was an American who stole the Armlet? Didn't it disappear just when the base was really opened and most of the men came?'

The little colonel said, 'Precisely at that time . . . But think, my child! You know it belonged to the Saint himself. You know that it is one of the most sacred relics of Spain and of our Church, and the particular pride of Medina. Do you know that it was stolen before, and miraculously restored?'

Kit nodded vaguely. She did remember hearing something of the sort.

The colonel said, 'Do you know the particular circumstances under which it was stolen on that occasion? . . . No? . . . It was when foreign infidel invaders were at the gates. The Moors, A.D. 712. If it had not vanished when it did, the Moors would have taken it or destroyed it. And it reappeared under the altar when the Moors had been thrown out of Aragon.' He nodded his head, his small eyes fixed intently on hers. '*This* time, it disappeared the night before it was to be shown in procession, on the arm of the Santo, in solemn ceremonies to dedicate the base ... As I said before, think, my child, and remember that in Spain the present is only the visible flower sprung from the roots of the past.' His manner changed. 'But don't think about such things now. There are only two or three young men here and you ought to be with them, not with me.' He took her elbow and gently guided her towards the corner of the room where Bill was talking to Major Dave Metch, his aircraft commander.

Bill saw them coming and raised his glass cheerfully. 'Hi, Kit. Good evening, sir ... Colonel, Dave and I were talking about a honey of a problem we haven't been able to lick yet. As you know, we're taking off and landing sometimes with a slight down-wind to avoid flying over the city. Here's the thing. How many degrees of cross-wind crab to compute for a forty-five-degree quartering cross-wind.'

'But with a ten-knot wind, or less,' the little colonel said.

'Right,' Bill said, 'and because of the low wind velocity we never have to crank in very much. The real question is, what direction do you crank it in and how much is the landing roll factor increased?'

Colonel Portuondo began to give his opinion. Kit carefully sipped her Martini. The three men had forgotten she existed and the colonel's hand had dropped from her elbow. For all his gallantry, a woman didn't really matter compared with a thoroughbred horse or this strange world where aircraft and mathematics seemed to merge into each other. It was a shame, because she had meant to find Bill and make up to him for her grumpiness of yesterday. But in this world Bill also changed. No longer a boyish 'vanilla American', he was on his own ground now, a place where she could never stand with him, even if she accepted him; and he was not boyish at all, but mature, professional, highly trained, highly expert, confident, and calm.

Suddenly it was the mayor and Señor Núñez and the rest of them who seemed gauche. And suppose this wasn't a house but a jet plane in flight? Then they and all the rest of them would be passengers, and Bill and a few more would be the bosses.

That must be the reason for the tension she had noticed whenever civilians got to talking with men of the U.S. Air Force, especially of the Strategic Air Command. The civilians could think that they themselves were still ultimate bosses – at least, Americans could – but only in that way that the passenger is the ultimate boss on a commercial air line; nevertheless, when the door thuds closed and the motors start he's just a passenger, a load of human freight that the crew doesn't need, and which is actually in their way. And in the horrible reality of the world no one knew when the door was closing, or who would close it.

_She turned away abruptly. Fenced in and locked in. Twenty-two, an honours graduate; and where on earth, or off it, was happiness? Or the liberty to become what you had it in you to become? And what was that?

Moving restlessly away, without direction, she bumped into someone, spilling some of her drink. 'Oh!' she gasped. 'I'm sorry.' She looked up.

'It is I who should apologize.' The man's voice was deep and flat, and he had prominent ears and a long, dark face.

She said, 'Señor Aguirre.'

He bowed slightly.

She said, 'I'm Catherine Fremantle. I threw you a carnation . . . I hope you didn't mind.'

He bowed again and she saw that his left arm was in a sling, the black silk lying smooth across the front of his dark grey suit. He was wearing a white shirt and blue polka-dot tie. She dropped her hand and asked, 'How is your wrist?'

'It is broken,' he said. 'In a very complicated manner. It was a beautiful flower that you honoured me with.' His voice seemed bored and his face never relaxed its air of removed melancholy.

There was a short silence. She thought, he's from Medina, so he'll know all the Spaniards here – no point in talking about them. 'You and your sister speak English very well,' she said.

He said, 'Thank you. We had an English governess from the year I was three until my sister was seventeen, that is, three years ago. Do you speak Spanish?'

She said, 'Rather well, as a matter of fact. Two years in high school, four years in college, and now five weeks with Señor Damas. _Puedo defenderme._'

Separated from her by the _callejón_ and the theatrical brilliance of the suit of lights, he had been exciting in the way a famous actor is exciting on the stage. Now he had come down into the orchestra to talk to her; and he was bored.

36

'I hope your stay in Spain has been enjoyable,' he said.

She saw his dark eyes stray momentarily. There must be some man he wanted to talk to. But she looked good tonight – Ramos Portuondo had said so – and she was no longer a college girl.

She said, 'No.'

He looked startled, and his eyes came into focus on her. They were black and deep. 'What is wrong, señorita?'

She said, 'The fence. When you came here you drove in through it. I'm inside, and I can't get out, and if I do, then you all have fences round your houses and I can't get in there . . .'

'It is worse than that,' he said with a faint smile. 'Inside the houses we have fences round ourselves, each one of us a secret fence, much higher than the ones you can see.'

She said, 'You come to parties here and we go to parties in your houses – not much though, because you don't entertain in your houses, do you, but in the cafés, and that's a fence right there . . . and still neither really knows how the other lives or thinks, and not many even want to. That's what I think is so awful.'

After a time Aguirre said, 'I do not think "how" is the right word. It should be "why".'

She said, 'Yes, that's what I mean, really.'

'Kit, dear . . . I'm told you met these ladies yesterday.' It was her mother, introducing Doña Teresa de Aguirre, and her daughter Isabel . . . and how wonderful to meet her son, a real live toreador! She took Señora de Aguirre's arm and wandered off, talking.

Don César had stalked away during the interchange, after a word of apology, and Kit was alone with Isabel de Aguirre.

'What a racket,' Kit said gaily. 'Are your cocktail parties as bad as this? I mean, when there aren't any Americans?'

The girl said, '*We* don't have any. César does not like them. He is old-fashioned . . .' She hesitated, and then said, 'We were standing quite close behind you when you were talking to César. It sounded so interesting, but I couldn't hear everything because –'

'Because my mother was speaking,' Kit said, laughing. The girl laughed, and they were looking into each other's eyes, laughing together at the same joke, alone in a roomful of people separated from them by age or sex or point of view.

The Spanish girl said, 'I heard enough. I agree with you.'

Kit said, 'Yes, but what can we *do*?'

Isabel de Aguirre said, 'You know what some of the towns-people call the base? The Yankee Ghetto.'

Kit said vehemently, 'And it is! Our own church, stores, parks, pools. . . . If we could even live in Medina, it would be better . . .' She shrugged. What was the use?

Isabel was looking at her with an odd intensity. Then she spoke, in a rush. 'Miss Fremantle, would you –'

'Oh, please call me Kit.'

'And me – Bel . . . Kit, would you really like to live inside Spain?'

'I can't think of anything I'd like better,' Kit said cheer-fully.

Isabel said, 'Then come and live with us.'

Kit said, 'Why, that . . .' She stopped. She remembered Señor Damas telling them in Spanish class to be careful what they admired, because a Spaniard of the old school would give it to them. Now she'd done it.

Isabel was speaking eagerly, 'Please! It is a big house, old-fashioned, but comfortable.'

Many thoughts raced through Kit's mind. This was some-thing she had wanted to do ever since she first came to Medina, and felt the fervent, sombre pulse of Spain beating away there so close and so far from her. And she could stand away from Bill Lockman for a little time, and see what was in her mind about him.

Isabel said, 'You could invite anyone you liked to the house, whenever you liked.'

Suddenly the base and the fence and her position at home weighed on her with an intolerable burden. She was supposed to be a free agent now. Then why couldn't she act like one?

She said, 'If you really mean it, I'd love to. For a few weeks. I must speak to my parents, of course. What about yours?'

'Our father is dead, several years ago,' Bel said. 'Mother will be pleased that I have a companion, I am sure. And César will give his permission.'

'César?' she said. 'Of course . . . I forgot.'

Of course. If the father was dead César would be master of the house.

Bel said, 'I'll go now and speak to them, and then my mother will find yours, and ask her, but you and I must be there. You will not be leaving the party for a little while?'

Kit said, 'No . . .'

She was alone. Her glass was empty. Better change to tomato

38

juice now, though. The Martinis had done their work. She felt elated, and guilty. If she had a duty, it was to stay here, but she damn well was going to get out for a while.

*

'If your stomach gets upset, you must come back at once. They cook in olive oil the whole time.'

'It won't,' Kit said cheerfully.

She was sitting on the sofa, with her mother, in their own living-room. Her father was sprawled in one chair, Bill Lockman sitting upright in another. They'd got back from the party ten minutes ago, and it was nine o'clock. Her father groaned, 'These Spanish hours are going to bring my ulcer back.'

Her mother said, 'And you must never drink water. I suppose we could ask Major Johnson to test it.'

'No, we couldn't,' Kit said abruptly. 'If they can survive on it, why can't I?'

'They're used to it,' her mother said. 'They've got immunity.'

Her father pulled himself upright in his chair. 'Hadn't we better decide whether she's going at all, before we worry about the water and the olive oil? We'll miss you, you know.'

He smiled at her wearily and it was on the tip of her tongue to say, I won't go. An information officer was not normally anything very important in the Air Force, but here it was different. Here, Dad was in a sense Colonel Lindquist's right-hand man, and he wasn't up to it; that's why she had come to Spain immediately after graduation. She remembered how much she wanted to run away while Dad was stationed at Westover, because it had seemed intolerable that they should lean on her when she wanted to lean on *them*.

Her father said, 'As to the family, they're fine. Portuondo says it's a very old family and a very important one. Another branch used to be counts or marquises or something, until it died out a couple of centuries ago. Don Ernesto Aguirre, the father, was mayor of Medina three times and a very upright man, greatly respected. The eldest son was killed in the Civil War, and so were a couple of daughters, in a Commie bombing raid, right here. This son, César, was supposed to follow in father's footsteps – they have a big house the other side of town, own some farms, have shares in a wine business and a bank and the olive oil cannery ... but he becomes a bullfighter. His

39

father died a year later. From the disgrace, a lot of people said, according to Portuondo. Most bullfighters come from poor families, not of much account socially – I mean, like the average ball-player – however much they might be national heroes.'

'You must have typhoid inoculations,' her mother said.

Her father said, 'There's no reason why you shouldn't go.'

'You can take some DDT bombs, hidden in your suitcase so they won't be insulted,' her mother said. She got up. 'You must talk to Bill. After all . . .' Her voice trailed off. She left the room. From the hall they heard her voice, 'A hundred and twenty-two. I can't have eaten three pounds of canapés . . .'

Her father sighed. 'I'm going to get out of uniform. See you both at supper.'

After a while Bill said, 'Want to take a stroll in the yard?'

She jumped up. 'Oh, yes!' She put out her hand to him, he took it quietly, and they walked out across the patio on to the bare earth. The fence formed black striations against the pyramid of lights of Medina Lejo. To the left and behind them the arc lights of Medina West made a white glare in the sky, and the jet engine was still screaming on the test-bed.

She said, 'About this . . . I've been feeling so cooped up, Bill. I'll see just as much of you as before. And not on the base. It's like a goldfish bowl.' She pressed his arm lightly. She would have liked to say, Please, but that would have been to make a promise to him.

He said slowly, 'I don't know, Kit. It's not me I'm thinking about. You know how much Ham depends on you. Peggy too, really.'

She became impatient of him. It was not his business to tell her where her duty lay. She said, 'I'm not going to carry the problems of the U.S. Air Force round my neck for ever. They're not my problems. I've got problems of my own.'

'And you want to escape from them?' he said gently. 'Problems like me?'

'Yes, you. And other things,' she said. 'Damn it, Bill, I want to be free for a time, free of the old food, the old thoughts, the old standards.'

'They're pretty good standards,' Bill said.

She said, 'Suppose I asked you whether I should go or not. Mind you, I'm not, but suppose I did – what would you say? Honestly.'

He was looking at her with a worried frown creasing his

forehead. Twice he seemed about to speak, but did not. The third time he said, 'I'd say you shouldn't.'

She said, 'Well, I'm going to.'

He said, 'O.K., Kit. Don't . . .'

'Don't what?'

'Nothing.'

'What?'

'I was going to say, don't change. But I guess that's not what I mean.'

*

She got up early the next morning, and at one minute to eight was hanging round outside the Lindquists' house when the colonel drove out in his car. She waved to him and he stopped beside her. 'Lindy,' she said, 'can I talk to you for a minute? On the way to the office. I'll walk back.'

The colonel opened the door for her without a word, and lifted a bulging brief-case from the front to the back seat so that she could sit down.

She said, 'It's about an invitation I've had . . .' Rapidly she told him of Isabel's invitation. 'Peggy's going to ring Doña Teresa later this morning – but I still haven't made up my mind. Do you think I ought to go?'

She saw his lips tighten momentarily and said quickly, 'I *am* sorry, Lindy. I have no right to bother you when you've got so much else to think about.'

'I'd feel pretty miserable if you or anyone felt you couldn't,' he said. 'What were you going to do at home, before Ham and Peggy asked you to spend the summer over here?'

She looked at him in surprise. 'What has that got to do with it?'

'It might have a bearing.'

'Well, I didn't really have any idea. I was so glad that I was going to be out of college, and grown up, and free to do whatever I wanted, that I was just taking deep breaths and wondering exactly what it was that I *did* want to do.'

'And then you found there was a job here for you.'

She said slowly, 'It's not my job. I mean, I can't go on being a sort of pillar of the household for ever. But you know I love them.'

'I know,' he said. 'Here we are. Come into the office.' She preceded him past a saluting sentry into his office. Lieutenant Colonel Davenport was there and the colonel said, 'In a couple

41

of minutes, Jim.' The door closed behind him. 'Sit down, Kit. You're prettier than an honours student has a right to be, even though your mouth is too big . . .' He looked out of the window for a moment, his thin hands resting immobile on the desk. He swung back to her. 'A lot of people say, Never give anyone any advice. No one's God, they say, so wash your hands of everyone else's problems except your own, and too damn often wash your hands of those, too. No officer of the services can do that, of course, and if he wants to he's not much of an officer. I say you should go.'

'But . . .' she began doubtfully, yet wanting to be persuaded.

He said with the gleam of a smile, 'One or two young men will be sorry to see you go – but not if you're getting something out of it and they really like you. As to the rest . . . well, sure I think you have a job here. Your father's carrying more of a load than anyone in that branch of the service, any service, has ever had to carry before, and your being at home means that he's working out of a place that's that much more comfortable for him, more secure.'

'But I don't *do* anything,' she said despairingly. 'I just *am*.'

'Exactly. What you are is more important than what you do, always, and if you're not sure what you want to do, it's all the more important to make sure first what you are. Anyway, if you want to look over the fence, you ought to . . . because maybe what you're looking for will be over there. Besides, I can see this place is getting you down. Discipline, restrictions, duty . . . You'll accept them when you need to . . . and I think it will be a help to us out here to have someone inside the enemy camp.'

'Enemy?' she said, startled.

'In some ways,' he said grimly. 'Don't make any mistake about it, when foreign troops come into your country in peacetime, they're enemy – especially in Spain – until they prove they're not . . . Yes, you could do a job, Kit. You know, there's a good deal of friction between us and the Spaniards, and about all we can do is try to remove the sources of friction, one by one, as we discover them, and patch up the damage that's been done. A lot of this trouble is something that always happens between the military and the civilians – I mean, it's no better at Westover or Rapid City than it is here. But here there's also the element of nationality, and we need to find out the roots of the difference between them and us – what it is that makes us see the same thing in different ways . . . and even that's only a stage, because then we have to go deeper still, until we get to a place where we're *not* different – and try to ensure that we all look at things from that level.'

She listened eagerly. 'That's wonderful,' she said. 'I'll try to find out . . . so that all the time, instead of just looking *at* things like a tourist, 'I'll be looking *into* them . . .'

'Don't take it too seriously,' the colonel said dryly. 'Some of the best brains in both countries are wrestling with the same problem – and you're young and pretty, and you're supposed to be having a good time.'

The telephone rang and he picked it up. 'Lindquist. Yes I'll be down at nine o'clock. Have Carney take the internal temperature of the steel right away and try to work back from the heat-loss coefficients to what it must have been when it cracked.' He put down the receiver.

'No, I think you should go.' The telephone rang again. 'And of course you can come back any time you want to. Don't be ashamed of doing that. No one will be sneering at you. Spain's pretty strong meat.'

He picked up the telephone. Kit kissed him quickly on the top of his bent head and he winked at her as he began to talk. 'Lindquist. Yes . . .'

She opened the door and crept out quietly, and walked home, and told her mother to telephone the Aguirres and accept their invitation with thanks. Her mother looked at her and said peevishly, 'I can't make you out, Kit. Bill was just ready to . . . and here you go doing . . . well, I don't know . . .'

*

The two men were seated at a table outside the Bar Gallego in the Calle Ináñez. Crowds passed slowly back and forth in front of them, full of voices as a river is full of water. The sounds from two contending radios, both at full volume, met over the two men – from the left, a frenetic imitator of Elvis Presley, guitar a-twanging and alto-saxophone honking, from the right the blare and crash of a bull-ring pasodoble. An old man's voice made a staccato, irregular accompaniment as he peddled lottery tickets: 'For today! For today!'

The marble table top was littered with shrimp shells, an empty saucer, two glasses, two ashtrays, and a religious book. One of the two men was a young, round-faced priest of twenty-six or twenty-seven; the other was Don César Aguirre.

43

The priest sipped his whisky and put down his glass. 'Soon we will be making sherry only for the foreigners,' he said. 'And I hear that already half the pretty girls in the *feria* at Seville are likely to be American tourists. The Spanish watch the show – drinking whisky.'

'Not me,' César said, lifting his manzanilla.

A passer-by stopped, and asked him about his wrist. 'All the small bones shattered,' he said; and in response to another polite question, 'Not before San Marco.' The passer-by shook hands again and passed on.

Father Francisco said, 'By the same token, you had better start training some foreigners for the bull-ring. Already half our matadors are Mexicans, Peruvians, Venezuelans. Why not an American?'

'Franklin,' César said.

'Of course ... but more, lots more. Girls. Why not Miss Fremantle? What is she like, by the way?'

'In forty-eight hours I have not been able to probe her character to those depths which your priestly office enables you to plumb at a glance ... But she seems a nice enough young woman. Good figure. Too much make-up. Lively, energetic. An earnest seeker, like all Americans.'

'For what?'

'That we don't know. I don't think she does. Bel likes her very much.'

'Bel's a good judge. She has never yet, to my knowledge, formed one of these passionate attachments to the obviously trivial which are so common among young women. Well ... if you don't want to turn the American into a lady matador, don't turn her into a lady bull.'

'Just what do you mean by that?'

'I mean that you are susceptible to the sex – to put the most charitable interpretation on it, as a man of God must do. But, since you have assumed a pose of ruthless libertinage, as befits a matador, you pretend that you are hunting them, instead of the other way round.'

'I am extemely unlikely to fall for an American, any American. I did not ask this one to the house. You know my views about them.'

'And several psychologists have recently made the earth-shaking discovery that hate and love are closely connected.'

'Nonsense.'

'Have it your way. But I am fond of you, for some inscrutable reason, and I do not wish to see you get into trouble. You should know better than anyone how easily a triumphant *faena* can turn into a fatal goring ... So, you will not be able to fight again till San Marco?'

'That's what the doctors say.'

'Why fight then?'

'Because I am a *matador de toros*. Perhaps you have noticed a sort of small pigtail that I put on, and a rather garish suit of ...'

'Please! Your irony has the delicate charm of an elephant dancing, seen from behind ... Don't you think you are old enough now to give up this matador act and try another? There are many things of Old Spain at least as well worth preserving as the *corrida*. Now, don't close your face against me, but listen ...'

'Yes, Father Franscisco.'

'And don't call me father when it is as a brother I speak ... Waiter, another whisky, please.'

'Allow me to persuade you to have another drink? Please.'

'Now you are giving a feeble imitation of what *I* used to say when you helped yourself to the *churros* that I used to steal from old Pepe ... You must have noticed that you are not popular as a matador.'

'Because I am rich.'

'No. Because it is an act, and the people know it. Have you read Barrera's criticisms of your fight last Saturday?'

'No.'

'There! You are the only matador in Spain who wouldn't have had the accounts brought up to him still wet from the press. Because it is an act.' He took out a folded newspaper from under his robe and handed it across. 'Read it.'

'No, thank you.'

'Go on. Read it.'

'I do not wish to, Father.'

The priest thrust the paper into his hands, and said, 'Well, read it later ... The point is that you have great talents which you could use for the preservation of what is of real value in Spain. For a year or two it was rather a gallant and youthful gesture, even though it did seem ridiculous or positively disgraceful to some ... but now that you are nearing maturity you must consider whether you really wish to spend your life play-acting, either in the suit of lights or with, uh, other anachronistic societies ... The deputy chief of the secret police

45

came down from Madrid last week, by the way, apparently for the sole purpose of seeking out people with whom he could praise the virtues of our good Evaristo.'

'How interesting.'

'I thought you would find it so ... Well, I must go.' He picked up his hat. 'You have six weeks to think over your further career in the bull-ring – and out of it.'

'There is nothing to think about.'

'How fortunate for you. Till the next time, César.'

'Good-bye, Father.'

Several minutes after the priest had left him, César picked up the newspaper, opened it nonchalantly, and began to read :

César Aguirre presents the problem of a *torero* who is not a *torero*. He does not have to fight the bulls, like most, and he does not want to, like the rest. As a result his art, though plastic and delicate and full of valour, seems to be imposed from without, not growing from within. He can do everything a full *matador de toros* of his standing is expected to do, and does it with grace and skill. But in his case his art in the ring does not cause true emotion to flow out from him to the *aficionados*. It cannot, because it has in some mysterious sense already flowed in the opposite direction, from the past and present tradition of bullfighting into him, guiding him as to what to do. Indeed, his ring name, El Rondeño de Aragon, is indicative of this fault, if fault it be. He has set himself to be a matador in the classical style of Ronda, and though he has succeeded, it is the projection, the deliberate act, that we see in the ring, not the inner man, César Aguirre. There is thus a permanent conflict between what he intends to be and what he actually is. The roots of this conflict are deep, deeper than he knows, so deep that it will take a calamity or self-discovery of the first order to bring them to the visible surface. But some day come it must, in or out of the ring, and then we shall see the end of Don César Aguirre as a matador – or the beginning.

César carefully folded the newspaper and called for the waiter. While the man was adding up the account in pencil on the marble table-top, César glanced at his watch. Then, having paid, he got up and strode slowly down the street, leaving the newspaper on the table among the shrimp shells and the dirty glasses. The black sling on his left arm felt exactly like a dress cape, and all the people he passed recognised him.

*

The meeting was in the drawing-room of a large apartment on the Calle Contrabandistas, and the other three men were already there when César arrived. After a few words of greeting and handshakes all around, the four stood up, facing each other across the empty fireplace. The oldest among them, a grey-faced man in his fifties, said quietly, 'Let us pray for the Soul of Spain.'

For three minute they stood with heads bowed. Two children were squabbling in another room of the apartment and farther off a radio was giving out blurred, unintelligible news. César tried hard, in the three minutes, to blot out all the disturbing elements – the screams of the children, the bla-bla of the radio, even the presence of the other three men, and think only of Spain. He tried to bring to life before his inner eye the vision of a knight, dark and closed of face, implacable for the right, totally uncompromising and unafraid, possessing no wealth but virtue and faith, armed with the Cross; but the bull-ring came before him, and then crowds in the street, and women's faces fleeting; and then the grey-faced man broke the silence.

'Sit down, please, gentlemen . . . *El Baturro,* of last Friday.' He spread out a copy on the occasional table. A heavy black headline announced: AMERICAN TRUCK CRASHES INTO HOUSE. The story below the headline recorded that a U.S.A.F. truck had gone out of control on the Medina-Lérida road, crashed into a barn, and burst into flames. The driver had been slightly burned, the stone barn undamaged.

The grey-faced man said, 'I think that's excessive.' He was wearing a conservative dark grey business suit, white shirt and black tie. His thin hair, grey at the temples, was brushed straight back from his forehead, his face was smooth and grey and pouched under the eyes, his hand, resting on the newspaper, was smooth and manicured.

César said, 'Nico is a fool to use so much black ink on a thing like that.'

The man on his left said, 'If *El Baturro* keeps crying Wolf! when no one is hurt and no damage is done, except to the Americans' own property, and hints at drunkenness when there obviously was none . . .'

He didn't finish his sentence; César finished it for him, in his own mind. First of all, the people would begin to nod and wink at each other, and hint that *El Baturro* had it in for the Americans. Then the censor's office in Madrid would reach the same conclusion and soon one of those men with blank, hard eyes and smooth faces would come down and drop Nico some hints about the importance of not making too much play on the

Americans, one way or the other. And if Nico didn't use more discretion he'd find himself a reporter in Ecija.

The man on César's left said, 'There's no need to press so hard. They are their own worst enemies.' He was a thick-set man in his thirties, with dense, curly hair, butcher-blue eyes, and strong, open features. He went on, 'Remember their fanfare about that rocket last year, the one that was going to answer the first Sputnik! We had more jokes here after that – and better ones – than since Primo de Rivera's time.'

'You were a little young to appreciate *those* jokes, Ricardo,' the fourth man said smoothly. He was short and plump and his voice was a little nasal, and beautifully modulated.

Evaristo said wearily, 'That rocket business is a long time ago now, Mario.'

The plump man, Mario, said, 'It is. And in any case, we would be foolish to regard them as babes-in-arms, however much they sometimes force the comparison. Remember the T.W.A. incident.'

All four men laughed shortly, each after his fashion – Evaristo with an effort, Ricardo openly, Mario with a smooth chuckle, César abstractedly. He was remembering the details. Some fools, people not connected with this group, has started chalking *Yankee go home*, on walls all over the city. But two or three days after the first scribbles appeared, and when you could hardly move anywhere in Medina without seeing them, the city awoke one morning and found that underneath every cry of *Yankee go home* there had been pasted a large red sticker, saying simply, *By T.W.A.* The city laughed itself sick – secretly of course; and privately scored it as a victory for the Yankees.

Evaristo said, 'What is coming up in the next week or two?'

Ricardo said, 'The Day of the Jota tomorrow week. I don't suppose many of them will be coming to that.'

'You are wrong, my friend,' Mario said smoothly. 'They will be there in force, with Leicas and Contaxes and flash-bulbs. Major Fremantle will be there, wondering whether he can get together a U.S.A.F. team to enter the competition next year ... But there is nothing to be arranged.' He shrugged gently.

César glanced at him impatiently. He could never rid himself of the idea that Mario had been a priest once; and he didn't like the way he walked or talked, either, especially about women. Mario was a *maricón*, a fairy, and that was the truth of it,

48

thought no one said it aloud. It was a pity, because his membership in the group somehow degraded it. Yet he was very useful. Fairies always seemed to hear rumours long before anyone else did, and were wonderfully adept at spreading them, too.

Evaristo said, 'Of course nothing is to be arranged. Let them do the pushing. They will trip themselves . . .'

'And we will be there,' Mario said. 'With a sword.' He bowed slightly towards César. 'There is something very like a brave bull about the Americans – the straight charge, the strength, the inability to catch a fast-moving man with *banderillas* . . .'

'Bulls have been known to jump the *barrera* and kill a sword handler,' César said.

'Exactly!' Mario said, his eyes sparkling. 'They were the cowardly bulls, the sly ones, the . . .'

Evaristo interrupted with a raised grey hand: 'Agreed, Mario, agreed, many times and long ago. But remember that our secret police are not Americans. They know perfectly well what is going on and they probably know fairly well who is involved in it. They cannot prove anything, of course . . .'

'They don't have to,' César said abruptly.

'That is correct, and right,' Evaristo said. 'They are authority . . . We are wasting a little time, I think . . . I have a note about the *paseo*. Have any of you watched it recently?'

Ricardo squeezed his hands together slowly. 'You mean the changing, the loosening of the pattern? Yes, I have noticed.'

Evaristo said, 'What is happening is that more Americans are coming to watch. They are nearly all unmarried and they have heard much about the passionate Spanish señoritas . . . and the girls, though they keep their eyes down looking at them. I think there will be trouble soon.'

César said, 'Has our friend in the police seen?'

Evaristo said, 'Yes. But he doesn't think he need take notice just yet. It will be a matter of chance which comes first, some kind of trouble, or his having to notice and take action which would prevent it.'

Ricardo said, 'I should have thought he could turn a blind eye long enough.'

Evaristo sighed impatiently. 'Isn't this what we have just been talking about? It would be folly for him to take any risks in a petty matter like this. Don't forget that the Americans are not the only enemy we have to fight.'

49

'Not even the most important,' César said. 'It is our own slackness, our materialism . . .'

Evaristo said, 'I agree . . . But even if the Americans were all-important, Ricardo, do you imagine that a riot between a few American airmen and a score of our young lads over some silly girls is going to cause the Caudillo to revoke the treaty?'

'Everything adds up,' Ricardo's words kept repeating themselves in César's mind. Everything adds up. His wrist was hurting with a dull, unpleasant ache, and he had nothing to do for six weeks. The time stretched in front of him like a void. He must do something with his days, and whatever he did would add up, adding its quota of good or evil to the hours spent in the bull-ring, in these meetings, in the cathedral. It would present God with a hard sum when He came to make the reckoning – so many imponderable units of courage displayed and cowardice hidden, so much faith held and so much lost, so many virgins despoiled, so many orphans fed.

Well, something would turn up. Meanwhile, the discussion was nearly over, and the next meeting would be at another place after Mass on Sunday week. Only Ricardo from today's committee would be present. There were moments when this campaign to save the soul of Spain resembled a sinister and slightly comic opera, and his comrades in the society a rabble of ill-rehearsed actors. But Evaristo had told him it was just like this before the Civil War, on both sides. The war had been no opera.

It was time to go home. He'd promised to show the American girl the library, after dinner.

CHAPTER 4

Kit came swinging down the street at a good pace, much aware of the sunlight and all that it shone on. She was carrying a shopping-bag, and felt like singing as she walked. Here, opposite the alley called Penas de Juan, the Casa Aguirre began to emerge from behind the nearer houses on the same side of the street. She saw the window of her own bedroom, on the second floor . . . then Bel's . . . then the other guest-room, empty now. César's and Doña Teresa's rooms were on the other side of the passage up there. The high wall would hide the garden and all the ground floor of the big house until she came level with the tall wrought-iron gates. The garden was very green and the formal flower-beds very beautiful, because Pedro worked seven days a week from dawn till dusk in the sun, under a battered straw hat like a carthorse's, for twenty dollars a month.

Beyond the Casa Aguirre the narrow street curved away between the houses, but so gradually that she could see the last houses on the outside of the curve, and they were two hundred yards away. Beyond them the yellow earth began, sloping gradually up into rolling hills covered with olive groves. Three miles away a tower stood alone on a bare knoll, and to the right of it a curve of road lay like a loop of white rope across the hill. This was the Calle de los Obispos, the Street of the Bishops; where the houses ended it became the Camino de Roldán – Roland's Road, the road to the beautiful Valley of Roldán that Bel was always telling her about, and the Pyrenees. Once, from the window at the end of the third floor passage, where the servants lived, she had seen snow along the crest-line.

There was a small, chipped, blue enamel plate beside the gate, with the number 93 on it in white figures. One half of the tall gate was open, and she walked in, swinging her shopping-bag. Soap, bread, half a kilo of the string-like pasta called *fideos*, half a dozen boxes of matches.

In the kitchen she found Juana the cook and Eloísa the maid sitting huddled side by side at the huge, scrubbed table, a paperbacked book between them. Juana was forty and thin, dark rings round her eyes, a widow; Eloísa had a small nose and full red lips and sang when she scrubbed the floors, and was twenty and plump like a well-fed little bird.

Kit put her purchases on the table, and asked, smiling, 'What are you reading?'

Wordlessly, Juana turned the book over to show the cover. It was titled *Esmeralda*, and there was a garish picture of a servant girl holding open the door of a great mansion, and a young man of unbelievable beauty standing in the opening, staring at the girl, transfixed, and behind him the shape of a huge chrome-gleaming automobile.

'It's a beautiful story,' Juana sighed. She peered into the shopping-bag. 'Thank you, señorita. How much did you pay for the soap?'

'Five pesetas a bar,' Kit said.

51

Juana nodded gloomily. 'That's right. I suppose he knew it wasn't worth trying to cheat.'

Eloísa looked up. 'Señorita Bel says you are going to watch the *paseo* with her this evening. Is it true?' She giggled cheerfully, hardly waiting for Kit's reply before she rattled on. 'I'm going. I shall wear my blue dress.'

'You'll see your *novio*?' Kit asked. She had not been in the house an hour before Eloísa had told her about her boy friend, a shop assistant called Pacito – how clever, how passionate, how strong he was.

Now the girl tossed her head. 'Him? Pooh, no. I shan't look at him. What is an American with three stripes, and one across the top, like this?'

'Technical sergeant,' she said.

'How much does a technical sergeant earn?' the girl asked quickly.

Kit said, 'About twelve thousand pesetas a month.'

'*Mi madre, es fantástico!* A sergeant, twelve thousand! ... You will laugh at the *paseo,* señorita. It is very dull, old-fashioned. The boys will make rude remarks about us if we allow strange boys to speak to us, even. One day they will find out that times have changed. *We'll* show them. Do you think the sergeant has a car of his own?'

Juana said roughly, 'Don't bother the young lady with silly questions. The sooner you get married, the safer for you.'

'And for the boys?' Eloísa said.

Kit glanced at her wrist-watch. It was after seven and Bel had said they'd better leave the house before eight.

Her bedroom had a huge old-fashioned ring latch on the door. Inside it was cool and very dark, for the metal shutters were folded across the single tall window and the curtains were drawn. She opened the curtains, pushed back the shutters, and stood in the window, looking out over the city.

To the left, atop the rising rows of houses, was the cathedral. To the right, as far to the right as she could see unless she leaned out, was the topmost row of the Moorish arches of the bull-ring. In the centre, but much farther off, past the slope of the city and across the river, were the twin water towers, on their tall stilts, of Medina West and Medina East Air Bases. Between and under those three – the dome and sword, the Moorish arches, and the water towers – lay the ochre city of Medina Lejo, with many roofs, and washing hanging high across the streets; and far off she could see a woman in black leaning out of a window to look down into a hidden alley.

She turned back into the room and thought, This is really Spain. The room was big and square and high, the floor of wide oak panels, the walls of plain, fine-cut stone. There was very little furniture beyond the necessities and nothing at all of frills or decorations, except a Virgin hanging over the head of the high old-fashioned bed, and, on the wall to the left of the window, a dark oil painting of a young man in early eighteenth-century costume. He sat at a desk with a quill in his hand, and stared at her with a surprised look. Don Alfonso, Bel's great-great-great-great-grandfather. He had a resemblance to César about him, and Kit had found herself turning her back to the picture when she undressed. She did so now, smiling, as she began to change.

An hour later, at Bel's side, she was walking through the narrow streets behind the cathedral on her way to watch the *paseo*. Here were the little bars with sanded floors. Here, on the marble counter tops, were the fish – small shrimps and big shrimps, ordinary prawns and huge dark red ones, crayfish and lobsters, *almejas* and mussels, oysters and snails, squid and octopus, small sharp-spined *langostinos, cigalas,* and red *cangrejos del río*. There was the house jutting out into a street that had everywhere else been recently widened. The old gentleman who owned it had lived there for seventy-three years and no one would think of pulling it down till he had gone. This was Spain.

At the corner of the Cathedral Square, the Plaza San Marco, the *paseo* began, and it was called that because in it took place the daily parade of the young people of the city, the *paseo*. Kit knew it well, because it was on the main route from the base to the Plaza and because, at this upper end, it was lined with the few quality-goods stores in Medina. From here it sloped down, straight for over a quarter of a mile, to another square, the Plaza del Mercado. Beyond the Mercado were the railroad tracks, and then the New Bridge across the Milagro River – new because it was built in 1704 to replace the Roman bridge destroyed in the floods of that year; but the ruined Roman arches still spanned half the river, three hundred yards downstream.

The Paseo consisted of two narrow carriageways split by a broad central mall. Three ranks of sycamore trees marched all the way down the mall, as far as the Mercado. The sycamores were trimmed square and flat on top, and under them, in the failing light and the dust, a great crowd of people walked up and down.

Bel said, 'We are going to the Café Madrid. They have an upstairs room where it is all right for us to sit.'

In the café they sat at an upstairs window, with milk shakes, among two or three obviously engaged couples who took no notice either of them or of the parade going on in the wide avenue below.

Kit sucked at her milk shake and watched with interest. Parade was the right word. The girls walked one way round the mall, the men the other. All were in twos and threes and larger groups. Under the central rank of clipped sycamores there were benches facing outwards, and on them older women sat comfortably, with baby carriages, and babies, and there were some couples holding hands, and an old man reading a newspaper.

'If you see a man and a girl actually walking round together,' Bel said, 'that means they're engaged, or at least going ... going ...'

'Steady,' Kit said.

So, if she wanted to walk in the *paseo*, she'd have to walk with Bill. If she walked alone, that was a way of announcing that she was fancy-free. Nice and straightforward, an odd mixture of licence and discipline.

The paraders were fascinating ... two teenagers, one with a pony tail, both with high heels and dress luxuriously tight across their fannies. Big fannies too. In front of them, three girls abreast; then two; then four. One of them was Eloísa.

Dark glasses, dark glasses all the way, though the sun was down and it was getting dark. Most of the men wore their coats hung on their shoulders, the sleeves dangling. Every now and then a young man would remove his glasses and give some girl a burning, direct stare as he passed. That look meant *bed*. At home it would be a flagrant insult. But then, at home, the man would stop and whistle, or say something that would start the process of turning the look into action. Here ... nothing. She could just see Lindy's dry grin when she tried to explain this to him!

Now two taller men were walking slowly up the centre mall. Surely they were Americans. And one of them was Master-Sergeant Olmbacher, wearing black shoes, well-cut gaberdine slacks, and tan coat.

'Look,' she said. 'There's Sergeant Olmbacher. There, sitting down now, right opposite us. He was sitting beyond me at the *corrida*. Well, I must say I never thought *he'd* walk up and down in the *paseo* looking for girls. I suppose we'll see Bill Lockman next . . .'

She turned to Bel, laughing cheerfully. Bel's face was pale and woebegone, and she was twisting a handkerchief in her hands.

'Why Bel, whatever's the matter?' she asked. 'You look as if you'd seen a ghost.'

Bel whispered, 'Kit . . . how can you forgive me? I pretended a little . . . I mean I pretended to like you more than I did, and now I really do, and I feel awful . . .'

'What on earth are you talking about?' Kit asked gently. 'Are you sure you wouldn't like to go home, and talk about it there?'

'No! Not until the end of the *paseo*. This is the only time I can even see him these days.'

'Who?' Kit asked.

'Pete. Sergeant Olmbacher.'

Kit cried, 'What?'

'Please!' Bel muttered in agitation. 'Speak softly. The people behind us will hear.'

Down below many more Americans had joined the crowd. Four or five, including two Negroes, were sitting ouside a café opposite, beer glasses in front of them. Some were walking in the *paseo* itself – crew cut or sporting as much of a Presley hair-cut as the U.S.A.F. would permit, chewing gum, smoking thin cigars, all young and loose-slouching in their walk, moving like a fresh, riffling breeze in the dark parade.

Kit said quietly, 'Well, tell me about it, if you want to – not if you don't. We're both past the age of consent.'

'Consent? Oh no, there is nothing like that . . . has been noth-ing. I love him. I will tell you. He came here a year ago, and he has a car, of course. A black Dodge . . . I had borrowed César's car. He had just taught me how to drive it, but that time I had taken it without permission, because he was not here. He was fighting in Almería. But it broke down on the way back from the farm where I had gone. It just coughed and stopped five miles out in the country.'

Her voice faltered and Kit saw that Olmbacher, on the bench, had glanced up at the window where they were. Bel slowly raised her handkerchief and held it in her hand. Olmbacher looked away.

Bel said distractedly, 'That is all ... or nearly all. Have you ever been in love?'

'You didn't give the slightest sign at the *corrida*,' Kit said.

'That is what hurts so much ... The car was broken down and he came along. He stopped and asked if he could help me. I said, Please. I felt very shy already. He looked under the hood and then he looked at me, right in the eyes, and he said, "There is water in your carburettor," and I – we, fell in love.'

Kit let out a sudden snort of laughter and Bel looked at her reproachfully.

'It is not funny, Kit,' she said.

Kit quickly touched the other's hand. 'I know it isn't, and I am sorry ... but it was rather sudden, you must admit.'

'He was there half an hour, fixing it,' Bel said indignantly.

'That's plenty of time,' Kit said seriously. She felt forty and twice widowed.

Bel said, 'It is true, though, and we both knew it at once. ... He told me later he could have fixed it in five minutes. *I* knew.' She smiled and blushed. Olmbacher and his friend got up and moved away. Bel turned her back to the window. 'That was a year ago. In all that time I have seen him alone five, no six times, when I have slipped away when I was supposed to be doing something else – shopping, visiting a friend ...'

'And this time?' Kit asked.

'This is not alone. This much we can have more often. He slipped me a note as we were leaving the *corrida*.'

'Boy, am I blind!' Kit said. 'But the other meetings, what do you do about them, where do you go?'

'He waits for me in a room above Rafael, the blind cobbler's shop in the Calle Lope de Vega. Rafael knows, but no one else does. Twenty times Pete has waited for me there and I have not been able to come. And, when we do, we hold hands, and talk of the future, when we shall be married, and ...'

'But what's stopping you? Why don't you tell your mother, and have her invite him to the house?'

'A sergeant?' Bel said despairingly. 'A mechanic! That's what he is and that's what he is going to be when he returns – when *we* return to Huron Corners. Huron Corners, New York. It is by the shore of Lake Ontario, he says. The Hurons are Indians, but there aren't any there now. But of course you know all this ...'

56

Kit said slowly. 'I wouldn't think Doña Teresa would mind so much as you think, about him being a mechanic. Besides, he is rather special. All of us on the base know him, and we all think he's the nicest man there.'

'Really? How wonderful!' Bel said. 'He is!'

'I don't think anyone could object to him after they'd met him,' Kit said.

Bel said, 'César could, and he will.'

Kit began, 'But what . . . ?'

'He is the head of the family,' Bel said. 'I would be very unhappy without his permission.'

Kit said, 'Surely he won't object once he's met Pete, and when he's seen that only Pete can make you happy.'

'Happy?' Bel muttered. 'César thinks there are more important things in the world than happiness. There are ideals, duty to follow, at whatever cost. He never forgets that we were marquises once, leaders of Spain. César says it is our responsibility to keep Spain loyal to the Faith, and the old traditions. Whenever there has been change in Spain for the past five hundred years, some Aguirre has been standing in the way. Peasants have murdered us, townspeople burnt us in effigy, kings tried to get rid of us, even the Church has excommunicated us. An Aguirre knows better than any cardinal, than the Holy Father himself, what is right. Aguirres don't bend, they only break . . . César would rather kill me than see me marry an American mechanic. Don't *ever* let him know, or guess.'

A thought struck Kit and she asked, 'Is Pete a Roman Catholic?'

'Oh yes,' Bel exclaimed. 'Otherwise, I could not dream of marrying him. His family were from Bavaria, and went to the United States a hundred years ago.'

Kit stared wonderingly out of the window. Bel was wrong about César, surely? She regarded him as though he were a Victorian father, but he was only twenty-six, and a matador, and a musician, and an artist . . .

The girls down there, with the pony tails and the wriggling fannies and the spike heels, prinked along as tirelessly as ever. A bunch of airmen had fallen in alongside some others, probably Eloísa's row. Sure enough. The airmen were obviously talking about the girls, and the girls were giggling at each other. The young Spanish men, going the other way, stared with poker faces, and passed on.

Bel was seeing nothing. 'The last time we met alone –' she

said, '– it was nearly a month ago – Pete said he wasn't going to tolerate it any more. If I couldn't think of a way to get César's and my mother's permission, we would elope . . .'

'And would you?' Kit asked.

After a long hesitation Bel said, 'Yes, if Pete said I was to. But if only I could see him more often, so that we had time to think, I could make him understand that we must be patient . . . Now, we meet for an hour at the most, and for forty-five minutes of that time we cannot think of anything, but only look at each other, and then it is time to go, and nothing has been decided. *You* know.'

I know? Kit thought. Do I? To have a love so big that it filled your whole life, and simply blotted out doubts and selfishness and worry about personal freedom, personal aims. If that were love, she didn't know it. Perhaps Bel meant really that they spent the first half-hour making physical love and were too spent after that, to talk. But she'd said not. It must be plain love, with the sex there but held back.

'Will you help us?' Bel whispered. 'That was why I asked you to stay with us – my first reason, I mean. Please! It's been like getting out of prison only to talk to you. I swear not a soul in the world knows, except Rafael, and now you.'

'Of course I'll help,' Kit said slowly.

'Oh, thank you, I can't tell you . . .'

'But wait a minute. I'm not sure what's the best way of doing it.'

She fell silent, staring out into the street. If she helped Bel in her intrigue, she would be accepting responsibility for the consequences. Responsibility again, and she'd just walked out of the base and the house and away from Bill and her family. She felt a small spurt of annoyance against Bel.

The problem was to see that Bel found happiness. She really need not worry about Pete Olmbacher's suitability, or anything like that – it would be an impertinence on her part. She must assume that Bel really loved him, and that her happiness lay in being his wife. She looked at the girl and said suddenly, 'You haven't slept with him? Really? I think I have to know.'

Bel said earnestly, 'I swear by the Holy Mother that I have not, nor with anyone else. I am a virgin.'

Kit said a little awkwardly, 'Well, I'm not. I asked because it really does mean a lot. The man was awful really, but for a few weeks I was absolutely infatuated. I couldn't see anything wrong with him.'

Bel said, 'Of course I *want* to ... you mean, am I being carried away? I don't think so. Really, I am sure I am not, though I suppose I have been specially thrilled because this is the first time, the very first, that I ever felt anything at all – though of course I know how to flirt like a young lady – and it is quite overwhelming to have a man, and a man like Pete, who loves you so much.'

'And meeting him above a blind cobbler's doesn't make him any less exciting,' Kit said dryly.

'No ... Oh, I see what you mean. No, I do not see myself as an Andalusian maiden meeting a bandit lover by moonlight. I just want to marry, and settle down in Huron Corners and have many, many of Pete's children.'

Kit said, 'Well, let me think what's the best thing to do.'

'You are so much more experienced than I am,' Bel said.

'Yes,' Kit said grimly. 'Much.' And, she added to herself, also so much more uncertain. 'Shall we go now?'

She was thinking of Bel's problem while they paid the check and went down the stairs. As soon as they stepped on to the sidewalk another distraction took her mind off it. Something was happening to the *paseo*. It was falling into confusion as the parade of women piled up behind one row of three pert girls who could not move because three American airmen had stopped in front of them. The men were bowing with exaggerated sweeps of the hand. Clear across the carriageway Kit could hear the one in the middle, a big darkly handsome Italian boy – 'Ma'am, do us the honour of having a milk shake with us. *Batido? Con* us. Aw, c'mon, our dogs are barking, we've been walking round here so long.' He held up one foot and barked plaintively.

More Americans strolled up, laughing. Bel muttered, 'Those girls are seamstresses. They do not have a good reputation ... Those poor boys! Look, look! They *are* going with them!'

The disorder in the *paseo* increased. The three girls went defiantly off with the airmen, towards the wood and glass and copper façade of the Café Texas, across the street.

Bel said excitedly, 'Eloísa's going too, with her friends! She's not a bad girl.'

'She likes men though,' Kit murmured.

Bel said, 'And money and bright shiny things ... but when she goes, and her friends, that makes it different. That's revolt.'

Everyone had stopped moving. The Spanish young men were

gathered in groups under the sycamores. Some pretended not to see what was happening. Some stared after the half-dozen girls who had gone with Americans. Outside the Texas there were already twenty airmen drinking milk shakes, and now others were bringing Eloísa and her friends, like trophies. All the airmen stood up politely.

A young Spaniard stalked past in the middle of the carriageway. Opposite the Texas he turned his head and called politely and distinctly, *'Qué tal, puticas?'* Two Guardia Civil marched purposefully down the road, in the opposite direction, rifle and sub-machine-gun slung. On the other side of the mall stood two of the grey-and-red Armed Police, looking anxious.

'What did that man say?' Kit asked.

' "How's it going, little whores?" ' We had better go home.'

Kit noticed Olmbacher and his friend walking slowly up the central mall. Keeping level with them. She muttered to Bel, 'Don't look now, but we're being followed.' She motioned with her head.

Bel looked, and quickly away. 'He won't let me come to any harm. Perhaps if there were a fight, a bad riot, he could rescue me and take me home. César would have to recognize him . . .'

She sighed. Kit said nothing. Heroics were't going to help here. Patience, common sense, and a little reasonableness would do it. Those, and on admission that Bel ought to be free to find her own happiness. They were crossing the Plaza now, passing the statue of the saint and the defiant bull. They turned into the Calle de los Obispos. The narrow streets lurking to right and left were not named after pretty Elm or Maple, but spoke of the binding ever-present chains of history, of strong, strange individuals – Santa Teresa on the right, Caudillo on the left, Contrabandistas on the right, Penas de Juan . . .

Common sense? A little reasonableness? Freedom? Happiness? There wasn't a street in the city named for anything to do with freedom, or happiness.

CHAPTER 5

At half past ten, twenty minutes after they had finished dinner, Kit was sitting in the smaller drawing-room, reading. Doña Teresa was knitting a brown sweater. She knitted most of the time, always sweaters or socks, for the Society of the ladies of San Marco. During the festivities of San Marco, they would be distributed to the poor of Medina, in readiness for the bitter Aragonese winter.

Bel also was reading, but Kit noticed that she turned the pages almost haphazardly, sometimes two or three in quick succession, then five minutes without turning. Dreamy! If no one knew she was in love, they were blind. Doña Teresa, at least, *must* have seen; and decided to say nothing until Bel spoke. César – well, he was probably too busy, and anyway he was a man. He had excused himself with a word, immediately after dinner, and gone off to the library.

As regards Bel, Doña Teresa might be thought of as a sort of umpire who mustn't be allowed to see anything underhand actually going on, but who would accept the result once it was in the open, and might then become an ally. The enemy was César, because he was the head of the house, and old-fashioned. Her own part was to arrange more meetings with Pete Olmbacher. That shouldn't be too difficult, but ... this was a strange, new world. It was not like the reality of the twentieth century, but like renaissance drama, complete with dark-visaged brothers to be circumvented, rope ladders to be affixed to upper windows, cloaks and swords. César had a sword, and actually used it. That alone practically pushed common sense out of the window.

She wished she could see it plain and simple, the way Bel thought she could because she was twenty-two and not a virgin. They had secretly dumped a load of responsibility on her, and also a sense of duty towards all of them – including César. If César were an American elder brother he'd have said, basically, that Bel's love life was no damn concern of his, that she was an independent human being, she'd got to lead her own life, and she was free to find her own happiness. But he wasn't and he hadn't, and so no one was free – all were interlocked with each other ... He was nice, in a faintly distant way, friendly enough and terribly polite. If he would just stop being so damned polite he would come to life. So far, he impressed her as rather a striking painting – a Velázquez; not demonic enough for a Goya – of the personification of the Soul of Spain. He kept changing: now he stood with sword and suit of lights in a circle of blood and sand; now sat like a grandee in his library, now like Portago, in his Hispano ... And here she was, turning over pages as distractedly as Bel; so if someone were sur-

61

reptitiously watching her might they conclude that she too was in love?

There was a knock on the door and the 'man' came in. Butler was much too formal a word for his matter-of-fact ubiquity. From a pace or two inside the room he announced: '*Teléfono para la señorita americana.*'

Kit put down her book and got up. Doña Teresa raised her head and said, 'Octavio, are you so stupid that you can't remember Señorita Fremantle's name for an hour on end?'

'I can remember it,' Octavio said. 'I can't pronounce it. She should marry Don Alfonso Gonzalaz Zuluago de Alcubierre y Tardienta. That would be easier.' He was holding open the door for her; closed it carefully behind her, and followed her into the hall. He jerked his head at the telephone and went away.

Kit picked up the receiver and held it to her ear. '*Allo!*' she screamed. '*Aquí Señorita Fremantle. Diga!*'

'Señorita Fremantle?' Her father's voice at the other end was clear and close. 'Why . . . Kit, it's *me*! I'm speaking *English*.'

Kit lowered her voice. 'Hullo, Dad. How are you?'

'Fine, fine. Listen, this *jota* competition next Saturday. It's supposed to be a big thing in the life of the city, a great folk-lore event, and you know what, I can't find out where or when, exactly, it's going to be held. A week ahead and no one seems to know. Can you beat it? . . . Can you find out?'

'Bel told me. It's going to be in the Plaza San Marco. We have a team in it.'

'We? We don't.'

'Oh, I mean the Aguirres. Men and women from the farms out at Saldavega . . . It starts after dinner.'

'After whose dinner?' her father shouted. 'Well, now I can put something on the bulletin boards. This is the kind of thing our boys ought to see if they want to understand Spain.'

'What if they don't?' she asked.

'What? I can't hear you . . .'

'Nothing.'

'Oh. Listen, I've an idea, Kit. It's a sort of home and away double-header – a fair here on the base and a fiesta in the city. We throw the base open one Saturday and have a real American-style shindig – softball, baseball, swimming, sideshows, a barn dance . . . We'll elect a Spanish girl queen of that. Then the next Saturday, the city will have a fiesta, see, and processions, dancing in the streets and so on, and they'll elect an American girl queen of *that* ... How's that strike you? It's still in the talking stage, it just came off the top of my head yesterday.'

'It sounds fine,' she said dubiously. The events during the *paseo* this evening had not been encouraging. 'What does anyone else say?'

'I haven't talked to anyone else yet, except the colonel, of course. He's not so sure, but he's willing to hear more. But we've *got* to do something, and he knows it. We're getting fouled up, the Spanish and us – that Armlet being stolen, the B-52s balling up the bullfight...'

'And the *paseo*,' she said.

'What's that?' he said. 'I haven't heard about that.'

She told him briefly what had happened. At the end – 'It's getting faster,' he said soberly. 'If we don't do something ... We've got to take risks to grab their attention and hold it on to the selling point – that we're ordinary people, the same as them. We've got to break that downward line on the graph. You talk to César, and get his opinion about the double-header, his frank, honest opinion, eh?'

'I'll try,' she said. 'He's not very easy to talk to, you know.'

Her father said, 'Well, try, Kit ... Peggy sends her love. She's on a bridge jag at the Hills' ... How's everything? No belly-aches yet? ... O.K. ... 'Bye now.'

'Good night, Ham.'

She hung up the receiver slowly. The double-header sounded rather risky. It might turn out to be a good idea, the sort of 'eyepatch' that Dad was always quoting as a stroke of genius. But selling shirts wasn't the same as getting Americans and Spaniards to live together in peace. If people laughed at the eye-patch ads, or resented them, they would still remember the name and buy the shirts. There, failure was for no one to notice. Here, that sort of failure might be success.

She was standing in the middle of the hall. Soon it would be bedtime. She ought to talk to César tonight, if she could. Tomorrow, heaven knew where he'd disappear to. He never announced where he was going, or when he was coming back. He'd told her she could use the library whenever she wanted, hadn't he? She might go there now, to get a book to read in bed.

She went into the drawing-room and picked up her book, cigarettes, and matches. She said, 'I'm going to get another

63

book, then I'm off to bed. Good night, Doña Teresa. Good night, Bel.'

'Good night, Kit. *Que duermas bien!*'

She was out in the hall again, moving quickly along the dark passage, her loafers clacking on the worn stone floor. This was the Men's Department of the house, Doña Teresa had said, only half smiling. 'We women only go there on invitation.'

She walked more slowly. The first door on the left was the small office where César dealt with the management of the properties and estates, helped by a part-time secretary. Next was the library. The door was solid oak, in large square plaques. She knocked. César's voice said, '*Adelante!*' and she went in.

She stopped short. 'Oh! I'm sorry.' Another man was with César. César was sitting at the small desk in the corner, under the portrait of himself in his bull-ring *traje de luces*. The other man was leaning against the wall, a cigarette drooping from his lower lip. The french windows were open.

She recovered herself. 'I hope I'm not disturbing you. I just came to get a book to read in bed.'

The man stood away from the wall, and César said, 'This gentleman is José, my bullfighting agent – *apoderado*. You may have noticed him at the *corrida*.'

José took his cigarette from his lips and gave her a short bow. This was the man with the blue suède shoes and the Broadway manner. Her eyes strayed down – yes, he was wearing the same shoes, and the same sharp, pin-striped suit, rather dirty blue shirt, and loudly patterned tie. Perhaps he didn't have any other clothes.

'*Encantado,*' the man said. 'You threw the maestro a big carnation.'

'I did,' she said. 'Well, I'll just get my book . . .' She turned away. This was a nuisance. Now she wouldn't be able to talk to César.

César said, 'In a minute I will help you choose one. José's just going. We have been discussing my next appearance in the ring.' He spoke in Spanish, and she guessed that José could not speak English. 'José is annoyed with me for damaging my wrist in such a detailed way.'

'For six weeks I shall have to hang around this putrid city,' José said. 'The rest of the *cuadrilla* will go to their homes. Gordito will get fatter than ever. The Bull of San Marco couldn't satisfy Gitano's girl, but Gitano will do his best. The others will try to drink Segovia dry, and that can't be done

64

either.' He relit the stub of his cigarette, which had gone out. The smoke from the cheap black tobacco and near-brown paper was acrid and familiar. César smoked the same brand. José turned to César – 'You'd better take some exercise, man, or you'll get the horn where it hurts. They always have Martos bulls at San Marco.'

César offered her a cigarette from his pack and, when she refused, lit one for himself, one-handed. He said, 'I shall. I shall be out of the plaster by Saturday. After that I shall go to the cliffs of Roldán and get some exercise there, the same as I do before the season begins. I shall play the calves at Saldavega. And you?'

José sneered. 'Man, what exercise do I need? Sending telegrams to hotels for this *caudrilla* and keeping that wreck of a Hispano of yours going is enough exercise for me ... Don César is an expert in all the useless arts, señorita. He can do anything, as long as it's old, Spanish, and produces nothing, or – better still – destroys something. He can kill a bull on his feet or *rejoneando*, write a pasodoble, play the guitar, ride a horse, and put a bullet in a mountain goat's eye at two hundred paces. In other words, he is a parasite ... If you're going to be a parasite, man, why not do something that's popular? Why don't you take up football? You could make a great centre half. Bullfighting's dead, and you know it.'

'Spain is rotting away,' César said with sudden sharpness. 'Football, rock-and-roll – anything, as long as it's cheap, easy, and safe. They'd sell their Faith for a rise in pay.'

'So would you,' José said, 'if you were starving, like most of them.'

'I would not,' César said quietly.

The *apoderado* pulled angrily at his cigarette. 'No, you're right. You would not. That's why you're the only *torero por principios* in history. That's why we shall have to have another civil war in Spain before anything gets changed. And you know what side you'll find me on ... and, man, I don't want to put a bullet in *your* tripes, but you understand, at long range, you may be difficult to recognize.'

'I shall wear my black *traje de luces*,' César said with a smile. 'And you, stand on your head and wave your blue suède shoes in the air ...'

'Certainly ... I'll be about. You know where to get me if you want me. Take care of that wrist. Go carefully at first, you understand? I'll get the *cuadrilla* back here two, three days before the fight, if I can drag Gitano off that girl and Gordito out of the kitchen at the Hornos ... Good night, señorita. A pleasure.'

He stepped out through the french windows, and his thin shoes crunched away, quick and nervous, on the gravel.

The sound died. A truck ground past in the street, and it was again silent. Kit said, 'Did he really mean what he was saying about a civil war? And what is a *torero por principios*?'

César looked at her curiously. 'Mean it? Of course he did. He's an anarchist. A *torero por principios* is a "bullfighter on principle" ... Don't you want to sit down?'

She sat down carefully in one of the straight-backed chairs. The cigarette smoke drifted up in front of César's dark eyes. He said, 'Everything José said is true. In twenty years there will be no more running of the bulls. We will all be playing football – what you call soccer – and perhaps baseball in the summer. The only thing that can save bullfighting, or the *jota*, or any traditional thing, is for someone to prohibit them.'

She said, 'You said Spain was going rotten. Do you really mean that?'

He said, 'Yes. We had a way of life in Spain which was based on each man being independent and different. Nothing could be mass-produced because no one wanted exactly the same as anyone else. A man had nothing but his freedom and he could say, *Apenas podemos existir, pero sabemos vivir* – We can hardly exist, but we know how to live. Now he wants to eat three times a day and have a television set and a car, like America. To get them he'll have to serve the machines and fit his way of life to theirs. The *jota* and the *sardana* and the *flamenco* will die. There'll be no more bagpipes in Galicia or guitars in Andalusia, except as music hall turns, and no one will wear *alpargatas* or *fajas* or Córdoban hats. A crowd in Gijón will look the same as one in Granada, and both the same as a crowd in Manchester or Buffalo – the same trousers, coats, shirts, dresses – all screaming for their own Séptimos to win the league title.'

He stopped suddenly and looked at her almost anxiously, as though apologizing for his outburst, but all he said, in a wry voice, was, 'Séptimos is Medina's football team. The Seventh, named after the legion. Nicknamed also Gemina – that was the Seventh Legion's name.'

He was giving her an opportunity to change the subject, but

66

she didn't want to. His point of view was fascinating and kind of helpless. She said hesitantly, 'But, César, *you* eat three times a day. Don't you think everyone ought to?'

'At what price?' he said. 'For your virtue, would you? Some would. They are called whores. For your freedom, would you? Some would. They are called slaves . . . But in fact most of the world has accepted slavery and the rest is eager to, slavery to the machine, to the mass market, to communism or democracy. I do not believe in democracy, nor does any Spaniard at all, without any exception. Authority or anarchy – that is the Spanish choice, and anarchy only means that each man is his own final authority. I would like that best, for myself – but there would be no more Spain . . . I am boring you. Let me get a book.' He jumped up abruptly.

She cried, 'No, *please*! . . . I want to learn.'

César said, 'I know. It is a very flattering American trait. It enables the most ignorant of foreigners to become professors.' He sat down slowly and lit another cigarette. 'The other night, in here, you were interested too, weren't you? When I showed you the books.'

'Of course I was,' she said. 'Why do you sound surprised? Do you think women are too stupid to appreciate books?' She smiled at him. This was the man who held Bel's fate in his hands. She would start at once to disabuse him of the idea that all women were silly, fluffy things who needed looking after. Besides, tonight he was speaking to her for the first time as though she were a person, and responding to her. His mouth was twisted down now in a cynical grin, as he said, 'Young ladies of your age are not usually enthralled by old books. American girls, in particular, don't have that reputation. Did you do well at college?'

'Pretty well,' she said.

'Because you wanted to learn. And where will your learning take you? Will you teach Spanish literature in a college for women? Or join the experts in the State Department, who know so much about the foibles of the backward races beyond your frontiers?'

She looked at him quickly. Yes, the hint of a smile was still there behind the taunt. She said, 'I don't think *you* want any foreigners to understand Spain.'

'You may be right,' he said, not smiling now.

'I don't expect the learning to *take* me anywhere exactly,'

67

she said slowly. You couldn't throw words out lightly with this man. 'I expect it to make me something, someone better equipped to live fully, happily . . .'

'Life, liberty, and the pursuit of happiness,' he said. 'And you have come to *Spain*?'

She looked at him for a time without speaking. There was a lot to be discussed in what he had just said; but it would take weeks, and she didn't really understand precisely what he meant. She might find out later.

She thought, instead, that she would draw him out on a subject nearer to the problem particularly at hand. She said, 'And of course I hope to get married.'

He said, 'It seems rather a waste of so much education.'

She answered firmly, but with a smile, 'Oh, nonsense! To me marriage is not an end in itself, not something that turns me into a new person who is only one thing all the time, a wife. I'll still be a citizen, and a voter, won't I? I'll still go to the theatre and read books, I'll still be *me*. Married women don't spend their *whole* time making cakes and having babies, at least not in America. What are they going to do, and think about, the rest of the time?'

'In America – bridge,' César said.

'You're impossible,' she said lightly; but she found herself blushing, because at this very minute her mother was playing bridge. On the other hand Grace Lindquist was probably stretching a canvas in the guest-room at the back of the house which she had turned into a studio. And Mrs Hughes would be working for her PH.D., so that she could teach at Hollins College when George got his next overseas posting.

'You look quite beautiful when your temper gets the better of you,' César said. He was on his feet, smiling openly. 'Perhaps we had better find a book now.' He turned to the shelves. 'I have something here that you might like ... Here is the *Hamlet* in English, and here is the Luis Astrana María translation. Why don't you read the two side by side?'

'Shakespeare!' she said.

He turned slowly, the books in his right hand. 'You don't like him?' His tone was faintly contemptuous, as though he could have added, I might have known.

'Not much,' she said.

He said, 'You speak the language of the greatest artist, the greatest creator the world has ever known. You could understand him directly' – he touched the books to his heart – 'not lessened by the translation of a smaller mind . . . and you don't like him? Is this general in America? Or is it only you?'

They were standing close, facing each other, the tall shelves of books on her right. Suddenly he had stepped out of the paintings, and become wholly real and alive. She began to explain about Shakespeare, gesturing animatedly . . . Of course the language was gorgeous but the people, the situations, were out of date. César cleared his throat, and she hurried to find a better word – 'Unrecognizable. Untrue,' she said. Shakespeare was larger than life, any life. Shakespearean men and women fell in love like diving over thousand-foot cliffs into a raging ocean, not as it was when you wondered whether a man you liked preferred you in blue or green. They shouted their passion in coruscating floods, and stabbed themselves or their women with jewelled daggers, and drank mead by the flagon and went roistering and bawling in and out of inns and on and off horses. She ended, her arms flung out in a strong gesture and the language flowing strong, her eyes sparkling.

César said, 'You are saying that Shakespeare frightens you.'

She thought quickly. 'Perhaps . . . Suppose I'd gone steady in high school with Hamlet? Suppose I was engaged to Othello? Wouldn't that be frightening?'

César said, 'I wonder whether you are really frightened, or only think you ought to be. You have come to live with us, haven't you?'

'What's that got to do with it?' she asked, puzzled.

He shrugged slightly. 'Spain is Shakespearean. The food is strong-tasting and strange to you. Nothing is hygienic or temperate. People feel big feelings, and kill each other for them. People rip their backs with metal whips on Good Friday, in penitence for something they themselves didn't do. You could have seen this from a distance, homogenized and predigested like your food – but you have come here.'

Staring into his eyes, very close, she could not think of anything to say. Perhaps he was right. No, damn it, she'd come here to shake off the last bonds of responsibility still weighing her down, to be free to find where happiness and life lay for her.

The cathedral clock tolled twelve heavy strokes. My God, she'd been in here over an hour. She reached out her hand for the books and said, 'I'll take them.' He handed them to her without a word. She said, 'I *must* go . . . but, César, there is one thing my father wanted me to mention to you.' She told

69

him about the double-header, and ended, 'What do you think? I mean, Dad's anxious to have an honest opinion before he really starts to organize it.'

'Has he spoken to the mayor yet?' César asked.

'He wanted your private opinion first.'

Cesar said, 'I see. The mayor *is* an easy man to persuade ... I think it might be a good idea.'

'But . . .' Kit began. She stopped.

'What?'

'Isn't it rather, well, risky? I haven't been outside the base long, but already I wonder if we aren't trying too hard, and ...'

César interrupted her with sudden abruptness. 'Possibly. I can only tell you what I think – that it might be a great success. There is always the chance of misunderstandings.'

Now she had insulted him somehow. He was unpredictable. She said, awkwardly, 'Well, thank you. Good night.'

He said, 'Good night ... You needn't read the Shakespeare if you don't want to.'

'I know,' she said. 'But I do. Good night.'

'Good night ... I shouldn't read tonight. You look a little tired.'

'I am, I suppose. Well . . .' She smiled, and closed the door gently behind her. He was standing, unmoving, by the shelves, looking at her. She walked very slowly along the dark passage and up the stairs, wondering, testing, trying to pin down her emotions.

*

The intercom at his elbow buzzed softly. Without raising his head Colonel Lindquist said, 'Yes.'

'Major Fremantle, sir. Can he come in for a second?'

'Give me ten minutes.'

'Right, sir.'

Colonel Lindquist went on reading. The paper, a top-secret intelligence brief on Russian progress in air-to-air guided missile systems, could not be put down and taken up again at will.

In ten minutes he reached the end and sat back in his chair. Ham Fremantle. He sighed. The job here was really too big for Ham; but on the other hand the only way a man could grow was in a job too big for him. Look at Harry Truman. Come to that, look at Kit, thinking she was avoiding responsibility and instead walking into a post as unofficial ambassador to Medina, besides her personal problems. Perhaps he'd been heartless to advise her to go; but he wouldn't advise her differently if she came again. You had to learn some time that standing alone was the biggest responsibility of all.

Major Fremantle came in, saluted and spoke with tight deliberation. 'Colonel, someone's knocked the balls off the Bull of San Marco.'

Lindquist stared at him in astonishment and then broke into a wide grin that suddenly made his face boyish. 'Well now, that's as fine an introduction to a military conference as I've heard for some time.'

'Someone did it in the middle of the night, knocked them off with a sledge-hammer.'

'The pride and joy of Medina,' the colonel said thoughtfully. 'Second only to the Armlet, which has already disappeared.'

'Yes, sir. They've got a lot of proverbs all over Spain, making out the men here are the prize goats of all time, on account of the Bull.'

'And now the jokes will be going round to the opposite effect,' the colonel said. 'Who did it?'

'Nobody knows. There's a rumour that it was some of our boys, drunk . . . wanted to take them home as souvenirs.'

The colonel said abruptly, 'I don't believe it. Didn't I hear about some trouble at the *paseo* yesterday evening, some of our men persuading a few girls to have a Coke with them, for the first time?'

'Yes, sir. I was going to tell you about that . . .'

'Sure. I'm not accusing you of anything, Ham . . . It seems to me that this is a gibe against themselves, for letting our men take their girls. I think some Spanish kids did it.'

'I hope so, sir, but . . .'

'I don't. I'd rather they attacked us than lashed themselves into a frenzy.'

'And there are these rumours . . .'

'Yes. But, Ham you mustn't get so worked up about rumours. There are always rumours, and we've got to hear them and collect them, track them to their sources if possible, and study them for trends. You're doing a fine job there. Very good.'

'Thank you, sir.'

'But we mustn't let them divert us. After our SAC mission our first task here is the maintenance and improvement of Spanish-American relations. Unless Kit finds some secret key

71

to the problem, I am damn sure that our only course is to go ahead in a straight line, doing our duty . . . If the city police bring up a clue that points to our men having knocked off the bull's balls, we'll cooperate in catching them. But I'm not going down there screaming *mea culpa*.'

'No, sir. Of course not. Uh, colonel. I've been working on that double-header idea. I'd like to talk about it pretty soon. I've got a prospectus made up, and . . .'

'This afternoon. Four-fifteen. How's Kit getting on, by the way?'

'Fine, sir.'

'Perhaps she'll hear something about the bull's missing equipment. She's not shy.'

'Shy, sir? She'll talk about anything. She keeps shocking Peggy, especially since she's been here. You know the way the Spanish girls call a spade a spade. Kit thinks it's a fine idea.'

'And yet she's as unworldly as a child, in some ways . . . O.K., Ham. This afternoon.'

'Yes, sir.'

Alone again, the colonel sat a moment looking at the door. Then he pressed down a switch and said, 'Jim, I'm ready.'

CHAPTER 6

The night of the Day of *Jota* one had a snack at the barbarous hour of eight, in Medina Lejo. In the *posadas* and restaurants every male member of the dancing teams would already be wearing the *baturro* costume, and so would as many others as possessed it, which was not many. In the houses, the women would change into costume after supper. That was the custom . . .

At a quarter to nine that evening Kit found herself alone with Bel in the small drawing-room of the Casa Aguirre. Doña Teresa had just gone to her room to change.

The two girls were alone. Bel lowered her voice. 'Is everything arranged?'

Kit said, 'Yes. He'll be in the upper room by half past ten. Mind you're back in the Plaza by half past eleven, though.'

'I will,' Bel whispered. 'I must change. He's never

seen me as a *baturra* before. César doesn't really like me to wear the costume – after all, it's a peasant dress – but this year I insisted. I wanted to show Pete.'

She hurried out of the room. Slowly Kit followed her. She must remember to take her light-weight coat, hung inconspicuously on her arm, because Bel was going to throw it over her shoulders when she slipped away from the Plaza San Marco to go to the blind cobbler's. In the side pocket of the coat was one of Bel's black suède court shoes with the heel broken off. In America shoemakers were seldom open at half past ten at night; but this was Spain. It was all very clandestine, and vaguely troubling.

She opened the door of her bedroom. It was César she had been deceiving when she telephoned Olmbacher. And César was a human being – twenty-six years old, who smoked too much cheap black tobacco, so that it stained his fingers, and had as many doubts and problems as the most disturbed girl she'd met in college, and *that* was saying something.

She'd better get going. She opened the doors of the tall wardrobe, and stared at her clothes. Tonight everyone in Medina was dressing up, and she ought to. Earlier in the week she had thought of getting Señora Arocha the dressmaker to make her a *baturra* costume like Bel's – ballet-length red and black skirt over five vari-coloured petticoats, white cotton stockings, white blouse, red and black shawl. She'd asked César, and he'd said, 'You would look superb.'

But that was all, and his voice absolutely neutral, so she'd pressed him. 'But *should* I? You know what I mean.' He said, 'You are old enough to make up your own mind, aren't you? In Spain, an adult person is presumed to know what he is doing, to know the possible consequences, and to have decided it is worth it.' And she, insistently, 'Well, I'm not Spanish and I *am* asking your advice.' Then he said, 'The Day of the *Jota* is not a fancy dress parade, but a part of our life.'

That was that, and she'd been pleased to find that her qualms had a sound base. She though of Jo-Ann Goodwin, who had spent three months with her husband in Pakistan, and now always went to cocktail parties in harem trousers and a long bright skirt down to her knees.

She looked into the wardrobe. The full-length white organdie was too girlish, and too 'indoors'. The green didn't really go with her eyes and she should never have allowed her mother to buy it for her. This was it – the red velvet sheath, slim, and

73

severe, and she'd wear the big black brooch Bill had given her, and black shoes . . .

Half an hour later, as she reached the foot of the stairs a deep sigh from close by made her turn round with an involuntary start. The girl Eloísa, in *baturra* costume, was standing in the deep shadow under the stairs. She said, 'Ah, señorita, you were beautiful, coming down the stairs.'

Kit smiled. 'Thank you, Eloísa . . . but how did you see?'

The girl pointed to the long mirror in the wall beside the front door. She said, 'Juana and I often hide here to see a guest coming down the stairway, if it is a handsome man, or beautiful, rich lady.' She leaned forward confidentially, her eyes dancing. 'And we are not the only ones.'

Kit said, 'Oh?' It was about time Bel came down, or they'd be late. She glanced at her wrist-watch.

Eloísa said, 'Don César sometimes watches . . . *you!*'

Kit jerked into full awareness of what the girl was saying. 'Me? Don't be silly, Eloísa.'

'You,' the girl repeated. 'He watches you, and I watch him. He likes you, señorita. And you like him, eh?' The pert little face was alive with the eagerness of intrigue.

Kit said. 'Of course, but . . . oh, Eloísa, I just like him, as I like you or Señorita Bel.'

Eloísa shook her head slowly from side to side. 'Impossible,' she said. 'Men and women cannot like each other that way. I know what you feel, because I have watched you with Don César, when you two are alone. Don't be afraid, though, I shan't tell anyone. Never, never!' Dramatically, she held her lips together.

Kit thought in exasperation, Really, these Shakespearean romantics! The girl was leaning forward again. 'My sergeant is coming down to watch the *jotas*. Many Americans are coming, he says. He told me, at the *paseo* yesterday. We have a Coca-Cola with them most days now, I and my friends. It is better than marching up and down, and round and round.'

'What do the young men say?'

'They do not like it. We tell them to mind their own business.' She pouted prettily. Her face became alive again. 'Tommee, that is my sergeant, earns two thousand five hundred pesetas a week. If I married him, I would never have to work again in my *life*! I would have servants of my own, American servants, and I would say to them, clean that, bring this . . .' She gestured imperiously with her arms, the *baturra*

74

shawl jumping to her movements. 'But I would be kind to them, like Doña Teresa.' She slipped away, smiling.

Kit looked after her, wishing that she herself could find so much excitement in life. So César had been watching her. Or fixing his tie, or looking for his matches, or something . . .

Bel came, and then Doña Teresa, stately as a galleon, and ten minutes later, as they walked into the Plaza San Marco, the tenor bell of the cathedral clock was striking ten.

'Just in time,' Kit said.

Doña Teresa said, 'In Spain, only one thing begins on time, the *corrida de toros*.'

A clatter of many voices, and the broken phrases of guitars being tuned, broke over them. The wide stone steps, running the whole length of the south façade of the cathedral, were thickly crowded with people – standing, sitting, moving about. People swirled in throngs about the Plaza, and people leaned out of the windows of the houses all around, above the arched collonade. The street lamps cast thin pools of yellow light in their accustomed places, but the dominant light in the square pulsed out in orange and scarlet waves from a dozen flaming torches set on tall poles around the Plaza and up the sides of the cathedral steps. Where the flames ended, columns of black smoke wavered on upwards into the sky. Moving slowly along the lower steps behind Doña Teresa and Bel, Kit saw Americans among the crowd, easily recognizable by their light shirts, light coats, and the cameras in their hands or around their necks. There were Spanish airmen here too, and stunted infantrymen, long red tassels dangling down from their caps in front of their eyes. But all these were small drab islands in a heaving sea of colour – the people of Medina Lejo, in their traditional costume. Atop the huge plinth it was no bull but an emasculated ox that guarded San Marco. She had heard that it would take two weeks to cast new testicles and weld them into place.

Doña Teressa said, 'Why, César, I didn't know you were dressing *a lo baturro* tonight.'

Kit turned quickly as *César* answered, 'I am bored with sack suits. Besides, I wish to show that it is not the height of every Spanish aristocrat's ambition to look like a New Yorker.' He was standing on the step below, dressed in the Aragonese costume.

Kit said, 'You look wonderful. Why don't you wear that every day?'

75

He glanced at her, and smiled briefly. 'Or the suit of lights? . . . You have left your camera. How will anyone know you are an American?'

She said, 'Now, don't try to annoy me. You know it doesn't work. Dad will take enough pictures. I just want to watch.'

César turned to go and they called after him, 'Good luck!'

A moment later as they stood on the steps, Doña Teresa said, 'There is Doña Luisa. I must talk to her. You will be here?'

'Oh, we may walk around a bit,' Bel said carelessly. The clock struck a single note, the quarter past the hour, the heavy tones falling thunderously into the stone pit of the square. Bel sat down on the cold step and carefully Kit followed suit. Bel whispered, 'I shall go in a minute . . . Here are the judges.'

Three men in business suits, very Western and drab, sat down in a row on the fourth step up from the square. A priest was there, in long cassock and biretta. The music of guitars and *bandurrias* and castanets grew louder. Suddenly, the dancing began.

Bel muttered, 'Now.'

Kit handed over the coat. 'Be careful,' she whispered, smiling. Bel threw her an agonized look. Her eyes were huge and dark, seemingly sightless in their inward-turned intensity. She moved off along the steps, and in a moment was lost among the people. After a moment of anxiety, Kit turned her attention to the dancing.

The cleared space was thirty or forty feet square, and ringed with spectators and other competitors. The dancers whirled and met and whirled again; the castanets clattered in the tremendous, tripping rhythm of the dance; the guitars plucked out the resonant chords. The dancers met, for a moment danced together in an intricate, violent, kicking pattern. An unintelligible cry rose from the crowd, a single voice crying, *Hola maño!* . . . and wailing off into a low gabble. The crowd murmured in approval, and a man in the front rank, by the guitarists, held a leather bottle high in the air and squirted a thin stream of read wine into his mouth. The guitars slowed and transposed to the minor key. A woman at the side stepped forward two paces, flung out her hand towards the judges on the steps, and began to sing.

Her voice was strong, not resonant but lined with metal, deep in pitch, and very loud. She sang two lines, and at the end of nearly every note she dragged the note down in falling steps

76

and slurs. The crowd murmured and a voice yelled, '*Y además de verdad!*' A long pause, and she sang again, throwing the couplet at the packed steps, at the towering cathedral, at the sky.

It's such a simple tune, Kit thought, I ought to be able to sing it myself. She tried, but it wasn't as simple as it sounded. The woman sang again, the same tune, different words. Kit put her hands over her ears to keep out the other sounds and hear only herself singing. That was better. Now the woman stepped back and the dancers burst into a final brief frenzy. They ended among shouts and cries and the passing round of leather bottles. The judges scribbled in pencil on the stone steps. For a moment there was no other distraction. Kit put her hand over her ears, closed her eyes, and tried again.

When she put down her hands a voice beside her said in Spanish, 'That is almost right, señorita.'

Kit turned with a smile. It was the woman now sitting next to her on the steps who had spoken, and the face was familiar. Almost at once she recalled that it was Señora Arocha the dressmaker. She was dressed in *baturra* costume, her shawl of scarlet silk with a pattern of widely spaced yellow roses. Kit said, 'I can't get the small notes, and they seem to be part of the melody.'

Señora Arocha nodded. 'It is not easy. Listen.' She leaned close and sang very softly. Her hoarse voice held the tune, then slid slowly off, not smoothly as in glissade, but in steps, like a stream dropping over a series of small falls of different heights.

Kit said, 'You make it sound so easy ... I saw you at the *corrida*. Aren't you Señora Arocha?'

'Marcia Arocha.'

Kit said, 'I'm Catherine Fremantle ... I nearly came to you to have a *baturra* dress made for tonight, but César thought it wouldn't be a good idea, so I didn't.'

The woman smiled pleasantly. 'You do not have to introduce yourself. Everyone in Medina knows who you are. You are the young American who is staying at the Casa Aguirre to see what the Yankee Ghetto looks like from the outside ... Now we have the Falcons.' She nodded down at the open space, now filled with another jota group. 'The first team were the Children of the Miracle.' She sank into silence. Kit glanced at her wrist watch. Nearly ten to eleven.

'How many more teams are there after this?' she asked her companion.

'Four,' she replied. 'The White Goats, then the Jabalí . . .'

'That's César's society,' Kit interjected.

'Yes,' the woman said gravely. '. . . Then the Pyreneans, and lastly, the Roses of Aragon, which is my team.'

The dancing continued. The noise from the crowd grew louder and less patterned as the leather bottles continued to pass round. Camera bulbs flashed like a battlefield round the cleared space where the dancers were, but no one seemed to mind. Five airmen were sitting quite near her, in a row on the steps, not drinking, absorbed in the spectacle and the noise, looking like so many cowboys on a non-existent corral fence.

Kit kept looking secretly and with increasing frequency at her watch. The dancing music and the clapping of hands and the clatter of castanets were numbing her faculties. She didn't want to have to worry about Bel. She wanted to dance and sing and drink red wine like everyone else.

A moment or two before the half-hour she saw Bel, and could not hide a small sigh of relief. Her companion turned to her inquiringly, but Kit said, 'Look, here are the Jabalí!' Bel was on the edge of the crowd round the cleared space. All was well. 'And there's César. But of course you know him.'

The woman nodded. 'Everyone in Medina does.'

'His wrist isn't mended,' Kit said. 'That was a terrible toss he took. I can't think how he managed to kill the bull after it.'

'By courage,' Marcia Arocha said.

Kit said, 'He's very brave. You must all be very proud of him here in Medina.'

The woman said, 'Some are.'

The guitars had started, thrumming slowly, now the beat quickening. The men and women were in the starting pose, arms raised, elbows bent over their heads. The Jabalí singer, a man, stood with his hands on his hips. César stood at the edge of the crowd, directly below her and beyond the dancers.

They began to dance. Kit cried, 'I do hope we win. Let's clap hard to influence the judges . . . Oh, I am sorry. I forgot, you are on another team.' She laughed happily at her companion. She was a nice woman, very calm and friendly. A widow perhaps.

The woman smiled. 'It does not matter. I will clap with you for a moment, señorita – because it has been an enchantment to meet you . . . You like Spain?'

'Oh, yes, everything!' Kit said. 'I love it. In the base, I didn't, but here . . . the colours seem brighter and the wind stronger, and . . . I can't explain.'

78

The woman's hoarse voice was low. 'How old are you?'

Kit said, 'Twenty-two.'

The woman said, 'Spain *is* strong wine, I think, for an American girl of twenty-two. I am thirty-two . . . Good night.' Kit had hardly time to answer before she was gone.

For a brief moment she stared after her. Those were slightly odd remarks. Oh well, they would have been odd at home perhaps, but this was Spain. And Bel was coming up the side of the steps, settling down beside her, in the place Señora Arocha had been in.

Kit muttered, 'O.K.?'

Bel whispered, 'Yes. Take your coat. Does it look as if I've been crying?' Kit glanced at her and said, 'Not in this light. Shh!'

'Hi, Kit! Good evening, Miss Aguirre. I've been looking all over the place for you. Say isn't this something?'

It was her father. Kit pushed closer to Bel. 'Sit down, Dad. You're blocking the view.'

Her father squeezed himself into place. César was watching her. Or just looking in this direction?

Her father said, 'That singing, it's enough to break your eardrums when you're close to it.'

The Jabalís were nearing the end, the pace quickening, the white stockings flinging up and down, in and out, the red skirts whirling.

Her father said, 'Kit, I've got . . .'

'Shh!' she muttered. 'This is *our* team.' Her father muttered, 'O.K., O.K.,' and lit a cigarette.

The Jabalís ended. For a moment, while the echoes of the guitar died, they held the classic pose that began and ended all the dances. Kit leaped to her feet, clapping and shouting. After a time she realized that though others around her were making the same demonstration, the applause was fading. In a moment, she would be alone. She sat down slowly.

'Rah for Aguirre U!' her father said. 'Can I speak now? . . . About the double-header. The mayor's enthusiastic and the colonel's agreed. I had to do a lot of talking, but finally he said he'd let me give it a whirl. We're in business. The American fair's slated for Sunday, 3 August, and the Spanish fiesta for the following Saturday, 9 August. The mayor wondered whether we could get it arranged in time, but hell, there's nothing to it. And here's the icing, Kit. There's going to be a little private election, the mayor and me and a couple of others,

79

to choose the queen of the fiesta. Of course they don't usually have queens at an ordinary Spanish fiesta, but the mayor thought it was a great idea. Well, we're having *our* election the day after tomorrow – and you've been chosen.'

Kit listened with half an ear. The Jabalís had done well, perhaps the best so far, judging by the applause. She shouldn't have been making such a row herself and then she would have been able to gauge better what the experts, the crowd here, thought about them.

'You're going to be the queen,' her father repeated.

'Really?' she asked with forced enthusiasm. 'How wonderful!'

9 August was two weeks from today. She couldn't get the shape of the fiesta into her head, so she couldn't feel very excited. Were they going to pick a court of other girls, put them in bouffant white dresses, choose them escorts from the young men of Medina, and send the whole lot slowly through the streets in open Cadillac convertibles? And then seats on the fifty-yard line at the *corrida*? But there was no *corrida* until César fought again, on San Marco . . .

'I'll have to have some clothes,' she said. That at least was a reality.

'Sure,' her father said. 'You think about it. You might wear this *baturra* costume, eh? I guess that would be a popular move, señorita?'

'Yes,' Bel said. 'I'm sure people would be very pleased.'

Kit looked at her suspiciously, but Bel's face was perfectly open. Perhaps it would be a good idea in the special circumstances. She must ask César.

Her father said, 'I've got to go down. You know what? I've got Airman Gralinski down there with a note pad, and two guys from the Photographic Wing with movie cameras. Gralinski was studying choreography before he came into the Air Force. He's noting the steps down, and the cameras will catch what he can't. It doesn't look too hard.' He lowered his voice and bent his head closer to hers. 'Next year, we're going to enter a team. But keep that under your hat till I give out the release.' He stood up. ''Bye, señorita. *Hasta la vista!* Night, Kit.'

He hurried off up the steps, along the façade of the cathedral, at a brisk walk, past the green and black statuary group of the cloaked Guardia Civil, down the steps at the side. Kit watched him go with a pang and a spurt of familiar exasperation at her heart. Poor Dad wasn't young and he wasn't clever, but he had to act as if he were. He wasn't cheerful, but he had to pretend to be, because at home pessimism was worse than halitosis He should have been a Spaniard, and worn his uselessness like a black hat and cloak, with dignity, a man universally respected for his failure. Well, she must play her part in the fiesta, and play it well, for his sake.

Now suddenly the time began to pass quickly. She asked Bel how the assignment had gone, and Bel muttered, 'The same. Everything, and nothing.'

Kit thought she was going to cry again, and changed the subject. 'Look,' she said. 'Señora Arocha is singing. You know her, don't you? She was sitting up here for a bit.'

Bel said, 'We know her slightly. She has been a widow for seven years. She has no children.'

'She sings really beutifully,' Kit said.

Marcia Arocha dominated the cleared space and the whole Plaza. The dancing torches threw strong light and powerful shadows on the agony of love and misery in her face as she sang, her hand achingly outstretched. Her singing was in a different class from anything that had gone before. Her voice was deep and loud and lined with metal, as theirs had been, but with fire in it that set the skin at Kit's neck crawling.

Bel said, 'She is singing of the Virgin saving the shrine of Pilar in Zaragoza from the French.'

'She's ... *fantastic*,' Kit whispered, awed by the singer's passion.

'She can dance, too,' Bel said. 'She is the best dancer in Medina. All kinds – *flamenco, jota, tango, sardana, castellana ...*'

'César should get her for the Jabalí then,' Kit said. 'Then we'd always win.'

Bel said nothing. Suddenly the song ended, and it was all over. The crowd milled across the cleared space, and in a moment, without sign or order, the three judges and the priest on the steps had become the focus of the Plaza. Bel and Kit stood up to see better. Everyone was on his feet and the melodies and patterned dances of the *jota* societies had died to a single guitar, played by a drunken man leaning against the plinth of the statue, and a child of six, *a lo baturro*, whirling alone in the street.

The three judges and the priest rose to their feet. To the melancholy notes of the drunken, hesitant guitar the judge in the centre spoke, in a voice hardly above conversational level. 'We, the adjudicators, have seen and made judgement, according to ancient custom and the classical and correct way of dancing the *jota* of Aragon, we now declare that the prize dancers for this sacred year of grace, 1958, are the Roses of Aragon. Second the Jabalí. Third, the Children of the Miracle.' There was a burst of clapping and shouted cries. Now many guitars started throbbing and voices rose in song. The priest gave the blessing. Men took the tall torch poles out of their sockets, shouldered them – still flaming – and trudged off. The dim street lamps and the lighted open doors of the cathedral were the only illuminations in the Plaza San Marco. The music and singing grew louder . . .

'What now?' Kit asked.

'We should go to César,' Bel said. 'Mother's with him . . .'

They went down, and Kit congratulated César on his team's showing, adding, 'The Roses of Aragon only won because of Señora Arocha.'

César looked at her for a moment. 'Señora Arocha sings and dances very well.'

One guitar, among the dozen or so now throbbing among the slowly swirling crowd, was plunking a new beat, a steady twanka-twanka-twanka.

Doña Teresa said, 'I'm going home. No, no, child, you and Kit can stay here . . . until half past one.'

César said briefly, 'I will take them, Mother.'

Doña Teresa said, 'Good. Then of course you can stay out as late as you like.'

Bel said, 'I'm very tired, *hermanito*. I think I'll go home with Mother. You stay, Kit . . . Of course!'

César bent to kiss his mother on the cheek. Then she and Bel left, they were alone.

Two more guitars had joined the first in the new, pounding rhythm. Soon a voice rose above the plunking, strutting guitars, and César said, 'What's that?'

The voice was not singing but calling, in English. The caller, a plump young man with a crew-cut and a big bottom, stood on the lowest of the cathedral steps, clapping his hands and calling the steps of 'Dive for the oyster, dig for the clam.' César moved slowly forward, his lips tight. Kit said hurriedly. 'They're only square dancing. It's an old dance, a folk dance, Elizabethan, I believe . . . I'm rather hungry.'

César said, 'In a minute.'

82

The space in front of the statue had become clear again. Twenty or thirty American airmen were there, and as many young Spaniards, including a dozen girls. Three armed police were there, watching interestedly. Her father was there, on the steps, beaming and clapping his hands. One airman was playing a harmonica and three were using borrowed guitars, the *baturro* owners leaning over them, smiling. In the cleared space four airmen, including a tall, strong Negro, were showing the steps of the dance to four giggling Spanish girls, one of whom was Eloísa.

Everyone was having a wonderful time. Eloísa's head was thrown back and her mouth was open, and the man opposite her was laughing down into her face. The caller changed to 'Turkey in the Straw'. More men and girls, Americans and Spaniards, were swept into the dance.

Her father saw her and shouted across, 'Look at this, Kit! Isn't this something?'

César watched, silent, and when she stole a glance at his face she could read absolutely nothing in it. The Plaza San Marco rocked to the beat of the dance and the caller's rapid, nasal call. In the upper rooms people leaned out of the windows to watch. The *baturra* skirts whirled and the girls shrieked as their partners swung them in the air. The white woollen stockings tripped round and round and the turbaned heads – it was nine hundred and twenty years since the Moors held rule here – turned and bobbed.

A little distance off, standing with his friend Dick Holmes, she saw Bill Lockman. Dick was a fighter pilot, a man from Iowa, angular, bony face, blue eyes, brown hair, big hands – American Gothic. He was watching the square dancing, but Bill was looking at her. Perhaps he's been watching her for a long time. She felt a pang of guilt, for she had hardly thought of him since arriving at the Casa Aguirre; and yet, seeing him now, she was glad and pleased. She beckoned to him and they came over. She made the introductions.

César said, 'I had the pleasure of meeting you at Colonel Linquist's cocktail party, did I not? I believe you were also sitting next to my sister at the *corrida*?'

'Yes, I was,' Bill said awkwardly. 'And I guess I ought to . . .'

Kit cut in quickly. 'Look at them now!' He was going to apologize for his behaviour at the *corrida*, and it was all over now. Still, it was nice of him. He *was* nice, period. Nice. What

83

kind of a word was that to use about a man you were thinking of accepting as a husband?

They watched the square dancing for a few minutes. Then abruptly César spoke. 'All right,' he said; and again, 'Very well.' He looked down at her, his eyes bright and hot. 'We shall go and have something to eat.'

Bill glanced up at the clock. 'At a quarter past one?' He laughed. 'That's late even for Spain, isn't it?'

César threw out his hands and hunched up his shoulders in a gesture Kit had never seen him make. His voice was slightly sing-song, rising on the ends of the words, like the standard way of telling a 'Mexican' story, the vowels dragged out ... but nothing more than the hint of a suspicion. 'Eet ees a custom,' he said, 'to eat after thee *jotas*. We would be so happy if you could come with us. We are going to the Casa Córdoba, a very nice restaurant, *muy típico*.'

Bill and Dick looked at each other. Dick said, 'I think that's a fine idea, sir.'

César cried, 'Wonderfool! Thees way!' He flung out his hand, bowing a little. Together they walked towards the Calle del Alcalde. They passed under the frowning mass of the city hall, the Ayuntamiento, and as they entered the narrow street the sounds of the dancing and singing behind were caught for a moment by the ornamented stone and the black arches, and hurled back and forth in a maniacal echoing and re-echoing that broke the rhythm into a crazy syncopation and the song into the jangle of lunatics. Then it was quiet and they heard only their footfalls on the cobbles.

CHAPTER 7

The street lamps cast light in isolated pools on the street. Upwards, in the violet curtain of the dark there were squares of yellow light, and in the squares black silhouettes, always motionless, always women. On the street the doors were closed, then came a sudden vista down a tunnel into a central patio lit by candles, aflame with geraniums ... and here another alley, a mounting criss-cross tangle of clothes hanging on lines, strung from window to window; and a child reading a book alone

84

under a pale lamp beside a barred door. The cathedral clock on its hill boomed a distant, deep two strokes.

'Look at that kid,' Bill muttered to Dick Holmes. 'He can't be more than ten, and it's two o'clock.'

Kit thought, Please ... don't say anything wrong tonight. This was a night for adventure and excitement.

César stopped in front of a low open doorway set down three steps from street level. The windows beside the door were grimed with dirt. There were many people inside, and someone was playing a guitar. César said, 'Here we are – the Casa Córdoba. It is a very primitive sort of place, I'm afraid, captain, but very typical.'

'Fine,' Bill said heartily, and followed César down the steps; but Kit knew that he was not overjoyed at what he saw. The room was long and narrow, the bar occupying half the length of the left-hand wall. The floor was covered with sand, stains of spilled wine, spittle, and a pink debris of shrimp shells.

They moved forward in single file between the men crowding the bar and the tables squeezed against the opposite wall. The man behind the bar, who was wearing a dirty blue shirt and a beret and had not shaved for a week, raised his hand and nodded as César passed. César leaned over the bar and shook his hand. '*Qué tal?*' he said. 'I've brought some of our American friends to see how we live below the surface in Medina.' The man shrugged and turned to a customer, and César led on.

Past the end of the bar, where the room widened, a gipsy with a guitar was sitting on a rickety wooden chair. Beside him a woman leaned against the wall, and her kohl-rimmed eyes stared stonily at the visitors as they passed her. In the gloom at the end of the room César pulled back chairs from an unoccupied table. To the side, at similar tables, three women sat alone, all three heavily made-up and all showing a great deal of leg as they sat with thighs crossed in short skirts. At two other tables were two men, also alone. Kit saw Bill throw Dick Holmes, a tight-lipped look, and Dick make a small shrug. Through an open door filtered a strong smell of hot olive oil and a clattering of pots.

She sat down, César muttered to the waiter and turned to them, his hands spread. 'It is a place of character, this. *Muy español.* I don't suppose there is anything quite like this in your country, captain?'

Bill said, 'We have places like this.'

His face was set and cold. Obviously he thought that César had no right to bring her here.

César called, 'Marta!'

The gipsy woman came over, her cat-like face splitting in a smile to show broken teeth; but she had been good-looking once and still walked with a scornful litheness.

César said, 'Sing for us. Something special.'

The woman said, '*Lo que quieras, maestro.*'

Glasses of sherry had appeared on the table – dirty glasses. She saw Bill hesitate fractionally before he stretched out his hand. César saw too, and cried, 'Ah, I am so sorry, captain. I never thought. Waiter! Pssst!'

Bill said, 'It's O.K. Don't bother, please.'

'But of course,' César said. 'You don't drink manzanilla, do you?'

Bill said, 'Not usually, but look, don't . . .'

The waiter was there and César was speaking to him. 'Take these away, and bring two Scotch instead. In *clean* glasses. On the rocks?'

'Sure, that'll be fine.'

'On ice, Manolo.'

'There isn't any ice.'

César smiled apologetically. 'Spain is so primitive.'

'Plain water's O.K. with me,' Bill said, and then, quickly, 'Make that soda.'

Kit had seen his eye light on the thumb-marked, clouded water jug in the middle of the table. It did look rather disgusting . . . but this was Spain, wasn't it? If the Spanish could drink the water, why couldn't he?

The guitar wandered up and down the scales, searching for a melody, and found one in a minor key. The woman began to clap her hands, slowly at first, then quicker. Someone at the bar let out one of those sudden shouts, '*Eso es! Anda, anda!*'

Dick Holmes was enjoying himself in his calm, sensible way. César asked him politely about his home and family. Dick told him of his father's country store in Iowa, and described the land, and the distance, and going as a boy to fish in the creek.

César's attention suddenly focused. 'And from this, you fly at a thousand kilometres an hour through our sky, shut up with ten other men in a winged prison full of instruments, twelve thousand metres above us . . .'

Dick said, 'Alone. I fly an F-104 ... And I guess I'd just as soon fly through the Iowa sky, if they'd let me.'

Kit tapped her foot to the rhythm of the guitar. Bill was still looking cold and angry, but she would *not* let him spoil her evening. She was no longer bound to feel disgusted by the dirt, the grubby glasses, the smell of oil, the surly man behind the bar, the whores in the corner. She was a free agent.

The song ended. César said, 'We must eat. *Pssst!* ... What would you like?'

Bill said, 'A sandwich, maybe. A ham sandwich. Something plain.' Dick nodded agreement.

César turned to the waiter. 'What is there, Manolo?'

The waiter said, *'Sesos, callos.'*

César turned apologetically. 'They only have brains and tripe. Very typical dishes, of course. They do them quite well here.' He looked anxiously at Bill.

Kit said, 'Oh, try one, Bill. It won't kill you.'

Bill shook his head. 'I'm sorry, Mr Aguirre. I just can't eat them.'

César said, 'I *quite* understand. And I'm afraid the ham will be country ham, even if he can get it. Very tough and spicy ... Manolo, you must have some hamburger.' The whores and the fairies and the men at the bar were watching and listening.

The waiter said stolidly, *'No hay hamburguesa.'*

César said, 'Well, please get some. My friends want some. Tell Luis to send out for some.'

The waiter shrugged and trudged off. César said, 'For us ... I think tripe is heavy on the stomach at this time of night. The brains?' Kit nodded and César shouted after the waiter, *'Y dos raciones de sesos!'* He shook his head as he turned back to Bill. 'We shall get some civilized food, never fear. And milk to drink with it?'

'This will do me,' Bill said shortly, indicating his whisky and soda.

'Good!' César sat back and lit a cigarette. 'Tell me honestly, how did you enjoy the bullfight?'

For a moment she thought it was bad of him to inject that old hostility into the evening; but then she thought, Bill did call him a fairy practically to his face. And besides, if they disliked each other so much it might be best to bring it into the open.

Bill answered the question – 'Not much.'

César said, 'It is a barbaric spectacle, I agree. We call it, you know, the *fiesta brava*, and that explains everything.'

'What does *brava* mean?' Dick Holmes asked.

César said, 'It means brave, but also wild, untamed.' Kit thought that he spoke no more politely to Dick. 'It is a hard word to translate with precision. Wild horses that run free on the range, and have not subjected themselves to harness, are *caballos bravos*. The fighting bulls, which will die, fighting, on the sand, among brilliant colours, but will never do anything useful, and will never wear the yoke – they are *toros bravos*. When you say that the bullfight is the *fiesta brava* you have said everything, for and against.'

'I've never been,' Dick said. 'I wouldn't like to see the animals deliberately hurt before they were killed.'

César said quietly. 'You are honest not to go, then. For us Spaniards it is a little different. We are cruel people, and feel no one's sufferings, even our own. And you, captain, you will not go again?'

Bill said, 'I feel the same as Dick. Kit made me go.'

César said, 'Of course ... and yet, when your time comes would you rather die in air combat or be shot against a wall?'

'The cattle in the stockyards don't know what's going to happen to them,' Bill said.

'Nor do the bulls in the ring,' César said. 'Nor do I ... I am one of a number of matadors who are trying to have the protective padding taken off the horses. It was only put on for the foreigners, but it is not fair on the bull. How can he fight well, and feel brave and strong, unless at some time he stabs his horn into flesh and blood? But I see you are pained by this talk.'

Bill said nothing, but Dick would not let the subject go. He said slowly, 'I think, sir, that what I don't like is the intention. Sure, the cattle have a bad time in the stockyards. They can smell the blood and hear the squealing, and they're in a panic. I've seen them. But we need the meat and we're doing our best to kill them as painlessly as possible.'

César said gravely, 'Suppose we need, not meat, but art – an art *bravo*, a spirit *bravo*?' The gipsy woman began to sing again, and he raised his voice to be heard.

Kit saw that Bill closed his ears to the discussion. He had just winced, but it was because the gipsy was singing raucously almost into his ear. The noise in the café was terrific. Several men were having a loud argument and the barman had switched

88

on the radio, which was interspersing jazz music with deafening French commercials.

César had seen Bill's involuntary movement. Tonight Bill didn't seem to be able to draw a breath without César noticing it. César exclaimed, 'Really, I do not know what has come over us all tonight! You must excuse us. It is the Day of the *Jota*. Spain is a very noisy country and Aragon noisier than the rest of Spain . . . Marta! Marta!' The woman stopped her singing. César said, 'Can't you sing something more up to date?'

'Of course I can,' she said. 'For El Rondeño de Aragon I can sing anything.'

'Something modern, popular,' César said. 'There's a good girl.'

The woman turned to the guitarist and muttered something to him. In a moment she was singing 'Hound Dog,' as loudly as ever. Bill's face was pale with anger. The waiter returned with two plates of brains and two pieces of beef that had recently been chopped into a few large hunks and then overcooked in unrefined olive oil. That'll teach him, Kit thought. He'd asked for American food, and he'd have to eat it, and it would be awful. The brains didn't look too good either, and they had been cooked in the same olive oil, but she was determined to show nothing but pleasure.

The gipsy woman sang, 'I Want to Be Happy,' and César beat time eagerly with his hands. She sang 'White Christmas' and Bill pushed his plate away, the meat half finished. Dick Holmes carefully finished his portion. The atmosphere was a dense blue blend of burning olive oil and black tobacco fumes, and it was half past three. All the *baturro* costumes except César's had gone, and the people left in the tavern looked tough and very poor. The whores had each left the room twice, with men, disappearing up a narrow flight of stairs beside the door to the kitchen. A smooth young man had been talking to one of the 'rough trades' for the past half-hour, heads close together. Now they were holding hands. Kit thought she had a headache coming.

Suddenly César jumped to his feet. 'Excuse me . . . a friend of mine.' He was waving towards the far door, where a short, plump man had just entered, well dressed and alone.

Bill said, 'I think . . .'

César cried, 'One moment! You must meet Mario.'

He struggled towards the door, and returned a moment later, talking eagerly with the stranger. He made the introductions,

89

calling the newcomer only Mario. 'Mario has a last name,' he said, with a wink. 'But not in the Casa Córdoba, eh?'

Mario sat down in the chair César pulled up for him, next to Bill. César said, 'Our American friends are seeing some typical things here tonight, eh?'

Mario asked in Spanish, 'Do they speak Castillian?'

César said, 'The young lady, yes, very well. The gentlemen, no.'

Mario rubbed his hands together. He was very smooth, and his hands and wrists and face were hairless, but his eyes were alive and as he smiled at her across the table she thought, He could be amusing, very decadent, but fun. The womanish intonations of his voice came through clearly in spite of his broken English. 'Medina has very much *fascinating* things,' he was saying. 'Very, very much. I knowing all.' He turned to Bill. 'Spain *fascinating* place. Very rude.'

Bill said, 'I haven't seen much of it.'

Mario smiled softly. 'No? Some times you and me going see more fascinating things, *verdad*?' His plump right hand fell on to Bill's knee and gripped it.

Bill jerked his knee away. 'That would be great ... Señor Aguirre, I'm afraid Dick and I have got to go. He's due at the sheds at seven.'

The plump man edged his chair back close to Bill. 'Spain *more fascinating* for you than others, captain. Very handsome man. *Muy machote!* Everyone *loving* you in Spain ... girls, and *everybody*.' He gripped Bill's knee again. Kit pulled out her handkerchief and blew her nose to hide the laughter that was rising in explosive bursts to the surface.

Bill stood up abruptly. 'We've got to go, now.'

César stood up. 'Of course ... I was forgetting the time. Manolo, the bill!'

Marta was yelling, 'Three Coins in the Fountain' at the top of her hoarse flamenco voice, and Dick Holmes had just finished the last of his bread.

Bill said, 'We'd like to pay our share.'

César brushed him aside. 'No, no, please! You are my guests. I am so sorry that everything was so poor. Next time we must go to the Texas ...' He gave money to the waiter, pressed some more into Marta's hand, without interrupting her singing. Mario was on his feet, smiling that smooth smile, his tender voice caressing. 'My address is Penitentes 37, ground floor, captain . . . Telephone 6969. In French, *soixante-neuf*, twice over, eh? Please coming see me, call me!'

Then they were out in the street, a quarter to four in the morning. The street lamps were dark, there were no men singing, no guitars, a footfall here and there, two dim shapes under a tree. The Day of the *Jota* was dying at last.

César said, 'We are lucky in one thing. There is a taxi, at least. Hey, driver, wake up!' He banged on the door of an ancient Dodge sedan drawn up against the kerb, its driver curled asleep across the front seat.

Bill said, 'It's not far. We can walk.'

César said, 'If you wish, of course. A little fresh air is good for the lungs after an hour or two in the Córdoba. But Kit is a little tired, I think . . .'

The driver awoke, grunting and yawning. César said, 'Where have you left your car, captain?'

'In Penas de Juan Street.'

'Good, that is very near to our house. We shall go there. Driver, Penas de Juan!'

The driver staggered out, stretched, and began to wind the starting-handle. They were all four hunched up in the back of the car, César and Dick on jump seats. The motor roared into deafening sound, lurched, clanked into motion, and heaved away over the cobbles. A thick silence filled the inside of the car.

Bill said to Kit, 'Coming out to the pool tomorrow? I can come for you about eleven.'

She hesitated. It was impolite of him to ask her without asking César. Also she didn't know whether she wanted to go. He'd been awfully priggish this evening. Being with César seemed to bring out the most stuffy side, the side that worried her most when she thought of marrying him. But she did like him, and perhaps it would be different out at the base. She said, 'All right.'

'Don't put yourself out,' Bill said in a low voice. The taxi had stopped in the Calle Penas de Juan. Dick Holmes was holding the door open for her. She got out. 'Then I won't bother,' she whispered coldly.

César was standing with the driver in front of the taxi's headlights, fumbling in his pocket.

Bill said briefly, 'I've got it.' He pulled out some money and without looking at it, thrust it towards the taxi-driver.

'Please,' César said. 'You are my guests.'

'Not now,' Bill said curtly. 'Here.'

Kit saw that he was holding out two one-hundred-peseta notes – four dollars in all. César said quietly, 'Please allow me to fulfil my duties as your host.'

Bill said, 'I'm not your guest any more. And while we're on the subject, I don't want you to take Miss Fremantle to that joint again, or any place like it. I notice you didn't take your sister. I don't know much about Spain, but I know that nothing there is "typical" as you call it. It's just plain decadent –'

'Un-American?' César interjected politely.

'Yes, thank God,' Bill snapped. 'And Miss Fremantle doesn't need to have any part of it. Here,' he pushed the notes towards the taxi-driver. The taxi-driver looked inquiringly at César.

César reached out his hand, took the notes, tore them carefully across, and threw the pieces into Bill Lockman's face.

Dick Holmes took a quick step forward, but he was too late. Bill muttered, 'You son of a bitch!' and hit out with all the force of his right arm and doubled fist. César's feet didn't move, but his head swayed gently to the side and the blow passed by without touching him. Bill fell into him, recovered, and grunted with the effort of a left hook which thumped into César's body. César stepped back, his hands down.

Kit jumped forward screaming, 'Stop it!'

Dick Holmes had Bill in a strong hold by then. 'Take it easy,' he said. Kit found her hands out, and she was lashing Bill across the face with all her strength, left right left right, the blows cracking like pistol shots in the street, and high up a window slamming open and a voice yelling something in Spanish.

'You . . . you . . .!' she gasped. 'His wrist isn't healed.' She stood away at last.

Bill said, 'O.K., Dick. Thanks.' Dick let him go. Kit found herself trembling with a passion such as she had not known since the terrifying reasonless outbursts of childhood. She said, 'Who are you to tell me where I'm to go and not go? I'll go wherever I want to with whoever I want to. I'm not your property and I'm not a schoolgirl. I'm a free agent, a woman.'

Bill said quietly, 'Yes.'

Kit shrieked, 'Well, go on, get out, get back to the base, and stay there. I never want to see you again.'

Bill walked past her to César. He said, 'I meant what I said, but I shouldn't have hit you. I apologize.'

César bowed slightly. 'Your apology is accepted.'

Bill turned and climbed into his own car. César paid off the taxi-man, his hands steady as he counted out twenty-five pesetas. The motor of Bill's car started up.

César said, 'Come. It's time we went to bed.'

They walked in silence up the street. The lights of Bill's car sprang out behind them, passed them, turned the corner, and vanished.

Kit found tears in her eyes. She said, 'I'm sorry, César.'

He said softly, 'You should not be sorry, Kit. You are, as you said, a woman now.'

CHAPTER 8

She awoke slowly. Her head ached, and she had been having a long talk with him, about bicycles. It was urgent and un-finished and terribly important. She'd go back and continue where she left off. Somewhere in the house Eloisa was singing softly, *Yo te quiero mucho*, a lovely little tune.

She staggered out of bed, opened the shutters, and fell back into bed again, on top of the bedclothes. The light and heat beat against her screwed-down eyelids. Then as she slowly opened them the colours she saw changed from grey and green to blue to the full warmth of their actuality, in honey and pink.

She stretched out her legs in the shorty nightdress, and look-ed at them. Bill liked to ogle them when she was in a bathing suit, pretending they made him feel terribly lascivious; but they didn't really.

Bill. She had told him she never wanted to see him again. Since she had liked him, she ought to be feeling depressed, or at least angry. But she wasn't.

What on earth would César think of her, screaming like a fish-wife?

César. She had been here two weeks now. César did not look at her legs, or make joking remarks. Sex was no joking matter for him. He'd treated Bill, last night, exactly the way he treated a bull in the ring. Cruel, maybe? But Bill deserved it, César was attractive, in or out of the bull-ring; and there was a sense of adventure in being with him, a sense of danger. It was he about whom she had been dreaming when she awoke. Where was he now?

93

She picked up her toilet bag and went quickly along to the bathroom that she shared with Bel. Fifteen minutes later, dressed, she dropped into Bel's room on her way downstairs. Bel lay propped on three pillows, wan of face, her dark hair spread across the white linen, deep rings under her eyes. She held out her hand quickly. 'Kit . . . did you sleep? César was in to see me. He told me there had been a quarrel. Is it true?'

'Sure,' Kit said lightly.

'But it was only because you were all tired,' Bel said anxiously. 'And perhaps you'd had something to drink. You must telephone him, dear.'

She laughed. 'I'm not going to telephone him.'

'But –' Bel began anxiously.

'Don't talk about it,' Kit said firmly. 'It's all over and done with. What's the matter with you?'

'A bad headache,' Bel said. 'And I have, as you would say, the curse. I have taken two aspirins and Mama says I am to stay in bed till after dinner . . . Seeing Pete always exhausts me. I long for him so much that when we part I feel I have been wrestling for an hour with a giant far stronger than I.' She touched the crucifix hanging on her bosom by a thin golden chain. 'Without the Virgin to help us, that giant would defeat us, and we would sin.'

Kit looked at the crucifix and thought, It really helps her. To her it's not an idol, hardly even a representation or symbol, but an actuality. Christ and His Mother were actually present, through it, to comfort and sustain her.

'How was it this time?' she asked.

'The same, I told you. Peter said again that he could not stand doing nothing for much longer. He must bring it into the open, ask formally for my hand, ask the advice of Father Perreira at the base, something . . . Oh!' She sat up. 'Kit! César said you told Bill you were never going to see him again. But next Saturday you are going to dinner at your parents' house, and he was going to come in afterwards. You told me the day before yesterday.'

Kit said, 'I remember.'

'Will you still go?'

'I don't know. I haven't thought about it. Why?'

'Could you tell my mother that I have been invited too?'

'I can do better than that,' Kit said. 'You *are* invited, from this instant.'

'No, no,' Bel said. 'If she thinks I am invited, but really I am

94

not ... I could meet Pete, and when you are coming home, you could pick me up ...' Her large eyes overflowed with single-ness of purpose.

Kit said slowly, 'It's a little risky, Bel. Suppose my father meets César later and it comes out that you weren't there? ... Can't we just tackle César? Really, he's not so stuffy.'

Bel said firmly, 'On no account ... As to the other, we will have to take the risk. Sooner or later, we will be discovered. Pete almost wants it. I am playing for time, praying that God will help us so that Mama and César and Holy Church will be pleased and proud. It is a miracle that I pray for, to break down the barriers ... and if there is no miracle, many people will be hurt, and I will be one of them. Pete understands, so now it is he who suffers, for my sake. How much longer he will be able to, I don't know. We will have done our best.'

She sank back on to the pillows. Kit glanced at her watch. 'Want me to draw the curtains?' she asked.

'Yes, please. I think I shall try to go to sleep again.'

Kit hurried downstairs. She was hungry, her headache was better, and a fresh wind blew down the street below her win-dow. She would have some breakfast, and then walk past the window of the study and see whether César was working. If he wasn't she'd get him out for a quiet game of pelota in the private frontón beyond the kitchen garden. It would help get his wrist back in shape.

But when Eloísa had brought her coffee and croissants to the small drawing-room, and she had finished them, Doña Teresa swept in, smiling, and kissed her warmly. 'There, you foolish girl ... wandering round till all hours with César. You are looking much better than my silly daughter, at least. I am going to do a little shopping. Would you like to come with me?'

Kit did not hesitate. Doña Teresa was a part of this won-derful home too, and the day was long, and sunshine and shad-ow swept across the city under dramatic white clouds. She ran upstairs, grabbed her pocket-book, looked at her lipstick, and ran down again.

*

Bill stood at attention in front of Colonel Lindquist's desk. The Old Man continued to write a note on the foot of an official document, his handwriting large, precise, and steady flowing. Bill waited. The Old Man never kept you standing there merely to emphasize his power to do so.

The colonel put down his pen and looked up. He said, 'A report has reached me that you've had a fight with a Spanish civilian.'

'Yes, sir,' Bill said.

'It was a non-official report,' the colonel said with a small emphasis. 'I presume the fight was, too.'

'Yes, sir,' Bill said. 'I was not in uniform.'

'So I understand ... At ease ... I gave Kit a job to do in Medina, Bill.'

Bill said, 'I know, sir.' He knew he should say nothing more, but anger against Aguirre began to rise, and he said, 'The whole thing's personal, sir.' Lindy would not expect him to sit back with folded hands while this spic of a matador tried to take Kit away from him.

The colonel said gravely, 'I know that, Bill. All the same, I gave Kit a job to do, as I told you, and I don't want her attempts to do that job hampered by this kind of ... violent emotionalism. Aguirre didn't fight back, did he?'

'He couldn't ... I don't think he would have even if he could. Unless he used a knife.'

'You're old enough to know that a sock in the jaw is not the answer to each and every problem, the way it is in the comics. ... Have you seen the new crew ratings?'

Bill stiffened. 'Yes, sir. I'm responsible for that. I made several goofs on the radar runs and two in the flight simulator. We'll do better next time.'

'You will,' the colonel said. 'The six crews at the bottom of the wing list are going to be put to work.'

Bill glared at the colonel in angry disbelief. This meant that the crew would be practically confined to the base – at any rate they'd be working twice as hard as before, and that was hard enough. And Lindy was doing this merely to keep him away from the city and Kit. Again his suppressed anger boiled over. 'Dave Metch and the rest of them haven't got in any fights, sir.'

Lindquist said, 'Much as I like Kit, I wouldn't allow her to affect my decision on an Air Force matter for one fraction of a degree, and you know it.' He ended with a sudden cold enmity – '*Don't you?*'

'Yes, sir,' Bill said at once. 'I apologize. But ...'

The colonel interrupted him. 'For Christ's sake, Bill, do you think I've never been in love? ... We're professionals. We've got a job to do, and we're drawing pay for doing it. If you don't like being a professional, get out of the Air Force. The crew ratings of your aircraft have gone down because you have a personal problem and this job is so damned complex that any lack of concentration shows at once, unless you're seasoned enough and tough enough to have a reserve of efficiency in hand to absorb the loss. *You* don't, yet. At the same time the rest of your crew know you're having trouble and they sympathize with you, because they're a good crew, and that affects their efficiency – just an infinitesimal amount, but we work to infinitesimal clearances ... I can't solve your private problems and I wouldn't if I could, but I can see that they don't show in your work. Metch says the drop in the rating is his fault. It's certainly his responsibility, as he's the commander. If the crew remains in the bottom third of the wing ratings next half month, Metch is out as commander of an aircraft.'

Bill stared for a moment into the blue eyes. Unfair, blazingly evilly unfair ... A commander has power, and balancing responsibility. Dave Metch was his commander.

'This is a SAC base,' Colonel Lindquist said quietly.

'We won't be in the bottom third of the ratings, sir,' Bill said at last.

Lindquist nodded in dismissal and bent again to his paper.

Bill saluted, turned, and went out.

*

All the hams hanging from the beam in the store looked exactly the same to Kit, but Doña Teresa examined them with care, muttering to herself as she did so. This one was stringy, that one too lean, the third had been indifferently smoked ... Kit's mind wandered. A weight had been lifted from her, and that must be why she felt so light-headed. What weight? Did the mere fact that Bill liked her – loved her, then – impose anything on *her*? If it did, no one could ever be free.

'I'll take this one, Pedro. Will you weigh it, please.'

'*En seguida, señora!*'

Out now and slowly down the street, peering into windows and opened doors. Onions had gone up a peseta a kilo, bread the same, veal six pesetas. There were two American women in the butcher's. They knew her, and one pointed to a piece of veal in the scales. 'Look, Kit, it's only a dollar a pound, at least that's what I work it out at. I never remember whether a kilo is two pounds or two and a half.'

F.H.–D

A dollar a pound, about fifty pesetas, or a hundred and ten pesetas a kilo. Doña Teresa was looking at the portion from which the veal had been cut. The butcher murmured, '*Setenta y cinco, señora.*' Seventy-five – the kilo, of course. So they were running two price boards now, one for the Americans and one for their own people.

She turned away. What did it matter? Perhaps it was fair enough, considering the different income levels. Doña Teresa was ticking the man off for raising his prices and he was saying, 'It's not my fault, señora, believe me.'

Supply and demand, she thought. Inflation. Too much money chasing too few goods. The economics professor had had a long nose and long hair, and had tried hard to breathe life into his figures.

She ought to tell Dad and Peggy that she'd quarrelled with Bill. She ought to tell Lindy. He'd understand. Peggy would tell her she'd been hasty. She'd say that Bill was a fine, upstanding young American and she was an unreasonable and flighty girl. Nevertheless, she was free, and ready to let the breeze that hurried round the street corners tug at her skirt and send it whirling round her legs, and herself whirling into a dance down the street to the sudden edge of the city, across the yellow hills, music in her ears, someone singing behind her, now dancing with her, and a guitar in the secret valley.

Into another shop, this one tiny and dark and smelling of spice and meal and sacking. Out again. On down the street, the basket on her arm heavy now. She found that she walked with her hips swaying slowly to counteract the weight of the basket; but she must keep her head up and her chest out if she were to have the wonderful carriage of the Spanish women.

Doña Teresa was speaking to her. 'Did you notice Pilar in the shop there?'

She thought back. A small girl, about her own age, sulky-looking, but perhaps that was the way she put on her lipstick. Doña Teresa said, 'She had a quarrel with her fiancé a month ago, and still they have not made up. Did you ever see anyone so unhappy?'

Kit agreed, but privately she thought the girl didn't look so much unhappy as discontented.

Doña Teresa went on, her high heels clacking accurately on the sidewalk. 'The young man – he is a carpenter's apprentice – goes about looking just as unhappy. Yet neither of them will take the first step.'

Kit said, 'Perhaps they found out they really aren't suited.'
Doña Teresa knew more than she let on. Perhaps the scene in
Penas de Juan was common knowledge all over the city by now.

Doña Teresa said, 'It is possible. But my dear, that is not
often truly the case. A woman can learn to please any man if
she tries. It is a matter of discipline. A woman must have pride,
otherwise no man will think anything of her, but then, once she
has shown she has pride, she must subject herself to the discipline of our sex. She must take the first step. That is the
woman's part.'

Kit kept an obstinate silence.

'That is the trouble with César,' Doña Teresa said.

Kit started. 'I beg your pardon? What is the trouble with
César?' Doña Teresa was clacking steadily along, peering into
shop fronts, just as usual.

'Lack of discipline. I have brought countless girls to him, of
the best families, from here and all over Spain. He is attractive
to women, I see these girls put their own pride in their pockets,
and long for him to take real notice of them.' I know, Kit
thought. 'But he does not, and I think it is because he has some
idea that he will lose his freedom . . .' She shook her head, stopped, and looked at Kit. 'Until he understands that there is no
such thing as freedom in this world, I fear he will not marry
anyone.'

'I think there are a lot of men like that,' Kit said. 'But most
of them do in the end, don't they?'

'*Claro, claro!*' Doña Teresa said. 'But César . . . A happy
marriage is a gift from God, but César can only make women
unhappy. It is a sadness to me, but it is true. Whatever men
dream, we women must face the truth, my child . . . Now let
me see, we'll try for the olive oil in here, but if the price is more
than twenty-three pesetas a litre, I won't take it.'

She led into a large, bright store. Kit thought, I don't think
she understands César better than anyone else does. *She* understood perfectly. Marriage, as such – no. One particular person –
that would be different. Then you wouldn't be thinking about
Marriage with a capital M, but about the exact shape of that
relationship with this special person.

Her thoughts drifted comfortably on as she accompanied
Doña Teresa through the round of marketing; then home, but
he was not in; through an hour in the kitchen, and Juana teach-
ing her how to make Aragonese *empanadas de jamón;* through
lunch, which she ate alone with Doña Teresa.

After lunch Doña Teresa usually disappeared into her own room, and she did so today. Kit sat awhile, looking out of the window at the flowers against the wall on the far side of the garden. It was a rare day, like the best of October at home. She lit a cigarette and went restlessly to the door. She might read. Or go to sleep ... She must need sleep, but she didn't feel tired.

A distinctive roar and burble broke out from the back of the house, where the stables had been converted into a garage. Wheels crunched on the gravel. She went slowly to the window, her heart beating faster. César, bareheaded, wearing dark glasses and a sports coat of light English tweed, swept round the circle of the drive at the wheel of the Hispano Suiza tourer. He stopped at the front door, got out, and strode towards the house and out of her sight. She stayed where she was, looking out of the window, seeing nothing now. The front door opened, his footsteps crossed the hall. The drawing-room door opened.

She turned, the window behind her, making herself smile. He was in the middle of the room, picking up a pack of cigarettes. For a moment he did not speak or move and she thought, he is so sad. She wished he could always wear the *baturro* dress, or the *traje de luces*. In them the melancholy fitted, and was not noticeable. In the English coat and grey flannel trousers he looked like a sports-car driver who had heard for the first time of Death.

He slipped the cigarettes into his pocket, and said, 'I am going to the farms of Saldavega. I have some business to talk over with Don Emilio. Would you like to come?'

'Yes,' she said.

'I'll tell Octavio so that Mother will know where you have gone.'

He went out and she heard him call in a low voice, 'Octavio!' Then she was in the car, her hands in her lap, waiting for him. The engine muttered and throbbed and the car shook gently. He came to the door, looked at her, went back, and came out again with an old coat and a *baturra* shawl. 'It'll be cool later,' he said, as he climbed in beside her.

He drove slowly through the almost deserted streets. It was the hour of the siesta. A few young children were playing under the sycamores in the Paseo and weary waiters sprawled asleep in the chairs under the awnings of the cafés. Kit waited patiently for the city to come to an end. Not long now, for they were passing the Mercado and beyond that there was only the New

Bridge across the river and then the Mournful Plain began.

The car slowed and stopped. A freight train was standing on the grade crossing at the near end of the New Bridge. The engineer sat on the ledge of his window, facing the rear of his train, reading a newspaper. Beyond the train she heard a low continuous screaming sound, like a tortured bird. The box-cars hid the source of it but she knew what it was – an ox-cart, grinding slowly across the bridge towards the train and the city.

The squeal of the cart was close now, and a continuous angry blaring had suddenly broken out with it. The old woman with the flags, the crossing keeper, was peering under the cars. The blaring and hooting became frantic, as the unseen driver pressed on his horn in a series of short, hysterical blasts. The grinding scream of the ox-cart continued.

César leaned far out and peered between two box-cars. He said, 'The cart's reached the end of the bridge now. The car's passed it . . . It seems to be an emergency.' He opened his door and got out. Kit followed suit.

A man in U.S. Air Force uniform was running along the track towards the locomotive, shouting, 'Let us pass. Urgent. I'm a doctor. Urgente, hospital, Krankenhaus.' She recognized him as Captain Mason of the Medical Corps, the surgical specialist at the base. Now he was shouting up at the engineer, '*Urgente!* Move forward, or backward. Just to let me pass . . . please!'

César said, 'They'll think he's drunk.' He glanced at the Hispano, now hemmed in by two cars and an ox-cart, walked a few unhurried steps towards the locomotive, and called, '*Eh, amigo!*'

The engineer's impassive face appeared on that side of the cab. César said, 'Friend, can you move her? It would be a great kindness to me.'

The engineer peered down the train. Then he shrugged and said, 'There's a red light back there, Don César. But most of these R.E.N.F.E. wagons should have been broken up years ago, anyway. It should make a good noise.' He disappeared inside the cab. The whistle shrilled twice, the locomotive puffed heavily, and the wheels began to turn. The train ground backward off the crossing, and she saw the doctor scrambling into his car. It shot forward, its horn again blaring. Opposite the Hispano it slowed and Captain Mason leaned out. 'Thanks, Kit. Emergency operation – trepanning. I'm helping.' The Buick bounded forward.

Kit climbed back into the Hispano. She said, 'Well, the train didn't back into anything, anyway.'

César engaged gear and the big car moved slowly forward, climbed the ramp to the tracks, bumped across them, and entered the bridge.

She said, 'You'd think all our people could learn a few words of Spanish, at least, wouldn't you?'

César said, 'I do not see why. The people of Medina are not expected to learn English, and in fact only those who want something out of you do. In any case the engineer would not have understood any American's Spanish just then, because he was being shouted at.'

Kit said uncomfortably, 'I suppose it was an emergency . . .'

César said, 'There is no emergency great enough to require one to forget good manners. In Spain it is not the *thing* that matters, but the form of presenting the thing.'

They came to the end of the bridge and began to accelerate, very slowly.

César said, 'In America there would be no bullock-cart and no narrow bridge. The engineer would know at once that there was an emergency, and he would do all in his power to help, and he would not care whether the doctor said Please or Damn you . . . but what *could* he do? Nothing, absolutely nothing. He could not back off against the signal because he might be run into by the Twentieth Century Limited at eighty miles an hour.' He took a firmer grip on the wheel, and said in a louder voice, 'But now – that's behind. We're in the open.'

She raised her head, shaking out her hair so that the wind rushed through it. So he felt it, too, the importance of getting into the open. The city was behind, and in it the tenacious facts of their existence. The towers of the base rushed towards them, and flung back, and with them the last responsibilities. The road unwound beneath the wheels and the motor thundered in a rising pitch. The gate flashed by, and the sentries, the long wire fence began, blurred past, ended. A mile ahead two figures stood together by the side of the road, unmistakable in their shape, their watchful immobility. The Guardia Civil . . . soon one of them would step out into the road and raise his hand. Anyone could tell that the Hispano was doing over ninety. But they didn't move and it was César who raised one hand as he passed, and she saw the white teeth smiling under the winged black hats. El Rondeño de Aragon was expected to drive at breakneck speed, especially with a girl beside him.

102

The tempo of the day rose to match her quickening emotion. The wind whipped her hair around her face so that she wanted to shout, and because she wanted to she did. 'Look at the clouds, look at the fields!' The wind snatched the breath from her lungs and the wind stung tears from her eyes. The Mournful Plain ended, farmlands spread out before her across rolling hills and a broad shallow valley between. Under the slanting sun the wheat moved in waves of paler and darker gold down the wind.

Time ran fast in the car, and faster still the meeting with Don Emilio the steward, tall and stately in his whitewashed room. His wife wore the long Pyrenean dress that fell in a hundred pleats from under the armpits to the floor, and seven big keys hung from a chain around her neck. A glass of wine and then the steward's wife showed her the kitchen with its huge central fireplace and conical chimney while the men talked in the parlour; then out alone to watch five horses in the field and the bull calves in the paddock, and to wonder at a yellow cloud hanging over the hill above the farm.

César came out of the house, an old canvas haversack slung across his shoulder. She saw him go to the car and open the huge trunk that occupied the whole width of the luggage carrier. He pulled out a shotgun and a few cartridges and came to her. He said, 'We will look for pigeons in the wood,' pointing across the wheat. Half a mile away a few trees made a rare pattern of green leaves and violet shade in a rocky gully that did not seem to hold any water. He tapped the haversack. 'And this we have in case we get hungry. Doña Maria thinks I am still thirteen, and cannot go an hour without eating. But first, we have something to see up here.'

They walked slowly up the hill towards the yellow cloud, by the edge of standing wheat, among poppies, on a lumber track. On the farther side of the wheat two men worked with long, slow sweeps of their scythes to cut it. At the brow of the hill César stopped. The white farmhouse lay behind them in its stone-walled enclosure. A red-and-black cock in the yard supervised his twelve hens as they searched for food under the wheels of the Hispano. Beyond the farmhouse the road divided the wheat from the plain. There was an iron bridge over the gully below the little wood, and a mile beyond the bridge the houses of Saldavega clustered round a square church tower on top of an outcrop of rock. Far beyond and above, a quadruple streak of vapour barred the sky, burrowing in and out of clouds

103

in a ruthless, ruler-straight line; at the end of it, drawing it thus firmly across heaven, a silver triangle glittered momentarily in the higher light, then became invisible.

Northwards the ground fell first in wheat, standing and cut, and then rose in a powerful pauseless sweep until it heaved above the skyline, and there many trees stood. To the left a line of snow peaks made a thin white fire against the flecked sky.

The threshing floor lay in the hollow directly below them, a circle of hard, beaten earth, covered now with the thrown wheat. Two mules trotted round and round drawing a sledge. A man stood on the front of the sledge, holding the mules' reins, and behind him a buxom woman, and three big girls with sunburned faces under wide-brimmed straw hats; and behind them two little children. The blunt knives in the sledge slid through the wheat on the threshing floor. Chaff rose, and the wind blew it away and up in swirls into the air, where it hung, a yellow cloud.

César spoke suddenly. 'Next year, the year after, the mechanical reaper and thresher and binder will come, with the tractor. Then half these people will be out of work. They will go to Madrid and Barcelona, to find work in the factories. Saldavega will die, and this will die . . . and so will these people, stifled.'

He stood a moment longer and she stole a look at his face. How could she comfort him when she knew that what he fought was the inevitable?

He looked down at her suddenly and she thought, He's going to kiss me, here on the hill-top, between the farmhouse and the threshing floor. She waited, her skin trembling.

He said, 'Come on!' took her hand, and broke into a run. At the threshing floor the men and girls called and waved to him, the people on the sledge and the others working with pitchforks in the cut wheat. César put down gun and haversack and cried, 'Change places, Juan!'

The sledge swept round, and as it passed the man stepped down and César stepped on and took the reins, all in a single motion. The next time round he called to her, 'Up!' and she took his hand and he lifted her on. The woman and the full-bloused girls held her, and the children shouted, and César snapped the reins and shouted, '*Arre, mulos!*'

Round and round and round, the children beginning to sing, César singing with them, and after a time she with them all, it being nothing that she knew neither words nor tune. The sun stood lower over Saldavega and every colour was softening to gold.

At last César hauled back on the reins, the mules stopped, and they got down. César picked up gun and haversack and the men crowded round him with advice, some pointing up to the high forest, some across to the wood in the gully. One of the big girls offered Kit a leather bottle, with a smile. Kit laughed. 'I don't know how to.' She would spoil her dress if she tried that trick; and she saw the neck of a bottle sticking out of one corner of the haversack. The woman wiped the sweat from her forehead, shouted, 'Very hot, this work!' raised the leather flask high in both hands, and pressed, to send a stream of wine squirting into her mouth.

César said, 'You'll get fat, Esperanza, and then what'll you do for a *novio*?'

The girl lowered the flask with a grin. 'Man, did you say I'd *get* fat? What am I now?'

'Fat, but pretty,' a man called. 'I'd take you.'

The girl snapped, 'Ah, but who'd want *you*? Look at your great fat bottom. Like a woman's. Worse than mine.'

The man shouted, 'It takes a big hammer to drive a thirty-centimetre nail.'

Everyone yelled with laughter and the girl clapped her hands over her ears. César said, 'Come on.'

The work was over for the day. The group at the threshing floor were breaking up, gathering patched coats and straw hats and leather bottles. In a chorus of good-byes and good lucks Kit followed César off the threshing floor.

They walked through wheat stubble, then along a path beside a dry-stone wall, and everywhere poppies flamed in the yellow wheat and under the wall. The men with the scythes had left the field. On the road she saw them, as small black shapes distinguishable by the broad flash of light on their shouldered scythes, going towards the village. The cut wheat lay in curved swathes in the ghosts of the wheat fields. In the saddle of the hill behind her the grain stood in pyramids on the edge of the threshing floor, and a man was leading the mules down the hill towards the farm, children on their backs.

She turned forward, shutting off all this too, for now even the place and the hour had become extraneous to her happiness. The wood was still a little distance off, and César strode slowly ahead. The wheat field, uncut, ran to the edge of the trees. She began to count ... seven, ten, fourteen trees. On the left, the downhill side, trees were rare – one or two beside the road, one standing in eerie silhouette on a far slope. Up the hill the trees possessed the land. Once the forest had held the earth as far down as the wood, farther perhaps, but in the centuries the ruthless droughts of Aragon, and more ruthless man with his axe, had attacked it, and cut the salient off from the main body. The fourteen survivors stood calm in their untenable position in the waterless gully, a mile from the nearest help.

They reached the edge of the wood and César turned to face the fields. She took up position, still behind him, a little to one side. César whispered, 'Any minute now.' She could just see the roof of the farmhouse, blue smoke drifting from the high stone chimney. The sun was gone, the threshing floor deserted, and she did not need César's telling her to know there was not long to wait now.

'Here they come,' César muttered.

The pigeons came in a flock, racing in high from the south, their wings beating the air with a hard-edged sound. They circled the wood once, high and far, and the second time passed lower and slower and nearer. César raised the gun and swung easily. The explosions bellowed in her ears, cordite haze drifted across her nostrils and made her sneeze helplessly. She put her hands over her ears, and was sneezing again as César fired both barrels for the second time. This time she saw the death of a pigeon. The bird was racing straight, with a rapid onward beat. At the shot its wings folded and the straight line of flight became a parabola. The pigeon dived to the ground, and landed with a loud thump on the edge of the wheat, bounced twice, and lay still.

César lowered the gun, blew through the barrels, and went out into the field. He returned with three pigeons. All were stone dead, their green and dove-grey feathers ruffling prettily as they swung in his left hand.

'Juana will be pleased,' he said. 'We won't get any more tonight.'

She followed him between the wide-spaced trees into the wood. It was evening and the wind lay sleeping in the wheat. She watched César kneel and lay the gun down carefully on the dry ground. She knelt facing him, waiting. He unslung the haversack and pulled out the dark, unlabelled bottle, and unwrapped a cold omelet from its white cloth. Beside them he set the loaf of bread and two ripe tomatoes, the skins a little

106

broken, and a length of white-flecked sausage, and a thick slice of quince jelly. In his pocket he found a knife, and opened the big blade, and put it down beside the bread. She knelt, waiting.

I have seen paintings like this, she thought. A hundred with the bottle and the gun and the dead birds, light lying like a blue bar along the gun barrels. Many of such a wood as this, unpeopled, shadowless and with a far view between the smooth boles. Several of the man and woman alone and kneeling in such a place, or in the edge of the wheat field hearing some sound from outside and far away, the bells of Saldavega, or only silence, or the whisper of distant calamities. Once, green wood and green grass, and food laid out like this on a white cloth, and a man and, lying on her side, a woman, waiting, naked.

He leaned out and took her hand. She felt it drawing away from her body, her arm stretching to a frightening length, the clasped hands so far away from her that neither could be hers. There were a score of reasons why she should not obey the pull of her hand, that went out to him and tried to draw her after it. But the hand was insistent and it sent urgent sensuous messages to her. Pervasive tremors were overwhelming the fear and the weak objections of her mind.

There was no other sound in the wood or the world but the beating of her heart. From the corner of her eye she saw the bottle and the gun and the still, pastel tints of the pigeons' feathers.

She leaned forward and closed her eyes as his lips met hers. After a long, quiet moment he said, 'We shall eat now, and then go home.' She opened her eyes slowly. 'Yes,' she said. 'Of course.' She looked down at the food. Had she got to wait now, feeling like this?

CHAPTER 9

The cathedral clock boomed one, a single cracked note. She neither sought sleep nor rejected it. She lay on her back, suspended between the floor and the pale ceiling, between consciousness and dream.

An American girl lies on a bed in a Spanish house, under a

sheet. The iron shutters are folded back and she has a view over the city, for the window-sill is low and the bed is high and old-fashioned. Then there is I, Catherine Fremantle, called Kit, watching the girl in the bed. The light of the city, a pale glow emanating like heat from the houses and the streets, shines dull in the fair hair of the girl on the bed, and what that girl feels and thinks reaches me in the same manner that the light reaches her, a glow faintly seen but strongly realized.

Slow notes of music stepped out of the darkness in a falling, sad rhythm, filling a place that had been left vacant for them in the scene, and giving it motion, as though the two girls in the room had been waiting in a boat, and the music had come to join them, its beat like oars, setting the boat moving on a deep river.

She thought languorously, This is no dream; or if it is the maker of the music is in the dream and the boat with me; because the tune was a famous *Jota* and the words, sung softly now, were:

> *Para mayor sentimiento*
> *Pasa el Ebro por tu puerta*
> *Y no me das de beber*
> *Teniendo el agua tan cerca*

And you hold the water so close to me, but do not allow me to drink.

The Ebro ran a long course through barren lands, the life blood of Aragonese passion, and it was upon the Ebro that the boat was launched.

Pasa el Ebro por tu puerta, and a cascading fall of the melody at the end. The girl on the bed and the other one were two pictures of one person now, a double image on a negative, or the photographer had jerked the camera.

I hear the music clearly, through the window, one told the other, her eyes closed. It's coming in through the window. From the garden below? From the street, beyond the garden and behind the high wall, where a young man serenades his lover? No, closer than that. From the roof of this house. It is César, with his guitar, on the roof.

The voice stopped, the guitar rowed on alone, carrying her farther into the stream of the wide river. The voice rose again.

The jota was born in Calatayud on the banks of the Jalon.
Aben Jot was its father, and a lonely woman its mother.

108

The voice sank low and died away. After a while the notes of the guitar ceased in actuality, in her consciousness carrying slowly on until the door of her room opened.

She heard the door open, and close again. After so much waiting he had come at last. If she lifted her head, she would see him standing beside her.

She opened her eyes and he was there. His head came down, his hand was behind her neck and his lips met hers. For a long time she did not move, neither did he move. She was joined to him only by her lips, his right hand gentle at the back of her head, her right hand stirring jerkily on the back of his. Open mouth to open mouth they stayed, tongues soft and inquiring, wandering against each other, passing, caressing, admitting. He pressed harder, forcing her lips wider, only a little.

Like the guitar notes, warnings of morality tried to form a more sombre tune in her mind. Morality failed. It could dissuade her from nothing, because this was what she wanted. But now a sense of her ignorance came, and distasteful memories of her first experience, and held her stiff and uncommitted against him.

He said softly, 'Are you ashamed that this is the manner of love? Open your eyes.'

She opened her eyes and saw that he was ready like a stallion beside her. He said, 'Either enjoy *this,* or send me away.' His voice was low and harsh.

She whispered, 'I . . . I don't know enough.'

He said, 'You know, if you're honest.'

She put up her left hand and caught him tight, and felt her legs moving of their own instinct under the sheet, first one drawing up, stretching, then the other, her knees sliding against each other. No turning away of the eyes, she thought voluptuously. The unmentionable was the texture of the act, and the act of the emotion – sexual love.

She clung to him, arched her body so that he could slip off her nightdress, whispered his name into his ear, made a clasping serpent of spread thighs for him, touched, stroked, held open, and at last heard her own explicit groans.

A time later she moved her hand and found her face wet with tears. She turned to him and smothered him with gratitude, until again he mounted her and completion overwhelmed her like a draught of hot soporific.

She awoke later, searching for him in the bed, but he was

not there. She got up and lit a cigarette. Three o'clock. She sat down slowly in the chair by the open window.

My God. My God.

If that was sex it was the most important thing in the world. Suppose she'd gone through her life, like plenty of women, apparently, and never discovered it?

But the act, with César, was immoral. He had seduced her. She had got herself laid. Her mother, if she were fool enough to tell her about it, would say that what she had experienced was not Love but Lust. Then why did she want to give and go on giving, not just sexual pleasure but everything she had or was or could become? She felt the same now, her senses calmed, her heart bursting.

And what would be the difference if she were married to him? Would it still be lust? The act would be the same, and without the act what difference was there between married love and mother love, or love for your children, or your country? Love always meant wanting to give.

Total love. Animal lust. She's been laid. She'd found the secret of happiness. She'd acted like a tramp. She'd been lifted wholly above selfishness for the first time in her life. Take your pick.

She stubbed out the cigarette and lit another. Why had he waited so many hours, when they both knew in the wood, in the evening, that they would make love? There was no reason why he should not have had her then, and again now. He certainly had had the desire. But he had disciplined himself, and waited. And made her wait. 'In Spain it is not the thing itself that matters but the form of the thing.'

Sitting by the open window she came to the slow, almost unwelcome realization that she was going somewhere. The girl who left the base two weeks ago had been running away from, but now she was going towards, something. Like Bel. No, not as clearly defined or as simple as that. Bel was running towards marriage, while she herself could not yet think of marriage. The goal was positive in the distance, but so far away that it was hard to see its exact shape; she only knew that it was a person, still to be called Kit Fremantle, who was as 'large' in all love as she now felt in this one branch of love.

She had experienced an extraordinary exaltation of giving, aroused in the sexual act. But the sexual was obviously only a part of a personality – perhaps only a small part. Suppose one could expand the exaltation of giving, of love, to include the whole personality ... The thought overwhelmed her, and she got quickly back into bed.

It was César who had given her this ... César was her partner, without whom she could not move forward, and to whom she would offer the whole person that was to be forged. They would go on from here to the hearts and depths of each other, and when no words would do for the love and understanding, this act would replace words, and go farther than words could take them. For a man and a woman, *this* was the language of love.

CHAPTER 10

Without altering his even pace César turned off the broad street into the narrow alley. The old houses rose four and five stories high on each side and the pavement was less than six feet wide from wall to wall. At the far end, by the Calle Gopa, an ornate iron lamp bracket hung out over the alley, casting a dim yellow light on the hot stone.

Tonight he ought to be wearing an Andalusian cloak and a Córdoban hat, he thought sourly, the cloak wound around and flung across the lower half of his face. It was always like this when the meetings were held at Mario's – an air of intrigue, and this skulking down medieval alleys on the semi-respectable edge of the Barrio, always after dark. Mario liked intrigue for its own sake. That was why he had been so good at baiting the hulking Yankee in the Casa Córdoba last week.

And look what had happened as a result of that evening. He'd got another woman on his hands. Whose fault was that but his own? Did he have to mount every single girl who followed him round like a moon-eyed heifer, not knowing what she was doing until she'd done it?

In Mario's apartment, Marcelino, Carlos, and Mario himself were waiting for him. He greeted them politely. A different group of the members, as arranged. Very efficient.

The cards were spread out on the table, and he glanced at the hand opposite his chair. This was another of Mario's little pleasures – he had a pad of paper at his place, and a pencil, and the pencil had been used the right amount, and the scores of three hands of *tresillo* were written down on the pad. If anyone asked him, Mario would be able to recite the cards and the

111

bidding and the play in those three hands that had never been played.

Mario said, 'Your turn, Carlos.'

Carlos threw his hand down on the table. 'Stop fooling, Mario. I can't think and play at the same time.'

Mario laid his cards down gently. 'Very well ... I have a report from Gerona, and one from Valencia, to pass on to you gentlemen. And there is the question of a meeting at Covadonga.' He talked, his hands now joined in front of his chest, now twining in and out of one another, now smoothing the wood of the table.

In Gerona Communist cells were beginning to organize themselves afresh, with help from across the border in France. Did the authorities know about it? Almost certainly not – yet. What was being done?

Mario said, 'As yet, nothing. *Our* people will wait and watch. By the end of a year we should have the names of several new concealed Reds on our lists, for use at an appropriate time ... The report from Valencia is a little less, ah, weighty ...'

It appeared that the leader of the organization in Valencia had noticed that some of the young girls, not whores, were wearing slacks on the streets. It had not been difficult to see that they were jeered at. There had been quite a scene near the port about a week ago, and now the girls weren't wearing slacks any more.

Good, César thought. The female rump was not meant to be displayed in trousers. Not even Kit looked at her best in them, for all her long American legs and ... He frowned.

'While we're talking about clothes,' Carlos said, 'has anyone been up to Anisclo recently? I hear that the last old woman has decided she's had enough of being photographed by French and American tourists as though she were in a zoo, and has put away her dress.'

The extraordinary dress worn by the women of Anisclo had animated researches by anthropologists, sociologists, and historians all over Europe; now they had agreed to become like the Americans, César thought grimly, in deciding that difference was a crime in itself ... These sumptuary matters were a nuisance. Women were a nuisance. Kit's regional and historic costume would be fringed deerskin trousers and a fringed jacket, a long rifle on her shoulder, a powder horn round her narrow waist, and her hair in a bun. So it was all right for women to wear slacks if it were a regional costume?

Mario was talking again. The subject was the annual pilgrims' Mass, celebrated in September, at the shrine of Our Lady of Battle at Covadonga, in the Asturias. The purpose of the rites was to give thanks to God for that greatest moment in the history of Spain, when the hinge had turned and the Moorish infidels had been stopped there at Covadonga, and the long defeat had turned into the longer, harder victory, which ended 780 years later in Granada. It had now been suggested that every chapter of *this* organization should send one or two representatives to Covadonga. While there they could secretly meet, and discuss some of the major problems facing them, such as the growth of Communism, the power of Opus Dei, and the Americans, for example. These three subjects were all too big to admit of settlement on the basis of local decisions, and they were all urgent, or becoming so.

'I think it would be invaluable,' Mario summed up. 'Of course, our pilgrims would have to recognize each other. They might all wear lapel buttons with the cross of Santiago.'

'So might several hundred others,' Carlos said.

'Our representatives could wear them in the *right* lapel, in specially made buttonholes,' Mario said eagerly, his eyes sparkling.

César said, '*Cojones!* They might also walk on all fours, or wear white robes like the Ku Klux Klan, with a big red monogram of our initials . . .' Mario held up his hand deprecatingly, always grinning. César went on, 'For some of us to go as pilgrims, independently, with nothing in our heart but thanksgiving for the deliverance of Spain – yes. But to go by arrangement, for the meeting of cabal – no. Our strength lies in our shapelessness. Those who have heard of us think of us as an octopus, with tentacles everywhere, but we are not – we are a jellyfish, an outlook, a spirit which lives, large or small, in the hearts of *every* Spaniard, and only reaches the solidity of a recognizable human shape in a few – in us, who call ourselves . . . what we do. It is a spirit, an all-pervading spirit that we must remain. Tentacles can be found, and cut off, however many there are. Tentacles must spring from a central heart and and head and brain, and then – one needle between the eyes, and pouf! But the spirit cannot be killed . . .'

He stopped, breathing deeply. Carlos said slowly, 'You are right . . .'

Marcelino frowned heavily. 'I don't see quite what César means, about spirit, and all that. I wish we could get these Reds
113

out into the open, and put them against a wall as we did in '36 ... but I think he's right about not having a big meeting at Covadonga. It would be disrespectful to authority.'

César smiled a little grimly. Good, stupid old Marcelino!

Mario said, 'I see your minds are made up, then I will pass the information along ... That is all that we have of any importance.' He put down his pencil and César saw that four more sets of figures had been added to the score pad. So they'd played four more games, had they? He wondered how much money he had lost. Mario always had him lose.

Mario had turned to a few local matters. César tapped his fingers idly on the table. Members were urged to subscribe to the fund for the preservation of the Moorish tower outside Calabarre. Nico was going to give it an editorial in *El Baturro* ... American picture magazines, comics, and lurid paper-backs were filling some of the kiosks along the Paseo. They were childish, of course, particularly the comics – but their very childishness enabled young Spaniards to leap over the language barrier. Children, for instance, now wouldn't wear anything but blue jeans. The behaviour patterns shown in the comics were more corrupting than the actuality of the visible airmen ... Better leave it to the Church and the civil authority, Carlos said. 'They're just as concerned as we are, for slightly different reasons. Never pick up your own sticks.'

Marcelino said, 'Talking about the Americans ... How were they allowed to turn the *jota* competition into a square dance? A lot of people were impressed with them – the way they jumped around and were full of good humour, and all sober.'

'So?' César asked, his temper rising.

'I don't think it should have been allowed,' Marcelino said heavily. 'Nothing like that has ever happened before. It's not customary.'

'How can we stop it?' César asked shortly. 'I was there.'

'I know,' Marcelino said. 'That's why I was asking ...'

'I was there,' César repeated. 'And it just happened. How often do we have to say that the enemy is not outside, but inside? Do you think the Americans or anyone else could seduce Spain unless she half wanted to be? She's like any other woman. No girl's yet ever been laid under the river bank who wasn't wanting it at the time. It's afterwards, when it's too late, and her belly's swelling with a child that she's going to be stuck with for ever – *then* she wishes her father had locked her in, the way he threatened to. I tell you, if we regarded the Americans

114

as the enemy, instead of the temptation, we'll be in trouble. We've got to get rid of them, yes, but the enemy is the weak part of our own nature, yours, mine, everyone's.' He stopped, his fist clenched on the table. Marcelino was looking at him with that heavy, bloodhound face unchanged. 'I'm sorry,' César muttered. 'But believe me, nothing could be done to prevent that incident, the other night. But I think the effect can be erased, quite soon.'

Mario said quickly. 'You have something in mind?'

César hesitated. 'The American fair and the Spanish fiesta,' he said. 'The double-header,' he added in English.

'What is a "double-header?"' Marcelino asked.

'It's something to do with baseball or basketball, when they see two games for the price of one.'

'Ah, the blonde is being useful, after all,' Mario said, grinning.

César ignored him. 'You have heard about the fair and fiesta, Marcelino?'

'Yesterday, I heard,' Marcelino said. 'I don't understand. I mean, 9 August is not a feast day.'

'That is what a good many other honest *baturros* are going to think,' César said.

Mario said, 'Ah! So there will be no one at their fiesta? Or the wrong kind of people?'

César said, 'It is impossible.' He found he was looking down at the table, at the scattered cards strewn there, at the pack now in his hand. He'd picked it up and was pretending to stare at it. Why? Lack of courage, that he didn't want to look Mario in the eye? Because he felt ashamed? He put the cards down carefully and looked up.

'The fair at the base – that is tomorrow. We need not worry about that. It will be nothing. They will show off their electric washing machines and electronic kitchens, and someone will try to teach the children baseball, or perhaps even their football. All this only helps to confirm a good *baturro* in his belief that they and we do not inhabit the same planet. Therefore, that none of their solutions or answers are applicable to us. The following Saturday is the fiesta. The mayor has put the arrangements in the hands of Juan Bermúdez, the old one, at the Banco de Medina.'

'He isn't one of us,' Carlos said. 'Nor is the mayor.'

César said, 'No. But the mayor's a fool and Bermúdez has

only been here a few months. He doesn't know people. His arrangements could go awry.'

'Really, it is too much,' Marcelino said, slowly. '9 August has never been a fiesta day. Why should we dance in the streets just because some American says we are to? And there will be a queen, I hear, like we see in the movies, when they have those battles they call football and one girl is carried around in an open Cadillac.'

César said; 'A queen for each. At the fair, a Spanish girl. At the fiesta, an American girl – Miss Fremantle.'

Mario was nodding his head blandly. 'Very good, very good,' he said, his tone full of admiration. 'Nothing violent, nothing planned. But I imagine everyone in Medina will have something to laugh about the next day. You should have been born in the Inquisition, Don César.'

Kit wouldn't be laughing, César thought. On the other hand, she might; she might be preening herself on what a great success the fiesta had been. The delight of dealing with foreigners, especially Americans, was that none of them could read the Spanish face. The Yanks might all return to the base swearing that the fiesta had been great; and the Spaniards would go to their houses thinking, What fools they made of themselves, but *we* didn't give them an inkling of it, did we? Lindquist was obviously taking a calculated risk, for he was no fool, but he had to rely on Kit's father and the mayor – both of whom were. The only person who had the position and the temperament to give weighty contrary advice was Colonel Portuondo; and he had gone on leave. The officer temporarily in command was – one of them. His behaviour would be impeccable.

No, in all probability Kit was going to get hurt, because she was no fool. It was her own fault for having the impudence to ask herself into the house. That wasn't fair. Bel had asked her. Why had Bel done that, on such short acquaintance? Bel looked like a ghost some of the time and like a bride at others. It was time he talked again with Mother about getting her married.

Kit was ripe for marriage, too. Why were all women such fools? He'd kissed her, her silly virginal legs had trembled and parted, and now she was in love. Not a virgin, though, technically. Probably that clumsy, red-faced captain with the big fists, Lockman, had had the privilege of putting the first key in that lock, and certainly he'd made a mess of it, or the girl wouldn't be in the state she was in now. She looked at him, César, these days as if he'd handed her the Holy Grail . . .

116

Marcelino's words caught his attention. 'But . . . I don't like it.'

Carlos said patiently, 'The excommunication rests only on those, who, knowing anything about the theft of the Armlet, have not spoken. You know nothing.'

Marcelino said obstinately, 'But I do.' His face was pale and damp and he was very unhappy. César looked at him closer and thought he must be losing weight.

Mario said gently, 'Marcelino, my friend . . . We know nothing at all. Supposing you go to the bishop or your confessor, what can you tell him? That Evaristo said, that night before the base was consecrated, that it was time to bring home to the people of Medina, in the most forceful way possible, the iniquity of what was happening. We agreed, and he said he would see that it was done.'

Marcelino mumbled, 'He also said that the liberalism of the Church was as great an enemy as any we faced, and he reminded us of the unknown soldier who stole the Armlet to save it from the Moors.'

Mario said, 'So what? you may *think* that Evaristo went and took the Armlet, alone or with some other members of us – but what do you *know*?' He shrugged.

Marcelino said, 'Excommunicated! And going to Mass just as though I hadn't been. I never thought it would come to this.'

Carlos snapped at him, with sudden nervous viciousness, 'Shut up! You are a coward, as well as a fool.'

Marcelino said, 'I can't help it, Carlos. Aren't *you* frightened?'

No one answered. César said coldly, 'You've got to forget it, Marcelino. If you can't – get out of Spain. There are others in worse case than you.'

Marcelino looked at him and after a time nodded his heavy head and said, 'Yes. There must be. After all, I don't really know, and someone must. I am a coward . . .'

Mario said, 'Well, that's about that. About the next meeting . . .'

He gave the details. It would be at a different time, a different interval, a different place. Only one of those now present would be there. Carlos. They'd hear about it in due course. César got up.

'Won't you stay for a real hand?' Mario asked. 'Or must you get back to the señoritas?'

'Good night,' César said shortly. The others rose and shook

117

his hand formally. Mario hurried his pudgy shape and tiny feet quickly round the table to let him out. 'Good night, César.'

César strode slowly up Penitentes towards the Calle Pedro Romero. Nine o'clock. Bel and Kit were having dinner at the base. They had probably eaten three hours ago, but they wouldn't be back yet. It was a pity, otherwise the three of them might have played cards. Or he and Bel could have started to teach Kit the elements of the *jota*. She had the coordination for it, and the rhythm, and a lithe, free-moving body. A week ago he would have said that she could never sufficiently abandon herself, that she would always be conscious of herself and of the impression she was making – emotions that were death to the *jota* – but five days of making love to her had changed that.

The word 'excommunicated' sprang into his mind. It meant cut off from the communion of the Church, of Christianity. But who had the right to do that, except Christ himself? He pushed the thoughts and the word back down, deep, where they had lived for months now, and again turned his mind to Kit.

She'd be back by midnight probably, and he could go along to her at two. But he'd sworn to himself, only this morning that tonight he would not go to her and would not tell her to come to him. She was becoming like a drug, and if he wasn't careful the habit would be hard to break. He was the master still, because she, not he, was the one who begged. That must not change.

He stopped on the corner of the Plaza to light a cigarette. Half the passers-by smiled, and murmured to him as they passed. It was good to be known, better still to belong.

She was an American when all was said and done, and a Protestant, and what on earth was he worrying about her feelings for? She only seemed different, because she was here, and a woman, a young one with long twining legs and an innocent lust. In fact she was just like the rest of the Yanks – brave, doomed, direct . . . Moved well, came out of the pen firm and bold, head uplifted. Followed the cape beautifully. A wonderful animal to work with. She hadn't had the pic yet. That might be the night of the fiesta. That would be the night for her to show courage, pressing in against the lance, against the hurt. The pin-pricks, the *banderillas*, they'd come thick and fast, later. She was in herself America and all the Americans – butting in where she wasn't wanted, clumsy, generous, corrupting.

He glanced up at the cathedral clock. The surest way of pro-

118

tecting himself against the feverish compulsion to go to Kit tonight, which would be as dangerous as putting the sword into *her* hands, was to go somewhere else. He hadn't been there for a week; five days to be exact.

It was too late, really. Or too early. And there was a lot of work in the office at home.

He threw away his cigarette and set off at a rapid pace along the Calle de los Obispos towards his own house.

CHAPTER 11

Under one of the severe, goose-necked concrete lamp standards that lined the roads of the base, Bill Lockman looked at his watch. Quarter to nine. If the wind were in the east he'd be hearing the cathedral clock from the city. When that happened everything got fouled up, because it was never quite right. That bell must make a hell of a noise close by, in the Aguirre home, for instance. Kit must be used to it, or she'd get no sleep.

Peggy Fremantle had suggested he drop by around nine . . . 'Just for a chat, Bill.' That was fine, and he'd agreed, but he was damned if he was going to arrive early, and there was the Fremantles' quarters not a hundred yards away, the big black Hispano parked in front of it.

He turned and walked in the opposite direction. It was a fine, warm night, a breeze from the north at about ten miles an hour down here, though the meteorological section reported winds of a hundred knots at thirty thousand feet.

It was quiet out here, just walking. For once Maintenance wasn't running an engine on the test bed. The Casa Córdoba had been noisier than a J-57 under test – in bursts, though. And what with a long day and a headache he'd let himself be goaded into doing exactly what the son of a bitch wanted. The same way he could do it to the bulls, he had done it to him – made him charge a taunting cape, just moved slightly to avoid the charge, and not hit back; and sure enough, the applause was not for the victim but for the guy with the cape, strutting off with Kit.

With Kit. That hurt, still, though not in quite the same way now. At the time it had been anger, and he'd found himself

119

muttering, Bitch, stupid silly little bitch. She'd said she never wanted to see him again. O.K., so she didn't and neither did he, and the hell with her, there were plenty more girls where she came from et cetera, et cetera. The trouble was, there weren't. At least not for him. She kept coming back into his mind, until after a few days what he felt was not anger but dismay, and tenderness. When he had time to feel anything.

Instead of cursing Kit he'd do better to take a good look at himself. He could realize, for a start, that she was no college girl. He mustn't treat her like one, ever, by thought or inclination. She was a woman, with a capital W. He knew less about Women than he did about B-52s. Why? Because he hadn't studied them. He'd better start right away – only not on Women; on Kit.

She was a special person. He'd known that all the time, but he'd just called it love instead of trying to find out. It would be easier all round if Kit's specialness came out in art, like Grace Lindquist. That made people tolerant, and at the same time interested. Grace Lindquist is an artist, they'd say, and if she announced she was going to Barcelona and live in a fish market for a week, everyone would nod and see why she would have to do a thing like that. Kit didn't compose symphonies or paint pictures. But suppose she was an artist, and the thing she wanted to create was a better herself, or a fuller life? Suppose that in the end it was her life as a woman that was going to be the symphony? Then the man she loved and married would be – what? The conductor? No – another symphony, blending with hers to make something bigger and better still. It was a frightening and exhilarating prospect.

He found he was standing outside the Fremantles'. After a glance at his watch he rang the bell. Ham Fremantle let him in, and slapped him genially on the back. 'Hi, boy!' At Ham's side, Ham's arm draped lightly round his shoulders, he walked into the living-room. Mrs Fremantle was reading in the chair by the fireplace. Kit was on the sofa.

This was the first time he'd seen her since the quarrel in Penas de Juan. He went straight to her and said gravely, 'It's good to see you, Kit.' She looked up sharply, and her brittle smile altered slightly. He said, 'You're looking swell. Spanish cooking seems to agree with *you*, at any rate.'

He sat down, but not too near her.

'Drink, Bill?' Ham asked.

'Just a Coke, Major. Let me . . .'

'I'll get it. Same for you, Kit?'

Kit said, 'Please, Dad . . .'

Ham strode out of the room. Bill looked at the ceiling. He didn't know what Kit was doing. Looking at her nails, maybe. He'd have to speak to her in a minute, but he didn't want to say, Lovely weather we're having for the time of year. He wanted to say, Look, honey, I made a horse's arse of myself, and I'm sorry . . .

Peggy Fremantle looked up, lowering the book, at arm's length to her knee. 'Why do writers have to write about such horrible people all the time?' she asked querulously. 'In this book everyone's out of a job and two of the men are drug fiends and the heroine only likes other women.'

'A Lesbian,' Kit said clearly.

Her mother said, 'I'm sure I don't want to read about them. Why can't they write about something nice? And the language is *awful*. Half the words I can't understand, and those that I do are unprintable.'

'They seem to have been printed,' Ham cut in, entering with two Cokes already poured into glasses.

'The unprintable's the only thing that matters,' Kit said. Peggy looked up sharply, her mouth half open. After a moment she returned to her reading.

Ham slumped into his favourite chair and picked up the Martini on the table beside him. 'I was telling Kit that the double-header is coming just in time. Trying to keep this town informed about us is like pulling up dandelions. While you're uprooting one lie, another's springing up behind you. Now prices have gone up another five, six per cent and *someone's* spreading it around that we're responsible. We can prove that the cost of living's going up all over Spain, but do you think that's going to help? . . . Oh, yeah, Sergeant Mendoza heard another great one today. When they put the equipment back on the Bull of San Marco, they're going to be normal size, or maybe a little smaller, because the old set offended the ladies at the base.'

'That's ridiculous,' Kit said.

'Not so damned ridiculous,' her father said. 'Since we're on the subject, look at . . .'

Peggy said, 'I wish you wouldn't talk about those things in the living-room. It's as bad as this book. Can't we get away from sex anywhere?'

121

Ham said, 'Look at Elsie the Borden cow.'

Kit said, 'César was asking me why we put skirts on her.'

Ham said, 'Because lots of people felt embarrassed by seeing those big three-colour ads of her prancing around without a bra, and . . .'

Peggy said, 'Mrs Bohorquez was nursing her baby when I called on her yesterday. Right there in the drawing-room, and there was a *man* there. An airman. Her husband's servant. I think. I didn't know where to look.'

'I would have,' Ham said, grinning.

'Don't be disgusting,' Peggy said.

'It's not disgusting,' Kit said quietly. 'That's what our breasts are for. Why should we be ashamed?'

'Kit!'

Ham said, 'For the anti-Americans it doesn't matter what we do. They're going to find something against us either way. They complain that we're over-sexed, and they complain about Elsie being given an apron. These Reds are nobody's damned fools. They don't spread stories that are plain untrue. They hint at the worst explanation for what *is* true. They spread stories that are unprovable one way or the other. Like the one about Mason, when he went into the city hospital to help operate on that kid.'

'What are they saying?' Kit asked. 'I haven't heard anything.'

Ham said, 'This kid got his skull crushed between a truck backing up in the street and the wall of his own house, and . . .'

'I'm going to take my book into the other room.'

'Hell, I'm sorry, honey,' Ham said. 'But that's what happened.'

'I don't want to hear about it in such detail. It's quite unnecessary.'

Kit muttered, 'You mean he was shaken up on the play, Dad.'

Mrs Fremantle was on her feet now, speaking to her husband, 'And didn't you have some work to do before bedtime, Hamilton?'

"Oh, sure,' Ham said. 'In a minute.'

Peggy trailed out, the book in her hand.

Ham said, 'I'm just going . . . Where was I? Oh yeah, well, you know the boy died in spite of the operation? They're saying that Mason was drunk.'

'Jim doesn't drink,' Bill said.

Kit said suddenly, 'I remember. That's just what César thought people would think. He said so, right there.'

'Right where?' Bill asked sharply. 'And who did he say it to?'

Kit was a little flushed as she answered him – 'He said it to me, at the grade crossing by the Puente Nuevo, if you want to know. Captain Mason was shouting at the engineer to move the train off the crossing, and César said, "They'll think he's drunk," something like that, and then he . . .'

'Who else could have heard?' Bill interrupted.

'Or misheard,' Ham said.

Kit said, 'One or two people, perhaps. There was an ox-cart quite close. And the gate-keeper. But . . .'

Ham said, 'They're everywhere, these Reds, and cunning as monkeys. By God, it had better not rain tomorrow, to foul up our fair. We've got to *make* these people like us . . .'

For a moment longer Bill pursued his thoughts – César, dropping hints; César, spreading stories; César, holding the red cloth negligently, flicking it, whispering Charge, you clumsy brute . . . But Kit was looking defiantly at him, and Ham was talking about the fair. He said, 'Most of tomorrow's programme is indoors, isn't it?'

Ham nodded. 'Yeah. The dance is in B Hangar. But the soft-ball, the handball, the baseball, the band playing down there in front of the Enlisted Men's Club . . . people walking about, just enjoying themselves, finding out we're human . . . that depends on good weather . . . Well, I've got to get back to the salt mine for an hour or two. You know to help yourself to anything you want, Bill . . .'

He wandered out, still talking. He had hardly left the room when Kit said, 'I did not ask that we should be left alone.'

He ignored that. Now was the time. He said, 'I want to apologize for last Sunday. I lost my temper, and – I'm sorry.'

She said, 'I should apologize too.' She smiled calmly. 'I'm sorry, really sorry, Bill. I behaved like a washerwoman.'

He couldn't just sit there, just looking at her. He jumped to his feet. 'I still feel the same way about you. I want you to know that.'

She said, 'I'm sorry.'

From the middle of the floor he looked down at her. She was too calm, too little moved. She wasn't going to get away with dismissing him with a nod and a smile. He said, 'César was baiting me that night, and I was fool enough to fall for it.'

'Perhaps,' she said. 'If he was, I'm grateful to him.'

'Grateful?' Bill said angrily.

'Yes,' She looked up at him firmly. 'For making something

like that happen, something violent enough to break us out of this silly thing we had got into. We could never be happy together. It's better this way, to have it over and done with.'

'It's not over for me,' Bill said bitterly. 'I tell you, I love you. Don't you believe me?'

She looked at him steadily for a time. 'I don't think you know what love is yet.'

'And you do? You're the wise woman of Medina by now, eh, and I'm just a freshman from Hicksville U.?'

She raised her hand. 'Please!'

He struggled for control over himself, but the anger kept pouring up and out. 'You're making a fool of yourself, and if no one else will tell you about it, I will. Your hero César Aguirre is anti-American all the way. If he can stick a knife in our back, he's going to do it. And that goes for you personally, too.'

She had picked up a magazine and was riffling its pages. He swept it out of her hands. 'Listen to me! I'll try and speak plainly enough for you. You like plain language since you went to live there. I always thought you wanted to be treated like a lady, but if you don't that's fine by me. There's such a thing as plain American, too, you know, and I can use it as well as the next man ... César Aguirre is a prick, P-R-I-C-K, prick, an anti-American prick, a prick with the morals of a monkey, and cruel as a cat, or a matador, and full of Fascist chicken-shit about his family and the lower classes, which means me, *and you*. This is the guy you treat like he was Jesus Christ and Frank Sinatra rolled into one. When he said Jim Mason was drunk –'

'He didn't,' Kit interrupted.

'I'm goddamned sure he meant it to be heard,' Bill swept on. 'And . . .'

Kit snapped, 'And did he break up the *paseo*, and bring the B-52s over the bull-ring to spoil his own *faena*, and steal the testicles off the bull of San Marco, too?'

'He doesn't need *them*, I'm sure,' Bill snarled.

He stopped suddenly. He'd never lost his temper with Kit before, except that time last week, and very seldom with anyone – his mother sometimes when he was a kid, once or twice a special friend in high school. That is, only with people who mattered very much to him. Kit was sitting forward on the edge of the sofa, glaring up at him. They were like two fighting animals; and he loved her.

124

He said, 'I'm sorry. I guess you won't believe me when I tell you I only blow my top because I love you. I've found out that you can't do a thing that doesn't affect me as though I'd done it myself. You've always talked a lot about happiness, and being free, Kit, and I know it won't do any good now but I've got to tell you there isn't any happiness for you the way you seem to be looking for it, and there isn't any freedom either.'

Her voice was unsteady as she answered. 'Why must we quarrel? How have you done it? I came here feeling that I'd never quarrel with anyone again. I was so happy ... If you really love me, you'll leave me alone.'

For a moment he wanted to take her in his arms and cradle her bowed head in his shoulder.

He said in a careful neutral voice, 'I'll be around when you want me.' She did not look up, but he saw a wet streak on her cheek under the glowing hair and the broad, cream-and-tan forehead and the long, thick eyebrows. He said, 'Are you coming to the fair tomorrow?'

'Yes.'

'With César?'

'And Bel.'

'Good night.'

'Good night.'

'I love you.'

No answer. He opened the door and went out, past the parked bulk of the Hispano.

CHAPTER 12

The four of them – Ham, Bel, César, herself – were sitting at a table in a corner of the great hangar, among many others. She and Bel had danced every dance since they arrived, and now had begged to sit this one out, and the airmen were leaving them in peace. Bel was going to elope at San Marco. That had apparently been arranged last night during her clandestine meeting with Pete, here on the base, while she was supposed to be having dinner at the Fremantle's. She looked a little drawn, nothing worse. She herself must talk to Olmbacher about it tonight. She was getting out of her depth.

'The joint is jumping,' her father said with satisfaction.

She stole a glance at César, wondering what he was thinking. The joint wasn't really jumping yet, but the dance was going well. The hanger was hung with bunting in stars and stripes and yellow and red. Beyond the rolled-back doors, which were so wide and tall that the dance seemed to be in the open air, the apron stretched away under scattered inspection lights to four silver ghosts crouching the far side of the runway – some of the B-52s. The queen and her court, escorted by half a dozen airmen, were sitting at a large table across the concrete floor from the ten-piece band. Tables and chairs and benches were ranged two deep round the walls. Near the door, in rows, sat the mothers and aunts and grandmothers of the Spanish girls. There were plenty of young Spanish men here, too, though not so many men as girls. They mostly stood in groups along the wall, not mingling with the airmen. Nearly all the girls were dancing with airmen, some straight, some jiving. There was suppressed shrieking and giggling, and swinging out, turning and flinging slipping back into the jerking, shaking pattern.

César's face was empty, and as still as a stone. Two weeks ago she would have thought that he was noticing nothing. Now she knew better, and she knew what he was thinking, because she felt the same way. How bright it all was, and how shallow! The hangar blazed with strong lights, the trumpets screamed, and the drums went thud and swish, but the noise vanished up into the high, steel-strutted roof, and there was no depth or variation of sound, just as there was no variation of light – or feeling. How different was the *jota* dancing in the Plaza San Marco, with the torches flaring out smoke and yellow flames and the voices of the singers echoing back from the cathedral, from the Ayuntamiento, from the medieval arches, along the south side! And the music itself . . . In the plaza they had sung of death and poverty, of miracles and faith and passion, of the labourer who loved wine so much that he undressed before the laughing girls and took one of them and jumped into the vat for a swim with her, of the man who sang to a young boy –

> *When you go to Calatayud, ask for María.*
> *Give her this rose, and kiss her hand,*
> *For she is your mother, and was my lover.*

But on the bandstand the young man with the jiggling knees had seized the mike and was bawling into it –

Ready, set, go man go!
I got a girl that I love so.
I'm ready, ready, ready, ready, ready,
Ready, ready, ready, ready, ready,
I'm ready, ready, ready, ready, ready,
Ready, ready, ready, ready, ready,
To rock an' roll.

Her father's voice droned on. He was telling Bel of the success of the day. '. . . four hundred and fifty people went through the KC-135 during the day two hundred and forty-seven through the B-52 . . . The midway made over three hundred bucks for the Medina Hospital . . . There weren't as many spectators at the baseball as we'd hoped, but we had twenty-nine kids come to the softball clinic.'

César said, 'A very successful experiment, I'm sure.'

Her father said, 'Experiment is right. Next year, it'll be better, because we'll have today's records to help us.'

César touched the card on the table. 'These?'

Her father said heartily, 'You bet!'

Kit picked up the card and looked at it. It was a well-printed little job in Spanish, asking *nuestros buenos amigos* to reveal what they'd liked best about the American fair so that their good friends the United States Air Force could give them a better time next year. If they could spare a minute would they fill out this form? 'Did you visit – the aeroplanes – the midway – the sports field – the kitchen?' Mark X in appropriate box. Are you male, female? Over 21, under 21? Married, single? (There is no need to sign this card, *amigos*.) If you went to the dance would you like – more ballroom dances – more square dances?

'Remarkable,' César said.

Lieutenant Dick Holmes appeared at their table. Her father said, 'Hi!' and César rose easily to his feet. 'Señor Aguirre,' Dick said with a pleasant smile, 'I'd like to dance with your sister, if I may.'

César said, 'She is her own mistress tonight. God knows there are enough *dueñas*.' He motioned to the walls, where boutonniered airmen of the dance committee were plying the *dueñas* with cigarettes and glasses of wine.

Bel took Dick Holmes's arm and slipped into the dance.

'That finishes him for the night,' her father said with a grin. 'Officers aren't allowed to dance tonight unless they know a lady, and then only once, all night. On their honour. And now I'm going to take *my* dance if you'll excuse me, César. This one's just about my mark – not too fast, not too slow . . . Kit?'

She rose smiling.

Her father danced jerkily, though it was not a Charleston, and spoke jerkily. 'How's it going – in the town?'

'What?' she asked.

'The great entente, the affair Spanish-American. What do you hear – about us?'

'Nothing much,' she answered. None of them out here understood how remote and unreal the base seemed from that quiet house on the Calle de los Obispos.

'What did people say about the *jota* competition ending in an Ozark jubilee? Public-relations-wise it was great. Spontaneous combustion.'

'But . . .' she began. A gyrating couple bumped into her: an airman and a laughing Spanish girl – Eloísa.

'I thought César looked a little huffy at the time,' her father said. 'But if people prefer the square dance to the *jota,* what's wrong with that?'

She said, 'But what if the *jota*'s better, more important? The best things aren't always the most popular.'

'Who says what's best?' Ham responded. 'The buying public, the people. The *jota* crowd can learn the square dance, or the bongo or the balalaika fling, or whatever's popular.'

'And the vineyards can be replanted with cola nuts and the matadors become quarterbacks,' she said with sudden vehemence.

What is right *is* right, regardless of how many people say otherwise. What is bad *is* bad, votes or no votes. César's Spain said one thing, Dad's America, another.

She noticed Marcia Arocha, just entering the hangar with three younger women. More girls were coming in behind them, with more *dueñas.*

Her father said, 'Another truck-load. We've got four trucks on the job, and a few of them are coming in taxis they've hired for themselves . . . Of course we can't do anything about the taxis, but none of our trucks leaves without at least one *deuña and* one member of the dance committee in it. No one gets pregnant tonight.'

What about me, she thought suddenly. What would you say, my dear Daddy, if I told you that I was being made love to, not in the grass or in the back of a parked car, not hastily or

128

awkwardly, but in luxury, like a married woman, in my own bed, or in his, sleeping with my lover's arms round me until we part at four or five in the morning?

The dance finished, but she had hardly returned to the table before an enlisted man claimed her, and another, Bel. The band turned on the heat. Their star, a Negro clarinetist, leaned back in front of the stand, his spine arched, and streamed out hot licks into the blanketing arch of the hangar. Stomp and jive the dancers went, shoulders dipping, the men's left arms low and fingers clasped. There was Eloísa, red lips parted, dark eyes fairly snapping, haunches bouncing inside the tight skirt. The Spanish girls rocked and rolled as though they had been doing it from childhood. The young Spanish men stood thicker along the walls, watching.

Before the music started for the next dance Pete Olmbacher was suddenly at their table. 'Miss Fremantle, will you dance?'

She looked up. Bel must have seen him coming, for she had her face under control and was looking at him with a pleasant, polite smile. Kit said, 'Sergeant, I don't think you know my friends ... This is Don César Aguirre, Master Sergeant Pete Olmbacher.'

César, already on his feet, extended his hand. 'A pleasure, sergeant.'

'And Miss Aguirre, his sister . . .'

Pete said, 'Pleased to know you, sir ... Miss Aguirre.'

César said, 'Are you a pilot, sergeant?'

Pete said, 'No, sir. I'm a master mechanic.'

César said, smiling, 'I wish I could get you to look at my car. It is temperamental, an old Hispano Suiza . . .'

Pete said, 'I know it. Everyone knows that car.' He hesitated, and then blurted out, 'You ought to get her timing looked to, sir. She's way off. I heard it when you passed me in the street the other day.'

'I thought there was something wrong,' César said pleasantly.

Pete turned to Kit, and she went out with him on to the floor, far from the table where César was again sitting alone, for another airman had taken Bel away. Good – now Dick Holmes had returned to talk to César.

'I couldn't help saying that about the timing,' Pete muttered. 'I know I shouldn't draw his attention to me, but it hurts me to hear an engine being treated that way ... I want to thank you, Miss Fremantle, for everything you're doing for us.'

Kit said, 'I'm glad to do it ... but I'm not too happy about

129

it.' She looked up at him. 'You know, I feel responsible for Bel. What's this about eloping?'

Olmbacher said, 'I decided this hole-and-corner stuff won't do. I've got ten days' leave lined up starting 21 August, and a friend of mine in the draughtsman's office is forging a U.S. passport for Bel, and a civilian one for me, with another name.'

Kit danced round silently for a time. Forgery, abduction . . . and no one in the world less likely than Pete Olmbacher to be found involved in such things. The steps of the dance were becoming faster, more complicated, more charged with passion and meaning, and she was not a kindly spectator but an integral member of the fandango, who must do her part, keep her step, come out in the end at the right place at the right time, hand raised. And Bill Lockman was in the dance too – he had to be, even though he now seemed far away, because he had been in it when it started.

'Is Bel happy about eloping?'

'No,' Pete said. 'She hopes it won't come to that. She's praying for a miracle. So am I. But she's ready if the miracle doesn't happen.'

'She won't agree to speak to César, or her mother?' Kit asked.

Pete shook his head. 'No. She says that though César can't do much to her, he can prevent us getting married, because he's her guardian and she's a minor – and he can get me sent back Stateside, and then we'd be really finished. But, miss, the point is that Bel will be unhappy unless she can get his consent, and his blessing.'

Kit said, 'I can't help feeling that César is not going to be so stuffy about this as Bel thinks.'

Pete said, 'I guess it's like the farmer's dog, then, and the farmer telling the mailman he doesn't bite, and the mailman saying, "You know he doesn't bite, and I know he doesn't bite, but does the dog know?" ' His face crinkled into a quiet smile, and he said, 'Now I don't want to bother you with my troubles any more. Everyone's got his own load to carry . . .'

She said, 'Yes. I'll do my best for you both, only I hope there won't be any need for any more secret meetings. That's not a good part of town she has to go, often in the evening, and always alone.'

Pete said, 'Don't I know it? Sometimes I wake up sweating, thinking of her being mugged or something down there – and then I'm ready to grab the telephone right away and get Señor

Aguirre and bring the whole thing into the open, come hell or high water.'

They danced on without speaking. Kit thought, they have all cast César as the villain. No one but herself knew César. She would speak a word in the night to him, sometime soon, and of course he'd see that Bel's case was exactly the same as his own. She'd tell him her own life story, and this little thing about Bel would just be a part of it; and then he'd tell her his life. They'd share every thought and be honest and deep until they shared each other's hearts as wholly as they shared their bodies.

As the music ended Pete circled firmly but unhurriedly towards their table. Bel and her partner were a few paces away, Bel smiling, saying, 'Thank you, so nice.'

César and Dick Holmes were on their feet. Pete said, 'Thank you very much, Miss Fremantle. And now I'm here' – he smiled – 'I guess I'll ask Señorita de Aguirre. Would you?'

Bel said, 'Thank you. I would love to . . .'

Pete took her off, and as their voices faded under the music, Kit looked at César, and said, 'It's a waltz.' She looked at him beseechingly. She had never danced close with him, hand to hand and body to body.

'The Rock and Roll Waltz,' he said. He stood up. 'Will you dance with me, señorita?'

'Delighted,' she said.

His right hand held her, firm and warm in the small of her back. She felt herself relaxing, her body moulding softly to his. He knew how to dance, he knew how to lead without pulling or pushing, and she was his. The saxophone honked, the singer moaned into the microphone, but it was all dimming and her eyelids were sinking together, enclosing dreams. Don't leave me, don't leave me! She moaned it at night when he was ready to leave her body and she whispered it now. It will always be here for you, warmth and a place to rest, and my love.

She brought herself to with a jerk. She mustn't give herself away so obviously, or the reality of parents and moral values would intrude on their idyll before she was ready for them.

They were passing the bandstand again and she said, 'Aren't the music stands awful? So . . . insensitive.'

The music stands were hung with silver-fringed squares of pale blue velvet. The design on the pale blue, drawn in Mickey Mouse style, was a winged red bomb, with ears back and teeth bared, falling diagonally downward through the blue. Riding it was a cowboy with a hat raised and 'kerchief flying. Above

131

and below the design were the two words forming the name of the band, Medina Cowboys.

César said, 'It is honest, at least.'

She whispered, 'May I come to your room tonight? I want to talk and talk and . . .' She left the sentence unfinished, her hand moving gently on his shoulder. 'All night.'

He said, 'Tomorrow I am going early to Saldavega to start cape work with the calves.'

'Can I come and watch?' she said.

He didn't answer for a moment. Then he said, 'You and Bel.'

She pressed close against him, That would be wonderful – to lie on the stone wall of the corral behind the farmhouse, with Bel; two women in love, but only one knowing the other's secret. Or perhaps she would tell Bel tomorrow.

When they returned to the table Bel was already there, and Pete Olmbacher had gone. Kit's knees felt weak and she knew that dancing with César had altered her face. She must get away for a moment. She picked up her pocket-book and went to the toilet.

Inside, several Spanish girls were all talking at a great rate, the most voluble of them a bold-looking woman of about her own age, with heavy eyelids and an unhappy shade of orange lipstick. Her spike heels were too high and her skirt too tight even by Spanish standards, and she was wearing a bra that pushed her breasts unnaturally sharp and high, though there was no décolletage.

Señora Arocha came in, looking cool and chic, her black hair beautifully controlled but soft round her ivory forehead. She did not appear to notice Kit but turned to the talkative girl. 'Are you enjoying yourself, Rosario?'

The girl laughed. 'Certainly, señora. Why not? And you?'

Señora Arocha smiled. 'Very much.' She noticed Kit and smiled politely. 'It is Señorita Fremantle. I hope your father is pleased with the way the fair has gone.'

'Very,' Kit said.

'It is a wonderful place, this base,' Señora Arocha said. '*Fantástico!* . . . And next week you will be queen of the *fiesta*.'

'Yes,' Kit began, but the johns became vacant, and she went in. The *fiesta* was next Saturday. Time flew now, the days rushing past in dreams and housework, the nights filled with physical love. She was getting a slight purple-violet tinge under the eyes, and the eyes themselves had seemed larger and softer just now, when she looked at them in the mirror.

Marcia Arocha was looking at herself in the same mirror when Kit came in. She spoke at the mirror, as she brushed up her eyelashes, carrying on the conversation from where they had left it. 'What are you going to wear, as queen of the *fiesta*?'

'I have no idea,' Kit said. 'I don't have a thing. My father was talking about having a white ball gown made for me, but I don't think that would be quite right somehow.'

'Why don't you wear *baturra* costume?' Señora Arocha said.

Kit returned her lipstick to her pocket-book, and began to pat her hair into place. 'Well ... César – Señor Aguirre, you know – thinks that only women of Aragon should wear it. It's not a fancy dress but part of the people's deepest feelings, he says. Anyway, I don't have one.'

Señora Arocha said, 'I agree that it would not be suitable, in most cases, for an American lady to wear it. But this is different. I think the people of Medina would take it as a great compliment if you wore it, particularly as your attendants will be wearing ordinary clothes, I am sure. American clothes, so to speak.'

Kit thought, I'd love to really. Wouldn't César be surprised and, in the end, pleased – as long as she got every detail right, and *moved* right? Moving was a special accomplishment of Spanish women.

'What American dress size are you?' Señora Arocha asked.

'Twelve.'

'And the measurements?'

'Thirty-five, twenty-five, thirty-six.'

'Then I can lend you a costume. I would like to do more than that. I would like to give it to you,' Señora Arocha said.

'Oh, I couldn't! But if I could borrow ... or hire it.' The generosity of Spaniards was almost frightening. She hardly knew Señora Arocha.

The woman, smiling, said, 'It is a very beautiful one, with an eighteenth-century scarf to go with it.'

Kit thought, Boy, would he get a shock when she appeared in *that*!

'But you must keep it a secret,' Señora Arocha said. 'You can say your dress is to be a surprise, but the colour will be red. Your maids of honour will want to know that much. Then come to my shop an hour or two before you have to gather at the Ayuntamiento and we will put it on – and it will be yours.'

'I *couldn't* take it, as a gift, really,' Kit said. 'You're too kind, but please let me pay.'

Marcia Arocha shrugged lightly. 'Very well. You shall pay . . . You know where my place is? It is in the Pasaje de Aragon, the narrow alley leading off the Calle Zurbarán opposite the rose window of the cathedral, number six, on the right as you go down, a little before you come to the Casa Cuartel of the Guardia Civil. Leave a little extra time, so that I may offer you some wine and wish you good luck before you go to the Ayuntamiento.'

'I will be there,' Kit said. 'Oh, shall I bring shoes?'

Marcia Arocha slipped out of one of her shoes and said, 'Put your feet beside that. You won't be able to get it in.'

'I know,' Kit laughed. 'My feet seem enormous in Spain. We all have big feet.'

'That is from taking proper exercise and playing games when you were little girls.' Señora Arocha said. 'They are two sizes larger than mine. I have a pair of *baturra* shoes, with buckles, that will fit . . . And not a word to *anyone*, or you will break the secret, won't you, and then the people you would most like to surprise will not be surprised, eh?'

'Cross my heart!' Kit said, in English, and *'Entendido. Ni una palabra nadie.'*

'Good. Until next Saturday.' Señora Arocha held open the door of the ladies' room and Kit went out into the twanging and fiddle-moaning and non-stop nasal calling of a square dance, into the gigantic hangar and the jumping and romping and yelling under the merciless neon tubes.

She reached the table and for a moment caught César's eye, and hoped he read the flashed message of continuing love. A young airman with rather attractive dark eyes, but terribly tall, was begging for the next dance. The square dance ended. The Medina Cowboys took up their instruments. She was on the floor. Excuse me, please. Dance a turn. Excuse me, please.

After a time she noticed that César was signalling to her, and returned quickly to the table. César said, 'We are going home now.'

Delighted she gathered her wrap and pocket-book and at Bel's side led the way out to the brightly lit parking lot. As they neared the Hispano an ancient taxi, loaded with girls and old women, chugged out towards the exit.

She wedged herself carefully into the middle of the front seat, found a cigarette, and lit it. The motor hiccuped and began to turn over with a heavy, uneven sound. César climbed in and pressed the throttle up and down. 'The sergeant knows more about this car than I do,' he muttered. 'And he's only heard it once. Sergeant Olmbacher.'

The car moved forward, and out on to the street. César seemed to be talking to himself. 'Olmbacher has dignity, though he is not what we would call dignified. He smiles and grips your hand the way any other American does. Hands. They are important to him. He works with his hands, and I'm sure he believes no man can do more, if he does it well . . .'

They came to the gate and the sentry box in the middle of the road. The sentries waved them on, and César turned towards Medina. The tiny red tail-light of the old taxi prickled in the darkness about half a mile ahead.

César said, 'Olmbacher was interested in us.' Kit pressed her thigh warningly against Bel's. 'Perhaps it was because I own a special piece of machinery – this car.'

They were silent. A car was coming towards them from the city, its headlights small and very close together in the distance. They were almost at the Ríp Antiguo. The Milagro used to flow here, but in time long, long past, and now there was a valley two hundred yards wide, between shallow eroded cliffs of umber rock. There were scattered trees here, and a mysterious pool of brown water, that came and went for no apparent reason.

The tail-light of the taxi in front, now much closer, disappeared down the sweeping curve that took the road into the depression. On the far side the headlights of the approaching car swooped down into it at the same time. César slowed for the curve and in the comparative silence they heard the scream of tyres. 'Our friend opposite is in a hurry,' César murmured softly. Then they were down among the trees, on the straight again, the chugging taxi close ahead and the other lights coming on fast.

A small animal – a rabbit or weasel – darted out between the two cars, the taxi and the other. Instantly the approaching lights swerved. Kit jerked forward with a gasp. Tyres screamed and her own hands pressed hard against the dashboard as César stamped on his brakes. The approaching car swung round. In the white headlight glare she saw that it was an American car, a two-tone sedan, blue and black. It skidded sideways towards the taxi. The taxi swung right, the sedan crashed into it sideways.

The crash and jangle seemed to go on for a long time. Only the Hispano's lights lit the scene. It came to an end in a heavy silence.

135

'That's Bill's car,' she said dully.

The taxi was upright, but off the road to the right. Bill's Ford sedan, its side smashed in, was off the road to the left, its nose against a tree. The headlights shone on the face of the driver, and someone struggling to sit up beside him.

She said, 'Bill was driving.'

César bent down and turned a switch. The lights of the Hispano went out. 'You've been driving,' he said. 'Get over, now.' He opened the door, slipped out, and muttered, 'Count ten and put the light on again.'

He vanished. Kit slid over to his seat, counting dazedly ... three, four, five ... she couldn't see what was happening, but a woman in the taxi had begun to scream ... eight, nine, ten. She switched on the lights.

An old woman in black was wandering round in the middle of the road. Two young girls and a middle-aged matron were standing by the taxi. As the lights came on they saw the Ford. They all began to scream, but in anger now. The old woman shuffled forward, her hand raised in a claw. 'Murderer! Assassin!'

The middle-aged woman shouted, 'Drunken Yankees!'

César stepped out of the driver's seat of Bill Lockman's Ford. His hair was ruffled and his collar torn and she gasped when she saw blood on his forehead. Bill got out of the back seat. The other man was in the passenger's side of the front seat, his head in his hands.

César said to the old woman, 'Your pardon, mother. Is anyone badly hurt?'

'Don César Aguirre!' the old woman cried, peering at him in astonishment.

Kit got out and walked forward slowly, Bel at her side. There were three more girls in the taxi. One was bleeding from a cut nose, and the other two were trying to staunch the flow. 'The driver?' César asked. The driver crawled out, holding his head. He began to shout, 'Drunken Yankee son of a whore, you'll pay for this! It was your fault. The police ...'

'Are you all right?' César asked, holding him gently. Now they were all gathered in the middle of the road.

'Can we help?' Kit asked.

César said, 'In a moment ... It was all my fault, friend. It is Fernando, isn't it?'

136

The taxi driver peered at him suspiciously. 'Who are you? ... *Madre mía*, it is Don César! What are you doing here, *maestro?*'

'I was driving the Ford,' César said. 'It was my fault. The rabbit, you know ... and I was hurrying back to try to bring my friends here to the dance before it ended. They have been visiting the Barrio. What would you?' He shrugged meaningly.

Bill said suddenly, 'My friend and I were talking about women. He's an enlisted man.' His speech was blurred and slow, but he was not very drunk. Kit thought, If it hadn't been for the rabbit he would have got away with it. But he was in a sullen mood. 'An enlisted man,' he repeated, looking and speaking at her. 'A draughtsman and, boy, have we been talking.'

Kit started. She said coldly, 'Then you'd better not say anything more, either of you.'

She turned her back on him. The old woman said, 'We're all right, señor. And the *Americanos?*'

César said, 'We're all right. Aren't we?'

'Yeah,' Bill said morosely, and the other man said, 'I'm o.k.'

The taxi driver was looking at the front of his car. 'This is going to cost me at least five thousand pesetas to fix, *maestro.*'

'Of course I will see to it, Fernando, or my insurance company, eh? It will arrange itself. But for now ... look, it is my own car that is here, by chance. I think we can take all you ladies into Medina, and you, too, Fernando ... I had better do that, captain, if you will stay here. As soon as I reach Medina I shall telephone the base. What number?'

'Extension 290,' Bill said. He looked more tired than drunk, and Kit wondered how he had found the time or energy to visit the Barrio, with the extra work Lindy was supposed to be giving him.

César said, 'Then I will say good-bye, and I'm so sorry. So sorry.'

'Don't give it a second thought,' Bill said.

César kept talking, urging the women into the car, starting off, telling the taxi driver what to do about reporting the accident – that was nothing, it would arrange itself, neither Fernando nor the ladies want to get him, César, into trouble with the police, he hoped. No, no, not the police, the women chirped. They were recovering rapidly, but César kept talking and as soon as they had crossed Puente Nuevo he stopped, and they all piled out with thanks and *adios* and *buenas noches* and *muchas gracias*, and César made his phone call, and got back in.

In silence he drove across the Plaza del Mercado, and up the Paseo. Bel said timidly, '*Hermanito*, what did you do that for?'

César said, 'Fun.'

CHAPTER 13

César paced slowly up and down his big dressing-room, five steps this way, five steps that. He was wearing supple leather slippers, a black silk robe with a faint Paisley design in gold, and nothing else.

If she were going to come, she ought to be here by now. He should never have let her talk him into asking her to come tonight. She was becoming a damned nuisance. Infuriating that the thought, she is coming to me, could set his flesh creeping like this. She was a drug, more subtle than the danger of the bull-ring because she looked so innocent. He stubbed out his cigarette and lit another.

Damned drunken oaf, Lockman was. Drinking to drown his sorrow because Kit didn't love him any more. Typical Yankee. No pride. If he had any, he'd draw it round him and show nothing at all, absolutely nothing. Even women could do that, in Spain. Like Marcia, ignoring him, and fearing what she need not fear. Women didn't understand what pure sex was. They pretended to, but they didn't really. There wasn't a woman on earth who really enjoyed sex unless she had persuaded herself she loved the man.

Well, Lockman would get her back soon enough, and in pretty good condition, considering. Better condition than when she left him, if he only realized. Worn in, like these slippers. Knowing more of herself. But Lockman couldn't be expected to appreciate that. Lockman was . . . nothing. Then why did the thought of Lockman making love to her cause him to feel suddenly vicious?

He stopped, his heart beating faster. Very faintly he heard the latch turn in the bedroom door. He resumed his pacing, but more slowly. As he walked away from the open door of the dressing-room he could see, in the mirror over his dressing-table, a part of the bedroom – a corner of the wide high bed, the buhl clock on the mantlepiece, a segment of the oak floor that Eloísa, humming a love song, polished every other day, a strip of the red Turkish carpet beside the bed. But he could not see the painting of the battle of Lepanto on the near wall, or the crucifix at the head of the bed.

She was standing hesitantly in the bedroom, a strip of black velvet ribbon round her loose blonde hair, her feet in pomponned mules, the robe wrapped tight round her and the column of her throat rising out of it. His heart went out to her, against his wish.

She raised her head when she saw him and, as he came close, took a step forward, and wrapped her arms around his neck. The curves of her body fitted warm and close to him, and he began to kiss her, at first expertly, then with increasing, fumbling passion. His fingers dug into her back and he felt her sagging against him.

She pulled away with a jerk. 'César . . . Oh darling, darling.'

She sat down on the bed and put out her hands for him to take. She said, 'You were wonderful tonight, at the accident.'

César swore silently and let go of her hands. She wanted to talk. They were all the same. You could be in their bodies, mounting to transports of love and lust, and they'd whisper, 'Darling did you like the partridge I cooked for you?' He found a cigarette in the pocket of his robe, and lit it.

She said, 'You saved us from another of those headlines in *El Baturro,* about drunken Yankees. And when you went you didn't know how seriously anyone was hurt.'

César shrugged. 'I wasn't trying to save anyone but myself. I thought the driver of the car was drunk or reckless when I heard him taking the corners down into the Río Antiguo. Then during the accident I recognized the Ford. I decided I did not want to give evidence at any inquiry or court martial where Captain Lockman was involved.'

Her breasts swelled smoothly, forcing out the material of the robe in soft, full curves. If she'd only let go of the damned thing.

She was saying, '. . . you saved him from that. It would have been extra serious for him because it was an enlisted man he'd been drinking with.'

César said, 'There is no need to whisper in this room. We can make as much noise as we like, here.' He went close to her and slid his hand down the back of her neck, under the robe.

139

She pulled his hand out, and kissed it, and held it tight. 'One of my professors used to say that American's don't really like going abroad because, in the societies they see there, no one is free. In Europe or anywhere else in the world, he said, if a man isn't politically chained he's economically chained, and if neither of those then he's chained by convention and custom, by established authority. To get inside the society he's got to accept one lot of chains or another, and he doesn't want to. But I . . .'

'Which lot are you accepting?' César asked her.

She said, 'None! That was what I was going to say – that the professor had forgotten one thing – an American might fall in love, and then there wouldn't be any more chains.'

César said, 'In other words, you think that it's all right to make love to me because you love me.'

She said, 'I know it's immoral . . . but I can't believe it's really wrong. I try, but I can't. We're not hurting anybody.'

He said, 'You are an American all the way through, in spite of what you said about the dance. No, we're not hurting anybody . . . and I dare say most people would agree that we were not really doing wrong, either. But suppose I do accept the chains. Suppose I think humanity would be merely bestial without them. Suppose I think that right and wrong are absolute, and do not depend on whether people are hurt or not hurt, or on opinions . . .'

He walked away from her across the room, angry with himself for talking. Talking, in this vein, was just what she wanted him to do, and it was more dangerous than making love to her. Her hazel eyes were full of tenderness and awareness. He swung back on her. 'An ancestor of mine was hacked to pieces by a mob of peasants outside his estate near Jaca, in the year 1780. He was on his way to prevent them burning a certain woman as a witch. A large democratic majority, in fact all of them out there, thought burning her was the right and proper thing to do . . . A week later my ancestor's son went back with some of his men from here and Saldavega – who also believed that witches should be burned – and executed nineteen of the peasants.'

Kit said, 'But . . . it was wrong to burn witches.'

He said, 'It was and is, whether the mob, which means democracy, says it is or is not.'

Kit said hesitantly, 'But who does say what is right, then?'

He said, 'For an Anarchist like José – himself. For an

140

Aguirre, himself too, but also the past — history, the voices of Spain that are dead, the Church. For most, Church and State — authority.'

'But . . . but . . .' she said. 'There would be so many "rights". Democracy does at least have only one.'

'Which stands an equal or better chance of being wrong,' he said. He sat down beside her and slipped his hand inside her gown and cupped her breast. He said softly, *'Brr-ratat-ratata-ratta*, you are like a pneumatic drill, digging holes in the street. Is this the way American girls are taught to make love?' He bent his head close and bit her ear lightly.

She pressed his hand closer against her. 'Oh, César, I want to know everything about you. I want you to know everything about me . . . You mentioned the Church just now. Do you confess to Father Francisco, about us?'

'Wouldn't it be better not to know?' he said shortly.

' I couldn't face him next time he comes if I thought he knew,' she said.

'That's what I mean,' he said.

She said, 'It would be worse than meeting your analyst, if you had one. The analyst at least wouldn't be thinking I was *wicked* . . .' She paused and looked at him, shyly but full in the face. 'Confession is something I can understand, even though I'm a protestant, but some of the other things . . . please don't be angry darling, but I must ask because it's like a wall round you, the things you believe but don't talk about.'

He said, 'Didn't I tell you we all had fences around ourselves?'

She hurried on. 'The Armlet of San Marco, the pieces of the True Cross they've got at Pantela, the relics that are carried through the streets — do you *really* believe in them? I mean, you are so cynical in some ways, aren't you, and you know such a lot about people and the world, and . . . well, you know there are enough pieces of the True Cross to make one a hundred feet high . . .'

He said, 'The Cross *was* a hundred feet high then, obviously . . . Or perhaps it is true, as your professor said, that you have got to accept some chains before you can understand what their value is.'

Now she was fumbling away at mysteries of Faith that he could not, perhaps would not, have tried to explain to himself. For a moment his Faith seemed to be with him, touching him, as a tangible and real third person in the room. For a moment

141

he thought he would show Faith to her. It would be a strange attempt, far more exciting than a sexual adventure, and far more dangerous. He might lead her to believe. And then what?

It was impossible, ludicrous, and wrong. All that he wanted of her, she was sitting on. If he did not manage to keep this affair at that level, the prospect ahead was suddenly becoming so bright, and so obviously impossible, that the mere looking at it would destroy him.

He said lightly, 'And now may I kiss you, Miss Fremantle?'

Slowly she let her robe fall open, displaying before him, because he liked to see them, the motherly fullness of her breasts, the virginal flatness of her belly, and the direct animalism of the dark hair running down into the spread of her thighs, and the final all-embracing statement of the barely concealed lips – I am the half of humanity. For a time she watched him with a subtle Madonna-like smile of grace as he passed his hand over her skin, then she came seeking him with her lips.

All through the drawn-out processes of preparing for and consummating the sexual act he could not divert his mind from the insistent certainty that this was more than a female body. This was an immortal soul, and each second made him more positive that it was a great one. A sense of shame and self-disgust, combined with an increasing, almost frantic desire that the physical should totally obliterate the spiritual, drove him to excesses of animalism that left them staring at each other, exhausted, wordless, and abashed.

When she left him he lay staring at the ceiling, knowing that he had failed in everything he had set out to do with her. Each such act as this, however seemingly gross the lust of its symptoms, lifted them closer to a total union.

CHAPTER 14

Kit came back to the house, with Doña Teresa, about eleven o'clock. The daily marketing had to be done whether it was the day of the *Fiesta Americano* or not, and it had been fun to see what kind of preparation the city was making. Not a great deal, really. A number of Spanish flags, here and there an American one, hung from windows or were draped across window boxes. A gang of labourers was putting up a wooden bandstand among the fruit and vegetable stalls in the Plaza del Mercado. That was about all.

Sitting alone in the small drawing-room Kit thought, I'm to be queen tonight. Six days since the fair at the base, six days, each moving faster than the last, and herself sinking deeper into the river of love, retaining just enough strength to realize that time was passing, and sometimes to wonder where she was going. Not often though, because the fluid richness of the emotion in which she lived would try to answer for her – You're not going anywhere. You wanted to find happiness, didn't you? And you've found it.

At times such as this, when she sat in the living-room waiting for César, she knew too that she was going wherever he was going. No other prospect, now, had reality enough to project itself into even the farthest corner of her imagination.

Six days. They had gone to Saldavega again, she and Bel that time, to watch César working the calves with the cape in the paddock. They had visited the Roman camp and half a dozen cafés and restaurants, always with Bel and sometimes Doña Teresa as well. They had driven to Zaragoza.

And what, she thought ruefully, have I done about Spanish-American relations, for Dad or Lindy? I might be said to have established very good Spanish-American relations – but in a rather restricted sense. She smiled to herself. And Bel? She was certainly helping Bel merely by being here for her to talk to; but the moment when she could say a word to César and resolve the whole silly predicament never seemed to arrive. In truth it wasn't so silly, seen from inside these walls of the Casa Aguirre, or thought about while walking in the evening under the chestnut trees. She had an uncomfortable feeling that if she were to raise the matter now César would simply say, No, and that she would nod her head and say, Yes, I quite see your point. To alter that situation she must manoeuvre César into some position where he could not say No, which meant, really, becoming his wife. And then, by accepting him, she would accept also the chains he had talked about the night of the dance in the hangar. Among other things, she would have to become a Roman Catholic.

She glanced at her watch. He should be along any minute now. He had promised to show her the cathedral. She had been inside it once, with her mother and father, as a sightseer. This time she was going with a different purpose in her mind. It was strangely frightening, considering that she had hardly

143

been to her own church voluntarily in her whole life, to realize that she was now considering leaving it. It made her think of belief, and ask herself what, in fact, she did believe – or did she believe nothing?

She was going to the cathedral to try to understand what César believed. She remembered the previous visit – a cool, enormous cavern with pillars smooth and round sliding up to a black sky of stone; patches of coloured light in the gloom; huge pictures on the walls, in ornate golden frames, where angels swept down from violet clouds, saints in scarlet robes raised pointing fingers before an ochre Spanish city; the Virgin, a hundred times, the Babe in her arms – once with her breasts naked and the greedy Child kneading at the firm young-woman's flesh. ('Look at *that*!' her mother had whispered in horror.)

She remembered chapels round the side, each with a small knot of people bowed at the railing; or an old woman alone in black, torn slippers on her feet and her worn witch's face raised in adoration before the image hung with jewels and crowned with a diamond tiara, twenty candles burning around it and before its naked plaster feet.

She remembered the uncompromising bulk of the pillars; the only way you realized their height was that they faded into upper darkness, the shocking sound of human voices pitched at ordinary conversational level where two priests were talking to a middle-aged man in a smartly cut suit, the chairs huddled together in the centre of the nave, facing the steps mounting to the hight altar; the smells of dust and sweat and stone and incense.

She remembered the chapel of San Marco, not at the side like the others but built into the inner curtain wall round the high altar; the smells of dust and sweat and stone and incense. open both ways, so that worshippers in the nave saw it, and the people kneeling on the stone between the curtain wall and the outer wall saw it. The statue of the saint was silhouetted against the light whichever way you looked. The saint was kneeling, dressed in real clothes, the uniform of a Roman soldier, helmeted, facing the high altar, his right arm raised, holding a short sword a little below the hilt, so that it formed a cross. The walls of the chapel were brilliantly painted in blue, with a silver halo over the saint's head, on the ceiling. The guide had pointed out the white band on his left arm, just above the wrist, where the Armlet should have been.

The clock struck eleven. The bell tolled faster these days, surely? When she first came to the Casa Aguirre she could had sworn that time did not move here. Octavio and Eloísa and Juana were always seen in the same places, always doing the same thing, and the cathedral clock was like the Milagro flowing under Puente Nuevo, moving but always the same in a featureless landscape.

César came in and she jumped to her feet. He said, 'Ready?'

'Waiting.'

Octavio was polishing the handle of the front door with a chamois-leather cloth as they went out. César said, 'If anyone comes, tell them I shall be back in an hour and a half, two hours.'

'Bien. And the *señorita americana*'s going with you?'

'Yes,' César said shortly.

'I do not ask out of inquisitiveness, my little master,' Octavio said reprovingly. 'But because there may be inquiries for her from the base, from the Ayuntamiento, from heaven knows where. Do not forget she is a queen tonight, though queen of what, exactly, I couldn't say . . .'

They were out in the street walking down Obispos towards the cathedral. She longed to rest her arms in his, and to avoid the temptation she walked well separated from him. After a while she said, 'Did you have good exercise yesterday in the Valle de Roldán?'

He said, 'Not quite what I wanted. I intended to go up the cliffs on the north side, where one has to use the hands for a thousand feet on end – excellent for strengthening the wrists and fingers. But there had been rain in the night up there, and the cliffs were dangerous.'

'Take me to Roldán sometime,' she said. 'Soon. Everyone says it's so beautiful.'

'Sometime,' he said.

In the Plaza San Marco workmen were busy removing the scaffolding from the statuary group of the saint and the bull. The repairs had been effected.

'They look as good as new,' Kit murmured. 'And just the same size, in spite of the rumours.'

César glanced up at the statue. 'Yes . . . What are you going to put on your head?'

Kit stopped in dismay. She would have to have a head covering of some sort before she could go into the cathedral. Searching in her pocket-book she pulled out a tiny white handkerchief. It would have to do. She arranged it on her head with an apologetic smile. 'It's the only thing I have.'

145

César took it off her head and said curtly, 'It doesn't suit you.' Leading her into a store under the arches of the Calle Zurbarán, he bought her a black lace mantilla.

As they recrossed the Plaza among the cooing, sex-obsessed pigeons she thought, he has kept my handkerchief.

Then the cathedral rose more bulkily above her, the sun glaring on the great south façade. They entered by the centre of the three twenty-foot-high double doors, passing through a little wicket gate cut into the oak. She adjusted her mantilla while César removed his dark glasses, and put them in his pocket. He said, 'You should always wait a moment inside a cathedral, to let your eyes get used to the change of light.' His voice vanished among the pillars – there was no resonance and no echo. She waited, her eyes half closed, and after a time the tenebrous vastness began to lighten and the dim figures to take life. Half a dozen people, nearly all women, were kneeling or sitting in the central nave. Rays of dusty light slanted down through the tall south windows, giving life to the saints and angels in the pictures on the opposite wall. The floor shimmered faintly, like the bed of a shallow sea under dimly coloured waves.

César moved forward to a font at the foot of a pillar, dipped his fingers into the water, and crossed himself. He pointed up at the rose window in the western face of the cathedral. 'Only the very centre of the rose is original,' he said. 'And most of the right-hand panel. The rest, all fourteenth-century, was destroyed in the war. It cost us ten million pesetas to replace them – a quarter of a million dollars.' He was silent, and she at his side, staring at the rose and violet glory of the window, forty feet in diameter, and the tall bright panels on either side, each ninety feet tall and twenty feet wide. In the centre of the rose a Roman soldier lay asleep, his body following the curve of the window space, his helmet in his arms, and a mysterious silver light on his sleeping face.

They paced on, neither speaking, till César stopped at the reredos behind the high altar. He pointed down to the stones where they were standing, and said, 'These are the tombs of the early bishops. The later ones are buried in the cathedral yard.' He nodded to the north wall. 'And that's almost full now. No one but a bishop, or another Medina saint, will get buried there.'

They moved on, Kit peering down at the hardly decipherable names cut in the stone slabs. When they stopped again, she found that they were standing outside the chapel of San Marco. Through the arch she could see the high altar, unlit, long and dark like a giant catafalque against the pale marble background of the carved screen. Under the arch, San Marco's plaster face was lit from below by a score of candles. Three women, and a young girl all in white, knelt outside the circle of the steel chain that guarded him.

César said softly, 'A detachment of the Seventh Legion, Gemina, came here in A.D. 98. That year and the next they built their camp. There weren't many Romans from Rome in the legion when it first came, and by the time it left it was almost solidly Spanish. The emperor at the beginning was Trajan. He was a Spaniard, too. Marco was a legionary in the 4th Cohort. He was secretly a Christian. On 21 August A.D. 112, Christ came to him in a vision and told him that he must declare his Faith, and refuse to bow down before any other gods. Marco was frightened, and the next day he took his arms and climbed the hill near the camp to pray. This hill ... A party was sent after him, because he'd missed parade, but they couldn't get near him, where he was kneeling on the top of the hill, praying that Christ would not make him declare his Faith, because a wild black bull, a fighting bull, was guarding him. Here.' He pointed to the stone below their feet. 'Marco finished praying and knew that he had to do as he had been commanded. As soon as he reached his decision the bull went away and left him. He went down the hill, announced that he was a Christian, and refused to bow to the statue of the emperor, who was of course a god. He was tried, found guilty, and crucified the next day, 22 August, in the presence of the legion, on the top of the hill where the black bull had guarded him the day before – here. But there was no bull that day.'

She waited, staring at the stone, her eyes dim. Now she could almost believe. The cross would have risen there, where the statue stood, very close to her.

César said, 'Everyone forgot about the soldier Marco until two hundred years later, A.D. 312, when some shepherd boys found his bones, and the Armlet on them. Soon the first shrine was built. The bones and the Armlet were buried under the altar. When a larger church was built by the prince of Medina, in about A.D. 700, the bones had vanished, but the Armlet was still there. The prince had the Armlet kept on the high altar. Then the Moors came, in 734.'

'And someone stole the Armlet,' she said suddenly.

He looked at her quickly. 'Someone – it is only known that he was a soldier – took it,' he said. 'It has been revealed that he had a vision that the city was doomed because of its wickedness and self-indulgence ... The Moors pulled down the church and built a mosque. After the reconquest this cathedral was begun, in 1115. The Armlet was found in this very place, under the ruins, when they pulled down the mosque to dig the foundations for the cathedral.'

Kit said hesitantly, 'How does anyone know exactly what happened in A.D. 112 and 312? There aren't any written records, are there?'

'No,' he said flatly. He moved on slowly round the curtain wall of the nave.

Kit followed, thinking hard. The Roman soldier, Marco, was crucified in 112. His remains were found in 312, including an Armlet, and reburied pretty soon. They stayed in the earth for four hundred years, almost as long as since Columbus discovered America till now. A year or two later, a soldier stole the Armlet and presumably hid it somewhere, to save it from the Moors. But he couldn't possibly have hidden it in the earth under the altar, where it reappeared four hundred years later ... Inside the guard chain there was a large coloured picture of the Armlet, taken when it had been on the arm of the image. It appeared to be a broad band of gold, edged with small blue gems, and it had a golden clasp, so that it could be fastened and unfastened. How would Roman legionaries have left such a valuable thing on the body of a man they regarded as a criminal, or a mutineer? Now she remembered Grace Lindquist saying, sometime, that the Armlet, once again stolen, was definitely twelfth-century work ... There was so much detail in the whole story. How could anyone know all that if there were no records? Marco may have worn an armlet, but surely it would have been an ordinary soldier's one, of leather or perhaps iron to protect his wrist? The 'new' Armlet *must* have been 'planted' by the count or king who ordered the building of the cathedral. In fact there was no real proof that Marco himself had ever existed.

She stole a glance at César. He believed all that he had told her. He must believe in miracles, then. Or, better to say that he believed, period. It was obvious now in the way he looked at the images in the chapels they passed. It was obvious at the door, where he stopped and turned back, staring slowly round the cathedral, and as he said, with the harsh, uncompromising

148

edge to his voice that was always there when he spoke of what was deep in him, 'There is no sense to this, when we are so poor. There is no sense in Faith. God preserve us from sense.' He put on his dark glasses and pushed open the wicket door for her.

She remained silent and preoccupied all through lunch. The visit to the cathedral, in César's company, had posed more questions than it had answered, and thrown an almost impenetrable cloak of meaning about all that had occurred and was to occur between César and herself.

As the meal ended Doña Teresa said, 'Now Kit, you should lie down and have a good sleep. You must look your best tonight.'

Kit jerked her mind back to the trivialities of reality. She was to be queen of the fiesta; and wear a *baturra* dress that would show César, among other things, that she could adopt the Spanish way of thought, for his sake, as easily as she could wear the dress. There was much to be arranged. She signalled Bel to accompany her upstairs.

In the room she said, We're going to eat tonight, aren't we?'

'Only you,' Bel said, a little uncomfortably. 'The rest of us will be coming out to watch the procession, and I will see you in the Mercado ... but we shall eat at the usual time, half past nine.'

Kit said, 'Well, I'd like something at seven.'

'Seven?' Bel exclaimed. 'Surely eight will give you time enough to dress afterwards?'

Kit said, 'No, seven. Will you tell Juana for me? Remember my dress is an absolute secret ...'

'I know,' Bel said eagerly. 'I've been wondering where it is. Is it in that big cardboard box that came from the base yesterday?'

Kit smiled. 'No. That's only something that I'd ordered from home ... As soon as I've finished eating, I am going to say that I am coming up here to get dressed, and you are coming to help me, and no one is to disturb us, no one at all, for any reason.'

'Yes, yes, of course,' Bel said.

Kit continued, 'But when we get up here I shall go out by the fire escape from your mother's room, and you must come into my room here, lock the door, and stay here till half past nine. The you go down to dinner and tell them I'll be in soon, and please to wait for me in the drawing-room. I shall come in at

149

the front door then, and come straight to the drawing-room, and show you all my dress.'

Bel said dubiously, 'It sounds very exciting.' She wandered round the room while Kit took off her dress and lay down on the bed in her slip.

Kit said, 'I'd better try to get some sleep now.'

Bel said, 'Yes . . . Kit.'

'What?'

'You know that note I asked you to send out to Pete, on Thursday.'

'Yes.'

'It was to tell him I'd got to talk to him again, at once. He gave me the answer at Mass in the cathedral this morning.'

Kit said, 'I thought you'd both decided the meetings weren't worth it, especially as you're planning to elope at San Marco.'

Bel said, 'I . . . I have to tell him I can't elope. If nothing's happened by then, we'll just have to speak to Mother and César. I can't run away.'

Kit sat up in bed and lit a cigarette. She felt guilty and ashamed of herself. She should have spoken to César. Really, why hadn't she? Because she knew it would change the tone of sensual ecstacy, and something more, that was growing up between them. She had been selfish, thinking only of the continuation of her own happiness.

She said, 'I can't stop you, honey . . . but for God's sake make this the last . . .' Privately, she added, And I will speak to César this very night, so help me.

Bel said miserably, 'We – I, need your help this time . . . The cobbler's gone away. His mother's sick in Soria. The room is locked up. Pete can't get away until nine o'clock on Sunday night, tomorrow . . . He's arranged for a friend to take a room, in one of these so-called boarding-houses in the Calle Estrecha, for two hours, and leave it to us . . .'

'O.K.,' Kit said, 'You'll have to go there the same way you have been going to the cobbler's.'

Bel burst into tears with an awful suddenness. 'The Calle Estrecha is the whore's part of the city, Kit! Of course it's much the best place for Pete to get a room, just for that reason . . . and the city's so overcrowded with the base and construction workers . . . b-b-but there are always men hanging round there, ours, Americans . . . and girls in doorways, and I'm terrified of being recognized going there alone. Please come with me.'

My God, Kit thought wearily. She wasn't afraid of walking

through Estrecha among the whores; she could look after herself, and two of them certainly could. But the whole affair was becoming more involved, more sordid. Then she thought, here is the first time Bel's asked me to do anything that involves an effort on my part, and I try to think of a way of getting out of it. The purpose of the meeting was good. There was something almost indecent about those two having to elope. Then she remembered that she had vowed to speak to César about them tonight. She could undertake to go with Bel to the whorehouse but it would all be different after she's spoken to César. The meeting between Pete and Bel could take place here and they could declare their intentions to César and Doña Teresa . . .

She said, 'O.K., Bel. I'll be glad to. About nine we should leave here? In disguise?' She laughed and took Bel's hand. 'Now, stop crying and don't say thank you. I won't let you down. Run along now . . .'

Alone, she closed her eyes. She must look her best, as they said. Should she wear ear-rings tonight? If so, which ones? The *baturra* shoes would have big silver buckles. The ear-rings that Aunt Jane had given her last Christmas might do. Have to have the right underclothes on, too. Briefs, no slip, two or three stiff petticoats.

The cathedral. Dark, matter-of-fact, and overpowering. Catholicism. Professor Jansen, Comparative Religion – 'The essential difference between Protestantism and Catholicism is a matter of authority. Protestant believes his responsibility to God is personal and direct. Catholic believes his responsibility is to the Church, which is the voice of God. From this concept . . . readily understand why the Roman Catholic Church cannot and does not tolerate private judgement on moral matters, true religious freedom, or the separation of Church and State . . . in fact none of these liberties, or licences, exist in predominantly Catholic countries . . . to expect them to do so is as unreasonable as to expect a lay state such as ourselves . . . France . . . allow each man to conduct his own foreign policy, or to separate the armed services from the control of the civil government . . .' Something like that. Professor Jansen was a short, pudgy man with twinkling eyes, said he was an atheist.

Having a direct responsibility to God was a pretty hard thing to understand. You listened to the minister more carefully than you listened to someone else, when he was talking about religion, because he was supposed to know. It was his job, so to speak.

If you listened a little more carefully still, and believed what he told you the same way you believed what the mechanic at the garage told you about the works of the car, you could call him a priest. The Pope was much more likely to know about God than she was, and anyway, nothing that anyone said could be actually proved one way or the other.

It wasn't often that you got to worrying about God, and death, and living, and what you were here for, but when you did it was uncomfortable not to know and not to be able to believe anyone. The minister liked to imply he didn't really know any better than you, so you listened to what he said the way you listened to Dad telling you not to drive the car at more than forty today, or Peggy lecturing you on the importance of keeping your virginity, knowing that when the time came you'd have to decide for yourself.

The mantilla suited her. And César had secretly kept her handkerchief. Why shouldn't she kneel on the stone like the rest of them, and believe in San Marco's Armlet? It wouldn't be difficult. Suppose she asked César, tomorrow night, whether she could speak to Father Francisco? Just to find out . . . He, Father Francisco, would know about her and César. Or he would guess. So he would know why she wanted to find out. The priests were much more comforting than the Protestant clergy. Father Francisco drank wine and rode about on a Lambretta with his skirts tucked up, and he nearly always had a spaniel puppy in a bag on the handlebars, the pup's head sticking out and his ears streaming in the wind.

The priests were human, even if some of them were supposed to be homosexuals because they couldn't marry. You felt Father Francisco would really understand what had happened to you, and be nice because you wanted to put it right. And then, on the other side, where being human was no good because there was no human answer, they were totally inhuman, like slapping down the Armlet of San Marco, and the Pope never being wrong, and ten thousand pieces of the True Cross, and miracles all over the place (why were there never any Protestant miracles?) – slapping them down in front of you in a huge, dark place with robes everywhere and candles flickering, and saying, 'Believe!' no argument, no explanation.

She crossed herself cautiously, and waited. The ceiling did not fall on her and after a time her legs became heavy and then her arms.

CHAPTER 15

Her heels made an exciting clack, clack on the sidewalk and the fairness of her hair turned the men's heads to follow her. The policeman on the corner of Caudillo, opposite the Bishop's Palace, looked deep into her eyes and said audibly, *'Ahí va un ángel, caminando por Medina!'*

She wrapped her thin coat round her – it was a warm night, but it would hide the costume when she came back this way to the Casa Aguirre. The big parcel of petticoats made a loud crackling noise and was awkward to carry.

Behold, an angel is walking abroad in Medina! She hugged herself gleefully. These formal compliments to pretty girls had long since been forbidden, Bel said – so of course it was the police who most often gave them now. Wonderful, wonderful Spain!

> *Tonight, tonight won't be just any night,*
> *Tonight there will be no morning star . . .*
> *Oh moon, grow bright and make this endless day*
> *Endless night!*

Americans could write good music and wonderful words if they tried.

Left here, from Caudillo into Zurbarán, along the west side of the cathedral yard, under the high retaining wall of the cemetary, where now there was only room for bishops and martyrs . . . Now, right, into the winding Pasaje de Aragon. A guitar plunked in an upstairs room over her head and solemn and slow the boom of the cathedral clock shook the houses, bommmmm, the nasal ending of the bell tone hanging in the air.

She knocked on the door of number six and waited. The door opened and Marcia Arocha faced her from a dimly lit, narrow hall. She said, 'Good evening, Miss Fremantle.' Smiling, she held the door open. A door to the right, presumably leading into the shop, was shut, and Kit went quickly up the narrow stairs. A door on the right of the landing was open, and she went into a long, narrowish room, unusually well lighted by

153

half a dozen well-placed and shaded bulbs. There were four work-tables, many bolts of cloth, two foot-operated sewing machines and a smaller hand model and, hanging from a beam across the centre of the room, a dully shimmering red skirt. Folded negligently over the hanger was an embroidered silk scarf of the same colour.

Kit gasped. 'Is that it?'

Marcia Arocha closed the door quietly, and came forward. 'That is the one. We may have to do a little alteration at the waist as I have not been able to have fittings. Of course, it does not have to fit anywhere else. See.' She took it down and held it at her waist, swinging it lightly so that the light caught the faint pattern of black roses in the dull silk. 'And now perhaps you will take off your clothes? In there.'

Kit went to the cubby-hole in the far corner of the room, slipped out of her dress, and returned. Marcia Arocha eyed her appraisingly as she undid Kit's parcel and held up the petticoats. 'These three,' she said. 'The other is too stiff ... If you will put them on. And now this blouse. It is not the real one, but it will do for testing the fit. Now the skirt. Kick off your shoes, please.'

There was a long mirror against the wall, and Kit stood watching herself in a growing trance. The skirt was gorgeous, but Señora Arocha had given her half an inch too much at the waist, so in with the pins, and carefully out of the skirt. She smoked a cigarette and watched while Marcia spread the skirt gently on a table and with her small, white, expert hands worked the needle and thread. Her cigarette finished, she remembered the ear-rings. She put them on, and asked, 'Do you think I should wear these?'

Marcia Arocha glanced up. 'They are pretty. We can tell when you have everything on.'

Into the skirt again. Right now, exactly right. The stockings, ribbed in a pattern of twining vines, ivory coloured, of the thinnest and softest wool she had ever touched. She hitched the suspenders on to them and Marcia knelt on the floor to straighten the ribs. Now the blouse, the real one. She gasped again as Marcia brought out from a closet a blouse of ivory silk, the collar edged with lace and sweeping in a loose V over the bosom, and more lace round the cuffs of the long sleeves. Now the scarf. Marcia arranged it carefully on her shoulders and knotted it in front. Now the shoes. They felt a little heavy, and in-between in height, for they had thick half-heels. Perhaps they pinched a little at the sides ... but she could bear that for tonight.

She stood up. Marcia stepped back and examined her critically. A lock of her neat hair had fallen across her forehead and she looked a little drawn. But she must try again, tactfully, while they were having a drink, to pay for all this.

Marcia said, 'There is one thing. You must take off your lipstick and make-up, if you wish to wear the costume as a *baturra* should.'

Kit looked at her face in the mirror. No lipstick, as Miss Medina, 1958? She would feel naked. 'All right,' she said. Marcia brought a damp cloth and carefully washed her face and lips till they were clean. 'You can bite your lips though,' she said. 'And slap your face a little before you go out, quickly, with both hands ... *Ya está!* Are you satisfied?'

She turned away and began to pack Kit's other belongings back into the brown paper parcel. Kit stood in front of the mirror, staring. The silver buckles glittered on the black shoes; the stockings showed the shape of her calf and slid up, just below the knee, under the ordered froth of the three petticoats; the skirt was a dream, so simple and subtle and rich; the blouse and scarf, hiding yet showing the shape of her bust; her neck rose proudly out of them; and here was her face.

Who was this exactly? The lips were pink instead of red, and that made the eyebrows seem even darker and heavier than they were, and God knows her mother had told her often enough she ought to pluck them. She looked terribly determined, or capable of it. She must smile. There. That was better, but she still looked vaguely powerful. Pretty was definitely not the word. This was a woman she had never looked at.

She straightened herself and thought, I am a *baturra*. This is how César shall see me, and then he will know. The dress was a uniform, after all, and a woman could only alter little details here and there. So, wearing this, and without lipstick and make-up, there was only the woman to look at. What she was examining in the mirror was not the dress, as she had thought to, but herself. It wasn't what she expected, but all the same this *was* her, Catherine Fremantle. Wherever she was, here or there, in Spain or America, she had seen herself. Now she would show herself to him, and say, I have found myself, because of you, and for you.

Her eyes began to fill with tears and she thought exasperatedly, I am as bad as Bel. She put out a hand blindly to Marcia Arocha, for she was another woman, and must see and understand – at least a little. 'Thank you,' she whispered. 'Thank you. I can't tell you . . .'

'Don't thank me,' Marcia said with sudden harshness. After a time, her voice again under control, she said calmly, 'Now will you do me the honour to come upstairs to my apartment, and take a glass of wine with me?'

Kit said, 'Of course.' Hurriedly she dried her eyes, picked up her belongings, went out on to the landing, and waited there while Marcia switched off the lights in the workroom and closed and locked the door. Then, with a word of apology, Marcia passed her and led the way up the next flight of stairs.

At the head of the stairs there was a small landing and a door. This was the topmost storey of the house. The door was solid dark wood and no light showed under it on the polished bare boards of the landing. *'Un momento,'* Marcia murmured as she fitted a key in the lock. The key turned, she opened the door a little, put her hand inside, and turned a switch. Light poured through the crack of the door opening. She turned to Kit, her face now absolutely smooth and without expression, the eyes burning huge and dark in it. *'Pase usted,'* she said in her metallic singer's voice. Opening the door wide, she stood aside.

Smiling, Kit walked forward. After three paces she stopped. César stood at full height on the opposite wall, in an oil painting. He was wearing *baturro* costume, one foot raised on a sidewalk in a dark street, a guitar in his hand. He was looking directly at her, his lips unsmiling.

She took a step forward, another, her eyes turning away, for César was looking into her. Wherever she looked, he was there . . . on a side table, in a big silver frame, head and shoulders, smiling. On the right wall, this time the two of them, Marcia and César, in bathing dresses standing in shallow waves, holding hands and laughing . . . on the mantelpiece, in the suit of lights, the naked sword in his hand.

'You . . . know César?' she said, understanding fully, but her throat would not obey her command to keep silence. By speaking, she was showing this woman the place to wound her, and telling her how best to do it; but she had to do all that.

The door closed behind her and Marcia Arocha's firm steps

156

approached. 'I am his mistress,' her voice said. Kit did not turn. How like a *jota* this sounded. This was exactly how it was sung, the tremor hidden in the voice but there, and the same aching agony to hear it as to sing it.

'He owns this house,' the voice said. 'He gives me as much money as I need, when I need it. I give him everything he allows me to. I have loved him for five years ... A glass of wine? It is wine of Aragon, the strongest we make. Aguirre wine.'

'Thank you,' Kit said. She held out her hand and took the glass.

'Everyone in Medina knows,' Marcia said. *'Everyone.'*

She could say, Why are you telling me this? Or, How distressing for you. She said, 'Bel?'

Marcia said, 'Yes, Bel, and Doña Teresa, and Colonel Portuondo, and the mayor, and the President of the Diputación, and Eloísa, and Rosario Lima and the other girls who work for me. Everyone. Everyone except the Americans.'

Kit sat down suddenly, her hand shaking so that a little wine spilled on the carpet. She bent her head. Surely the woman would leave her alone now, seeing her misery. She was too hurt to show any more pain, however many times Marcia pierced her.

Marcia's uncompromising voice went on. 'He has had other women since I loved him, of course. The ridiculous governess, Miss Mowbray, for a time before she left. Society women who throw themselves at him in Madrid and Valencia because he is a matador, so they can forget he is also a gentleman. I do not like it, but I am a woman, and can put up with worse than that. I made it my business to find out what kind of a woman you were, when I heard you were staying at the Casa Aguirre. César is susceptible, though we must not tell him so, must we? ... Don't think you are different from the rest, in his eyes. Just a little exercise.'

In the greyness surrounding her Kit felt something brighter, like a dim flash; but it hurt. It was a momentary flame, coming in the darkness to one lost, hurting the more because it might have been a guide out of night but instead only burned and vanished.

Marcia Arocha went on. 'He cares nothing for you at all, do you understand? Nothing nothing nothing! He has come in

157

here to me a score of times and told me how you pursue him. He compares you to a big, clumsy young mare ... Drink some wine or you will faint.'

Kit humbly picked up the glass, carried it cupped in both shaking hands to her lips, and drained it.

Marcia Arocha said, 'And I am a fool, because I remember always that I am a woman, and even when stupid or vicious amateur whores throw themselves at him I cannot help thinking that they are women, too, so always I can understand. I know how you feel, at least, how you think you feel. At the dance last Sunday at the base, when you were dancing with him, when you were sitting at that table opposite him ... like a spaniel waiting to have her belly rubbed, ready to roll on your back and put your feet in the air. Have you no pride? ... It was then that I decided something must be done. Not for my sake, because he loves me, only me, not you, you understand? No, it was for your sake. You think I have been cruel? Well, if you forget him from now, it will not be cruelty. You will learn that one day.'

Kit said, 'I'm afraid I must go now.' She stood up and looked wildly round. Where was the door, a window, some place she could rush, jump, fall away from this voice, this darkness, yet still lit by the mysterious searing flashes of light?

The woman's face came into focus before her. Quite clear, beautiful, pale, the ivory skin covered with a fine layer of perspiration, the forehead shining under a light. She is suffering as much as I am, Kit thought. Another flash of light, another dull agony deep under her breasts. The image of Marcia was very clear, and exact. Therefore she herself could not be crying.

She gathered all her strength and said quietly, 'If you will excuse me, señora, I think it is time I went back now. I presume I have paid for the dress, as you intended?'

The other woman stared into her eyes for a moment. Then she said roughly, 'You can't go back there. The *fiesta* procession will be as bad as this, or worse. You know nothing. I will send word that you have been taken ill, and will call a taxi to get you taken to your parents' house at once.'

'I am feeling quite well, thank you,' Kit said.

'Ah, don't be stupid,' Marcia cried. 'You will be hurt again! Leave us to our cunning and our loves and hates. We are cruel and vindictive and mean. Go back to the base now, go back to America. You are too innocent and simple for us.'

158

Kit saw that the woman really was trying to help her. She was kind.

She said, 'Thank you so much, but I will return to the Casa Aguirre now, for I must be at the Ayuntamiento at ten o'clock punctually.'

Señora Arocha stepped back, and watched wordlessly as Kit picked up her coat and put it on, carefully, to hide the finery of the *baturra* costume, found her pocket-book and the brown-paper parcel. 'I think that's all,' she said. 'Good night.' She walked to the door and opened it.

Marcia Arocha ran to her and caught her elbow. Her voice was hoarse and uncontrolled, 'For the love of Mary, don't go back to him . . . please.'

Kit said, 'Thank you so much.' She walked firmly down the steps, head up, into a night so cold it made her shiver.

Book Two

ROCK

CHAPTER 16

The cathedral clock finished striking ten as she stepped out of the Hispano in front of the Ayuntamiento, flash-bulbs popping all about her. She smiled blankly into the green balls of light they created in front of her eyes. The alto and treble bells began to swing and ring from high in the dome. They were the signal for great rejoicing, serious fire, or invasion by the French. No one else. It had to be the French.

easy to hear what he said, answer, and smile. Perhaps that was

César said something and she answered. It was inexplicably because the grey pall still enveloped her, and was still shot with tongues of some obscure joy that gave only pain. No new set of rules, no new ways of behaviour, had had time to shape themselves. She had returned to the Casa Aguirre just when and how she had said she would, and gone to the drawing-room, and made her grand entrance. If Bel and Doña Teresa had looked at her more closely than usual, why, it would be the costume, or because the excitement of the occasion had made her a little pale. They'd exclaimed in admiration, and wondered where she got the costume – but that was a secret.

It was mostly airmen here outside the Ayuntamiento. With cameras, of course. 'Look this way, miss.' . . . 'Hey, Miss Fremantle, hold it a minute.' . . . 'Smile, wide.' . . . 'Thanks, miss.' There were a few Spaniards – soldiers, old men, teenagers – peering under the Yankees' arms at the cameras.

She went alone up the wide stairway. César had been offering to escort her up. That was what he had been saying just now, and she had answered kindly that she would go up alone. More impressive. The mayor's big reception room was on the first floor. No, the *second*. The first was the one on the ground. Anyone except these European clowns would know that.

The mayor met her at the head of the stairs, looking worried in a smart dark blue suit. He led her into the reception room and everyone there exclaimed over her costume, how wonderful, how suitable, how complimentary; how pretty she was. The mayor introduced her to an oldish man, very flustered. 'How do you do, Señora Bermúdez?' He had had charge of all the arrangements. Of course the good Major Fremantle had made the original suggestion ... Not her father? Well, well! How suitable! ... And then he, Señor Bermúdez, had taken over, with a small committee. She would understand. *Claro*. Major Fremantle had asked for the merest nothing, just a gesture of friendship. All the rest was his idea. And the committee's. *Claro*. Great admiration for America, Americans, American justice, American Air Force, American plumbing. Stinking hypocrites.

The mayor introduced her to a young man with his hair plastered down and a self-satisfied smirk on his dark face. Her escort. My what? Escort. She smiled brilliantly at him. She had never thought of that, but of course a queen always had an escort or a consort or something, a young man with a boutonnière; but this one had a shiny suit and a leer.

She had a glass of wine in her hand now. Señor Bermúdez introduced her to her court ... one, two, three, four girls in taffeta evening gowns, in various shades of purple. Provided by Señor Bermúdez out of his own pocket. Made by Señora Arocha? No, she was too good a dressmaker to bear it. Against the colours of her own dress they were specially awful. They all had carnations in their hair, and one of them was Rosario Lima, the seamstress from Marcia's. She suffered a momentary glimpse of César taking Marcia in his arms, and she bending pliantly against him. She closed her eyes quickly and opened them. Everyone was still here.

The mayor pointed out several men and a couple of women, all in *baturro* costumes. The Cabras Blancas. The White Goats, a semi-gipsy *jota* club from the Barrio, most of its girl members not much better than tramps, she remembered, and the men, pimps, lottery salesmen, guitar players, hotel waiters.

Was this all, the great procession? Oh, there is more, much more, but outside, she would understand. Orphans from Santa Eulalia. A band. Not the municipal band, there wasn't one really, but *a* band, the best. The mayor's four heralds came in, wearing black tights and pointed shoes, and tabards emblazoned with the whole coat of arms of the Most Ancient, Most Loyal, Most Indomitable City of Medina Lejo. The crest was not a mural crown, like any other city's, but a Roman helmet, plume and all. The motto, I DEFY THEE, TRAJAN, just about marked where their crotches were, behind the tabards, and they carried trumpets in their hands, resting on their hips.

Through the open windows she heard the shrill bells ting-ting, jingling away. The French must be invading. No, it was the U.S. Air Force, in town in force tonight, and they meant to enjoy themselves. She had heard the good voices raised in the streets, on her way back to the Casa Aguirre. 'Give me a drink, Mac. No, a real drink tonight. Some of that goddamn Spanish whisky.' There were half a hundred of them out in the Plaza below, several looking up at these lighted windows. She heard an appreciative wolf whistle and waved her hand gaily. The whistling increased.

Señor Bermúdez urged her politely towards the door. The heralds with trumpets gathered round the mayor. Where was her father? Out there in the street, for sure. He wouldn't want to interfere with her big moment, and he'd even managed to keep Peggy out of her hair. But he'd have the pictures to show everyone later.

She went slowly down the sweeping shallow stairs. Her hand rested lightly on the arm of her escort, who pressed it tight against him, so that his forearm touched the side of her breast. She'd deal with him in a minute.

A low roar welled up from out there in the street, in front of the huge, wide-opened doors with the brass apples as knockers, that could only be reached by a man on horseback. The sound was formless and punctuated with sharp cracks like pistol shots. For a moment she quailed. What now, in God's name, what now? Then she went firmly on down, one slow step at a time. She'd find out.

As she passed through the tall doorway she made out what the sounds were – laughter, and the cracking of whips. A huge farm cart stood there in front of the door, heavily caparisoned with the red and gold of Spain and hung fore and aft with Stars and Stripes. She saw her father and mother in the middle of the street, a policeman watching negligently as her father snapped pictures. The mayor and the heralds were taking their places in front of the cart. Ahead of that she had a back view of the band, in uniforms of dark blue with yellow stripes, and peaked caps worn at every angle. The *jota* team from the Cabras Blancas pushed into a sort of formation behind the cart. Behind them there were three or four women and a hun-dred little boys and girls in dark blue pinafores with red sashes.

The orphans, of course. They had to earn their keep somehow. Behind them – twenty Roman soldiers. Romans, for Christ's sake. But Roman soldiers *always* attended processions in Medina. It was the custom. They were members of the Society of St Anthony, which was the municipal employees' society – clerks, street cleaners, sewer men.

The carriage was drawn by ten donkeys of various sizes, in charge of four loudly swearing men with big whips. Rosario Lima's hard voice beside her exclaimed, 'Donkeys ... What are you trying to do to us?'

Señor Bermúdez said unhappily, 'My dear young lady, remember where we are ... the young lady, the American ...'

Flash-bulbs kept popping. Kit thought there must be two hundred Spaniards around by now, but none of them were laughing. They all looked interested and solicitous. The laughter was from the airmen. 'Look at the goddamn *burros*!' ... 'That little feller there should get a ride in the cart, and put the babe with the big knockers in the trace, the one with the black hair and the pink flower ...'

Rosario Lima said, 'I will not ride in that thing, behind those donkeys. I refuse!' She stamped her foot.

Señor Bermúdez said, 'There were going to be six horses, young ladies. Six *white* horses. But the man sold them. Only this morning did I learn. We could get no other horses ...'

Kit said, 'Of course, it doesn't matter, Señor Bermúdez. I'd love to ride in the cart. Please don't worry about it at all.'

There was no block or ladder for her to get up into the cart. She reached up to grab the side and hoist herself up the long step, and a photographer at the side dropped to one knee for the cheese-cake shot. She swung up, and her escort, perhaps in an honest effort to help her, goosed her. She trod on his fingers as he followed her, but his cry of pain was lost in Rosario Lima's grumbling. Señor Bermúdez hurried forward to join the mayor.

They had spread an expensive Oriental carpet on the floor of the cart, and placed four unmatched kitchen chairs on it. The maids of honour sat down quickly on the chairs. The band struck up a march, and moved off, followed by the mayor, Señor Bermúdez, and the heralds. The carters cracked their whips and yelled. With a jerk and a heave the cart ground forward. The airmen raised a tremendous cheer and their laughter swelled and echoed in the Plaza; but all the Spaniards continued to look solicitous. Kit grabbed hold of the

164

front of the cart to keep her balance. Her escort stood beside her, resting his hand on her waist to steady her.

The band turned left into the Calle del Alcalde, the mayor followed, and, in its turn and with blasphemy from the carters, so did the cart. Kit glanced round – Rosario and the other girls were sitting bolt upright on the swaying chairs. The *jota* group marched close at the cart's tail, followed by the glum orphans and the straggling Roman soldiers.

Kit turned again, smiling and waving her hand. They could make her ride a donkey through the streets, they could crucify her, but they'd get nothing out of her except this smile, this waving hand. The noise of the band blew back strong to her, out of tune and dissonant, the echoes flailing about between the buildings to turn the rhythmic beat into a porridge of sound.

The procession turned right, down the Calle Ibáñez, towards the centre of the Barrio. Scores of kids marched alongside the cart, gazing up at her as though they had never seen a girl before. There were people, but not many more than there would be on any other Saturday night at this hour, for the escorting police and the procession itself forced the people on to the sidewalk, compressing them into the semblance of a crowd. The airmen came along in strength, though, whistling cheerfully in tune with the band, crouching in the road to take pictures.

The Barrio ... groups of men with dark sardonic faces, women in carpet slippers, hands on hips. The flat faces of the houses and the expressionless, oblong eyes of light in them were exactly the same as they had been at three o'clock in the morning of the Night of the *Jota*. The same silhouetted women sat up there against the light, looking down, and there were the same sudden vistas down dark alleys and into silent patios, and the same boy, or his brother, reading under a lamp. But tonight she knew them, and what they were thinking in their dark Spanish minds – how slowly one could tear the wings off flies, whether a heretic would scream more loudly over a fire of oak or of beech, more subtle ways of torturing bulls, overloading horses, starving dogs.

The cart halted with a jerk. They had reached the foot of Ibáñez and were trying to turn the sharp right-handed corner into the even narrower Calle Arenas. The cart could not make it in a single turn. Before and behind the procession stopped, and the sound of the band died away in fitful blares and drumbeats. The carters tried to back up the cart but the donkeys had never worked together before, and began to squeal and buck and bite at each other. A little jack donkey at the back succeeded in mounting the jenny in front of him. He's been trying to do that for some time, Kit thought dispassionately. Too late to crack whips over him now. The bandsman came back, shouting advice. The mayor lost his temper, the carters lashed out at the donkeys. The corner had become a bedlam of voices raised in American and Spanish, in every tone of hilarity and anger. The jack donkey, having finished his mating, slipped down.

An American voice said distinctly, 'You son of a bitch.' From the corner of her eye Kit caught the sudden movement, the flash of a fist. A little Spanish infantryman lay on the ground, holding his face. More soldiers pushed forward, more airmen. The mayor was there, and two, three, four police. The soldier was on his feet, shouting, *'He dicho que es una puta, la burra. La burra, la burra! La señorita, nunca, nunca!'*

'I heard him,' the airman shouted. 'Goddamn it, I know what *puta* means. These guys are trying to make a pig's arse out of us.' He was good-looking, burly, slightly drunk. Not very, she thought, only drunk enough to have the second sight and know what the Spaniards were really thinking.

A friend was restraining him, and the mayor was crying, 'Please . . . please . . . please!'

The airman yelled, 'This gook pointed at Miss Fremantle with his chin and said, *Es una puta.* He said, She's a whore!' The police led him away, his friend going along, also the Spanish infantryman and two others.

Near her on the sidewalk an airman drawled, 'Whadda ya say we take this town apart tonight, heh?'

Another answered, 'Hell, no, they don't mean any harm. It was just a misunderstanding.'

The first airman said, 'Maybe so. Well, let's see how it turns out, heh?'

The cart bounded forward, made the corner, and ground slowly on over the cobbles of the Calle Arenas, diagonally over an intersection, up the long trench of the Calle Goya, past the Excelentísima Diputación, past the little church of San Lorenzo.

As it turned into the Paseo and went down towards the Plaza del Mercado she heard the dip and blare of jazz music. Looking down the street, under the pruned trees, over the donkeys and the heralds and the mayor and Señor Bermúdez, she saw that the crowd down there was much bigger. The dancing was not supposed to begin till the procession arrived, and the Medina Cowboys were only there in the bandstand to keep the crowd amused until that moment; but the United States Air Force was in a funny mood tonight. The right mood, she thought grimly, as she smiled round at the tramps Rosario and Pilar and Pilar and Pilar, or whatever their names were.

Tonight the Air Force didn't care. Perhaps it had been like this all evening, or perhaps it had spread, in the way such things did, since the fight at the corner of Arenas and Ibáñez. The U.S.A.F. had decided they were tired of being ambassadors. They weren't in a bad temper, but obviously they didn't give a good goddamn what the people of Medina thought. She approved ... it had been awful last week at the fair, no one putting a foot wrong, a kind of bogus European politeness going on everywhere. Now she could almost hear the collective Air Force voice muttering, 'Screw that crap! I'm going to have myself a ball.'

The airmen were dancing all over the Plaza and she could tell, as soon as the donkeys carried her close, that most of the girls with them were from the Barrio, and many were gipsies. The band at the head of the procession was still blowing away, but they had no chance against the deft frenzy of the Cowboys in the bandstand. Quite a few of the airmen were high and they didn't give a damn. Eight Air Police stood in a conspicuous group on the far corner, where the road led out of the Plaza towards the grade crossing and the Puente Nuevo. Their parked trucks faced the base, ready to whisk away anyone who made trouble – and the airmen didn't give a damn.

The cart stopped, her escort jumped down and stood ready to help her. She shot him a warning look and slid down unaided. Señor Bermúdez murmured, '*Mil perdones, señorita* ... This is the first time, you understand. Little things will go wrong. Next year ... Medina has never had anything like this before.'

I'll bet it hasn't, she thought, smiling blandly. Someone gave her a huge bouquet of roses. The greyness of misery had dissolved somewhere along the route of the procession, somewhere in the long ordeal of holding up her head and smiling. She felt obscenely angry.

Now there was supposed to be a demonstration of *jota* dancing by the Cabras Blancas; but Señor Bermúdez was having a hard time getting the Plaza cleared and the Medina Cowboys to stop playing. To the right, as she sat, wasteland stretched away to the scattered lights of the railroad station and yards. It was an eye-sore by day, that waste, covered with scrub, a few sand-pits, playing kids, often the caravans of gipsies, and their naked children and dark-skinned women cooking something under the high wheels, or searching each other for fleas.

The boys would be taking the whores in there tonight. Why didn't César do the same if Marcia wasn't enough for him? The pain of realizing that what had been to her the most wonderful moments of her life had been to him . . . another lay, was almost unbearable.

The mayor came and murmured his good nights. Work at the Ayuntamiento, municipal business. She smiled sweetly. Her father and mother came and talked to her under the screeching of the *jota* singers. She had been wonderful. 'Why did they have to have donkeys?' her mother grumbled. 'I would have thought they could have found an automobile. We could have lent them one from the base if they'd only asked. Lots of people have convertibles.' 'Hell, no,' her father said. 'It's more typical, the donkeys. More Spanish.' He spoke cheerfully, but he looked worried. Her mother kissed her good night; she was going back home. Her father would stay till the end. Someone would give him a ride home. He drifted off. She saw Dick Holmes and Bill Lockman at the edge of the crowd opposite. Bill was watching her, his face very grim.

Her heart closed in tight. Not now to think of anything at all, just to get through the next hour. After midnight she could sneak away.

Bel and César came with Doña Teresa. Doña Teresa kissed her, and told her she had looked so beautiful. They had seen the procession, just the last bit, as it came down the Paseo. Bel whispered, when her mother moved away with César, 'He is here!' Kit nodded. But who was 'he'? Of course, Sergeant Olmbacher. The poor guy had no idea what he was letting himself in for. She looked into Bel's eyes. It was almost impossible to believe that she had played her part in causing this hurt, she looked so innocent and lovely. But she had, for she must have known, or guessed, and she had said nothing. There must be some way of making her suffer for it.

The *jotas* ended and she danced with her escort. Danced again, with another young man. Whatever member of the committee was supposed to be in charge of entertaining the queen and her court had vanished, or got drunk, or perhaps there never had been such a person in the first place. Each time she returned to her place, after dancing on the cobbles, another of the maids of honour had disappeared, Rosario Lima first. For some reason only Spaniards were surrounding her. She prayed that Bill would come so that she could hear his honest voice instead of these cruel Spanish compliments. The loathsome escort was looking into her eyes with a burning, soulful stare. Was she supposed to keel over and sigh, 'Take me!'?

She decided she would go now. She didn't know what time it was, but the Aguirres had left, Doña Teresa telling her the front door would be left open for her, and kissing her again. The Medina Cowboys were really gone now. The rock-and-roll set were jiving it up round the bandstand, a larger group watching and beating their feet in time and yelling, 'Tough, man, tough!' The crowd had surged forward past the two chairs still remaining in place. Some old woman watching from the lower windows above and behind her would see her go, but no one else. Her escort had gone away.

She stood up, and walked through the crowd and into the narrow mouth of the Calle de Jaca. The first house on the left of the street marked the corner of the Plaza del Mercado and also the corner of the wasteland. It was a narrow street of tenements, old but ugly. The children were playing in the street, as usual, though it must be well past midnight.

The grey fog had totally dispersed, leaving her clear and cold, but still invaded by the unaccountable flashes of pain that were not pain.

He'd be either in the library or his bedroom.

CHAPTER 17

César sat in the library, reading *Atlas Shrugged* with scornful satisfaction. After a few pages his concentration waned and he let the book rest in his lap.

If she were Spanish, she would not come. She would leave him to ask the questions, What has happened? Why are you different to me? Or she might stick a small knife into him, burst into tears, and accept the position. But it was almost impossible to imagine a Spanish woman being so naïve. Anyway, this one

169

was very hurt, and very American, so she would come to have it out, man to man!

The procession had been perfect. They'd done well to see that Bermúdez was chosen, and then nothing more. Mario couldn't have improved on it even if he'd used all his fairy's spite and viciousness trying.

He scowled. It ought to have been as funny as the calves and the clowns at a comic bullfight – even the small bit that he saw, let alone the farce at the corner of Arenas and Ibánez – and it wasn't. Like the calves, the Americans had not understood that they were cast in the part of helpless, energetic victims. The *banderillas* had been placed with the maximum agility and comic effect – so why should he feel like a murderer? Because she had got herself mixed up in it. It was like having a calf as a pet and one day finding it in the ring as your first bull. It would never understand why you were wounding and, finally killing it.

It was her own fault. No one asked her to come to Spain, to this house. He jumped up in a fit of anger. To hell with her. Let her get out of his sight for ever, and quickly.

The door opened and the muscles of his throat tightened. He turned. He had somehow expected her to be wearing nightdress and robe . . . or an ordinary dress . . . The *baturra* costume and the absence of lipstick and make-up had changed her completely. It was all he had been able to do to restrain a gasp when she came into the drawing-room before dinner. Because she was blonde he had assumed there was a pretty emptiness about her face, but looking at it then, it might have been for the first time, he saw that she was no more empty than the cathedral – timeless, ageless, known, but never finally.

The level hazel eyes gazed steadily at him under the thick, strong eyebrows. The wide lips were a little parted and her throat held the head high and firm.

She said, 'It was Marcia Arocha who gave me this costume. Without payment. And afterwards, she gave me a glass of wine in her apartment.'

He said, 'I have seen the costume before.'

'Has she worn it?'

He said, 'How could she? It would not fit.'

'It seems that everyone knows she is your mistress. Except me.'

'Yes.'

'And I suppose everyone knows about me? Do you hold meetings in the cafés to tell your friends how I did last night?

'Don't be silly. You are an adult now.' He lit a cigarette, cursing his shaky hands. He must show nothing to her, allow her no hint that she could affect him.

'Does your mother ask you every morning if the little American girl is giving you lots of nice exercise?'

He did not answer. His mother probably did guess, and there was so much that she could have done without declaring herself, to send the girl packing, or make her want to go. But she had done nothing, except probably give Kit some vague indirect warning – which Kit, being American, would not understand. It was always impossible to tell what a woman was really thinking, even your mother.

'I feel as though I'd been crawling about in a manure heap. Filthy, Spanish manure. There was plenty of it about in the streets tonight.'

He said, 'The street cleaners don't get there till five o'clock in the morning. Some of them were in your procession tonight, as Roman soldiers. Of course it will be much cleaner when we all have American cars to ride, instead of mules and donkeys and horses – but for the moment I can only apologize for our backwardness.'

'You don't understand why I feel like a piece of dirty linen, do you?'

'No.'

'Because I was in love. Do you understand that? I suppose not ... Can you tell me why I had to fall in love with a man with the morals of an alley cat? I'd just like to know, that's all. You know so much about women, perhaps you can tell me.'

'I suppose because you wanted to. I do not recall that you were ever asked to fall in love.'

'A piece of tail was enough? Or don't you know what that means? Hasn't it struck you after all your conquests that a girl who gives you a piece of tail without being in love is a whore?'

'You pretend to be innocent and simple. That is all very well, but being simple is not the same as being simple-minded. You knew perfectly well that it was silly to fall in love with me.'

'Very silly. I just couldn't help it, that's all. But you could have kept me from it, if you weren't as cruel as a, a cat, as well as randy as a goat.'

'What do you expect? Do Americans first list the other women they are familiar with, and only then attempt to kiss you?'

He was shaking with anger, and yet he knew that he was also

171

deliberately arousing it. This was impossible, horrible beyond any nightmare. Her courage had brought tears to the very surface of his eyes, and in a moment he would succumb to them. He could bear her look no longer, and took a step towards her. 'Kit,' he muttered. His voice came out choked and trembling.

She stepped back quickly with an involuntary motion of disgust. Now she seemed to be whipping up her own fury even as he had been. She stammered, 'And, and, while you, you think nothing of sssleeping with me, you despise Pete Olmbacher. He's worth ten of you, a hundred, even though he is only a mechanic.'

He said, 'What does Sergeant Olmbacher have to do with us?'

She was white at the corners of the nostrils and the edges of the mouth. Her voice rose. 'He wants to marry Bel, and Bel wants to marry him. They've been meeting for a year. A whole year. I'm not the only one who's been deceived, am I? I'm not the only damned fool!'

She might have stabbed herself, the way her eyes half closed, and she swayed back on her heels. Again he took a step to her, for she was in deep pain and all her pain became his. But her eyes snapped open and she whispered, 'Don't touch me.'

Then he could think of what she had said. Olmbacher and Bel. A year. He said slowly, 'So my sister is having an affair. Olmbacher, having seduced her because she was innocent of people like him, is now saving money he would otherwise have spent in the brothels.'

She said fiercely, 'Don't judge other people by yourself. They haven't done anything. They want to get married.'

He said, 'And you have been helping them to meet, betraying the trust my mother and I put in you.'

She said, 'Trust? From you? That's a good one. There wouldn't be any need for secrecy if you'd treat her like a human being. She's twenty ... I don't care. He'll be lucky not to get tied up with anything Spanish.'

He thought, Bel had been behaving oddly for some months now, absent-minded in fits, not eating very well, colour coming and going, preoccupied, unduly excitable. He remembered that it was not long ago he had told Mother they ought to make a serious attempt to find a good husband for her. If she were in love, Mother ought to have noticed. He said, 'Is she pregnant?'

172

Kit said, 'I told you, it isn't that kind of affair. Pete isn't that kind of man. But you wouldn't understand.'

He thought she was speaking the truth. That would be worse, in a way. Bel would feel doubly in love, if there had been nothing to make her ashamed. He said, 'I do not think we need continue our talk any further. You may think you have hurt Bel, as you intended . . .' He looked at her and saw how much he was wounding her. He went on, '. . . but you have done her a good turn.'

Slowly, with head bowed, she left the room.

César lit a cigarette. He was very tired and his hand still trembled. He must get his nerves under better control before San Marco.

He must think about Bel. There'd be a day or two longer, to decide what was best. Tomorrow one must presume that Kit would tell the sergeant the secret was out . . . Sergeant Olmbacher, the mechanic to whom machinery was music. He had a direct gaze, rather like Kit's.

A fine figure he'd cut in the society if it became known that he couldn't keep his own sister away from the Yankee dollars. Mario would have material for enough jokes to last him a year.

And back to Kit. It was all finished, and it had been nothing like a *corrida* really, though he had tried to make it so. He felt sick and lonely, and quickly reached for the bottle of brandy standing on the corner of the table. If he didn't get drunk, he'd go to her on his knees.

*

Kit awoke painfully. Her head ached and her eyes were sore. So she had slept after all, and there had been no dreams. Yet when she lay down, fully dressed in the *baturra* finery, she knew she would never sleep, and knew that he would come to her, and that she would not be able to compose herself and would only go on crying in his arms.

Half past six, and still wearing the *baturra* dress. She crawled off the bed and opened the shutters and looked out at a fine morning dawn, the haze thinning across the Llano Triste and a cock crowing.

The hate and the pain of last night were small this morning, though still present. They had been replaced by growing self-disgust and shame, that she had been cheap enough to betray

173

Bel. Something was wrong with the scale of values as it was taught you by ministers and priests and parents. Making love to César did not feel like a sin at all, but this letting-down of Bel, with intent to hurt her, felt worse than murder. Surely selfishness and spite ought to be made dirty words, instead of the words of sex, and what they caused ought to be called obscenity.

She got up, and, making as little noise as possible, bathed and changed, and then sat again in her room, behind the closed door with her guilt. She might go to Bel and tell her what she'd done . . . She could call Olmbacher and tell him to come in at once and speak to César . . . She might ring Lindy. He'd know what was best.

Twenty-two . . . not a schoolgirl, not a college kid. A woman now. Free to make her own mistakes, carry her own responsibilities.

She went downstairs. The front door was open and Eloísa at work scrubbing the stone step. She chirped, 'Good morning, señorita,' as Kit passed. Kit walked along the grassy edge of the drive and, as she passed, glanced into the study. It was too much to expect that he . . . but he was there, sitting at his desk. The french windows were open and she went in, carefully closing them behind her.

César rose to his feet. 'Good morning. I trust that you slept well.'

She brushed his coldness aside with a small gesture. He was hollow-eyed and bloodshot, but freshly shaved, his clothes clean, his hands white and clean on the table, and the morning light gleaming in the blue skin of his jaw.

She said, 'I must tell you more about Bel and Pete Olmbacher.'

He said, 'I can't stop you.'

She said, 'Please, César, listen. Please forget about us . . . She's your sister and she loves you and admires you more than anyone else in the world.'

'Except Sergeant Olmbacher, presumably.'

'Yes. When you want to marry someone, you ought to feel like that, and she does . . . I'm sorry I brought it out last night the way I did, but I'm really glad it *is* out. Sergeant Olmbacher is not just a mechanic, but a master mechanic. That means something. I don't think I've ever heard anyone say a word of bad about him. As far as I know he's strong, and kind, and

174

unselfish, and he'll always make good money. He really loves Bel and Bel really loves him. They'll be very happy, and honestly, there's no reason, in 1958, why they shouldn't marry, so . . .'

'There are a great many,' César said coldly. 'For one thing he is presumably a Protestant, or perhaps a Jew.'

'He's a Catholic,' she said.

He seemed surprised. Then, recovering himself – 'It is not important. For a thousand years we have seen that the Aguirre blood mixed only with the best in Spain . . .'

'People aren't racehorses,' she interrupted.

'We have not bred for beauty or size or speed, but for courage, faith, responsibility, nobility. It is out of the question to consider a marriage between an Aguirre and the descendant of some low-class German immigrant who went to America because he was too lazy or too stupid to make his way in his own country.'

It was becoming harder every moment to remember that it was on Bel's behalf that she was here. She said carefully, 'It wasn't always the failures who came. It was just as often the most adventurous and bravest. And anyway we're talking about Pete, not . . .'

César said, 'Bel has been trained to be the mistress of a house and family, to run them with taste and discrimination. Olmbacher will watch baseball on television, insist that she treat as close friends people with whom she has nothing in common, and demand to be fed on hygienically wrapped instant-mixed half-cooked pre-digested deep frozen Tastee-Treets out of a glass case in a supermarket . . .'

'That's up to her,' Kit said. 'If . . .'

César swept on. 'No, it isn't, because you *have* no idea of quality in America, or even originality. Everything you have, from food to religion, is a debasement, a cheapening of what someone else discovered and did better.'

Kit said, 'And you know all this without ever having been there?'

César continued, 'I mean that you have nothing except money, and you know nothing. You live in God's own country, and God is a United States citizen, therefore you do not need to know anything except the exploits of Superman. Your university graduates couldn't enter high school here. As to knowledge of the rest of the world – less than nothing!'

175

'You know such a lot about *us*, don't you?'

'A very great deal. Hollywood tells us.'

She said furiously, 'I think you might take the trouble to learn something true about the country that's keeping you going, with our money, our taxes, our help.'

He waved his hand irritably towards the windows, and she saw that Eloísa was scrubbing the stone outside them, her head well down and close to the glass. She looked up as the talking stopped, and quickly picked up the pail and went away, with a mournfully encouraging look at Kit. When she had gone César began again.

'Why should we be grateful for your kindness in helping yourselves? I have never seen foreign aid mentioned without some American explaining that really it's for your own benefit. Why should we be grateful because you can come over and teach us to drink Coca-Cola and wear blue jeans, and can send out your soldiers to get drunk on every liquor in the world? Why should we be grateful because your airmen can come here and mock the statue of our greatest hero?'

'You mean the Cid, in the Calle Goya? The one they call "He went thataway"?' She laughed angrily. 'Haven't you any sense of humour?'

'Haven't you any sense of reverence? ... These are the people before whom we are supposed to bow down and show gratitude. We are not Negro savages to fall on our knees for a handful of beads.'

'Negroes are no more savages than you are. Less.'

'Tell them that in Little Rock ... What nauseates us most is your hypocrisy. All men are born free and equal, but your Mr Bunche sits at the back of the bus, behind Presley and his collection of teddy bears. If you have a national religion, that's it – hypocrisy. No respectable woman is safe near an American base – but your movies mustn't show a husband and wife in the same bed, not even if they're playing chess. Sex is perfume and nylon and a permanent wave, the limit of a fourteen-year-old boy's erotic imagination ... Someone has to apologize because a doctor on television mentions that women have breasts. No one's allowed to show a woman in a whisky advertisement, while drunken American women are only one degree less common in Europe than drunken American men.'

'Women have as much right to get drunk as men.'

'And a stronger duty to stay sober, if they have any pride
176

in their sex. But obviously American women want to be recognized as inferior men . . .'

'You're as bad as Hitler. You're . . . you're a Nazi, a Fascist! My grandfather always said we should have stepped in against Franco in the Civil War.'

He said, 'May I ask, if General Franco's government was bad then, why is it good enough for you to help now? He hasn't changed. We haven't changed . . . You can't answer. Because you know it is not we who have changed, but you. Now you need us, then you thought you didn't need anyone. You will always change, for your own self-interest, because you have no moral standards. You will keep no promises to anyone. Any excuse will do – the Constitution, the Red threat, a few unemployed. We sign a trade treaty on which a whole industry depends, and a year later some fat man in Cincinnati, with three Cadillacs and a boat in Florida, will complain that he can only make a million a year instead of two million, and you will put the tariff up, ruining us so that men *starve*. You'll ask for open bids on generators worth millions of dollars, but when a European firm wins, you'll find some reason why it can't be given the contract. You want everyone to love you and no one does. You say you love the French, and send arms to Algerian rebels who are killing Frenchmen. You'd do the same in Ifni if Franco weren't clever enough to stop you. If Panama had seized the canal the way Nasser seized Suez your parachutists would have been there much quicker than they arrived in Little Rock, but because Suez was only the property of allies you sold them for Arab friendship, and more oil. You'd sell the Constitution for oil. We are not surprised. What more can you expect when you collect the scum of Europe and make them rich beyond the dreams of kings here?'

She said, 'You're just plain jealous, and spiteful . . .'

He said, 'Jealous of what? That we haven't won the competition to be the richest? That we haven't *won*? When will you understand that it is not the place you get to that matters, but how you get there? To you, only winning matters. Do you think we never see an American magazine here, in the unexpurgated home edition? Nice guys finish last. Break any rule, if you can get away with it, just as long as you win. Win what? At the end of the race there is only one certainty, for men, women, nations, the world – DEATH. So you can't really win, can you? That goddamn son of a bitch God fixed the referee, and in the end all that will matter is the way you did what you did, what you stood for, and believed. We were ahead in your kind of competition once. We left the Prado, the Escorial, Don Quixote, Santiago de Compostela. What will *you* leave, as the mark of your spirit, the sign of your intention, to tell the future that in this age you could do anything, make anything? ... A billion rusted automobiles, a pile of rotting nylon stretch girdles rising from the ruins of Manhattan to the moon. These will be the monuments of the great republic – fat, mannerless, insecure, hysterical, hypocritical – the lowest common denominator of the common man.'

She waited a time, head bowed wearily. She could not match his arguments, because she was no longer as angry as she had been a few minutes ago. He had become almost hysterical in his bitterness, and anger in herself had become out of place. She felt only sadness, and wonder, and sensed also that by this raging about nations he was saved from talking about people. It was no use trying to discuss Bel now. But, whether she liked it or not, he had forced her in some part to assume the role of ambassador for her country, and she could not leave him without trying to grope for words to answer him, and on a different level from that to which he had deliberately descended. Whatever she said would have no effect on him now; later, it might.

She said slowly, 'I don't think anyone has a monopoly of hypocrisy, César. You hate us, but to our faces you pretend to like us. I think that's the kind of good manners, or form, or whatever you call it, that we have tried to do away with ... I think we don't want to leave behind cathedrals, or even heroes, but something you can't put up a statue to, or write a good book about, only if you could it would say, No one starved here, people lived here the way they wanted to, everyone here was equally important to himself and to his neighbours ... You said we had no quality, that we cheapened everything. I suppose we do in a lot of ways, but in the end, instead of only a very few people being able to have the very best, nearly everybody can have something pretty good. You talked about the man having three Cadillacs. I believe ... I hope, that we don't really work *for* two cars or three boats or whatever it is, but *with* them, so that we can achieve the rest ... You said the scum of Europe came to us, and perhaps they did, but the strong ones came first, and made something so that later ... well, there's a poem on the Statue of Liberty ...

Give me your tired, your poor,
Your huddled masses yearning to breathe free,
The wretched refuse of your teeming shore,
Send these, the homeless, tempest-tossed, to me,
I lift my lamp beside the golden door . . .

The tired and poor came and after a while they weren't so tired any more, and not so poor, and . . . we haven't done much right, we're always failing ourselves, our own standards – but we do know it, and I think feel humble and human and wrong . . . Do you?'

For a time they stood, almost side by side, looking out of the windows at the freshness of the grass. Then Kit said, 'I'd better go home now.'

'Home?' he said sharply.

'To the base. I'll tell Doña Teresa Dad needs me out there. He does . . . I'm going to go and talk to Bel . . .'

'There is no need. I have spoken to her.'

Kit stared at him dully. It was still very early. He said, 'I could not sleep . . . and I found that she couldn't either, when I went in. I spoke to her. It is better that she should not suffer any longer under the delusion that it is possible I shall agree to her marriage with Sergeant Olmbacher. She needs comfort, not complicity . . .'

Kit raised her head with a reflex, vehement jerk. César lifted his hand with the ghost of a smile – 'Don't charge again, Kit! The fence is too strong for you, and you are outside it . . . Do you know a girl was assaulted last night at the *fiesta*? By some airman.'

'Oh.'

'It has some bearing on my argument, I think?'

'No . . . Then there's nothing I can do for Bel . . . or for you?'

'Nothing.'

'Good-bye.'

'Good-bye . . .'

*

Colonel Lindquist, standing a little in front of his staff and the OD, surveyed the ranked airmen paraded on the tarmac. This was the first half of the identification parade; over three-quarters of the total complement of the base were present.

179

When it was finished, and the urgent jobs had been taken over, the rest would come on. Lindquist kept his face severe, but he could imagine the comments that were being passed about in the ranks, and the suggestions as to the best methods of helping Rosario Lima to recognize the man who had assaulted her on the wasteland last night.

He glanced at his watch. She ought to be here by now, the stupid little bitch. Anyone would think one of the men had raped the Queen of England, instead of making a pass at a chick with her skirt drawn tight across her fanny and, from all accounts, ready to drop her pants at the crinkle of a five-dollar bill. But she was a woman, and she had a right to say just how far she was going to go, money or no money.

He looked with cold affection along the lines of men. There were potential murderers in there, and thieves, sodomites and saints, Olmbachers and punks, all wearing the uniform of the United States Air Force. And perhaps a rapist. The girl was a tramp, but Hanley said she'd been really frightened when she first came to him in the Mercado and made her complaint. The idea of a rapist gave you a bad feeling, if you liked women sexually. Well, they stood a good chance of getting him now; but, by God, if his troops hadn't been visitors in a foreign country they wouldn't be in a line-up like this. Stateside he'd have been able to handle the matter differently.

A battered taxi rolled up, and the girl got out, followed by a Spanish police officer and a priest. Lindquist moved out in front of the men and glared at them. It would be just like them to raise a low appreciative wolf whistle. How could they be expected to understand that the girl had been really frightened, when half of them knew her as a sultry amateur whore? He shook hands with the priest. It was Father Francisco, whom he'd met once or twice before. A young man, smooth of manner but probably tough beneath. He took him aside and said, 'Father, it's very important to us, and to all of you down there, to get this man identified. Tell Miss Lima to pick out everyone who she thinks is even vaguely like the man, and we can narrow it down later. Tell her to have a good look at me and my staff first.'

The priest nodded, and after he had spoken to Rosario, the inspection began.

Lindquist saw at once that the girl was annoyed and unco-operative. She hardly looked at some of the men, but hurried prinking along on high heels, her nose in the air and her lips made up into a sneer. She obviously thought the parade had been arranged for exactly the opposite purpose – to let the airmen look at her – so that they could decide whether they wanted to put their names on the list or not.

He was about to speak to the priest, but Father Francisco forestalled him, touching Rosario's arm and saying something to her quite sharply in Spanish. After that her pace slowed. Lindquist watched her with concealed moroseness. Had she really been assaulted, or was she inventing in the hope of making a few bucks? Or perhaps an airman had short-changed her sometime, and she was getting her own back on the whole U.S.A.F. She'd gone to the wasteland of her own accord – and alone, according to her. Why? *Para orinar;* what else? O.K., there were no public johns in the Mercado, or the rest of Medina, come to that. Then the man appeared out of the darkness and started talking, and perhaps she had been willing to talk. There had to be preliminaries, maybe even a day or two of them, otherwise she'd be forced to classify herself as a whore. But the man didn't talk long enough, and she began to scream – so she said. There was enough noise going on so she could have screamed her head off, God knew. But she did get away from him. And then made no complaint for over half an hour. Stupid, brainless . . .

'That's the man.' She had stopped and was pointing at an airman. 'Only he didn't have glasses on.'

Sergeant Winikoff. About five feet ten, slightly protruding eyes, thinnish hair, a thinnish kind of face, a bit of a stoop. A B-52 ground crewman and armaments technician. Lindquist turned to Vin Jones, the man's immediate commander. 'Where was Sergeant Winikoff last night?'

Jones said, 'On the base, sir. His mother . . .'

Lindquist remembered. Winikoff's mother had been taken seriously ill, in Chicago. The signal about it reached Medina late yesterday afternoon.

Jones said, 'Winikoff spent the whole evening and night working on the bomb nav system of aircraft 1927. He wanted to fix it before he left.'

Winikoff said in a studious voice, 'That is so, sir. I am sure that either Colonel Jones, Captain Goulette, Master-Sergeant Fitch, Sergeant Cwazka, or all four of them were with me the entire time.'

Jones said, 'His emergency leave papers are made out, sir, and he's booked on the Bread Run to Torrejón this afternoon,

181

and out of Torrejón at 1950 tonight as passenger of a KC-135 tanker flight to Loring. Loring's going to see that he gets on to Chicago before noon tomorrow.'

Lindquist thought, Perhaps I ought to tell her now that Winikoff can't possibly be the man, so that she'll keep on looking. But there was this doubt about whether she'd really been assaulted at all – the Spanish police were convinced she hadn't – and telling her she'd picked an impossible candidate was inviting her to pick someone else, just as definitely – someone who might have a much harder job proving he was innocent.

Lindquist said, 'Proceed with the inspection.'

Rosario stamped her foot and stabbed her finger dramatically into Winikoff's face from a foot away. 'That is the man! Haven't I just said so?'

Father Francisco told her to get going, then, but she'd turned really sour. The rest of the parade, and the next, was a farce.

Lindquist returned to his office in a bad temper. The hell with the girl. The rapist was still free. While Rosario waited in an empty room, he called in the police officer, Father Francisco and the interpreter, Sergeant Mendoza. His own Spanish wasn't good enough for this. Then, in the presence of the Spaniards he cross-examined all the witnesses who could vouch for Winikoff's presence on the base during the night. At the end he turned to the policeman. 'Sergeant Winikoff cannot be guilty.'

The policeman said, 'No, colonel. Obviously not.'

Lindquist sat a moment, staring at the priest. It wasn't hard to imagine what would be said in the city if the Yanks slapped Winikoff on a plane and flew him out of the country within twelve hours of his being positively identified as the assaulter of a Spanish girl. On the other hand Winikoff's mother was dying. The priest was being no help. Or perhaps he was, by just sitting there, saying nothing.

Lindquist sat up. 'I'm going to send Winikoff back home, as planned.'

The priest stood up at once. 'Very well, colonel. No man of goodwill can see that you have any other course open to you. We'll take Rosario back now.'

Lindquist said, 'All right ... don't be rough on her, father. She's pretty upset.'

The young priest nodded and left the room with a handshake and a warm smile, followed by the police officer.

Lindquist sat down, picked up the telephone, and called

Sixteenth Air Force in Madrid. To them he explained the circumstances and his decision. Sixteenth Air Force sounded agitated and told him to wait while they called JUSMAAG. JUSMAAG came back soon with about what Lindquist expected: he was the man on the spot and he must do what was right in his own judgement. In other words, they weren't going to accept any responsibility and they'd be happy to join in crucifying him if there was trouble. 'You're damn right I'm going to do what I think is right,' Lindquist said to himself, after saying the same thing in military language; and hung up.

Men of goodwill, eh. There were some about, somewhere. Plenty, really. Most, by and large, and if you worked at it.

He saw Lockman walking along the path outside the offices towards his parked car. He was in civilian clothes, and that was a pretty rare sight nowadays. Lindquist had an impulse to send for him; but no, he'd better leave them alone. He thought moodily, I should have advised Kit to take it easy. Anyone who was any good was likely to take things too seriously, especially at twenty-two. And yet no one could have done more than she did, in that ludicrous *fiesta*, to show that you can't lessen the naturally great. You only lessen yourself if you try. Lockman had something on his hands there.

He shook his head and pressed the buzzer switch. 'Captain Hanley.'

The commander of the Air Police came in. Lindquist said, 'What's the score on Airman Nugent?'

Hanley said, 'They're going to charge him with insulting the armed forces. He says he hit the soldier, sure, but only because he thought he was calling Kit Fremantle a whore. He had no intention of insulting the Spanish uniform.'

'It's the law,' Lindquist said. 'Dictator's law, but we've all been told about it ... Go and see General Guzmán's aide and try to hold off the actual charging until Colonel Portuondo gets back next week. I think he may be able to talk General Guzmán into letting us have Nugent, so that we can charge him under our law ... O.K.? ... Ask Colonel Davenport to come in as you go out, will you?'

For a moment he stared resentfully out of the window at the brilliant sunshine. Sunday morning, and a glass of beer at the pool ... He picked up a file and opened it at the marked place as Colonel Davenport entered.

*

183

César bumped over the grade crossing at half past three in the afternoon, and whipped across the Puente Nuevo, accelerating all the way. The faster he went, the quicker he would get there, and get it over. He hadn't slept all night, thinking of her, and himself, and love and evil. And then the talk with Bel this morning, Bel crying quietly, and repeating over and over again, 'But I love him, I love him.' And then Kit in the library, and he trying to arouse in himself such a hate against all of them that it would be big enough to sweep her up in it, as flood water first disfigures and then sweeps away a loved pool in the stream. Worst of all, he had known as he spoke that he was failing, and would fail.

He swooped down into the Río Antiguo. Very close now. She would be at her home. Or perhaps at the Officers' Club pool.

She might have gone out. He'd have to go round asking for her, and everyone would know why he'd come. Don César Aguirre coming back on his knees begging for forgiveness.

He jammed on the brakes, and turned the car off the road into the hot shade of a stunted tree, and lit a cigarette.

What was he going to say? After a hundred rehearsals, each time assuring himself that now he'd got it right – it still didn't make sense. 'I love you. Forget what I said last night and this morning, just remember I love you. I won't see Marcia again. In fact, I haven't for nearly a month – ever since you came to the house. Before we made love even.' And she could say, supposing she believed him, 'Very well, I believe you.' And, supposing she loved him – 'I love you too. Marry me.'

'I can't. Anything but that. Don't ask me to marry you.'

He could see the wondering scorn in her eyes. But she didn't know about the Gentlemen of Covadonga, and could not guess what his position would be among them if he married an American, or even gave Bel his permission for her to do so. Not only among the Gentlemen, either. It was generally known that he stood against everything America stood for.

A low droning scream filled the air and he looked round in alarm. Then he remembered, with irritation. He would never accustom himself to the futuristic sound the monsters made when they were coming in to land. The plane was sliding in over Medina from the direction of the city, of which nothing could be seen from down here in the Río Antiguo. Soon it passed over, a little to the north and so low that he could clearly see the pilot's head.

Will you marry me? There was no other basis on which he

184

could expect her to return, after last night – except to replace Marcia. That was out of the question. If she could consider that, he would not be here smoking furiously in Río Antiguo, the fingers of his right hand beating a tattoo on the steering wheel.

The noise was coming again. He swore furiously. How in the name of God could he think, in this heat, with their terrifying bats moaning over his head?

Marriage: just like Bel. Love: just like Bel. Impossible: just like Bel. Except she wasn't even a Catholic. Impossible, impossible.

Another B-52 was coming in, and as it passed over he heard two shots from farther along the Río Antiguo. He stared through the scattered scrub and low trees for a moment, wondering whether the hunter had got his hare. Then another B-52 came in and, cursing at the plane, he slammed the Hispano into gear and raced back towards Medina as fast as he had come.

CHAPTER 18

Bill Lockman lay on his side on the strip of grass surrounding the Officers' Club pool, watching the arch of the gate-house and changing room, through which everyone coming to the pool had to pass the wooden fence surrounding it. Sunday, 10 August, three o'clock in the afternoon, dry and hot, and over the fence a grey haze half hid, half revealed the barren hills to the north, and dust devils blowing across the Llano Triste under an unsteady west wind.

The grass round the pool was a brilliant pale green, the only grass of that colour for eighty miles in any direction. A score of men and women and a dozen kids splashed about in the chlorinated metallic-blue water, and the Spanish waiters from the club building behind the gate-house were bringing out cans of beer and trays of Martinis and whisky sours. Two or three muscular young officers sprawled at the water's edge, all heads in towards a portable radio that was tuned, through heavy static, to a play-by-play account of the ball game taking place at Bushey Park, near London, between teams representing the

U.S. Army in Germany and the U.S. Sixteenth Air Force here in Spain.

'Lieval's doubled in two,' one of the young men called to a friend across the pool, '. . . and Walsh has flied out.' He dived neatly into the pool and swam away.

Besides Bill, Dick Holmes snored lightly, asleep in the sun, a towel over half his face.

Here she was. Bill got up slowly. Mrs Fremantle had telephoned him late this morning that she was home, and would probably go to the pool. He knew he had to be careful.

He came up to her as she as looking for an empty cubicle on the women's side of the changing-room, and said gently, 'Hi, Kit.'

She stopped and looked at him with a sort of smile, but he couldn't see her eyes through the dark glasses. She was wearing a plain linen dress and high-heeled white shoes, very clean and neat and American. He remembered the look of her in the local costume last night and thought miserably, it isn't only one woman I've got to find out about, but two.

He said, 'I've got Dick Holmes snoring away over there. If you want to come and join us, we'd be delighted.'

'Thank you,' she said, and then after a small hesitation, 'Wait till I get changed.' She disappeared inside a cubicle.

Five minutes later she came out, wearing a white cap and a form-fitting white bathing suit. Watching her flowing stride as she walked towards him, Bill caught his breath and thought, Oh God, why not me? She dived into the water, and he watched with love as the white cap ploughed steadily up the pool, back again, up, back . . .

Dick Holmes woke up, rubbed his eyes, yawned, and looked around. He mumbled, 'Boy, am I cooked. What's the time?'

'About a quarter past three.'

Dick said, 'I've got to go. Be seeing you.'

Bill said, 'You don't have to go.' He knew that Dick, in that moment of waking, had seen Kit in the pool, and her pocket-book and towel beside his own.

Dick grinned. 'Yes, I do, kid. I'm on a night mission, remember? I've got to talk to Freeman. So long. Tell Kit I'm sorry.' He strolled easily away across the grass.

Five minutes later Kit came to the near edge of the pool and swung herself up and out. She lay down beside him, pulled a cigarette from her pocket-book, lit it, and dragged deep.

Bill said, 'You want to get on the Olympic team, or something?'

She shook her head and took another pull. She said abruptly, 'Dad didn't get back from Lindy's office till one, and he was soused by two.'

'What happened?' Bill asked. 'Did he want to talk?' He lay on his belly beside her, not looking at her.

She said, 'The *fiesta*, mainly. Nothing in particular, just the whole thing. Lindy said it was a worth-while experiment, but it had been a mistake. In future we aren't going to get into anything in the city unless we are asked, by responsible groups, and after plenty of time to find out what the Spaniards really think. He didn't blame Dad. It was his responsibility, he said. I guess it was.'

Bill said carefully, 'I suppose, if you're going to blame anyone you've got to blame the mayor. He's been told he's got to get along with us ... so he just says whatever he thinks we'd like to hear. There are plenty of guys like that in the world, especially politicians.'

She said, 'Poor Dad expected so much of his double-header. He just didn't realize how much they hated us ...'

'I don't think ...' Bill began.

'Some of them,' she said.

She relapsed into silence. He said softly, 'You were great last night, Kit. I don't ever remember feeling so proud of anyone, or of being an American ... Do you think they – anyone – did it on purpose? I mean, made a mess of the procession and everything, the way they did.'

'I don't know,' she said. 'The same sort of thing could have happened if they'd really meant to make a good show out of it. They're not the best organizers in the world ... I don't want to talk about it.'

'O.K.,' he said. 'I just wanted you to know.'

A low, hollow sound filled the air now, everywhere, close to the ground, towards the arch of the entrance, up in the sky. A wing flashed silver low in the sky to the east. They were coming in a little north of Medina – one on the landing run, flaps and wheels down; one, two, three circling, the rest not in yet. This was his own squadron, and one of those aircraft was his, being flown on this mission by a reserve crew on a shake-down. It wouldn't be an easy landing, wind turning gusty and strong heat turbulence below two hundred feet ...

She said suddenly, 'César is fanatically anti-American. I

187

can't make out why he took the trouble to save you from a court martial, and stopped another anti-American story getting into the newspapers – when you were drunk and ran into the taxi.'

Bill picked his words carefully. 'I'm afraid that wasn't his intention. You know, the true story is being whispered all over Medina by now. Of course one of those women was going to remember, when they got over the first shock, that they'd seen you and Bel and César at the dance a minute before they left – so how could he have got to Medina and be coming back? In the long run it would have been better, not for me but for the U.S.A. and for the base, if I'd been court-martialled. Instead there are rumours that I bribed César – that you begged him to save me and he did because . . . or that the police have told all the prominent men in Medina they've got to shield the Americans, Franco's orders. None of *us* thought of all this at the time. But I'm afraid it's very likely that he did.'

After a long silence she said, 'You were with an enlisted man that night. How much did he tell you?'

He said, 'Sergeant Boone. He told me all he knew. He was making out a phony passport. Olmbacher hadn't given him a photograph for it then, but I guessed who the girl must be because, I don't know, it just seemed fitting.'

She said, 'César knows about them now. I told him.'

Bill waited. There would be more.

She said with sudden vehemence, shouting into the grass, 'It was too much!'

Bill said, 'Does Olmbacher know that César knows?'

She shook her head, and he said, 'Would you like me to tell him? Just that he knows.'

She said, 'All right.' She sat up suddenly and shook her head so that her hair settled more loosely round her face. 'No, I'll tell him myself. That's my job. I'll telephone him as soon as I get back to the house.'

She picked up her towel and Bill instinctively reached for his own. She said, 'No, Bill. I'm just going home.'

He dropped his towel back on the grass. He must be careful. But she looked very lonely, and he said with careful diffidence, 'If you don't want to sit by yourself this evening, I'll sit with you.'

She said suddenly, 'Yes. I want to get out somewhere, anywhere. Can we go to Lérida?'

He hesitated. Flight line at 7 a.m., for crew emergency

drills. He hadn't made out too well on that last time ... To hell with the Air Force. It wasn't going to make him lose Kit by default, when she needed him most.

'Sure,' he said.

She looked at him quickly, and away. 'I don't know why I drag you out just because I'm feeling pretty lousy.' She was standing now, a little away from him.

He said nothing. She turned her head. 'Will you pick me up about seven o'clock?'

'Sure. See you then.'

She left him, with a small, tired smile, and he lay down again on the grass. The ball game was over and the sun just beginning to lose its full fierceness. He felt strong and much happier than he had for weeks. To *hell* with the Air Force. Jumping up, he dived into the pool and swam energetically up and down, as Kit had when she first came.

As he climbed out he noticed Bob Anstell, the Special Agent, hurrying out of the pool enclosure, carrying his towel. The officers and women who had been sprawled all over the grass and in the beach chairs were gathered in two or three groups, all standing, all talking. Bill picked up his own towel and on his way to the locker room stopped at one of the groups and asked idly, 'What's the excitement, George? You all look as if war had been declared.'

The officer answered without smiling, 'Maybe it has. One of the 52s got a bullet hole in it.'

'Where?' Bill asked, startled.

'Through the lower rim of Number 4 engine nacelle.'

'I mean, where did it happen? Some Arab blast off at them as they were taking off from Slimane?'

'No. Some hidalgo blasted off at them while they were coming into Medina, just now.'

CHAPTER 19

Kit stayed in her room long after she was ready. Even so, her mother came in, advised her to change the colour of her lipstick, and said, 'I'm glad you're going out with Bill again.'

Kit said, 'He's all right,' and went on fiddling with her hair, though it was done. She had put on a chemise, dull orange in colour and slightly hobbled below the knee. Her mother left the room. Kit sighed with relief, sat back in the low chair in front of her dressing-table, and stared out of the window.

She wondered whether the evening would end by Bill making love to her. It wouldn't happen unless she led him on very strongly, and maybe not even then. She didn't feel a bit like it . . . but perhaps it was the only fair thing to do, and the only way she could escape from the feeling that César was the *only* man in the world. Cruel, immoral, anti-American . . . but the only man. It couldn't be true, and if it were – that didn't bear thinking about. And yet, there'd be something awfully wrong in deliberately trying to seduce Bill.

The only thing was it might help her to forget what she'd done to Bel. Sergeant Olmbacher had said nothing when she phoned him, except thank you.

She heard Bill's car outside, took a last quick look at herself in the mirror, and hurried downstairs. Bill was waiting in his borrowed Plymouth.

As they drove slowly along the barren avenues towards the gate and the main road, Bill said, 'It's quite a way to Lérida. Would you like a drink at the Continental before we go on?'

She said, 'All right.' She would have preferred to pass straight through Medina without stopping – or even to go in the opposite direction – but it didn't matter.

They turned left out of the gate and headed for Medina. The sky to the east lay like a grey wash behind the city on its hill. In the faces of the climbing houses, in their walls or the curve of the dome, there was nothing of light or life, only a stark patterning of pale violet and dark purple shadows; and between and around stretched the Mournful Plain. What a country, she thought, what a people, existing between the burned grass and the glare of day and by night this other purple-coloured and stony death.

In the Río Antiguo Bill slowed down and she saw two Guardia Civil standing in the road, one with arm raised. Bill muttered 'They're searching all cars ... in case the guy who shot at the 52 tries to bring the rifle back in, I guess. About four hours too late.'

The Guardias saluted and carefully searched the car, peered into the trunk and under the hood, and asked to see Bill's licence. By the side of the road two other Guardias stood over a small fire, their rifles at rest, green cloaks hanging in straight folds from their shoulders. The uneven light from the fire shone in their winged black hats. The smell of thyme and sage drifted into Kit's nostrils, and she moved impatiently.

The Guardias waved them on, but it was too late. The scented wood smoke was at work, hunting out a hundred memories, running them down and killing them before her eyes. She smelled the wheat on the threshing floor at Saldavega, and the dry heat in the stubble. She saw other dark faces, as immobile as those of the cloaked men, but suddenly smiling because she had come among them in love. The land was utterly harsh, but she had seen warm red wine spilled on it, and the brilliance of pigeons' wings spread out on it. In the silence she had heard the creak of ox-carts grinding down the road in twilight, as she walked back with César from the wood.

Away with the memories. They were false. They had not happened.

Outside the Continental she caught Bill's arm and cried with forced gaiety, 'I shall have two drinks. Extra-dry Martinis with a twist of lemon, no olive.'

He grinned down at her. 'You've been listening to your father order.'

While the waiter was bringing their drinks she looked carefully around the room. César never came in here that she knew of; but then she didn't know much about him, as she had learned the hard way. Perhaps this was where he always came with Marcia. A group of youngish Spaniards were sitting in the far corner, all in Ivy League suits, farther away, two older men with the typical grey skins, dark grey suits, and pouches under their eyes; at the next table, some Americans, their heads bent together.

The waiter set down the Martinis. A low voice from the next table said, 'If they're going to start shooting at us, I don't know that I'm going to blame ...' The voice sank and she heard no more.

She drank deeply. Two more Americans entered and Bill said, 'Sergeants in my squadron.' They leaned against the bar and one rapped a coin imperatively. 'Hey, Mac! Two double rye on the rocks, and make it snappy.'

'*Va enseguida!*' the barman said. 'Coming up!'

The sergeants leaned their backs against the bar and surveyed the room. They were both smoking long, thin, black cigars. 'Hi, captain,' one called as he saw Bill, and Bill raised his hand in acknowledgement.

'They wouldn't mind a fight tonight,' he muttered. 'So far it's the Spaniards who've been angry, if anyone has, but now . . .'

Kit said, 'I heard that Lindy was going to put the city off limits tonight, while everyone's so excited.'

Bill said, 'He can't. It would be like saying that we suspect everyone of wanting to shoot at us, instead of one criminal crackpot.'

From her seat near the window only the sword and the top of the cathedral dome showed above the near houses. The *paseo* was in full swing, and she noticed that no Americans were taking part in it this evening, though there were several in the cafés.

She and Bill sat, almost in silence, through two Martinis. Then she was in a sudden hurry to go, and obediently Bill paid the check and followed her out. The motor purred under the key and she rolled down the window and leaned back. Bill turned into the Calle Pontevedra. It was dark there, with few people, and the lamps like far-spaced soldiers. Bill drove slowly, for the road was full of pot-holes.

Behind the tall houses, somewhere in the medieval alleys on the left, someone was shouting. They were always shouting. One night while she was in César's bed two men in the street had shouted at each other for over an hour – a taxi driver and his fare – bawling at the tops of their voices over four pesetas, or eight cents.

There were more men than one shouting now; more than two; and women's voices in there with them. It came from the next alley on the left. Bill was going very slowly. 'What's the row about?' he asked, peering intently ahead.

She shrugged. Louder, louder though, closing in from left and right and behind and in front, echoing off the walls.

A man dashed out of the alley ten yards ahead, turned left and raced towards them, his flying feet pounding the sidewalk, bang bang bang. Another followed, then another, then three in a bunch, then a running woman. Bill jammed on the brakes.

CHAPTER 20

Bel walked quickly down the narrow sidewalk of the street called Strait, Estrecha. She was wearing her plainest and oldest black dress, a shawl thrown over her head to hide her hair and most of her face, her head bent down. Estrecha had few lights and the houses in it were very old, with recessed doorways, and side alleys plunging off towards Goya on the left and Pontevedra on the right.

She heard voices above her head, as the women in the windows or on the old-fashioned balconies talked to each other across the street; but she kept her head down. Feet came towards her, nearly always men's. Each time she bent her head still lower, and walked faster. Always the feet passed without pausing. No one spoke to her.

She raised her eyes and looked quickly at the door she was passing. A woman in a tight skirt leaned there, smoking a cigarette. Her eyes flicked uninterestedly over Bel's face and away. The number beside the open door was 36.

Next time she looked it was 44. She hurried on, trying to control her breathing, trying to hold down fear. No one would harm her. She didn't look like a whore, and even whores weren't molested. They were only paid. Except Rosario Lima last night. It must have been her own fault for leading the man on. Men had a hard enough time controlling their lusts and a woman who encouraged them must expect what she got.

Mary, Mother of God, why had everything happened last night? Poor Kit must have been really in love with César. And she herself too blind, too absorbed in her own love, to see or understand what should have been plain . . . The two of them could have come down here chattering and pretending they were just walking through.

Sixty-eight. She stopped with a shock of new fear. She'd passed it. Now she'd have to go back, and that would be worse, if any man was watching her. She turned and looked quickly up the street. There was a man, but some distance up. She wouldn't have to go as far back as that. She *wouldn't*. He would be certain to think she'd come back just to go past him again.

She looked at every door now. Sixty-six. Sixty-four. This one . . .

She stopped. This was Number 60. There was no such house as Number 62. She pressed herself back against the wall and fought against a frantic need to run on down the street and away. The man was still there. She must keep moving, at all costs. Not towards him. Back. And think while she was moving. She could go on down the street to the far end and ask at the first shop where Number 62 was. But the woman in the shop might recognize her. *She* couldn't ask anyone where a number in Estrecha was.

There was an alley, no wider than the width of her arms spread, running down the side of number 64. There was no light in it for its whole length but at the end it ran into a lighted street. At the near end, at the side of the No. 64, there was a door. No, it was actually a separate house. She couldn't wait here any longer, the fear spreading downward and outward from her pounding heart. She slipped into the alley and hurried to the door. The white metal plate with the blue figures was stuck into crumbling stone beside the door, up three steps from the alley and recessed. She crept up on tiptoe and made sure that the number was right – 62. She leaned against the door with a gasping sigh.

She stared at the door. There was no bell, no door-knob. Should she knock? She looked up at the windows. Three floors up, one showed a faint reddish light behind a thick curtain. The other windows were dark. She looked up and down the alley. From the Calle Estrecha he was coming, striding down silently towards her.

She ran to the foot of the steps and called softly, 'Pete . . . oh, darling.'

The man was on her, his hand out to grip her sleeve, and she saw that it was not Pete. His voice was soft and hoarse, 'O.K., sister – but my name's not Pete. How much, and where do we go?'

She stepped back with a feeling that she was going to be sick. She said, 'I'm sorry. I thought . . . I was waiting for someone.'

He caught her hand and said urgently, 'Come on, don't you give me the run around too. You called me darling.'

'It was a mistake,' she whispered. 'Go away, go away, please!'

194

Bill jumped out of the car, and grabbed the running man's arm. He was an American airman. At the same time the man reached for the door handle of the car, screaming, 'Let me in, let me in. They're going to kill me!' Bill pushed him against the car and jumped in front of him as the leading pursuers came up. They closed in with a howl.

Bill shouted, 'Get back! I've got him.' A man threw a punch at him. Bill blocked it and pushed the man backwards, hard, so that he tripped and fell. Kit felt cold, and under the noise she could hear the fugitive's heavy breathing through the open window. A street lamp on the corner cast a yellow, strongly shadowed light on a score of contorted faces. There were the pursuers, shaking their fists, lips twisted and mouths wide, red gullets glaring, teeth bared. There was Bill, jaw set, fists doubled. There was the man, his back to her, a dozen hands on him, pushing, wrenching, pulling.

Up the street, down the street the people came, running, pouring out of the alley, bursting from the doors of the houses. The furious cries so close to her were becoming lost in a rising surge of sound that welled up from the whole city. It was like a forest fire she had once seen in California, where the little spark, the single cry she had heard so short a time ago, was now part of a roaring conflagration that none could control.

Two airmen appeared. They yelled, 'Want any help, captain? Want us to take this bunch apart?'

'No,' Bill shouted. 'Calm them down for God's sake. Kit, get out. Here. By me. Ask what's happened.'

She was out, in a sudden island of silence in the rising ocean of the city's hysteria. Kit spoke, and a man answered. 'There has been a rape. Down there. In that alley. This man did it.'

'They're lying, captain,' the fugitive said. 'What are they saying?'

'They're accusing you of rape.'

'Kill him! Matalo!' The crowd was dense and huge, and the car rocked as they shoved all around it.

Bill said, 'Kit – shout that he's under arrest, right now, and I'm a captain.'

She shouted out the message. The man was a prisoner of the

captain. He would be tried. Please go home, go home, now, keep calm.

The angry, harsh voices rose. 'Tried? By whom? . . . Prisoner . . . captain . . . They will send him back to the United States . . . Punish him now . . . Kill him.' More voices in undertone, giving information. More, lower still, asking, 'What's happening? . . . Who's been run over? . . . Was the American drunk?' More voices, far off, miles away behind the crowd. 'Make way! Make way! Stand back there!'

Four peaked caps of the Armed Police slowly approached through the crowd, followed by two helmets of the Municipal Police. Soon they stood beside her, all with pistols drawn. The crowd was silent. The captain of Armed Police waved his pistol and shouted, 'More room!' The crowd shuffled slowly back.

The captain turned to Bill and said abruptly, '*Qué pasa?*'

Kit said, 'They say this man, here . . . has raped someone.'

From the back of the crowd the murmur of voices rose again. 'Here she is. Ah, the poor one! The murderer, the assassin!'

Like the Red Sea opening, the crowd parted. Three women came slowly forward, two older ones supporting a slim and younger one in the centre. The faces of the flanking women were set and angry, but their fat, soft arms held the girl and their fingers stroked her. As she came close Kit saw that it was Bel.

For a moment she could not move as the pervading cold turned to ice and concentrated in her heart and legs. Then with a huge effort she stepped forward, crying, 'Bel! You didn't go! Alone!'

'Back,' one of the women cried angrily, holding out a great arm.

'Bel,' Kit cried, 'Bel!'

Bel looked up. Her eyes were huge and dry and burning, her face white, her lower lip shaking like a lunatic's. A black streak and a cut marked her forehead, her dress was torn at the breast and side, and she held her right hand tight clasped. She opened it and there was a tuft of hair in it. The captain of police stepped forward, took it quickly, and brought it close to the prisoner's head. The voices rose. 'There it is, on the left! High up! Look!' The prisoner turned the left side of his head towards the car.

Bel jerked herself free from the women's arms and clung to

Kit. Kit held the small head tight while the silence beat in close waves over her, and all around the dark eyes stared.

Bel's whisper was dry and intermittent. 'What will Pete think? He wasn't there. What happened to him?'

'Don't worry,' Kit whispered. 'Don't worry. We'll get you home in a minute.'

'Pete,' Bel said. 'He wasn't there.'

The two women stood, arms folded, staring at her. Kit beckoned to the police captain, behind Bel's back. 'Captain, let me take Señorita de Aguirre home.'

The captain nodded, and said, 'She must identify the man first though, and make a charge.'

Kit bent her head to Bel's. 'Listen. Don't worry. Nothing's going to happen. Pete will understand. Of course he will. You must identify the man, so that he can be punished. Look up, Bel. Look up, and tell the captain which he is.'

The dry small voice trickled on, 'No, no. They're all staring at me. I don't want him punished. Anyone. I want to get home.'

'You must. Please.'

Slowly Bel raised her head. The captain stood silent, fat and grey and red, blue automatic back in the black holster, and behind him the eyes, the faces, the tall houses, and the halted ranks of street lamps.

'Point to the man, señorita.'

Bel pointed at the fugitive, backed up against the car.

'Touch him,' the captain said.

Bel stepped forward, Kit supporting her, touched him, and stepped back.

'What did he do?' the captain asked. 'What is the charge?'

The fugitive caught Bill Lockman's arm. 'I didn't do anything, sir. It's the Spaniards, after us all the time! It's a frame-up. The girl's a whore, and . . .'

Bill said, 'Shut up! Name, rank, and number?'

The man hesitated perceptibly before mumbling, '19040500, Airman 2nd Class Roy E. Smith.'

'Identification card and pay-book, airman.'

The man handed them over slowly. Bill made a note in his diary and handed the cards to the police captain.

Smith said, 'But, captain, I'm entitled to be held at the base, anyway.'

'That will be decided later. Right now you're in Spanish police custody.'

Kit said, 'Let me take her home now!'

The captain said, 'She has made no charge yet.'

Kit burst out, 'Can't you see she's half demented? Come to the Casa Aguirre in an hour, two hours. Bill, I want the car.'

Smith cried, 'Don't leave me to them, sir. They'll torture me and make me confess, but I didn't do anything. I've never seen this lady before in my life.'

Bill said, 'I'll have to stay with him until they get him to the police station and I can telephone the base.'

She said, 'Then I'll take the car. I'll be at the Aguirres'.'

She eased Bel into the passenger's seat. Bel sat with her head in her hands, huddled forward, and Kit whispered, all the time, 'There, it's all right. Don't think about it.' The Armed Police were at her side, walking along, brusquely waving open a path for her. The faces passed in a frieze of emotions, at first all taut, closed, and angry, gradually becoming inquisitive as she reached the outskirts where few could have known exactly what had happened.

Gradually she accelerated. By Arenas and Pedro Romero she reached the Plaza, slowly across among the crowds, far bigger than usual, everyone talking, and into Obispos. Carefully into the narrow gateway, past the lighted windows of the study.

She ran to the door and pulled the heavy rope. The bell clanged deep in the house. The door opened and César stood there.

'César,' she whispered. 'It's Bel. She's been ... attacked.' The true word had slid back into the recesses of her mind and would not be said, because she was guilty. César came quickly down the steps, passed her, and opened the door of the Plymouth. Kit stood back against the wall, out of the way, while Octavio passed her and hurried down after César. Doña Teresa's familiar footsteps entered the hall, passed her.

Alone, she went to the drawing-room, sat down in the middle of the sofa, and stared straight ahead of her. The house came to life around her. The footsteps moved faster, the sounds came closer together, louder, more urgent. The telephone bell rang and someone upstairs ran the length of the house over her head. Doña Teresa's voice was near the door, sharp and emphatic. 'Eloísa, stay in the kitchen with Juana till you are called for. Octavio, admit no one except the doctor when he comes.'

The cathedral clock tolled, but she did not count the strokes. A car came and someone went quickly upstairs. Later someone came down and the car left. Before her eyes the colours of the wall and the heavy curtains blended, whirling slowly together.

She had Bill's car here. Bill was at the city police station. At the corner of Pontevedra and Arenas.

Octavio was at her side, 'Telephone, señorita.' Her father.

What happened? We heard you were . . . assaulted. No. Bel was. Not you? Not me. Thank God. Jesus Christ. Now her mother – Are you sure you're all right? Come home at once. We'll come and fetch you. No, Peggy, no. NO!

Dad again, City off-limits. Air Police sending everyone back to the base at once. Some airmen already attacked in the Paseo, stones thrown, a shot fired somewhere by the Armed Police, no one killed.

No, I'll stay here. I must.

Doña Teresa and César were in the room and the door was closed. César said, 'Tell us what happened.' He was standing opposite her, lighting a cigar. Doña Teresa sat beside her on the sofa, while she told them what she had seen.

At the end Doña Teresa's hand rested on hers. 'Thank you, Kit. The doctor has seen her. Although the man entered her body, and she is torn, he did not emit seed. The doctor has given her a sedative.'

César said coldly, 'What was she doing in the Calle Estrecha?'

Kit said, 'Trying to meet Sergeant Olmbacher. They'd arranged it some days ago. She was going to tell him she couldn't elope with him yet. Because she wanted your permission.'

Doña Teresa said, 'She talks of "Pete", when she cannot control herself.'

In the hall the telephone rang. After a time Octavio knocked and came in. He said, 'It is Señor Chenel of the newspaper.'

César walked towards the door, Doña Teresa said, 'What are you going to tell him?'

César stopped. 'Everything.'

Doña Teresa said, 'You will tell Señor Chenel that you have nothing to say. Nothing at all.'

César looked taken aback. Doña Teresa went on. 'I have not decided whether we shall allow Bel to go into court.'

'But the man has got to be punished, Mother,' César said.

'Why?' Doña Teresa said sharply. 'If you had been there, you should have killed him, instantly. Now, it is too late, and it is only Bel who concerns us.'

César said, 'But, Mother, the police know. Everyone knows. The people are out in the streets now. The city's in a turmoil. Listen!' They sat silent and through the open windows flowed the deep murmur of fire, earthquake, massed emotion, just as Kit had heard it when the car stopped. The police had damped it then, but only in that place where they were, and now it had grown and spread.

Doña Teresa said, 'My son, you will tell Señor Chenel that Bel is under the doctor's care, and we have no further statement to make, none whatever. I will not have Bel's future influenced by headlines in *El Baturro*. Now I shall tell the servants that they too are to say nothing. After that I shall be in Bel's room.' She bent suddenly and kissed Kit on the forehead. 'There, there, my child. Don't look so sad. It is not your fault, nor your people's. Wicked men are the same everywhere.'

Kit cried, 'But it was!'

Octavio came in. 'The police, my lady.'

Doña Teresa went out and a minute later, as they sat in the silence of the room, they heard a car drive away. Doña Teresa came back. 'I told them she was asleep and we knew nothing. They will return in the morning.'

The doorbell rang. Octavio came in. 'It is an American, my lady. No one we know.'

'What name?' Kit asked suddenly.

Octavio said, 'I can't pronounce it. Ollambach. Like that.'

'Show him in,' César said.

Sergeant Olmbacher came in, slow, white, and collected. He stopped a pace from César and said, 'Señor Aguirre, I want to see Bel, if I can.'

César said coldly, 'You may not see her.'

Doña Teresa said, 'We have met, the sergeant and I, at the *corrida* ... Tell him she is all right. Tell him she is asleep, and the doctor has seen her, and she will suffer no permanent harm.' Kit saw that though her face showed no emotion, either of hostility or welcome, she was examining the sergeant closely.

Sergeant Olmbacher said, 'Is she all right?'

César said, 'As well as can be. Now you may leave.'

'Señor Aguirre, I would like you to tell your mother that I want to marry Bel, and that she wants to marry me.'

'This is not the time for such an announcement.'

'Tell her, please.'

'*Qué dice?*' Doña Teresa asked

Kit said, 'Sergeant Olmbacher, Pete Olmbacher, says he wants to marry Bel, and she wants to marry him.'

Doña Teresa sighed.

Sergeant Olmbacher said, 'Thank you ... Señor Aguirre, I

want you to know that Bel and I intend to get married, and that we will get married with or without the permission of yourself and your mother. Both of us would be much happier if you gave it, though. I'm not asking for it now. I only want to tell you.'

'We will not,' César said.

'Very well, sir. I have told you.'

César said, 'You are responsible for what happened tonight.'

Olmbacher said, 'I blame myself sir. Urgent work on a B-52 kept me for a quarter of an hour . . .'

'If you really loved her, as you say, you would have left it.'

Olmbacher was dead white and having a severe struggle to contain himself. 'I couldn't do that, sir. It's my duty.'

César made a sharp motion of disgust. 'I shall inform Colonel Linquist of your conduct,' he said. 'It amounts to attempted abduction, and is a crime. If you try to see my sister again, here or elsewhere, you will be arrested. But I think you will be out of Spain before you can do any more damage. Now leave the house.'

Olmbacher turned to Kit. 'Please tell Bell I called. Tell her I love her, and we're going to be married as soon as she's well. I'm going to speak to Father Perreira as soon as I get back to the base.'

'*Es Católico?*' Doña Teresa interjected.

'*Si,*' Kit said.

'Good night, ma'am. Good night, sir.' Olmbacher turned and left the room.

Doña Teresa said decisively, 'That is a good man.'

César said, 'A mechanic. What are you thinking of, Mother?'

Doña Teresa rose. 'We have enough to think about, César. Remember, no information to anyone. Kit, I shall wake you at one o'clock to sit with Bel. Get some sleep before then.' She left the room. César followed her and again Kit was alone.

I blame myself, Olmbacher had said. But there was no one to blame except herself. She had promised to go with Bel to the appointment in the Calle Estrecha, and she had failed her. She'd remembered, several times during the day, that Bel was supposed to go to the Calle Estrecha, and every time said to herself, She won't go, or She won't be able to get away now, or What business is it of mine?

She got up and went quickly to the library. César was standing there, near the far wall, alone, under the oil painting of himself in the suit of lights.

'Now what?' he said coldly.

201

She said, 'What happened to Bel was my fault, I am responsible.'

'You are,' he snapped, 'and so is Sergeant Olmbacher, as much as the criminal who did it.'

She said, 'No. Only me. I promised to go with her, and if I'd gone, nothing would have happened. She wouldn't have been ... assaulted.'

He said slowly, but with gathering force, 'You mean *raped*, don't you? What do you have in your mind? You see Bel going down the street and then – something unpleasant happens, which you hide under a word, the wrong word, because even the right word's too real for you ... You're not in America now to dodge reality by giving it a nice smell and a patented name. You are responsible for *rape*, not a word but an act. This act – listen ...'

Brutally he spelt out the bloody and sordid details. He ended, '... her forehead was cut and a handful of his hair was in her hand and her thighs were clammy with blood, she had blood in her mouth and remembered something crunching. Men and women were shrieking all round her and running past her. The women helped her to her feet and she vomited over the steps where she'd been raped ... Do you understand? Do you know what responsibility is now?'

Kit opened her eyes painfully. She said, 'Thank you,' in a low voice. César was right. She had admitted guilt, but her mind had refused to present to her the actuality of what she had caused, even the word. Already she felt different – not better, nor happier, but different. The cold was gone, replaced by a sharper pain. The windows stood like blurred ghosts against the far wall and César's taut white face hung shapeless, a ball of light, before her.

She said, 'What can I do?'

He said, 'You might ask your God for forgiveness if you had one. Or you might give yourself a penance. But you're an atheist, a lying, self-indulgent American bitch.'

She cried, 'What can I do?'

He had gone away from her to the far end of the room, and was turning now under the painting, now coming towards her. What was the matter? All he had to do was hit her, rape her, rip her back with the matador's sword in its case there.

He said, 'Walk to the police station and tell them what you know.'

She said, 'Is that all?'

He said, 'Yes. Go on.'

She opened the door, walked along the passage, opened the front door, turned right, passed the lighted windows of the study, came to the open gate, turned right.

Her knees buckled and she grasped at the wall for support. The city shook with an uneven heart-jerking rhythm. She could hear no cars, and then suddenly a blaring of horns two or three streets away, and a high faint revving of engines. There were people in Obispos ahead here, many of them, black shapes in the open street between the houses, and lights high in the old tenements beyond the last of the walled mansions. The cathedral dome stood grey and unmoved against the purplish-black sky, but there was a yellow tint below, from the lights of the city, and some faintest touch of light shimmered on the sword at the summit.

The police station was at the corner of Pontevedra and Arenas. Right across the city. A taxi was coming and she pressed back into a doorway. Bill was in it, leaning urgently forward. Come to get his car.

He must not see her. He would come looking for her along the direct route, if César told him where she had gone. She'd go by the back streets, the narrow ways. Right here, into Penas de Juan.

The first man drifted closer. Drifted, for they were all still, like logs on the surface, and she moving slowly through them. She must not look into the man's eyes, but he had a cigarette drooping from his lip, and he looked at her. His eyes were bloodshot and he was unshaven ... tattered blue shirt, high narrow forehead and fine-chiselled nose of these provinces. She passed him. Heavy shoes, she remembered. She would hear if he followed.

Now two men and a woman, the woman's voice raised in angry talk, the men listening. Beyond, more men, women. There were dark shadows against the houses on the right, and the cathedral dome rode along above the houses on her left. She could run in there for sanctuary, and fall on her knees at the high altar. Too far. They'd never let her get there. The crowds were growing. Policemen were few, and between them she would not be heard when she cried for help.

Down Zurbarán for twenty paces ... turn here into the Pasaje de Aragon. Marcia Arocha's street. Past the sentry outside the house of the Guardia Civil. Across Toros, and suddenly they were so thick she could hardly move through them. They were like swarming bees, and the disturbed roar of their voices hurt her ears.

Two women stood in front of her – not young, not smart, not dowdy, not old. Spanish women. The lighted street was far behind now, and there were no police, only the people, the noise, and a smell of fish.

'Ah, why did you have to come here?'

One of the women was shouting at her, finger pointed. And the other – 'Yes, why? Go on back, go home to your place.' She reached out a hand and grabbed at Kit's dress. Kit's arm came up and down, the flat edge of her palm striking the woman's wrist in a savage release of fear.

'Don't touch me,' she said fiercely.

The women's faces changed ludicrously, from scornful anger to startled fright. Then their heads moved quickly, right and left, and they saw the other scores of Spanish faces closing in, and Kit saw it all. One of the women cried, 'Did you see? She hit me. The American hit me. Who does she think she is?'

They were both screaming at her, claws raised to her face, tearing at her dress. The mind screaming, Run, you can run faster than they. But she stood still, facing them, brows bent and hands drawn back at her sides, ready.

A man's voice grunted. 'Let her go, you silly cows. She hasn't raped anyone.'

As suddenly as the attack had begun, the women turned on the man. Their voices rose. For the moment the crowd was not there in front of her, but gathered round the women and the man. Kit moved forward, first slowly, then faster.

She crossed the Paseo, wide under the lights, full of people. Car headlights bored the dust under the sycamore trees, and huge trucks ground slowly through the crowds on the long run from the sea and ocean to these cities of rock and night. The dust made haloes round the street lights. Kit looked quickly to the left, judging her distance to the cathedral, but an immense crowd was gathered under the arches of the Ayuntamiento and on the steps of the cathedral itself. Along the top step, a wide cleared space below them, she saw a long row of Napoleonic winged hats of the Guardia Civil, motionless above the eddy and surge of the people.

She entered Estrecha. How many minutes had passed since Bel lay spreadeagled here, her tenderest flesh ripping, her gentle soul shrieking? Every face was turned towards her now, every eye examining her. Twice women shouted names at her. Three youths called derision at the sack she wore. The faces passed, closed against her, and yet she knew she had only to ask for escort and it would be given, because this was Spain, but she was old enough to know for herself why she chose to walk through the streets at a time like this, old enough to speak out if she needed it, to demand and face hostility as a matter of choice, to suffer what she must, because she must have need to.

Here diagonally across the Calle Goya, and on down into the lower reach of Estrecha. Here was the edge of the Barrio Romano and a further recession in time, back from the medieval, past the Roman to the primeval. Here these men and women had stood and watched the Romans in just this way. San Marco himself they had watched, as sullenly. Here San Marco was a newcomer and a stranger, of no influence. The churches could give no sanctuary here, because this was older, and, in the secret hearts of the people, stronger.

The bellows roared in the blacksmith's forge and the hammer clanged in the anvil. It was a cave in there, and here another, a woman squatting on the steps, her baby at her breast.

Dark noisy shapes blocked the road. A drunken man turned and saw her floating down on him in her dull orange chemise and pale hair. He cried out in terror, 'A witch, a witch! She has the Evil Eye!' and jabbed his right hand in and out towards her face, forefinger and little finger extended, and with his left hand grabbed at his testicles in the ancient incantation, and jumped up and down on the cobbles.

As she passed him he saw her more clearly, and changed his mind, and staggered along beside her, shouting, 'It's no witch, it's the American! Make way for the queen of the *fiesta.* Make way!' He grabbed drunkenly at her pocket-book. Not a man or woman stirred as she stopped and faced him.

She said distinctly, 'Go back to your cave, you drunken animal.'

He stepped back from her, and as she walked on she heard his voice wailing behind her. 'Animal . . . drunk . . . she's right. They're right. We're all animals, live like animals!' His voice rose to a scream, '*America buena! España mala, Medina mala, Franco malo, la vida malo, todo malo, malo, malísimo!*'

The light strengthened and she stopped. She was here. Right here beside her a policeman lounged against an arch. She turned in. Men in uniform came forward and asked her what she wanted, but that she could not tell them, because she had forgotten.

Here was a fat sergeant, his heavy jowls beaded with sweat,

his pouched eyes suspicious, then puzzled, almost apprehensive. She remembered now, she had to tell them that she had failed Bel, when she needed her.

She told the sergeant, and he wrote it down carefully. At the end he said, 'Is that all, señorita? You have come here to tell me this?'

She nodded.

He stared at the paper and muttered, 'Very important. It was gracious of you to come . . . Your friend, the Captain Lockman, did you not see him on your way here?'

She shook her head.

The sergeant said, 'He went to fetch you, from the Casa Aguirre, as soon as he could leave.'

Kit stood up. The sergeant followed suit. She turned for the door. The sergeant said, 'You are going – where, señorita?'

She said, 'I'm walking.'

'Walking. Precisely. Walking.' She was at the door now, now under the arch, now in the street. The sergeant was beside her, speaking insistently. 'Please to sit down, señorita. On this bench. Please to come back. I will telephone the base and they will send a car for you. The Captain Lockman will return.'

He laid his hand on her arm and she shook it off with a nervous spasm. She had to walk in the city. But where? Back to César, to tell him she had done what he told her.

César's voice was close. 'All right, Sergeant. I'll look after her . . . Come home now.'

She stared at him, unbelieving, 'César. You are coming with me?'

'Yes,' he said. 'All the way.'

A pair of bright headlights swung and stopped close in front of them so that she put up her hand to shield her eyes from the glare. A car door slammed and a man was there, silhouetted. 'Kit!' Bill's voice cried. 'Are you all right?'

'Yes,' she said. 'Quite all right.'

'Where have you been?' Bill was saying. 'I went to the Casa Aguirre and they told me you were out and no one knew where you were. I've been out of my mind driving up and down the streets looking for you. They had to put a policeman with me at the end.'

She said, 'I walked here to tell them something.'

'You *walked*? Through the city? With César?'

'No,' she said triumphantly. 'Alone. He said I must, and I did.'

206

Bill turned violently on César. 'You made her walk alone through the city, tonight? Is this some kind of revenge for what happened to your sister? Because if it is, I'll . . .'

'It was no revenge,' César said.

'What the hell do you mean by it then? Everyone's got their blood up, the city's full of rumours, that five women have been murdered and God knows what else, all our guys are in a bad mood because of the shooting . . . Yes, the shooting! What were you doing when the B-52s came in this afternoon? You were somewhere near the base. The police say . . . What were you doing?'

César said, 'There is a gipsy girl who frequently takes her jousts out to the Río Antiguo. I was . . . you understand?'

Kit could not help smiling, because happiness was welling up and the overflow spreading through the dryness of her spirit, watering and softening the containing flesh. César with a gipsy girl in the Río Antiguo, that was funny. Funnier still if it were true, because a bigger truth was that gipsy girls and mistresses didn't matter one small damn. César loved her. That was what she had sensed in Marcia's anger, that was what had lit her misery with mysterious arcs of ecstasy. Marcia knew. Perhaps Bel knew. Eloísa, Doña Teresa. Everyone . . . He loved her, totally. They were both going to suffer because it was that and nothing less, but – she was happy, and must smile.

Bill saw her smile, and cut off his anger at once. His jaw tightened and he said, 'Do you want to be taken back to the base? I have to go right now.'

She considered a moment while the two men waited in silence, one on either side of her. Of course she wanted to go to the Casa Aguirre, but her father would need her at home; and, above all, she must find a little time, a little aloneness away from the relentless pressure of love, to study the shape of the future and what it would take of will and patience. Bill had to go, because of his duty. She had duties, too.

She turned to César. 'I should sit with Bel, but . . .'

He said, 'It is not necessary. She is under sedatives.'

'Can I come in for lunch tomorrow?'

'Whenever you wish.'

There was no need for any other words, for both of them understood clearly the position they were now in. She climbed into the Plymouth, and Bill drove her back to the base, neither speaking on the journey.

CHAPTER 22

César lay on the couch in the library, a cushion under his head and his hands behind his neck. The lamp on the desk, itself hidden by the low central bookshelf, cast a mesmeric pattern on the ceiling in the far corner. It was nearly midnight, half an hour since he had returned from the police station. He should sleep, but he would rather lie here and survey the cell he had locked himself into.

He was a prisoner of love. And so was she. If she had any knowledge of theology, would she have walked through the city? When the church gave a penance it was not a punishment, but a renewed declaration of love for the sinner. The sinner's acceptance of penance was also a declaration of love.

Someone knocked gently at the french window and he thought lazily, They'll open it, when they know, and let me out. Don't push, pull.

If he hid under the couch, they wouldn't find him, and so couldn't rescue him. But he must want them to, mustn't he? No one but a lunatic wanted to be a prisoner for ever.

They knocked again and he realized that the sound was here and now, and real, of the world, not of the mind. He got up, walked to the window, and pushed it open.

Evaristo came in, and Mario with him.

Evaristo said, 'Ricardo is coming in a minute.'

César motioned them to the two chairs beside the desk. He said, 'This meeting was not announced?'

Evaristo shook his hand. 'No. It is an emergency. May I inquire after your sister?'

'Well enough,' César said.

'Please allow me to offer to your mother and yourself my sincere commiseration.'

'And mine,' Mario said.

César inclined his head. Ricardo came in, shook hands, and murmured words of condolence. Then Evaristo said, 'With your permission, gentlemen – we have no time to waste. Some lesser matters first, but they are all connected. At his house Mario has the rifle from which the shot was fired at the American bomber this afternoon.'

'Who was it?' César asked.

Evaristo said, 'Pedro Lima. The father of that wretched girl Rosario.'

'But what did he expect to achieve?' Ricardo asked. 'Anyone knows those big bombers are armour-plated in vital parts and have self-sealing fuel tanks.'

'And you and I know that a table is made of oak, but does that prevent us from smashing our fists into it when we lose our temper?' Evaristo said. 'Of course, the rifle is unlicensed – a war souvenir. When Lima heard that the man Rosario identified was to be flown out of Spain, he took the rifle, hid it in a bundle of sticks, and went out to shoot an American – any American. He forded the Milagro below the Roman bridge, and was crossing Río Antiguo north of the road when he heard the bombers coming. So he shot at one of them . . . Then, as anyone else would have, he realized what a position he was in. He'd done no harm to the Americans, that he could see, his daughter was a whore, and there he was out in the open with a rifle he had no licence for. He scurried home as fast as he could go, and put the rifle back where it had been before, tied to the underside of his bed.'

Mario chuckled and took up the tale. 'We heard about the bullet hole in the bomber as soon as anyone did. My intuition told me it would be just the kind of thing the father of Rosario Lima would do. Almost feminine, eh?'

Evaristo said impatiently, 'Aróstegui of the Secret Police had the same idea half an hour later. But by then Mario had been to Lima's house, talked to him – he was in an absolute dither with fright – took the rifle and the ammunition, told him to deny everything, and came away. Mario's going to get rid of it.'

Ricardo ran a hand through his thick hair. 'Why take the risk?' he asked. 'What is this man Lima to us?'

Evaristo said, 'For the benefit of the Americans. They and the police and the secret police are investigating a case that appears very simple, and if they caught Lima – it would be. A shot fired by an angry man, that is nothing. Now it will appear to be a shot fired by the city. The Americans will mistrust everyone. The airmen will look for fights. The officers will not believe that our police are doing their best . . . I hear you drove out of the city shortly before the shooting, and back again shortly after, César – going in that direction.'

César said, 'Yes.'

'Can you prove that you did not do the shooting? If the police come?'

César said, 'No.'

'This might be important. What were you doing, then?'

'Driving around,' César said.

Evaristo looked at him sharply. 'I see.' He tapped his yellow-stained fingers lightly on the edge of his chair. 'Now we must talk about matters painful to you, César. You will forgive us. I hear that your sister was waiting to meet an American when the other man raped her, and that she loves him and hopes to marry him.'

'It is possible,' César said coldly.

'Is it true?' Evaristo insisted.

'Yes,' he said. 'I shall oppose any further meetings between them with all my strength. In any case, there can be no talk of it until my sister has recovered.'

'And your mother?' Evaristo said.

César said, 'I have not discussed the matter with her.'

'Precisely,' Evaristo said. 'I only wish to emphasize what I am sure you realize as well as any of us – that for you to countenance such a marriage would have a disastrous effect for our purposes and goals, here in Medina and all over Spain. You are a national figure.'

'Only in the suit of lights,' César said. 'And I understand the man is a Catholic. You realize I may have the Church to fight, if she persists in her intention?'

Evaristo said harshly, 'The Church! . . . The good lady, your mother, must be made to see that that is only a part of the problem. To accept this marriage is to surrender to everything we stand against. It is coming to terms with the enemy. It is compromise. It is treason.'

César thought, I know, in the name of God, *I* know. Do *you* know? He looked into Evaristo's dark, always-tired eyes and thought, 'Yes, I think you do; you aren't really talking about Olmbacher and Bel at all, but about me, and the girl I followed through the city tonight, a pistol hidden in my pocket.'

Evaristo said, 'My next point also concerns you closely. I think you should make no charge against the airman who raped your sister.'

César said, 'Why?'

Evaristo said, 'We must regard it as a case exactly parallel to that of the shot at the bomber. If no culprit is found and punished there, the base will become bitter against the city. If no culprit is found and punished here, the city will become bitter against the base. If the Americans have a licence to rape the

210

daughter of the most influential family in Medina, what can the rest of them hope for?'

Ricardo said, 'What about the protection of our women, all women, from this man in the future – and from others like him?'

Evaristo said, 'Again, I ask you – is another assault what we wish for, or not? We are in a war, I remind you.'

Ricardo said heavily, 'I do not like it ... Do you realize that if no charge is made, and if on the other hand no announcement of Señorita de Aguirre's engagement to the other American is made, it can be thought, and it will be whispered, that she is silent because she *has* no case. Don César and the señorita herself must be permitted to take this into account, since the honour of the family is concerened. They must be left to make the decision on their own.'

Evaristo said coldly, 'The truth is as true for Señorita de Aguirre as it is for my wife. Do you think I am not aware that she might be the next woman to suffer? Then – do I speak the truth, or do I not?'

After a long time César said, 'You speak the truth.'

Evaristo said, 'Thank you.' He stood up abruptly, and his hollow voice was low and distinct. 'We have agreed, a hundred times, that we must not jeopardize our position for small causes. It has been understood, though not said, that we *will* take risks when the cause is great and the result commensurate ... If word came now that the Caudillo had abrogated the treaty with America, the people would dance in the streets. They would turn the morning Mass into a service of thanksgiving for deliverance.'

Ricardo said, 'And the young ones would go on wearing blue jeans, and drinking Coke in the Texas.'

Evaristo turned on him coldly. 'You are wrong! They would know that their ancestors were right. Never welcome the foreigner, even if he says he comes to help. Keep Spain inviolate, poor, proud, but always, in everything – Spanish ... But the Caudillo will not act to abrogate the treaty, and in a few days the present feeling will die down.'

César looked at him with wonder and fear. It must have been another person, not himself, who used to be so much moved by Evaristo's fanaticism.

Evaristo continued, 'The events of today have stirred the emotion of the city to a very deep level. We must take advantage of it.'

There was a long pause. Ricardo said tentatively, 'How?'

Evaristo said, 'That is why I called you here. I put it to you that we should engineer an anti-American riot. If it's serious enough it could force the Caudillo to reconsider his position.'

Mario said, 'That should not be too difficult, if we spend enough money.'

'I will provide whatever is necessary,' Evaristo said shortly.

Ricardo said, 'But ... some object is necessary, some particular occasion.'

'If only Vice-President Nixon was about to pay Medina a good-neighbourly visit,' Mario said, rubbing his hands together.

'It's too late,' César said slowly. 'Nothing could be arranged, to set off the demonstration, until tomorrow night at the earliest and by then ...' He stopped; he had intended to say, The people will have forgotten; but he knew they would not have forgotten; his real meaning was that he hoped they would have; and why did he hope that? He finished lamely, 'Besides, as Ricardo says, we need an occasion.'

Evaristo tapped his fingers fast on the table, and stared unseeing at the wall. Abruptly he made up his mind, 'You are right. We must wait for the circumstance, and pray that it will come soon, before the full horror of this has left the people's minds. But we must be prepared. All of you, make sure that the best contacts for the purpose are in good state, especially among the gipsies and in the Barrio ... If the result is big enough, and the Americans are really driven back where they belong, it would be an event comparable only to the expulsion of the Moors ... and Medina will have done it, led by us.'

They waited for him to speak again, but he did not. After a time Ricardo got up and said, 'Good night.' Expressionless, he opened the french window and stepped out into the darkness. Five minutes later, while no one spoke and César watched Evaristo's brooding face, Mario followed him, and they were alone, Evaristo and himself.

Evaristo looked at him. 'You understand that when I spoke of your sister and the American, earlier, I had other thoughts also in mind?'

'I realize,' César said.

'If I may offer advice, you should not see her any more or your natural feelings – of whatever kind – will make your duty doubly painful for you.'

'I shall consider it,' César said, looking with cold hate at Evaristo.

212

Evaristo said, suddenly gentle, 'I am fifty-six, my friend, but I was not born at this age. Do you think I do not know how hard it is to keep to one's principles when the blood runs hot? Also from all I hear, she is a very charming young lady, and no Spaniard could have shown greater pride and fortitude than she did last night, during the *fiesta*. So much so that the people's hearts went out to her. She is trebly dangerous . . . Good night.'

CHAPTER 23

Father Francisco said, 'Frankly, I don't believe it was an American who stole the Armlet – it can't be boasted about, or sold, or even shown.'

It was Tuesday morning, and they were pacing up and down the edge of the lawn, under the chestnut trees, the priest's spaniel puppy frisking at their heels.

Before César could speak, a car swept in through the gates and Major Fremantle stepped out. César and the priest watched silently as he went to the front door; then he noticed them and came across the grass with quick steps towards them.

César said, 'Good morning, major. You know Father Francisco, I believe?'

'We've met . . . a pleasure . . . that's about the only pleasure I've had recently. I, ah, dropped in to offer personal condolences, from Peggy and myself, for what happened Sunday night. I won't speak for the base because Colonel Lindquist will be coming in later today, but you understand he's pretty busy.'

'Of course,' César said.

Fremantle hurried on. 'But he did want me to say that, well, we want this man tried and punished, just as soon as possible. We heard something from the police about there being no charge yet, and . . .'

César saw that he was uncomfortable, and waited with cold politeness to the end of the sentence, and then said, 'The matter is under consideration, major.'

'Well, sure . . . That's about it . . . Someone's gunning for us. The Armlet. Rosario Lima. The shot at the B-52.' He looked at his watch. 'Kit sends her best wishes . . . Conference at the

213

Ayuntamiento in half an hour. The ambassador's been on from Madrid about the – your sister. General Wentworth's been on ... Well, I'm afraid I've got to go. *Hasta la vista!* Good-bye, father.'

Alone again, they continued their pacing. Father Francisco said suddenly, 'Do you love her?'

He said, 'Yes.'

'What is going to become of you, then?'

'I don't know. The difference in religion isn't the only thing.'

'Obviously not. She is seeing me every day, for instruction in our faith, but I fear that this crisis is causing her to fix beliefs which she hardly knew she had. Mistaken beliefs, of course, but that doesn't alter the fact ... Have you considered going to America, and having your children brought up as Americans?'

'There is no place for me there,' he said.

Father Francisco said gently, 'That is very much what she might feel here.'

'But that's different. The husband has to fit into the society in which he lives, the wife has only to make a place for the husband and the family.'

'That is not true,' the priest said. 'It is not true even of the kind of marriage you are thinking about, and it is not true at all for her kind ... Love will find a way. Love laughs at locksmiths. Those platitudes are only true for the weak, for those who have no other supports in life. Love would not find a way for a Nazi who believed in his doctrine and a Jewish girl who believed in hers. Your only hope is that her beliefs are not as inflexible as I have come to think she is finding them ... considerably to her astonishment.'

After a long silence Father Francisco said, 'You are not fully up to date in one matter, César. Bel *is* going to make a charge – of rape. You recall that I was talking to her before I came down here to you.'

César said, 'I see. Is this your advice?'

'It would have been, only her mind was already made up as a result of Kit's talk with her yesterday morning.'

'Kit? What business is it of –?'

'She considered it to be, evidently. That also is part of your problem, and hers. Bel was going to do whatever you and her mother advised, but she asked Kit to ask Olmbacher what *he* wanted her to do. Kit said she would, but if Bel was going to be an American she must learn to do what she herself thought right.'

214

'So they always hear a hundred voices on any problem, none with final authority,' César said, half to himself. 'I don't know that I could live under such conditions.'

Father Francisco said, 'Precisely.'

The bombers of Mission Dogsbody eased in trail along the taxi strip up to the edge of the runway. Bill Lockman in the right seat of the lead 52 picked up the check-list flip chart as Dave Metch set the parking brakes.

'*Parking brakes.*'

'*Set.*'

'*Standby pump switches.*'

'*Checked. On.*'

'*Air-brake lever.*'

'*Off.*'

'*Fuel valve selectors.*'

'*Set for take-off.*'

'*A-C power.*'

'*Checked.*'

'*Radio call.*'

'*Tower, Dogsbody four one requests clearance to take the active.*'

The tower radio came back clear and strong. '*Negative four one. Hold your position. Civilians on runway near 6,000 foot marker. An Air Police vehicle has been dispatched to clear the runways.*'

'*For Christ's sake,*' *Metch said,* '*I hope it isn't those gipsies again. Last time the APES had a hell of a time getting them off.*'

'*Yeah,*' *Bill said,* '*Druken Yanks Beat Peaceful Villagers.*'

They waited. Sweat began to trickle down from the forehead bands of their crash helmets, the salt stinging their eyeballs.

Metch ripped off his oxygen mask and wiped his face. '*Let's get with it for God's sake before we go blind.*'

'*Dogsbody four one, tower.*'

'*About time,*' *Metch said, hooking his mask back on.*

'*Dogsbody four one to tower,*' *Bill said,* '*go ahead.*'

'*Clear to take the active and hold.*'

'*Roger. Taking the active.*'

Metch released the brakes and the bomber wheeled heavily out on the runway and lined up for take-off.

'*Check-list.*'

'*Crosswind crab.*'

'*Set.*'

215

'Brakes.'

'Set.'

'Steering ratio.'

'Take-off – land detent.'

'Compass and gyros.'

'Checked.'

'Stab trim.'

'Checked.'

'Wing flaps.'

'Checked – full down.'

'Crew stand by for take-off.'

When the crew had responded the navigator's voice came over the interphone. 'Sir, you have forty seconds to take-off.'

'Dogsbody four one ready for take-off.'

'Four one cleared for take-off.'

Metch settled himself in his seat, curled his fingers over the eight throttles. Bill said, 'Acceleration check, 116 knots at three thousand feet, go, no-go 154 at 5000. Unstick 163.'

Metch slowly eased the throttles forward to full power. Bill placed his hand beneath Metch's as a guard and scanned the instrument panel.

'You've got full power. Everything in the green.'

'Five seconds... four... three... two... one... HACK.'

The pilot tapped his brake release with his feet.

'Four one, rolling.'

Close ahead, Bill saw the yellow-painted streaks down the centre of the runway move slowly back to him. Far ahead, no change.

'Air-speed check.'

'Coming up on ninety knots... NOW.'

'Check.'

'Checked.'

Bill raised his left hand from beneath Metch's on the throttles. 'Coming up on three thousand... NOW.' The hand curved down striking Metch's lightly. 'Reading 116.'

Two miles away the black strip converged into hazy nothingness. The plane lightened and the drooping wings lifted and straightened. The yellow streaks began to gallop, vanish underneath, always more coming. The gipsies were shaking their fists at him, the APES standing over them.

'Coming up on five thousand, everything in the green.' Bill's hand went up again, paused, and dropped. 'NOW.'

'Reading 156.'

'Check.'
'Checked.'
'Committed.'
'Coming up on unstick . . . 160 . . . 162 . . . unstick.'
Metch pulled back gently on the half wheel and the yellow streaks slowed, spaced farther apart and were gone. They climbed steadily out over the Río Antiguo, north of the bullring, having the city and the cathedral on their right.

Father Francisco stopped his measured pacing as the multijet roar rose in volume. A B-52 streaked in a flat climb across the northern sky, low beyond the houses. Soon it was followed by another. Plane followed plane into the east, and Father Francisco resumed his pacing.

The puppy fastened its teeth into the skirt of the priest's robe, and was dragged along, growling ferociously. Father Francisco said, 'Let go, you little beast. I shall dip it in vinegar if you don't behave yourself . . . You have not discussed with me the question of Bel's intention of marrying the American sergeant. I might say you have gone out of your way to avoid discussing it.'

César said, 'I do not consider it any of your business.'

Father Francisco said, 'You will have to face the bishop soon, so you might as well have it out with me first. You disapprove?'

'In view of what we have just been talking about, you should understand quite well why I oppose it,' César said coldly. 'You were not a damned fool when we used to play marbles in the road outside this wall. That crow's uniform you wear has addled your head.'

'Oh, a bit, certainly,' the priest said equably. 'No one can be thrown for long periods into the company of Father Pietro without turning into a drunkard or an amnesiac . . . The American Father Perreira has visited the bishop, who called me in. I think you have not taken the trouble to find out anything about Olmbacher, and I know that you do not understand Bel. I don't think you appreciate that she is not only willing, but actually desires, to give up her way of life for him. She is, in fact, a good Spanish woman, though possibly a miserable Aguirre.'

'And if I continue to disapprove?' César said.

'The Church has certain policies in such cases,' Father Francisco said. 'The bishop will doubtless make them clear to you.'

'I do not wish to discuss the matter further.'

'I am aware of that, my friend. But all the same I will repeat
217

my advice. First, examine your own feelings with honesty. All of them. See Olmbacher. Talk to Bel, like a brother, not like the head of the family. Talk to your mother. And give your consent, quickly.'

'I will consider your advice, father,' César said.

'Do so, my son,' the priest replied, as formally.

They covered two lengths of the lawn without speaking. The chestnuts were beginning to ripen on the boughs, in their spiked green cases.

The priest said, 'Before Major Fremantle came, were we not discussing the Armlet?'

'We were,' César said. 'Since it disappeared, the subject has seldom failed to come up in our talks.'

The priest said, 'I was saying that I did not think it was an American who stole it.'

'As you have said on previous occasions.'

'Precisely. But I was going to tell you about a new conclusion that I have reached – that the theft was a protest against the decision of Holy Church to sanction, by a religious ceremony, the inauguration of the air base for American use. You follow me?'

'I am not an idiot,' César said.

'Precisely . . . But what *is* such a personal decision, made in defiance of the decision of Holy Church, than Protestantism?'

'Protestantism consists of licence,' César said.

The priest shook his head cheerfully, 'Ah no, my friend! Because, in fact, Protestantism does usually lead to greater licence, of thought and action, we are too apt to suppose that that is the nature of it. The nature of Protestantism is to protest the right of private judgement, whether that judgement is exercised more or less strictly than the judgement of the Church.'

'Very interesting,' César said.

'Isn't it? If my theory is right the man who removed the Armlet is suffering from divided loyalty – divided faith, if you like – and it must be a real torture to him. I have been praying for him every day.'

'Do you have any more theological gossip to retail?' César asked. 'If not, I have a little work . . .'

'Nothing more,' the priest said. 'Except that I would advise you to leave your work, whatever it is, and get out into the country for a day or two. You are fighting on San Marco – Martos bulls, I believe?'

'Yes.'

'You are nervy, over-tired, and haggard. Not, as usual, with the appearance of simple debauchery. If you don't solve your worries by Friday, my old friend, whom I love, I fear a black-and-white bull might solve them for you.'

'It would be fitting,' César said quietly. They had reached the Lambretta, parked beside the front door.

'But inconclusive,' Father Francisco replied. 'Inconclusive in terms of eternity, that is. We black crows do have to keep cawing that there is such a thing, even for Aguirres.' He kicked the starter and the Lambretta sputtered into life. 'Get out into the country, César. Take Kit perhaps. Show her the Valle de Roldán.' He hoisted up his skirts, arranged them carefully, patted the puppy's head and roared off, turning the corner into Obispos at thirty miles an hour with his horn blaring.

Below and ahead of the B-52's nose perspex, the Llano Triste expanded, as a drop of oil expands on water. Distant village towers crowded into the view, then hills, mountains, and snow, all diminishing as they huddled together, all tilting now in the earth haze as the aircraft banked left. Beyond the thin line of snow the land was clear. Toulouse straight ahead. The Alps were clearer today than he'd seen them for weeks.

'Course?'

'Course 021.'

'On.'

'On 021.'

The Atlantic looked bluer then the Mediterranean today. A lot of smoke over Paris. It was blue everywhere, a pale blue, white lines down near the horizon ahead. That would be the clouds over Norway. Bad weather report at Oslo, first check-point and course change.

Here it was. One hour fifty-four minutes twelve seconds from take-off.

'Take her now, Bill. If I drop off, wake me five minutes before we change course again.'

Sleep. Stars. Coffee. Greenland clearly visible with snow and icebergs on the western shore. Refuelling. An hour's sack. North Dakota.

'Fourteen minutes to Rapid City, skipper.'

'Okay. Begin landing check.'

'Landing data, endurance speed and CG.'

'Computed and checked.'

'*Safety belt and harness.*'
'*Fastened.*'
'*Radio call.*'
'*Complete.*'
'*Altimeter.*'
'*Set.*'
'*Circuit breakers.*'
'*Set.*'

Off. Fastened. Closed. Checked. Adjusted. Set. Open. On. On. On. Checked. Stowed. Gear down.

Lining up for Rapid City, South Dakota, Tuesday night. Mountain Standard Time. Coming in. In. Phase one completed. Twelve hours, twelve minutes, eleven seconds. Two days' lay-over here.

Dave Metch said, 'Okay, Bill, you can sack out for as long as you feel like . . . You got Medina out of your mind?'

'Yeah. I mean, no. It's right here, too, isn't it? It's all part of the same earth.'

Thursday morning. Kit parked her father's car in the Plaza San Marco and walked quickly up Zurbarán and into the Pasaje de Aragon. The letter written in deep blue ink on cream-coloured paper, of good quality, lay in its cream-coloured envelope inside her pocket-book. *Please come for I am ill and must see you. Marcia Arocha.* It had arrived in the mail this morning.

She glanced at her watch. She had nearly half an hour before she was due at the little Church of the Redemption for another talk with Father Francisco, and after that she was to visit Bel. She tried to see Bel at least once every day now, and was delighted and a little awed to notice how quickly her friend was shaking off the effects of the rape. She was not trying to forget it – but had simply accepted it as a thing of the past.

At Marcia's place the girl Rosario Lima was reading a paperback, sitting in the small display window between two mannequins displaying Marcia's Modes. Kit climbed directly up the stairs to the upper landing, and knocked on the heavy door. Marcia's voice from inside was small and low – '*Quién está?*'

'Kit,' she said. 'Señorita Fremantle.'

'Please come in. The door is not locked.'

She went in. Marcia lay on a couch against the right-hand wall, a window behind her. Her head was propped on two satin-covered violet cushions, and a thin blanket only served to show that under its imperfect covering she was fully dressed, in a black silk frock. The small table beside her was covered with cigarette packs, full ashtrays, empty matchboxes, a jug of water, and a full glass. She was carefully made-up, though more heavily than usual or right, but the rouge could not hide the hollows in her cheeks and the oil could not give life to her dull hair.

She is ill, Kit thought, in the long silence while the woman on the couch stared at her with bright, feverish eyes. This is love-sickness that I am seeing. Shakespeare was right. It can kill, or send you leaping off high places to death. Why hasn't the disease struck me, so that is it I who lie in a dim room, near an open window, under a hundred portraits of my lover? After all, it is I who daily see less and less chance of keeping him.

Marcia said, 'Thank you for coming to me.'

Kit said, 'How can I help you?'

Marcia said, 'Sit down, please ... I wish I could hate you. God knows, I have tried hard enough, but it was never real, even before ... It was a terrible mistake I made, giving you the *baturra* dress.'

She spoke slowly, and, as before in this room, Kit thought how near to *jota* song such words came, when spoken from a sufficient depth of feeling. It was all there, the copper sheathing of the voice, the hoarseness, the quavering fall, fall of the pitch, but quiet, instead of the *jota*'s artificial loudness.

Marcia went on. 'We have a saying in Spain, "And who will beat father?" The women of a house all say it, with delight, when the head of the household does something wrong. I say it now, of César. I know one thing — you cannot marry him. Can you?'

Kit said, 'I don't know.'

'You can't! He can't!' Marcia whispered vehemently. 'As Mary hears me, I wish it could be otherwise, because I love him, and after six years I have seen him for the first time come to understand what love is. So I ask, who will save him? ... He came to see me yesterday. I sent him a note, that was the only reason he came. He saw that I was ill. He saw how ill. I begged him to take me to San Sebastián, anywhere, to save my life. I knelt before him. I reminded him that I have given him my life, my reputation, the position I would have in society as an honest widow — and all the love God gave women to give.' She paused, wheezing for breath, and reached for the glass of water.

I should try to calm her down, Kit thought sadly, but I

221

won't because that would be pity, and because this is what she must do.

Marcia said, 'He sat in that chair, there, and looked through me. Oh, he wasn't trying to. He was trying *not* to, but he was quite unable to make anything I said have the smallest importance or meaning to him ... So, who will beat father? There is only you. If you will break with him, I promise that I will leave Medina and never see him again. But if you don't, you will kill him. *Usted lo matará!*'

Kit waited a moment while the other woman collected her breath. Then she said, 'I love him, too.'

'I know, my God, do you think I don't know that?' Marcia cried. 'But I'm telling you, love won't find a way. For your sake, and his, go back to the United States. You have nothing else to keep you here?'

Kit said, 'My father needs me. He doesn't say so, and of course he would let me go back ... but I feel that he needs me.'

'I understand,' Marcia said. 'You are a strong woman. But don't you see what you are running into?'

Kit got up. She said, 'I can't say anything, except ... I have sometimes thought of – doing what you suggest.'

Marcia Arocha's head fell back on the pillow. She said, 'Before you go – look at me.'

Kit looked at the woman on the couch, and saw love in the shape of sorrow. She understood well enough. And surely Marcia, at her age, and loving so much, must also understand that she had no alternative? She said good-bye and let herself out of the room and the house.

Friday. Course 261. Bomb run over Hickam Field, Honolulu, T.H. Course 110. Refuel. Sleep and sun. Lining up for Tampa, Florida. Coming in. In. Phase Two, completed. Seventeen hours eight seconds. Forty-eight hours lay-over. Sack.
Saturday – go out in the Gulf on a charter boat.

On Saturday evening Kit sat in the Lindquists' living-room, a dry Martini in her hand. Grace Lindquist was at the desk in the corner, under a strong light, wearing a spattered smock and chewing the end of a pencil, her greying hair in its usual disarray.

Kit said, 'I don't know.' She seemed to have said nothing else all evening. Lindquist grinned suddenly at her and said,

'Don't sound so ashamed, Kit. If I had a buck for every time I have to say, "I don't know," I'd be a rich man.'

He had asked her whether her stay in the city had led her to think there might be agitators deliberately at work against the interest of the base and the U.S.A., or whether, on the other hand, she could be sure that there were no agitators.

Kit said again, 'I don't know ... but I do think there isn't any need for agitators. I mean, we don't have to look that far. If I've learned anything it is that we think differently from them ... I don't mean things like them preferring soccer and us baseball. I mean – well, we might look at a building and say it was old and they'd say it was new. There was a French girl at college and she was always telling us about *old* things in France, castles and châteaux and so on, so, if the Spaniards call the same things new, it must mean that they are looking at them from the other side – as though they themselves were still in the Middle Ages, or earlier.'

'I understand,' Lindquist said gravely.

Kit went on. 'And then an American and a Spaniard can look at a ruin, and the American will say, It's ready to fall down, and the Spaniard will say, It's standing up very well. And if we had to weigh murder against bribery we'd say murder was more sinful, but they'd probably say bribery was, because it corrupts the soul ... But what we can do about it, I don't know.'

Lindquist said, 'One answer would be for us and them to take as little notice of each other as possible, but I can't really accept that ... One thing's certain. We haven't found that common ground I was talking about with you, before you went to the Casa Aguirre.'

Kit rose to her feet, her drink finished. She said, 'I'm awfully sorry, Lindy. I don't seem to have been doing any good at all, only bad.'

Lindquist said, 'Forget it ... No, I don't mean that. One shouldn't forget anything. Make it valuable. There's always the other side of the coin ... You are really sure about Señorita de Aguirre – Bel?'

'Positive,' Kit said. 'She loves him and wants to marry him.'

'Then I shan't even consider sending Olmbacher home. César asked me to, you know.'

Kit nodded. 'He told he he was going to. Good night, Lindy.' She kissed him on the cheek. 'Good night, Grace.'

'Good night, Kit dear.'

Lindquist saw Kit to the door. When he returned, his wife swung round from the desk. 'You were awfully rough on her at first, weren't you, darling?'

Lindquist said, 'I guess so. But I think she deserved it. She acted like a fool over the sister's affair. Besides, I was pretty worried, early in the week, what with the rumours and Peggy's hysteria; it seemed that she'd gone hogwild – induced Olmbacher to plan an abduction, gone off the deep end with César, got Bel raped . . .'

'And you were thinking it was all your fault,' Grace said gently. 'So when you found it wasn't so bad, you took it out on her. And now apparently she's carrying the weight of the Protestant faith on her shoulders as well. Peggy's nearly out of her mind.'

'Out of her what?'

'Oh, darling! . . . Can't you fire Ham? That would get Kit out of a jam, save us from Peggy . . . and you from Ham.'

'I could, I guess, if I shifted my feet a bit and let the dung fall on him. But damn it, Gracie, it's not all Ham's fault – it's just as much mine. Do you think I'm not groping along, trying to find answers, making mistakes, just like everybody else?'

'Washington won't hesitate to shift their feet if anything else happens here,' she said grimly. 'And let the dung fall on you.'

Lindquist said slowly, 'I'm not at all sure, if that happens, that I won't use it as fertilizer.'

Sunday night, Eastern Standard Time. Course 083. A night celestial to checkpoint and the bomb run: the fountain in the centre of the Court of Lions, the Alhambra, Granada, Spain. Flight altitude, 41,000 feet.

The 52 rushed silently towards the sun through a pale blue night studded with stars. The air whirred endlessly by, and far to the right and left the starlight glistened on the fuselages of the other planes of the mission, and their vapour trails drew straight blue lines across the stars. The sun rose fast; a red ball bursting out of the ocean, and climbing fast, and fast surging yellow, and spreading below it numerous and intricate patterns of white clouds.

'Stand by for bomb run.'

The precise seconds and the steady count-down.

'Bombs away.'

Monday. Five hours, seventeen minutes, forty-four seconds from Tampa.

'Course 042, for Medina.'

'Medina control, this is Dogsbody four one. Request let down clearance and landing instructions.'

'Roger, four one, you are cleared for immediate descent. Call when over Medina at twenty thousand feet.'

'Begin landing check'.

'Landing data, endurance and speed, computed and . . .'

Medina control broke in, 'Dogsbody leader, upon reaching twenty thousand hold until further instruction. Wish to report we have an emergency in progress.'

Metch quickly checked his remaining fuel and turned to Bill. 'We're good for another thirty minutes or so. Find out how long it's going to be.'

'Medina, this is Dogsbody leader. Request nature of emergency.'

'Roger Dogsbody leader. Fighter aircraft just exploded on takeoff.'

'Jesus,' Bill said.

The 52s passed Guadalajara and turned once more into the sun on a new course. The gaunt land streamed by half hidden in ground haze four miles below.

Father Francisco folded his hands and looked at the girl across the table with a benign smile. They were sitting in a small room off the cloisters of the Church of the Redemption, on the Calle Lope de Vega, and it was nearly eleven o'clock on the morning of Monday, 18 August. The room was more comfortably furnished than a monk's cell, less so than a study. The door was open on to the cloisters, and the sun made bright the grass in the canon's plot. Father Francisco liked to look at sunlight; and the opened door allowed Father Pietro, across the cloisters, to watch the pretty American girl without being suspected.

This was the priest's seventh consecutive talk with her, either here or at Father Perreira's house on the base, and once in César's study. It was interesting, he thought, that she had apparently never considered discussing her problem with Father Perreira, who spoke her native tongue. It was perhaps a symptom of the trouble, that the religious matter was so closely connected in her mind with Spain and with César that she preferred to discuss it with him in Spanish, where she often did not know the appropriate words.

'Well?' he said, smiling. 'Do you understand?'

225

She said, 'I think I understand, Father . . . but I can't accept it. I just can't.'

'There's no hurry,' he said equably. 'Rome wasn't built in a day. Or even reached from New York . . . except by those beautiful planes your friend Captain Lockman flies.'

She had been asking him about birth control this morning, and he had been explaining the Church's doctrine on the subject. She said, 'I just can't accept it, Father. It seems to me that the Church keeps telling us we're children of God, not animals . . . and then, here which is practically the only way we can overcome being animals, it says No . . . If I marry César I want the sexual side to be important. I think it ought to be.'

'It certainly ought,' the priest said gravely. Ah dear, she was a delightful person.

'So I don't want it to be spoiled for us – for me at any rate – by thinking that perhaps I was going to have a baby when I didn't want one . . . just after I'd had one, for instance, and was too tired to have another. Or suppose César went to fight a season in Peru one winter, I'd want to go with him, and I'd plan not to have another baby till we came back . . . I mean, I can't agree that anyone, anything, can take away what is *our* right, his and mine, and by whatever means we think best. If the Church permits one method of birth control, it *is* permitting us to have sex for fun, because we enjoy it . . . so I can't see what the method matters. What the Church says seems to me to be like saying we mustn't fly because God didn't give us wings.'

Father Francisco sighed and lit a cigarette. He said, 'Well, young lady, in the past seven days we seem to have reached an impasse on whatever you have asked me about – the sole right of the Church of Christ's authority, based on his direct statement, *Thou art Peter, and upon this rock I will build my church;* on the Infallibility of the Pope when speaking *ex cathedra* on ghostly matters; on the bodily assumption of the Virgin; on divorce and contraception; and on the Church's authority in your daily life. There seems to me to be a wide gap between your concept of life and that which I have tried to expound. I recommend that we repair to the Casa Aguirre and have a glass of César's excellent manzanilla.'

'I can almost believe, almost accept,' Kit said half to herself. 'Then . . . I simply stop and, whatever it's going to cost, I just can't.'

A heavy earth shock shook the fabric of the massive building. It went on a long time and ended in a lighter, but louder and decisive air blast, and the roar of an explosion.

Kit cried, '*What was that?*'

Father Francisco listened. An unnatural silence had settled on the city. He said, 'It came from the direction of the Mercado. Come quick.'

*

César studied another line of the Saldavega account book spread on the desk before him, then pushed it irritably away. He looked at his watch. Not quite eleven. She might come along soon, after her talk with Father Francisco and before she went back to the base. He would see in her face that there was no improvement in the religious impasse. He'd been a damned fool to permit her to talk with Francisco. He ought to have simply told her to become a Catholic and believe what she wanted. But that wouldn't do, and she wouldn't accept it. There was no such thing as half faith.

He himself was excommunicated. Every morning and evening at nine the bell in the cathedral tolled twenty strokes, and would go on tolling at those hours through eternity to remind the innocent that the Armlet had gone – and to torture the guilty.

According to Father Francisco he and Evaristo, who had actually taken the Armlet that night, were Protestants. Then what was the obstacle to his marrying Kit? And what did the bishop's excommunication matter?

He jumped up and began to pace the floor of the study. Daily it was becoming harder to show an outward calm. Love built up higher each time he saw her, faith in his Faith built up, guilt mounted. Only an explosion was possible, only an explosion could break down the walls that always moved, closing in.

He saw José, the *apoderado,* standing outside the french windows, a cigarette dangling from his lower lip.

José slouched in. 'Good morning, maestro. Why the caged-lion act? You look worn out. Are you getting any exercise – out of doors, I mean.'

'I have been to Saldavega twice, and twice to Roldán, climbing by the old smugglers' path to strengthen my wrists,' César said coldly.

227

'That's better. One doesn't kill Martos bulls with the other thing ... What were you doing near the air-base last Sunday week, in the middle of the afternoon?'

César swivelled slowly round in his chair and stared at his *apoderado*. 'What precisely does that have to do with you?' he asked.

José rubbed his stomach and said in the whining tone of an Andalusian beggar, 'I am a poor man, mother's a whore, father's syphilitic, I only live by your excellency's grace and generosity ... If you end in one of your friend Franco's secret jails, I'm out of a job. You don't think I'm interested in you for any other reason, do you?'

César waited, lighting a cigarette.

José said, 'Aróstegui, the Secret Police fellow, has been making inquiries. The city policeman by the Puente Nuevo saw you go out, and come back about twenty minutes later – less. You didn't have time to reach the nearest village, even at the speed you drive. You didn't enter the base, according to the Air Police. So – where were you, and what were you doing?'

'Ruminating on the inscrutability of fate,' César said. He rose to his feet. 'How does this information on my movements reach you?'

'Friends,' José said. 'Not unlike Don Evaristo and Don Marcelino, but – similar, shall we say? Don't pretend you don't know.'

'I know,' César said, grinning suddenly. 'You're a damned Red and an Anarchist and a Communist – and a good Spaniard. Where do you want your bullet when the time comes?'

'The same place as you,' José said. 'Well, I've warned you. If you don't want a midnight ride to Madrid in a closed van, you'd better think up a convincing explanation of what you were doing when someone shot at the bomber – or produce the man who really did do it ... While I'm here – are you going to marry the American girl?'

César said, 'Doubtless any such decision would be announced in *El Baturro*.'

José waved his hand warningly. 'Look, man, I hate the guts of your politics, but I like you, God knows why. Also, I was lying when I said my livelihood depended on you. A printer can always get a job. I can see you're miserable, and I know the girl has something to do with it. I'm telling you – make up your own mind. You're a creature of God, aren't you? Why let those black crows make a puppet out of you?'

César sat down wearily and pulled the account book towards him. 'You'd better go now, José. You have no more hope of converting me than I have of converting you. We are, as I have said before, both Spanish.'

The *apoderado* surveyed him gloomily for a time. 'I suppose so . . . Who do you think stole the Armlet?'

'I have no idea,' César said shortly. 'Absolutely none. It's none of my affair.'

'It isn't, eh? Well, you know what I think?'

César leaped to his feet, his face twisted. 'Will you get out of here? . . . *What was that?*'

The glass was tinkling all through the house and the french windows rattling violently. The two men ran out on to the lawn.

*

Four of the F-104s had already taken off, side by side in pairs down the long runway. The B-52s of Mission Dogsbody were due in ten minutes and the fighters had to be off and away to the north before control could clear the big planes for final approach. Dick Holmes raised his hand to his wing man, Bickerstaff and Bickerstaff did the same. Dick dropped his hand and pushed the throttle forward.

Side by side, the two silver darts lumbered into motion. The sound of Bickerstaff's exhaust jet rose faintly in Dick's ears, piercing the helmet and earphones. His own exhaust he could not hear.

Calculated take-off point with his load, into a head wind of 19 knots from almost due east, was at the 4200-foot marker. Exactly at that point his air speed indicator touched 180 knots and Dick eased back on the stick and pulled up his under-carriage. Side by side the two fighters heaved off the runway and pointed their long needle noses to the low horizon. The cathedral dome was quarter right. They were going out over the bull-ring.

'Down ten,' Bickerstaff's voice came to him on the radio. Yes, he'd been gaining slightly on his wing man. He put his hand on the throttle lever and inched it back.

The instrument panel rammed back into his face and a loud roaring filled his ears. He could not move and a huge hot pulse was filling his eyes with red, so that he could not see. He shouted into the mike, 'Compressor exploded.' He could see

229

nothing, do nothing, the blood was in his mouth. The important thing, what had happened, had been said. The nose was way down and he could do nothing.

If it could have happened in war. If he could fight at least for his own life, for the lives of the people down there, where he was going in.

The blood choked him.

Bill stared silently ahead. He was coming down in a long slant out of the dreaming boundless world of engines and light. He was slanting down from the doubly sealed universe, inside the ship, inside the flying suit, where the works of God were made manifest only by His laws, and there was no experience but through the working of those laws – the *heat waves, the radio waves, action, reaction, and counter-reaction of a thousand forces, the light waves that brought now to his eyes the polarized image of the ancient kingdom of Aragon.*

He slid down into the bowl of dust. The wind ran silent over the metal skin and the cathedral rose slowly on its hill, a fierce touch of light glinting on its dome. From twenty miles away it formed the centre of a universe, this one, this flattening saucer of red and grey and heat. The cathedral grew as the whole arc of his vision, which did not change, took in less and less of the earth, but that less, larger.

A column of black smoke towered into the air from the foot of the cathedral hill, rose higher than the summit of the distant dome. The hard black runway raced up, and the drag chute billowed out behind.

CHAPTER 24

As Kit ran to the door, a priest with a long, quivering nose rushed in, shrieking, 'The church is falling down! The Fascists are bombing us!'

'They are not, Father Pietro,' Father Francisco said crisply. 'Nor have the Visigoths returned. I believe an aeroplane has crashed near the Mercado.'

Kit reached the street first. In the direction of the Mercado huge violet and green flames towered above the houses. 'Traffic will be jammed soon,' Father Francisco said. 'We'll go on foot.'

She began to run as fast as she could, the young priest beside her, his skirts gathered up in a bundle in his hand.

In jerks and spasms the city rose from its shock. When they left the church people were cowered in doorways, some still lying on the sidewalk, unhurt, but wondering. There were cars stopped in the middle of the street, the doors open and the drivers vanished or kneeling vacantly on the cobbles. There were men staring dumbly at the sky, and a soldier crouched in a doorway with a spent match in his fingers, and a woman holding a triangle of broken glass as though it were a dish of pearls.

When they reached the Calle de los Toros, the people were moving and talking – in the road, on the sidewalk, coming out of doors and down steps.

Half-way down the Calle de Jaca the people were running and shouting. Now everyone was going the same way, towards the column of metallic flame that could still, even here in the trench of the street, be clearly seen above the house-tops ahead. The heat began to touch her face. The high bells of the cathedral began to ring. From beyond the city sirens approached in wailing rise and fall across the Mournful Plain, the volume of sound growing fast.

They reached the corner of the Plaza del Mercado, and stopped, and Father Francisco left her, telling her to stay where she was. I sat here, in my chair as queen of the *fiesta*, she thought, and airmen were taking gipsy girls out into the darkness of the wasteland on the right. Now in the wasteland there was a lake of fire, nearly a hundred and fifty feet across. The flames did not rise from any distinguishable point, and nothing material could be made out in the lake – only the roots of the jungle of flames. They were lower now, perhaps only eighty feet high. From the tops of the flames the smoke rose in a continuing black column as big around as the lake, at first vertically, and then, where the upper breeze caught it, bending to the west in a gentle, oily curve and spiralling up, still in a collected column as high as she could see.

The sirens burst out of the narrow streets diagonally across the Plaza, that led from the Puente Nuevo and the base. Five red fire wagons of the United States Air Force roared across the Plaza. A fruit stall went flying, a tethered donkey crashed against a house front and did not move. The wagons climbed the sidewalk, bumped on to the wasteland, and stopped. Men jumped out.

231

Round her the crowd, who were using hands and hand-kerchiefs to shield their faces form the heat, gave a collective gasp as two men in bulky white asbestos suits walked heavily towards the fire, metal-hafted axes in their grotesquely gloved hands. By then streams of white foam were jetting out from a hose in a tank truck. The green and gold flames rose about the men and in irregular spasms they began to disappear, fading figures now half seen, now luridly lit, their Martian outlines further distorted by the white foam congealing over them.

'It was a small plane,' somebody said. Not Bill, then.

Then for a full minute there was no sound but the ting tang crash of the high bells, the roar of the fire, and the subliminal hiss of the chemical foam jetting from the pressure pumps in the red tank truck.

Then the men came back out of the fire as they had gone in, half seen, not seen, now plain and terrifying, undiscovered monsters born in fire and advancing to destroy the clustered, awed humans. One made a painful, slow gesture with his axe – washout: no hope: nothing.

City fire trucks shining in brass roared in from the Paseo, bells clanging. The firemen connected their hoses to half a dozen hydrants. The fire chief was talking rapidly with the leader of the U.S.A.F. fire crew.

A particular sound rose above all others in her consciousness. It was human, being a word spoken by the humans in this dense mass of crowd behind her, but the effect was animal or pre-human.

'*Omba-dro-heni . . . omba-dro-heni . . . omba omba omba, nico!*'

The sound burst out suddenly, an explosion from a cavern. A man's voice behind her, hardly recognizable as human, moaned: '*Bomba de hidrógeno!*'

A hydrogen bomb. The plane had been carrying a hydrogen bomb. She heard her own voice saying it, in English – 'Hydrogen bomb!' and did not know what tone of voice she had spoken in, whether shriek or whisper. She stared in a hypnosis of fright at the lake of fire, the flames now no higher than a tall man.

A hydrogen bomb. When it exploded she would be annihilated. Not just killed – annihilated, vaporized.

The Spanish fire captain and Father Francisco and an American were walking quickly towards the crowd, all with hands

232

raised, and mouths open. She could not hear what they said in the rising moaning shriek behind her. The Plaza was full of Guardia Civil, tangled hoses, trucks, overturned carts, straying horses.

With an enormous effort she stood still. A hydrogen bomb cannot explode from fire heat. Even if she ran as fast as she could, she would not get away. The American was here, crying out in good Spanish, 'There is no danger! The plane did not carry a bomb! No danger!'

But the noise behind her was like an animal house. When she turned she was aware that she and a few others were the only people not in a frenzy of attempted movement. She was looking at the backs of men and women clawing away from the Plaza del Mercado. They fought, they kicked, and leaped into the air like salmon, to fall on the heads of the crowd farther in. Only a very little farther. Those who had been at the front with her, and were now at the back, had been able to get ten yards farther from the lake of fire, no more. In front of them the Calle de Jaca was jammed with people, all now shrieking and fighting like animals caught by the fire in their cages. Above all, with all the effort, there was no movement. The people fought and jumped where they were, and fell where they were. Already half a dozen women and children lay in the road, most writhing like wounded snakes, some still.

A shot cracked at the far end of the street, then four more in quick succession. An officer of the Guardia Civil was beside her, his voice loud and harsh in the renewed silence. 'Turn! Walk out this way. There is no bomb.'

Three more Guardias stood in line across the street, sub-machine-guns at the hip, faces expressionless under the black wings. The officer walked forward, automatic in hand. At the back of the crowd he raised the weapon and smashed the flat of it against a fighting man's head. The man turned like a cat, blood running down his jaw, his eyes wild. The officer raised the gun towards the Plaza. The man hesitated. The officer raised the pistol and pointed it at the man's heart. The man gabbled something and began to run in the direction he had been told, but looking always at the lake of fire, so that he tripped over a hose and fell heavily. 'Walk!' the officer said coldly, and turned back to the crowd.

More men and women heeded his voice and the blows of his automatic, and followed the first. Another shot sounded from

233

the far end of the street. The drone of the Guardia Civil officer's voice rose higher: 'There is no danger. No bomb. Out this way. Walk. Back to your houses. *Walk!*'

A car burst out of the Paseo and rocketed crazily across the square. There were more Guardia Civil there, in line across the street that led to the bridge and the open country. One of them raised his hand, the others aimed their rifles. The car's tyres screamed as the driver jammed on the brakes. Skidding sideways across the far side of the Plaza, it hit the wall, and turned over. Another car behind it stopped more gradually, that one hardly visible under the dense mass of people clinging on to every door and window.

The stream of people from the Calle de Jaca passed her steadily now, where she stood pressed back against the house front. The time of panic was over. They were pale and their faces tight compressed, but not with fear. It could have been anger, or hate. The half-empty street was littered with the bricks and stones they had used in the time of frenzy; but now they were helping the injured. Women passed her, weeping quietly on men's shoulders. Four bodies lay still in the street, while the feet of the survivors of the panic dragged past them. Father Francisco was kneeling beside one of the bodies.

César's voice grated at her ear. 'What are you doing here? Come with me at once!' She turned quickly. He took her arm with a rough gesture. She clung to him, her face pressed into his coat, and his arm was round her shoulder. The skin of her face burned against the material of his coat. He said angrily, 'They told me at the church that you had gone to the fire. Why didn't you come home?'

She stood away from him, but held tight to his hand, and looked in awe at the dying fire. The dried grass and shrubs of the wasteland had caught fire. Some hoses of the city fire trucks were streaming water onto them, others on to the backs of the closest houses, those on the left at the foot of the Calle de Jaca.

César spoke to the officer of the Guardia Civil. 'How many were killed, Captain?'

The officer said sourly, 'In the crash, only the pilot, as far as we know. He could not have fallen in a better place. In the panic – who knows? We shall find out.'

The fire trucks formed a full circle now, some in the Plaza, some out on the rough land among the blackened spears of the bushes and the burned grass. The fire was out. Smoke hung

234

about the houses and smudged the sky, but only small wisps rose from the hillock of yellowish sludge that had once been the lake of fire. Small sharp-edged pieces of dripping metal stuck up from the sludge. The sludge heaved slowly, like porridge. Big bubbles rose in it, and burst, and the mess soughed back again. There was a man in there.

César's hand was firm under her elbow. 'I'll take you home.'

Home. The Casa Aguirre.

The Martian fireman quaked the quaking lake of yellow foam on the wasteland. From an empty café an untended radio blared a pasodoble through shattered windows. The voices of the people remaining were high and hollow and loud, like jets in the sky. Home. What did anything matter, when you looked at the quaking sludge? Love was worth a Mass.

From the house at the foot of the Calle de Jaca, on the left, the one nearest the crash, came a single howling shriek. The aimless movement of the people stopped. All stared at the slatternly tenement with the red geraniums in every window at the front, and at the back and sides the wet walls and curling steam where the hoses had played. Outside the front door of the house three policemen were standing in a close group with a woman in a black cotton dress. One of them supported her in his arms, the other two patted her with a childlike helplessness.

The woman howled again – 'My son!'

She sank to her knees and scrabbled with her hands in the dirt of the unpaved street. Her howls became inhuman and unintelligible. A young man in labourer's blue shirt and trousers walked slowly out of the house, accompanied by another policeman. The crowd began to coagulate towards the centre of emotion, drifting, running, dragging towards the howling woman. Kit went, because the crowd was pushing her, because her own feet were taking her, because César was going, as slowly, seemingly as unwillingly, his hands still fast to her elbow.

The young man reached the woman and put down his hand to her shoulder. Then knelt beside her, and carefully caressed her arched back. His face was raised, and as he stroked her he was looking past the crowd at the bubbling, yellow sludge.

'He was playing in the field,' a woman said.

'Ah, the poor little one, how could he protect himself?' another said.

César said to the first woman, 'Is it certain? The parents were not here.'

'She was buying bread from Alejo, who is her mother's
235

cousin. Ah, look where the child is now!' She crossed herself quickly. César touched one of the policemen's arms. 'Sergeant, is it certain?'

'It is certain, Don César,' the man said heavily. 'An old man in the next house was watching the boy playing from a back window.'

'Come away,' César said to her. 'Come home.'

The crowd voice was like waves, lifting her, dropping her, breaking cold over her . . .

Nine years old . . . The priest has come. It is Father Jorge . . . It is not to be borne, that monsters should hurtle down on us . . . My own child was playing at the time. Not here, at our house . . . Seven years old, he was . . . The American should have parachuted, then no one would have been hurt . . . He was trying to save himself . . . If he had turned back across the river, he could have landed on the Llano . . . He was dead in the air, I heard . . . I heard he was trying to save . . . Only eight years old . . . None of us is safe . . .

No one says anything about the hydrogen bomb, and the panic that killed many more than the two victims of the crash. Surely, they have not forgotten, already? As she looked from face to face she knew that they had not forgotten. This about the child was no more than a ripple on the surface of their emotion, when compared with the deep upheaval of the other. A boy had died, as thousands of others had died suddenly in this city through its history, but, in the other, the total fact of the atomic fear had suddenly leaped upon them. Those five seconds had thrown them forward five centuries, and they were not prepared for it. Now they were realizing the exact shape of the truth which America had lived with – in fear and doubt – for thirteen years.

César looked sombrely at the reeking sludge. He said, 'They should bring your bulldozers and push up earth over that place and leave it there. A joint funeral for two victims of the century.'

'And the others,' she said in a low voice. 'The people who were killed in the panic?'

He did not answer, and she saw her father approaching, picking his way quickly across the hoses and the spilled fruit in the Mercado. He reached them, and she noticed with happiness that César did not take his hand from her arm.

Her father said, 'Kit! Are you all right? Jesus, look at that . . . You've heard who it was? Dick Holmes.'

César said. 'I knew him. He was a gentleman.'

Her father said, 'A gentleman? I don't know that he thought of himself that way. His father keeps a country store in Iowa. His mother's alive too. We've sent the cable to Washington already. Schuyler Field's right there, and an officer will be at the store by the time he opens. Six o'clock in the morning out there, now. Nice opening. Great.'

She said, 'Does Bill know?'

He said, 'I guess so. He's just come in . . . At least ten killed and a hundred injured in the panic, according to the police lieutenant down there. Christ, it's hot here.' He took off his uniform cap and mopped his forehead. 'You were here, César – how the *hell* did that rumour get started, about Dick having an H-bomb on board?'

'I was not here,' César said. 'It could have been spontaneous combustion.'

Her father rambled on as though César had not spoken. 'This is the end. Everything I've tried to do, blown up in a second. Now they'll never believe we're just ordinary folks, the same as them . . . Some Red, some goddamn murderous Red spread that rumour . . . Everything fouled up, every single goddamn thing.' He looked at her. 'Where have you got the car? Let's go.'

César said, 'I think Kit is . . .'

She cut in heavily, 'I'd better go back to the base, César.'

Her father said, 'The next thing, the very next thing, is going to blow Medina sky high, and SAC, and maybe NATO. Me, I've gone already . . . What did you say? You want to stay on? Sure, of course. Just tell me where the car is. And give me the keys. I've got to go to General Guzmán's office. Portuondo's already there. The ambassador's coming again – on Wednesday. So's the Under-secretary. She's in Madrid already.'

She gently disengaged herself from César's hand. 'I'm not staying in, Dad,' she said. 'I'm coming with you.'

César had stood back and was watching her with a sudden ache of love and admiration blindingly obvious in his face so that she said to him, pleadingly, 'For a little while, César.'

'Of course,' he said.

Her father said, 'Fine then. If you're sure. We're in big trouble, honey . . . Let's get going. Maybe we can make something out of it. Suppose Dick could have parachuted, but didn't, trying to save the city, see? Suppose . . .'

CHAPTER 25

Bill watched silently while Major Bob Anstell, the Special Agent, poured out the drinks. Then Anstell settled his glass comfortably in his hand and looked at Bill. 'What's on your mind? Take your time. Bessie's out and we have the mansion to ourselves.'

Bill said, 'What made Dick's ship go in?'

'The compressor broke up. Dick got that out. I guess it blew the seat forward against the panel so that he couldn't move or control anything.'

'Could a bullet have done it? A rifle bullet?'

Anstell sipped his whisky, looking carefully at Bill over the rim of the glass. 'Cause the compressor to explode?'

'Yes.'

'No.'

'A bullet could have killed Dick, though.'

'Some shooting – and theoretically impossible. We'll never know.'

'Not from the aircraft. If we got hold of the rifle, or the man who'd fired, we'd know.'

Bill saw Dick, alive, squeezed like a pancake, blood and flesh pulping out and the wind screaming past, unable to move hand or foot, only his eyes. This was his first drink since it happened and it was having no effect at all, except that the sense of loss was growing more quickly in him, and a bitterness against everyone who was still alive – Anstell sitting there calmly opposite, alive, and himself, and beyond and outside the presence of thousands, of millions, Americans, Spanish, all nations, all alive, all heedless.

He spoke slowly but still could not keep his voice fully under control. 'Who started the rumour that Dick had an H-bomb on board? Who fired at the 52 last week? Who fouled up the *fiesta*? It was you who told me once to look at results, not intentions. Why don't we assume Aguirre's responsible, and put every man we've got on to the job of proving it? Offer rewards. I'll kick in five hundred bucks myself. Make it a thousand. If Mr Holmes can spend a thousand bucks to see the place where Dick died I can afford a thousand to catch the son of a bitch who killed him.'

'Aguirre didn't shoot at Dick. He was in his library, talking to his bullfighting agent.'

'The agent's going to say what he's told to say . . . Have the police been on to Aguirre?'

'Aróstegui has, tactfully. In a café this evening. As tactful as you can be in the circumstances. I pressed him to, because Aguirre was out near the base last time, and doesn't account for his movements. Yes, Aguirre's being watched. Watched – not followed. He's not a damned fool and no more are the people he's associated with. I don't *think* Aróstegui is one of them.'

'So Aguirre's going to be left loose, free to do something else against us, kill another guy?'

His voice rose and broke on the last word. Anstell stood up. 'Here, let me fix you another drink. A dozen of them won't make you drunk, not the way you are now. Sit back, relax, because there's absolutely no goddamned rush or hurry now. Dick's dead, Kit's on the base, and you know damn well your crew's going to be in the top third this rating, and you won't do yourself or anyone else any good by worrying about whether we're doing our job on Aguirre. We are, the way you and your crew are. O.K.?'

After a time, the second drink still fiery in his throat, Bill sat back. He felt very tired. 'O.K.,' he said, 'I'm sorry . . . I'll just finish this and go. I'm bushed, and I've got to go down to Torrejón tomorrow to meet Dick's parents.'

'Oh, that's what you meant about them paying a thousand bucks. They're coming over?'

'Yeah. They don't want anything done about burying him till they get here. They don't know whether they're going to take him home or not. It's all irregular as hell, but I guess no one's worrying much, because there's nothing to take home.'

'The parents know that?'

'They've been told. It would be hard for an old couple like that to believe.'

'What about the Spanish twenty-four-hour rule?'

'Lindy signed a certificate of necessity. The Spaniards didn't question it because of the same thing – there's nothing to bury. I guess they thought Lindy was nuts . . . What about the Spanish kid who was killed?'

'I haven't heard anything. But the people killed in the panic are being buried tomorrow. Separate funerals, separate churches. The bishop gave the orders – no demonstrations, no processions.'

'Is he on our side, the bishop?'

'Hell, no. I guess he's on the Pope's side. God's side, he'd say. It's the same, to him.'

'Not to me, necessarily. Or Franco, I suppose . . . What's the poop about this conference on Wednesday? I hear we got Dulles and Twining and Nixon and God knows who coming now, all on account of Dick Holmes getting killed. He'd be flattered. Maybe.'

'It isn't as high-pressured as that, but it's big enough. And it isn't really on account of Dick. They were all coming anyway.'

'To fire the Old Man?'

'Could be. What's happened here is everything that might have been spread out between here and Rota and Morón and Torrejón and Zaragoza. Then it would have looked so thin no one would be able to call it a mess. But you know the way you can draw a royal straight flush to one hole card? Lindy's done it, in spades. Off with his head. Personally, I'm for it – the mess. One big yell is better than a year of whispering.'

Bill said slowly, 'What gets me is everything coming to a head because of Dick. Dick! One of the best men I ever knew, and he didn't ask to be sent here, and he didn't want to be here when they sent him, any more than I did, but he had a job to do and he was even getting to love this country in spite of its being so different from everything he was and believed in. He was talking about it to me, two, three weeks ago . . . about the personal dignity of the Spaniard, something he had in him deeper than Communism or the Church or Franco can touch. Dick understood personal dignity very well.'

'He didn't understand it. He had it.'

'And because of him our trucks are getting bricks thrown at them from the roofs. You know what? Right now I feel that I hate and despise this continent and everyone in it.'

'Now you're talking like a European yourself.'

'I know. But Christ, Bob, when I think of Aguirre and what he's done against us, and I think that he's not alone, that there must be scores, perhaps thousands, of Spaniards who know what he and his pals have been doing, and none of them say anything, but shield them, and sneer and laugh behind their hands at us – at Dick, I guess I'm thinking of now . . . They can't all be that mean and spiteful, or can they? What have

240

we done to make so many of these people think of us as the enemy?'

'Got rich ... and don't forget the D.A.R. and *Time* magazine and the rest of our perpetual adolescents, always crowing, "We've got everything, it could only happen here." Of course a lot of people are going to want to see some of the piss and wind knocked out of us. But mostly it isn't us who've failed. It's them ... Look. What practically no one in Europe or Asia understands is what you just said – that we don't want to *be* here, not even to drink their vintage wines, eat their food, be waited on by their servants, or screw their hot-arsed adoring women, even though they're the best in the world, all of them, aren't they?'

'No.'

'Sure they aren't, but I bet you bow down before an *Imported* label like the rest of us ... But we want to be back home all the same, with frozen food and the frigid tails. So they get us coming and going. If we want to stay we're dollar imperialists. If we think we've got something better at home, then they get madder than ever. You want to see a real mad foreigner, you get hold of an Englishman who's been giving an American girl the best of London for six months and finally she says really she prefers Oshkosh, it's a better place to live ... And then a lot of them haven't found out the size of the time we're living in. Look at what they find to pick on about us – airmen getting drunk, Harry Truman's shirts, G.I. bastards, monkeys on television, AFEX privileges, Detroit cars the size of whales, tourists doing Yurp in five days and not knowing a Château Yquem from a bowl of horse-piss, Sputternik ... what kind of crap is this to have on your mind when we're *all* in a lifeboat, castaways from a ship that went down on 6 August, 1945, and *we're* the only one strong enough to make the lifeboat go, or even steer a course? There's only one thing an adult worries about at a time like that – what course are we steering? Every now and then a European wakes up and asks that question, but most of the time they act like a bunch of high-school girls, sitting on the floorboards with their heads together, giggling at the steersman's big feet and dirty toenails.'

'They give us a bad time about Little Rock.'

'Sure. Most of them because they think the same way Faubus does and want to force us to admit that we're hypocrites too, just like them, and that stuff about all men being born free and equal doesn't go for niggers and the lower classes.

241

Our niggers, their lower classes. But when a good European –
I mean a guy who really wants to know – asks about Little
Rock, then he's not throwing it in along with Nixon and Orson
Welles's panic as another gibe. He *is* thinking about the course
we're steering, and he has a goddamn right to ask ... You
know who never think small? Who never forget they're in the
lifeboat, too? The Russians.'

'I wish the Russians were here instead of us. If these people
think of us as the enemy, let's get with it, let's go home and let
them have a real enemy ... O.K., O.K., ... I know we've got
to get on with the job, really. But will it never end?'

'Ask the President. Ask Krushchev ... You ever thought
about what's going to happen if César Aguirre gets arrested?'

Bill nodded.

'And shot?'

'They wouldn't shoot him. He's a matador.'

'Franco can't tell the difference between a matador and a
cardinal if they're making trouble for him. If Aguirre gets himself shot, or even into serious trouble, you'll be in big danger of
losing yourself a girl.'

'I've just about done that already.'

'No, you haven't. At least, you don't know yet, and what's
more I bet she doesn't. Don't give up the ship.'

'I won't. I ...' Anstell was a friend, but not a particularly
close one, but he had to say the truth to someone, tonight of all
nights. He stood up. 'I love her, Bob. It seems to me that I've
done just about everything wrong a guy can do ... and now I
can't do one goddamn thing, just sit and get on with my work
and try not to think about Aguirre, and pretend I'm a flying
machine. It's driving me nuts.'

'You're dummy this round. Just watch the hand being
played, and wait.'

'Nothing to it ... I wish like hell that Dick was here.'

'So do I.'

'Good night.'

CHAPTER 26

Kit settled wearily into the seat of the De Soto and summoned a smile and a wave for César, standing on the steps to see her off. These days when she visited the Casa Aguirre he made no effort to hide his love for her and dependency on her. Doña Teresa and the household had accepted the situation without a word or a look. Even Eloísa was calm and soothing with them, so that, while in Medina, Kit's life became a slow-motion drama acted out before this hushed and respectful audience. She could not avoid the thought that tragedy would be a better word than drama. The more deeply they loved, the more they found that whole love was inextricably a part of each one's individual moral fibre. Many kinds of grafting and transplantation were theoretically possible, at the price of weakening or killing that fibre in one or the other; but it was the strength of it that caused and increased the love. The course therefore seemed inevitable.

She drove a little faster. There was always the gimmick, the explosive and unlooked-for interruption from outside, the *deus ex machina* of the English classes, which would wrench events out of their foreseeable sequence into a new happy channel. But then, in true Greek tragedy, it always turned out that the new course led, after all, to the same end, and the purpose of the *deus ex machina* was to show that in human affairs the inevitable could not be avoided ... Those were only plays, written for the rounding-out of a theory. It could not, must not be so in her own case, for this was real life, not subject to the dramatic laws of the Greeks.

Wednesday afternoon. 20 August. Hot again, and only two days to San Marco. A dummy giant was propped against the wall outside the Ayuntamiento and a woman was mending a rent in its vestments. The woman was old, and a dwarf. It was the hour of the siesta and the streets should be emptier than this. There were too many people about, few moving, and all the albinos, hump-backs, cripples, and blind of the city seemed to be among them. They stood sullenly alone in shaded doorways, and stared at her. They were gathered in clusters just inside the narrow alleys off the Paseo, in the daubed purple shadow among the wine barrels and the trays of prawns. They blocked half the street outside the end house on the left of the Calle de Jaca, whence little Pedro García had vanished suddenly, on Monday last, while playing in the wasteland at the back of the house.

There were too many people in the Mercado, and not enough noise. She remembered another silence that had had this same quality – the moments after Dick Holmes crashed, while the church was still shaking and before Father Pietro rushed in screaming. Others – six of them: the times at the *corrida* when each matador drew out the sword from behind the shelter of the red cloth, and sighted it for the kill. That was the only other occasion, before today, when the power of the grotesque in Spain had struck her; for the tumblers and the one-legged and the dwarfs had all been prominent at the *corrida*, too.

As the car left the Puente Nuevo, she let out her breath in a long sigh. Going into Medina these days was like going under water without a diving suit. You wanted to hold your breath.

After parking the car in the road she entered the house and walked into the living-room. She stopped in surprise. Two old people were sitting in the middle of the sofa, staring at the wall, holding hands, a newspaper fallen to the floor at their feet. The old man began, painfully, to rise to his feet and she said quickly, 'Please don't get up.'

The old man stood upright. 'I've been getting up for ladies sixty years now, miss. Since I was ten, I guess. Don't see no reason to change my ways.' He was tall, with a lean, lined face and a heavy shock of grey hair. His wife was of medium height, and angular, her hair drawn back in a bun at the nape of her neck, her dress bought from a mail-order store, her shoes comfortable and a little turned over at the heel, well worn.

'I'm Catherine Fremantle,' Kit said. She knew suddenly who they were, though no one had warned her they would be here.

'Everett Holmes, miss. And this is Mrs Holmes. This lady is the major's daughter, Mother.'

Their grief was in no particular sign, but in their whole being. They must be very much in love, she thought, to be able to sit in this room absolutely silent, their faded hands gently twined on the sofa between them, seeing nothing but each other, and the dead son in the pattern of the wallpaper.

Mr Holmes said, 'Don't you fret about us, miss. Your mother's upstairs, putting the house to rights. Your dad's up there too. There's a deal of work in looking after a big place like this.'

Kit said, 'Is there anything I can get you?'

The old man said, 'Not a thing, miss. We came in here this morning. A fine young man, Bill Lockman, brought us in from Torrejón, sitting with us in the aeroplane. He was our Dick's friend, he says, and we know it's true because Dick often wrote us about him. Your mother gave us a lovely room, and showed us where everything is in the house. We don't need a thing.'

Mrs Holmes spoke for the first time. 'Ask Miss Fremantle about the funeral, Everett. Like her mother said to.'

'I don't know that we should bother her, Mother . . .'

'Please,' Kit said. 'Anything. I liked Dick so much. Everyone did.' She sat down on a chair opposite the old couple.

Mr Holmes said, 'We were talking with your mother, miss. She says you've been living with a Spanish family downtown, so you would be able to help us more than she can, you knowing the Spaniards better. Is that right?'

Kit said, 'I was living with a family. Whether I can help . . . I'll try.'

Mr Holmes said, 'We were talking about putting Dick to rest. A major came to the store Monday morning and told us about him being dead in this accident, and after a time Mother and me, when we got to understand, we thought we couldn't decide a thing till we'd seen the place where he was. Dick didn't like being in foreign duty much, miss, but we thought perhaps he'd want to lie where he flew, now his time had come, him being a pilot and Uncle Sam sending him there. So we came over. Your dad told us more, this morning, about how Dick was killed trying to hold off his aeroplane from falling in the middle of the city, but then Colonel Lindquist he said probably Dick was killed instantly, but in the end just one boy was killed, besides ours, thanks to God. And Colonel Lindquist explained about how they are really in there together, the boy and our Dick . . .'

Keeping her eyes carefully on his face, in the corner of her vision Kit caught the tiny spasm of his wife's hand in his. The unhurried Midwestern twang dragged on. 'After that, Captain Lockman drove us in his automobile to the place, and we looked at that. There were a lot of Spaniards round the house where the little boy lived, miss, and Mother and I wanted to go right in and speak to his folks, them and we being in the same boat, but Captain Lockman tells us they're still right badly upset, and he doesn't speak enough Spanish to translate for us.'

He looked steadily at her. 'So we came back here, and sat

in our room. Now we've seen it, Mother said. It's a foreign place, she said – and she's right, miss. But I said, Dick knew this place, and he died here, what are we to do? We got down on our knees and prayed. The good Lord didn't say a thing to us, but when we got up, I knew that our Dick would lie as well here as anywhere, and Mother agreed. We thought he and the little boy should be put to rest together, like they died together. That's what we were asking your mother, and she told us to ask you, you knowing the Spaniards, whether they'd take it right.'

Mrs Holmes said, 'We wouldn't like to hurt the mother's feelings.'

Mr Holmes said, 'Those folks are going to be thinking our Dick killed their boy, miss. That's human nature, when the grief's on you.'

A joint funeral, Kit thought. César had suggested it, while Dick and the boy and the F-104 lay under the quaking sludge. Let a bulldozer turn fresh earth over the whole disaster, he'd said. That might have done, but the Holmeses didn't mean that. They meant a proper funeral and they couldn't have any idea of what 'the grief' meant in a city like Medina, among a people like the *baturros*. She imagined the Air Force officer coming to Iowa store early in the morning with his news. Mr Holmes would grip the edge of the counter, Mrs Holmes perhaps sit down suddenly in a chair. Here ... She had watched the boy's mother break her fingernails on the cobbles and scream and wail in chords of grief inherited from the Moors, deeper still, from cave women and naked hunters of the black bull. She knew, from her father, that the mood of the young couple had turned to a sullen, tormented anger against fate and the Americans who had been its instrument. She knew that the same mood had infected the whole city; and behind everything was the presence of the panic.

'We would be right grateful for you to tell us what to do,' Mr Holmes said.

She thought – I, tell him? Knowing that they would do it, and would not be deflected, because they trusted her, and because once they had found the right they would persevere in it?

In the end everything was personal, everything came down to the person. She looked from one to the other of the two people on the sofa. Americans – to be hated. Parents of the man who had wiped the young, playing life out of existence –

246

to be feared. Protestants – to be despised. Rich; yes, rich, here – to be envied. People, an old man and an old woman, full of love and grief.

She said, 'I think you are right. It won't be easy, Mr Holmes. It may even be impossible. The people are very disturbed. The boy was of course a Roman Catholic, and Dick was . . .'

'Methodist, miss,' Mr Holmes said. 'We knew it wouldn't be easy. But Mother and I had made up our minds that was the right thing to do, and now you tell us, so we'll do it. We'll go and see Reverend Knight right away, Mother. His house is only just up the block. Then I guess he'll take us to see the Catholic reverend downtown.'

'They'll say a Mass over Dick?' Mrs Holmes said, looking up anxiously at her husband.

Mr Holmes said, 'He doesn't have to pay heed to that now, Mother, any more than their little boy has to pay heed to Reverend Knight reading the Good Book over him. I've never been inside a Catholic church in my life, miss, and I didn't reckon I ever would or would ever want to, but this is right. When they're thinking of their idols inside that church, I won't be with them, though I'm standing right there in the front row, but when they're praying for our Dick and the little boy, and thinking that what we're all there for it to put the two of them to rest in Christ Jesus's arms, then Mother and I will be with them, those people, even after we've gone home.' He stopped, and stood up. 'Ready, Mother?'

After they had left the house, Kit went slowly upstairs. Her mother was in her own room, pulling a tiny handkerchief back and forth between her hands and staring out of the window. When she saw Kit she said, 'Those people. Poor old things! Have they gone out? Why did Ham have to say we'd put them up? There's nothing I can do for them, and they just sit. It's awful.'

Kit said, 'Where's Dad?'

His voice came from the bathroom. 'Shaving.'

'For the conference,' her mother said.

'Not for the conference,' her father shouted. 'Just because I need a shave, damn it! Oh, God! That's done it! Peggy, where in hell's the styptic pencil? And here's the Old Man. Peggy, go down . . . no, help me with this damned cut, get some tissue, I'm bleeding like a pig. Kit, tell the colonel I'll be right down.'

Kit went downstairs and reached the front door just as the

bell rang. Colonel Lindquist entered. 'Hullo, Kit. I'm a little early but I wanted to talk over a couple of things . . .'

'Dad's cut himself.'

Colonel Lindquist grinned wearily. 'That's O.K. Where are the Holmeses?'

'Just gone out . . . They've gone to the Reverend Knight's to tell him they want a joint funeral for Dick and the García boy. They asked me first, and I said it would be right, if it's possible.'

The colonel sat up slowly. 'You said that? Why? What were your reasons?'

His blue eyes were cold and intense. She began to stammer, 'Lindy . . . have I done something silly again?'

'I don't know yet,' he said. 'What were your reasons for saying what you did?'

She said, 'I . . . I wasn't thinking of the trouble in the city . . . or really about us being Americans and them Spanish. I didn't really think about Dick or the boy either . . . It was the old people. They were so sad and loving that what they wanted to do must be right. They're *there*. We aren't . . . If people didn't like it, took it badly, it's the people who would be wrong, not them . . .'

Colonel Lindquist was standing. He said, 'What if I told you that it was a very bad, very dangerous idea to put in their heads? That you should have put them off it, or told them to come to me first?'

Kit felt her lower lip beginning to tremble. She said, 'Oh, Lindy . . . I would have said the same, that it *ought* to be done. I told them it would be difficult and perhaps impossible, but . . .'

'O.K.,' the colonel said abruptly. 'Now forget about it. It's not your responsibility . . .'

Her father dashed in, a long strip of sticking plaster down the side of his jaw and a blood-spotted handkerchief in his hand. 'I'm sorry, colonel . . . everything's ready.'

The colonel made a brief gesture of dismissal. He was still facing Kit. 'You know Rachel Sternfield?' Kit shook her head. 'She was asking this morning whether someone couldn't give her a non-military angle on the position here. Have you got anything urgent to do? . . . Well, come along. I may call you into the conference after we've got going.'

They drove to the offices, the colonel and her father rapidly discussing some papers in a file while she sat silent in the back

248

seat. Then she waited for half an hour in the colonel's own office, alone with her thoughts, until they called her in.

In the doorway of the conference room she hesitated with a moment of nervousness. A woman in her mid fifties, wearing a very chic dark blue dress, was at the head of the table. Her hair was iron grey, beautifully coiffured, and she wore two gold bracelets on her left wrist. Kit went forward slowly. The woman looked oddly in place among the generals.

The woman said, 'Come here, Kit. Yes, I know your name. I'm Rachel Sternfield. Sit down next to me and then you'll be safe from having your leg pinched on one side at least. Do you smoke? Well, smoke then.'

Kit sat down. This was the Under-secretary of the Air Force, the famous Rachel Sternfield. Her father had been grumbling, last night, about the tactlessness of sending a woman, and a Jewish woman, twice divorced, to talk to the Spaniards, of all people, about politics and jet bases. But Kit, looking at Mrs Sternfield, thought, This is right. It's time to lay it on the line, all that we have and are. She glanced quickly round the table ... General Lyman, commanding the joint U.S. Military Assistance group in Spain; General McCabe from the Defence Department, Mrs Sternfield's technical adviser; Mr Henry Fowler, the U.S. Ambassador to Spain; a lieutenant-colonel who must be someone's aide; poor Dad with his plastered face; Colonel Lindquist. Excepting the aide, she knew them all by name and face.

Rachel Sternfield tapped the table lightly with her pencil and said, 'We agreed, I think, to have a general report on the situation in Spain now, as it affects us.'

The ambassador was a paunchy man with blue suit, bifocals, and a small mouth. He said, 'Well, ma'am, as I was explaining to you on the plane up here, the general situation's not too bad, taking Spain as a whole. There are a lot of our tourists in Spain, and only the usual number have been earning undesirable publicity for fighting, drunken driving, or indecent exposure on the beach. It seems to be mainly the Scandinavian women who get into trouble that way.'

'They've usually got more to expose,' General Lyman interposed. There was a short chuckle round the table, in which Kit noticed that her father tried, but failed, to join.

The ambassador went on. 'We're having an average summer, maybe a little better than average. But the trouble here is having an effect on the other bases. It seems to spread like an infection. There hasn't been much specific to get hold of, but they all report the same thing – a noticeable worsening in the relations between the bases and the cities nearby. What seems to be happening is that people, I mean both the Spaniards and our people, hear about what's happening in Medina, and start to pick on faults in each other that they overlooked before. I can't say the local newspapers here and the correspondents for the Madrid papers – they're probably local men, too – have been bending over backward to minimize the troubles.' He glanced coldly at her father. 'They don't publish our point of view. Or they don't get it.'

Her father shuffled his papers and said, 'They get it, Mr Ambassador. I don't think the editor of *El Baturro*'s against us. But he's a newspaperman. I mean, he wants to publish what interests people . . .'

'And what interests Europeans is the sex habits of American airmen,' Mrs Sternfield said.

'Those incidents ought to be kept out of the papers,' the ambassador said. 'That should be possible, if there was a good understanding between the base and the city.'

'It's not easy . . .' her father began unhappily.

General Lyman said, 'I'd say it was darn near impossible, Ambassador. Portuondo can give us a better line on these particular newspapermen when we meet the Spaniards after this, but I know one thing, none of our boys in England can tickle a barmaid's fanny without hitting the headlines in the *News of the World* – that's their biggest Sunday newspaper – while a Welsh farmer living in sin with his five daughters and the cat only rates a couple of lines at the bottom of page six. And I don't think the British have any conspiracy against us. It's news, and no one likes anything better than to read about foreigners acting dirty, just like we were taught they all do when we were kids.'

Mrs Sternfield said, 'You might tell us about the political situation, Henry.'

The ambassador peered at her through the half moons of his bifocals. 'I suppose this young lady has been warned not to divulge anything she hears? Well, the situation in Madrid is that the Central Committee of the Falange met last night and Medina was the main item on the agenda. We heard this morning at the embassy, from our sources, what was decided. They're going to use the troubles here to call for abrogation of the treaty.'

'A billion and a half dollars down the drain,' General Mc-Cabe growled.

The ambassador said, 'And the worst setback for our foreign policy since –'

' – last week,' General Lyman cut in.

The ambassador frowned and Mrs Sternfield said, 'Now, Charlie, you know we can have you investigated for being a Democrat *and* a general, so be quiet ... I don't think there's much chance that the treaty actually will be abrogated, is there?' Kit saw that she was drawing a woman's evening gown on her scratch pad.

The ambassador said, 'No. The Falange will respectfully ask General Franco to abrogate, on the grounds that the treaty is causing ill feeling and undermining Spanish sovereignty. General Franco will not accede to the request. But he will be able to tighten the restrictions he has put on our use of the bases, and on our men in Spain, and he will be in a very strong position indeed when he asks for more non-military aid, and if we want to come to him for anything else ... which I understand we might easily want to do?' He looked at General McCabe. The general nodded, and with the forefinger of his right hand described a parabola, from the table, up, and down again.

The ambassador said, 'That's about it.'

Mrs Sternfield drew in an elaborate bow on the back of the dress, and turned to Kit. 'Now, dear, will you tell us what you know. Rather, what you think, what you feel, about the troubles here. I'm sure we've got to go deeper than mere facts. Didn't it begin with someone assaulting a girl called Rosario Lima?'

'That wasn't the beginning,' Kit said eagerly. Everyone was staring at her. She stopped. She'd made enough trouble.

'What was?' Rachel Sternfield asked gently.

'When we got here ... being different ... having more money,' she began. Her father was keeping his eyes down. The ambassador's small mouth was pursed and even smaller.

Kit thought, I've got to say what I think. With a despairing glance at Colonel Lindquist, she began to talk. She told them about the first break-up of the paseo; about the *jotas* that turned to square dances; about the secret mutilation of the Bull of San Marco; about the rise in prices and the two price lists kept by some of the Spanish shopkeepers; about Eloísa and her three or four sergeants and her sulky boy-friend; about the doctor and the train on the grade crossing; about the time, just after she arrived in Spain, that Mrs Wakefield's car broke down

251

on the road to Barcelona, and fifteen dark Spaniards stood watching, not raising a finger to help her, and Mrs Wakefield's rage – but they were only respecting her privacy: if she had asked, they would have pulled the car ten miles. And ... She stopped suddenly, for she was about to tell them that the double-header had been a failure, and the *fiesta* a fiasco: but those had been her father's pride.

'That's all,' she said lamely.

There was silence. The ambassador said, 'Have you anything to add to that, colonel?'

Colonel Lindquist raised his head. 'One thing, sir. Major Fremantle and I have also, as General Lyman knows, been paying out of our own pockets the wages of a girl who has been taking an informal poll on what people think about us. She can't ask questions, because public opinion polls are forbidden in Spain. She spends her time listening. The figures, until the week before last, were fifty per cent for us being here, twenty-five per cent against, twenty-five per cent neutral. That was not quite so good as Zaragoza, but better than Morón and Torrejón. Last week our figures had changed to forty, forty-five, fifteen. This week will probably be twenty, seventy-five, five.'

'Not a very encouraging graph, colonel,' the ambassador said.

'No, Mr Ambassador,' Colonel Lindquist said.

There was something in his voice that made Kit look at him more closely. Her heart began to beat faster, for he looked different. In the big cool room, the purr of the air conditioner like distant engines, he looked like what he was – a commander of heavy bombers. He was holding his scratch pad in both hands in front of him, like a half wheel, and sitting back, mouth closed but not clamped, blue eyes cold and steadfast. As the conference progressed and the minute hand of the electric clock jerked forward, he was approaching his target.

Rachel Sternfield said, 'Miss Fremantle's given us an excellent and unusual view of the background. Now – about Rosario Lima.'

Colonel Lindquist said, 'Airman Smith has been charged with the offence. Miss Lima has identified him as her assailant.'

General McCabe said, 'What about the shot at the B-52?'

'That came next – the following morning,' Colonel Lindquist said. 'There is no clue.'

The ambassador said, 'But ...'

Mrs Sternfield said, 'If there's no clue, there's no clue, Henry. I've got an appointment with the hairdresser in two hours . . . Next there was the rape of Señorita de Aguirre.'

Colonel Lindquist said, 'Airman Smith is under civil arrest on that charge, too. The trial will be next month, the civil governor tells me.'

They went on . . . the theft of the Armlet; the crash of the F-104; no evidence, no evidence. The ambassador brought up the double-header, and her father's ears reddened and he put his useless horn-rimmed spectacles on and off several times. Colonel Lindquist agreed that the double-header had been a mistake on his part.

Rachel Sternfield finished drawing a high-heeled sandal, and said dryly, 'All in all, what we need in Medina is a flood or a famine.'

General Lyman drew on his cigar. 'By God, yes! Like those floods on the British coast in '53. I was commanding Burton-wood then. They gave us a chance to show what else we could do, apart from stealing the Britishers' girls.'

Colonel Lindquist said, 'It was fine to be able to help, general. I was there. But I do not think we should be accepted only when we show that we make a pretty good auxiliary emergency service.' Kit watched the clock, and sat very small in her chair, and hoped they would forget she was still here.

General Lyman said, 'Sure, but a disaster makes people think bigger. You know what the British were saying during the war? "The trouble with the Americans is that they are overpaid, over-sexed, and over here." They weren't talking like that in '53.'

Rachel Sternfield said, 'The position here is slightly different. As I understand it, if there were an epidemic here now, this group of right-wing conspirators who call themselves the Gentlemen of Covadonga would let everyone know that we had spread the germs, and if there were a flood, the last series of atom-bomb tests in Nevada would have caused it.'

'That's about the size of it,' the ambassador agreed. 'And I would like to know . . .'

He began to attack her father, not too gently. A large part of the trouble seemed to be due to a failure in the Information Services. And . . .

Colonel Lindquist interrupted with cold politeness. 'Ambassador, Major Fremantle is on my staff, and has done nothing

253

without my approval.' Kit ran her tongue over her lips. Ten, nine, eight . . .

The ambassador turned to him. 'Very well, colonel, perhaps you can tell us how you are going to remedy the situation you have here. I think we'd all be glad to have you outline the steps you propose to take.'

Four, three, two . . .

Colonel Lindquist said, 'I do not propose to take any steps.'

Hack!

Kit fumbled for and lit a cigarette. There was a long shocked silence. Mrs Sternfield stopped drawing.

General McCabe said, 'Now, Lindquist, you've had bad luck here, we all know that, but obviously we've got to do *something*.'

Then they were all talking, firing at Colonel Lindquist.

'What about making compensation to the parents of the García boy in some special way?'

The colonel said, 'Compensation will be paid in the normal way, at the normal scale.'

'Make some gesture towards the dependents of the people killed in the H-bomb panic.'

Colonel Lindquist's hands steadied infinitesimally on the scratch pad, his eyes turned slowly to the questioner. He said, 'The panic was no fault of the United States Air Force. Also, I think such a suggestion would be considered insulting by the people of Medina – if not now, later.'

'Give a hundred thousand bucks to the city for a new wing on the hospital. I can get the money for you out of the Special Fund.'

'I think that would be inappropriate at this time, general.'

'Hand that other airman to the Spaniards for punishment – the one who slugged a Spanish soldier. They have the legal right to deal with him.'

'They do, sir, but it was agreed a year ago between Colonel Portuondo, General Guzmán, and myself that fights between members of our services would be dealt with by their respective military codes, in the absence of special circumstances, such as a specific intention to insult the other man's uniform or country. There were no such circumstances here. The man is already doing twenty-one days in the brig.'

'Place the city off limits for six months.'

'In my opinion, general, that is what our enemies would like best.'

'Couldn't the angle of the runway be altered, colonel, so that the planes don't come in and out over the city? I know it would cost a lot, but I think the money could be found, in the circumstances.'

'Ma'am, the runway was sited in conjunction with the Spanish civil and Air Force authorities. It is in the best angle and position to enable this air base to fulfil its mission.'

The ambassador ruffled his papers angrily. 'What about this Sergeant Olmbacher, then? I presume you are sending him home, or have already done so?'

'No, sir.'

'They're in love,' Kit said suddenly.

'My dear young lady –' the ambassador began. Rachel Sternfield jangled her bracelet loudly and cut in. 'And he's a Catholic.'

'Madam –' the ambassador began.

Colonel Lindquist continued. 'The proposed marriage is permissible under those clauses of the treaty relating to the subject. Olmbacher has done nothing wrong, and I do not propose to punish him by sending him away from his place of duty, until his tour is up.'

The ambassador slammed his pencil down on the table. 'Very well. You choose to alienate the Aguirres, who are, I understand one of the most influential families in Medina, and that's about all you do choose to do. That's right, isn't it? You have a mess here that's your fault – you admitted it – a mess that could jeopardize the whole U.S. position in Europe, and you propose to do absolutely nothing about it. That's right?'

'Yes, sir,' Colonel Lindquist said.

'Wheels down, Lindy,' General Lyman said quietly. 'The ambassador's right. Something's got to be done. Or at any rate tell us why you disagree with us.'

'I think I understand, a little,' Rachel Sternfield said. 'And don't I hear that Señor Aguirre is not a leading pro-American, to say the least of it? So trying to appease him might be a waste of effort, besides being degrading.'

'That's it, ma'am,' Colonel Lindquist said. 'Every suggestion made so far would have the effect of degrading the United States and the United States Air Force, and I do not propose to be a party to any of them. We are here to fulfil a certain mission, as a result of a treaty freely arrived at between our government and a foreign government. We don't want to be here and they don't want us to be here, any more than we'd like foreign troops on American soil. The treaty may be unnecessary, or unwise. That's not my affair. But as long as I command here we will not slink about our business as though we were criminals. We will not hide on the base. We will not pretend we are Spaniards. We will not pretend to like what we don't like. We will stand for what we stand for, with good manners, I hope – but firmly.

'Colonel . . .' General McCabe began.

Rachel Sternfield said, 'One moment, general. I don't think we need Miss Fremantle any more, do we? Thank you so much, dear. You're terribly beautiful, you know.' She kissed Kit quickly on the cheek and whispered, 'Run along now, *Kindel*, before they start throwing spitballs.'

Kit got up. All the men stood. Colonel Lindquist's voice rose slightly. 'You will be interested to know that Captain Holmes's parents have asked that Dick be buried here, in a joint funeral ceremony with the García boy. In line with what I have decided is our best, our only policy – I suppose to do all I can to persuade the bishop to agree.'

'My God!' the ambassador said, and sat down suddenly in his chair.

General McCabe said, 'That sounds to me like letting off a rocket in a powder magazine.'

Colonel Lindquist said, 'It's a risk, sir, but I don't think we should accept tolerance as a basis for our being here. Our business here is survival and annihilation, and to bicker about anything less than that is not worthy of us, or of Medina.'

'Will you see the bishop yourself?' Rachel Sternfield asked.

'Yes, ma'am.'

'This I want to see. East is East and West is West, and two strong men meeting face to face, though they come from the ends of the earth.'

'Never the twain shall meet,' General McCabe said.

The Under-secretary said, 'You've got it wrong, general, like everyone else. That comes at the beginning. The end is the face-to-face bit. Look it up. But, colonel, isn't this the same bishop who arranged that the funerals of the H-bomb panic victims should be carried out with a minimum of fuss and publicity? Surely there isn't a hope of his agreeing?'

Colonel Lindquist said slowly, 'It's the same bishop, ma'am, but so am I the same man who would have opposed this plan, twenty-four hours ago. I've learned something in the meantime – from the old Holmes couple, from others . . . I've been forced, one way and another, to look below the surface of the trouble, and see the roots of it. I hope, and personally I believe, that the bishop has done the same. He's got the responsibility, too.'

The ambassador said coldly, 'I am going to have something to say to this proposal, sir . . .'

Rachel Sternfield said quickly, 'Wait for me. So am I . . ' Run along, dear.'

Kit let herself out of the conference room. Beyond the white-gloved A.P. guarding the door, the Reverend Knight, Father Perriera, and Mr and Mrs Holmes were waiting in the outer office.

*

The bishop's secretary, a thin and nervous young cleric, was waiting for Colonel Lindquist outside the door of the bishop's study. Inside the study Father Perreira, who had left the base an hour earlier, was standing at the bishop's side.

Lindquist bowed slightly, uniform cap under his arm. The bishop's eyes were small, deep set and very dark in a wizened parchment face. His ears were big and stuck out under the scarlet skull cap, and his throat was thin and wattled. He sat in a curule chair, his hands resting like claws on the arms of the chair, the fingers parted and curved, a huge ruby ring on his right hand.

Father Perreira murmured, 'I have given his lordship an outline of the circumstances, sir.'

The bishop spoke suddenly in Spanish. His voice was thin but strong, and rough, like frayed wire. Lindquist understood what he had said – 'Please explain why *you* wish this funeral to take place'; but he waited until Father Perreira had translated for him. He noticed a flicker of appreciation in the bishop's small old eyes.

As Father Perreira stopped speaking Lindquist said, addressing the bishop, 'I think that this is a proper occasion to assert, in public, ties that are deeper and more important than our differences.'

The bishop waited in his turn, though Lindquist knew that he too had understood.

Then, without hesitation or pause, he said, 'In that case, I agree.'

Lindquist said, 'Father Perreira has pointed out that Captain Holmes having been a Protestant, a Methodist, it could be difficult, even impossible for you to agree. If that is so, I do not wish to press the request.'

The bishop said, 'There is nothing but chemical-soaked earth and calcined bones to inter. A handful of it contains the earthly relics of the Catholic Pedro García and of your dissident pilot. I must bury the García boy in consecrated ground, and cannot do so without also burying the pilot.'

Lindquist said, 'That is so, my lord.' He insisted on his point. There were ways out. It must be clearly agreed that they were to be ignored. He said, 'But different portions of earth could be assumed to be the remains of each and buried separately. Or chemical and medical analysis could certainly isolate certain particles and state definitely to whom they had belonged.'

The bishop said, 'The first would be subterfuge. I presume you are here because you think the time for subterfuge is past?' Lindquist bowed. 'The second – I do not propose to invite the scientists to separate what God has fused.'

Lindquist waited. The bishop seemed to be marshalling his thoughts. After a time the jewelled finger moved slightly, and the secretary in the corner murmured, 'Ready, your lordship.' His pencil was poised over a writing-pad.

The bishop said, 'The casket is to be buried in the cathedral plot . . .'

The secretary stammered, 'I beg your pardon, my lord, did you say . . .?'

'The cathedral plot. It will not take up a deal of room . . . That will mean there is no space for a funeral procession between the place of the service and the place of interment. Let the procession form at the Mercado, and go to the cathedral.'

'By the direct route, my lord?'

'No – through the Barrio. Via the Paseo, Goya, Arenas, Ibáñez, and Alcalde. To the main south front of the cathedral.'

'The f-f-front, my lord? B-b-but it is customary for f-f-funerals to use the west doors.'

'The south . . . I shall preside at the Funerales Corpore Insepulto in the cathedral. Let the presidency be formed in the cloisters. You will wish to provide a firing squad to fire a military salute, colonel? And trumpeters?'

Lindquist said, 'With your agreement, yes.'

'I agree.'

The bishop brooded in his curule chair.

The secretary said, 'The time, my lord?'

The bishop looked at Lindquist, 'Five o'clock tomorrow afternoon – for the start from the Mercado?'

Lindquist thought, and said slowly, 'A mission of a squadron of our heavy bombers is due to start taking off at 5.10 p.m., my lord. The wind has been steady in the east for some days now, at that time in the afternoon.'

Lindquist waited. The bishop said nothing.

Lindquist said, 'I cannot promise, but I am almost certain that I could have the take-off time delayed. Or you could consider putting back the procession till five-thirty, when the bombers should have taken off.'

The bishop said, 'No.'

Their eyes met; Lindquist knew they understood each other thoroughly.

He said, 'That is all, my lord. Perhaps you will permit Father Perreira to fix the remaining details with the dean and the Reverend Knight.'

The bishop held up his hand in a gesture of detention. 'One moment, colonel ... The people of this city have allowed pettiness to enter into their relationships with you.'

Lindquist said, 'We are equally guilty.'

'These young people are annihilated by an accident of the air age, which is not petty, whatever its other faults. Is there not some symbol more appropriate to the age than the sound of brass trumpets, to make a salute to the dead, and to impress a larger understanding upon the living?'

Lindquist said, 'There is, my lord – an aerial salute by fighters such as Holmes flew. But we are forbidden to do it.'

'Is Colonel Portuondo also forbidden?'

'Not with the same strictness, my lord.'

The bishop waved his hand to his secretary, 'Telephone Colonel Portuondo and ask him to come to me as soon as possible – also my urgent respects to General Guzmán.' He stood up. 'I shall see you in the cathedral.'

Lindquist said, 'I shall be there, my lord.'

CHAPTER 27

César knocked and the door opened at once. Evaristo stood there. 'Come in,' he said. César entered the room.

Mario, Ricardo, Marcelino, himself, and Evaristo the zealot. Five Gentlemen of Covadonga. Eleven o'clock at night, for an emergency meeting in Evaristo's apartment. Something properly fanatic about that, because the place was being watched. There could be no doubt about the purpose of the man sitting half hidden behind a newspaper at a table outside the café on the corner.

They made the prayer, and then Evaristo excused himself – 'I must telephone' – and left the room.

Mario said, 'I met José in the street yesterday. Is all your *caudrilla* here now?'

César said, 'I think so.'

'Ah, what superb disdain! The day after tomorrow he is fighting for his life and he doesn't know whether his assistants are present, absent, dead, or drunk! José told me that the Martos bulls for San Marco are all monsters.'

César said, 'José says the same of all bulls. I have not seen them.'

Marcelino said, 'They were being herded to the *plaza de toros* when the plane crashed, just the other side of the wasteland from them. It is said they became very nervous and untrustworthy. Be careful of them on Friday, César.'

'I will.'

'And after San Marco? You will pick up all your remaining contracts of the season? Where do you go next?'

'Barcelona on Sunday, Badajoz, Wednesday and Thursday . . . I can't remember after that.'

'I'm lying, he thought. I should have said, 'After this moment, I know nothing.' Somebody had recently hammered the names 'Barcelona' and 'Badajoz' into his head, and they meant something fairly definite, because he had been to those cities; but Sunday and Wednesday and Thursday meant nothing at all. This was the only Wednesday, and he loved Kit. Those words contained all knowledge.

Evaristo returned and said abruptly, 'The García boy and
260

the American flyer are to have a single funeral tomorrow. You heard the eight o'clock announcement?'

'I cannot quite believe it,' Marcelino said.

'It is true,' Mario said. 'The bishop's secretary is a *great* friend of mine . . .'

Evaristo said, 'The bishop obviously does not intend this to be regarded as an ordinary funeral. Do you realize that the casket is to be buried in the cathedral plot?'

Marcelino said, 'I heard that. But it can't be true, can it? Only bishops and Medina's saints and martyrs can be buried there.'

Evaristo snapped, 'It *is* true!'

Marcelino said heavily, 'The bishop must be out of his senses.'

'And the García's have agreed to everything?' César asked.

Marcio said, 'The bishop sent for them then and there. They didn't like it, but what could they do?'

Ricardo said, 'I don't understand what the bishop intends. Is he trying to make us show respect to the Americans?'

Evaristo said, 'I understand very well. He, and I suppose Lindquist, intend to force both Spaniards and Americans to weigh their differences in terms of death and life, of annihilation and survivial.'

Mario said softly, 'And you, Evaristo? You have called us here to tell us that you choose annihilation?'

Evaristo's face was pale, pale grey. 'Yes,' he said, 'Not survival on terms of compromise with anyone, for any reason! If we accept that American dissident liberals and Spanish Catholic traditionalists are in the beginning and at the end only a single spoonful of the same earth, then what is the sense of fighting? Is it not possible that their way is as right as ours? Live and let live. All human beings are equal in the sight of God. That's what the bishop is telling us.'

Ricardo said, 'I don't know, Evaristo. The bishop is no liberal. He could be saying that though there is only one right – ours – we have got to learn to live with the misguided in the same sort of dignity that we will die with them – as these two did.'

Evaristo said, 'And what is that but liberalism? This American shopkeeper's son is going to lie between Bishop Ulibarri and Don Fernando de Bohorquilla!'

Bishop Ulibarri the Inquisitor, César thought, who sentenced one hundred and fourteen men and women to burn in the Plaza

San Marco between 1590 and 1605. Don Fernando the Martyr – the nobleman who stabbed a sightseeing Moroccan prince to death, in the cathedral in 1873, for no other reason than that he was a Moor and was in the cathedral – and who had been tried and executed for murder in those libertarian days of the First Republic. Strange companions for a jet pilot and a slum child. Yet Holmes in his silver dart was an inquisitor, screaming down at humanity from his place far higher than Bishop Ulibarri's ancient tribunal, 'Do you accept God's word that E equals MV^2? Do you renounce the pleasures of hate and ignorance? No? Then I sentence you to death by Strontium 90. And with you, myself.'

Evaristo said, 'The foreigner is the enemy, with his perversions, the same now as he always has been.'

César thought dully, He is so tired he is almost unconscious in his chair. He works all day at his successful and important business, thinks all night of the Gentlemen of Covadonga, and always his exhausted flesh must feed this heatless flame burning in him for the Faith, for the spirit of Spain, for the impossible, self-sustaining zeal of the old, enclosed world. Impossible? What was *he* doing here then, if he could use the word? He didn't know, except that he was a Spaniard and an Aguirre of Medina, and feasibility was an unimportant notion.

Evaristo said, more calmly, 'Tomorrow the Americans will march through the narrow streets of the Barrio, passing among us in their physical presence, an insolent parade of the rapists, the murderers, the drunkards, the infidels, the foreigners, the rich and selfish and careless and uncaring...'

Mario said, 'The men who play like children with our children in the street, the smiling wolf whistlers, the emptiers of pockets, the square dancers, the tall runners, the fat laughers ...'

Evaristo said, 'I have made it my business to see that all that is pushed down from the people's minds, at the funeral. There are ways.'

Ricardo said slowly, 'I don't know. I don't like it. Where could it lead?'

'Anwhere,' Evaristo said abruptly. 'Anywhere. You do not seem to realize that we are already being carried along on the current. If we do not help to direct the flow we will be overwhelmed and washed away by it ... If it goes far enough, tomorrow ... there is a chance that Franco will get rid of them.'

'You would martyr the city to get rid of the Americans?' César said slowly. 'The Armed Police will not be loaded with blank.'

Evaristo said, 'And when Pelayo turned at Covadonga, did he say to himself, There will be war where there could have been peaceful submission?' His thin voice cracked with passion. 'No! He fought. And the shepherds and cowherds fought, and were killed and their wives and children were slaughtered on the mountain. Certainly men may die tomorrow, in order that the soul of Spain can live pure and free. What else is any war?'

After a time Evaristo resumed in his normal voice, 'I have been finding out all that I can. The gipsies will be there, the *saeta* singers among them.'

Mario said, 'The *saetas* drive people beyond reason at a time of grief.'

'There are piles of bricks lying in several places along the south side of Arenas.'

'And cobblestones everywhere,' Mario said.

'Several rumours are already spreading. There will also be omens for the superstitious.'

'How do you know?'

'I have arranged them. That is all I have done, on my own initiative. The rest is there, in the spirit of the city.'

Again a long silence fell. Marcelino broke it, in his heavy, wondering voice. 'Who is going to attack who, Evaristo? I mean, I'd like to get the Reds out in the open and shoot them, but at a funeral, I don't quite see ... I mean, the Garcías and other Spanish mourners are going to be in the procession too, aren't they?'

'Until it explodes,' Evaristo said. 'Then they'll be the first to turn on the Americans walking beside them. That's human nature. You'll see.'

Ricardo said, 'So, we have sown the wind ...'

'And the Americans shall reap the whirlwind.'

'Others, too.'

There seemed to be nothing more to say. Either the bishop and Lindqvist were right in thinking that the funeral would establish a new foundation for relations between the city and the foreigners – or Evaristo was right in thinking that it would make all future relations impossible. He realized suddenly that Evaristo had to be right, because it was on Evaristo's philosophy that he had built his own life. Tomorrow would solve everything, and vindicate his unhappiness.

Marcelino said, 'Now I cannot sleep, thinking that I have been excommunicated.'

Evaristo said, 'The Armlet will return to its place tomorrow night – when Medina has shown it has the courage, and the will, to fight for its soul.'

Mario said, 'That is just what they are whispering in the Barrio!' He was rubbing his hands gently together, and there had been a dreamy half smile on his face all evening, particularly noticeable when Evaristo had become most ardent in his zeal.

Marcelino said, 'But the excommunication will still stand. It will be on us for ever, until we confess and make penance.'

Evaristo said fiercely, 'You were brave enough in the war. Show some moral courage, man! ... I have nothing else to say. Has anyone?'

Ricardo shook his head. Mario said, 'No.'

'You, César?'

The numbness still held him. There were so many thoughts running in different directions in his head, colliding, mingling, rebounding, that there was nothing to say. 'No,' he said.

'Then let us kneel here and commend ourselves and our actions to God.'

Slowly César slipped to his knees, and bowed his head. 'Virgin Mother, guide me' he whispered. 'Virgin of the Pillar, help me. Saint James the Apostle, Santiago of Spain, be with me.' He repeated the invocations over and over, being racked suddenly with an overwhelming sense of sin and sacrilege. 'Christ Jesus, who wert without sin, speak to me!'

There was no door open, no light anywhere, no voice speaking as he called. The Virgin, and St James, and the gaunt figure on the Cross were all gone and silent, and he was as cold as in the passage under the stands, the minutes before marching out into the sun of the bull-ring.

*

César found himself walking slowly down the Calle Goya. It was nearly midnight and he was alone in the street. That was something strange, when the streets were full of dwarfs and cripples at three in the afternoon, to be altogether alone at midnight. He imagined he saw human hair in the gutter, along with blood and strips of flesh, Eloísa's hair, cut off by her sullen *novio* because she loved all men as long as they laughed; Rosario Lima's hair, because she loved all men as long as they had money. Black hair it was that he saw, but why shouldn't some be fair among the black?

Two policemen came striding up the middle of the road, walking close. They peered at him as he approached and he saw that their faces were set and strained. 'This is not a comfortable night to be abroad, Don César,' one of them said. They all stopped together in the middle of the street.

'No . . . I am hot. Tired. I have a headache.'

'So has everyone. Perhaps it is the water causing that, too.'

Water? What water?

'You haven't heard? Of course we say it is not true if we are asked. In fact we threaten to arrest anyone who does ask, for spreading rumours.'

'What are you talking about?'

'You mean you really don't know, sir? Well, it's just a rumour of course, but they say the city water is contaminated.'

'With some disease? Typhoid? That has happened before.'

'Radioactivity. And here we've been drinking it for a year without suspecting anything. Our bones rotting away, the men becoming impotent. Now that it's out, everyone's realized just why there have been so many children born deformed these last months. My cousin's wife . . .'

'How is the water supposed to have been contaminated?'

'Why, in the pipe, sir. It comes down from the Lago Perdido in a big pipe, doesn't it? And the pipe runs just outside the fence surrounding the base, on the north side? And what's buried in those underground caverns with the ventilators, not far inside the fence? Hydrogen bombs – giving off radioactivity.'

The other policeman spoke for the first time, bitterly, 'The Yankees knew all the time. *They* draw their water off the pipe a mile higher up. And we're supposed to see they don't get hurt when they come into the city tomorrow. Well, a man's only got two eyes . . .'

They marched slowly on up the middle of the street. César stepped into a doorway and fumblingly lit a cigarette. Now he seemed to hear the whine of fretful, thirsty children from all the houses. They cried for water in the heat and their frightened mothers gave them some wine. Hate built up, no one slept, heads ached.

Tomorrow there'd be a denial, complete with facts and figures. The day after it would be believed. That would be too late.

He walked on. Evaristo had to be right. His own fate was in Evaristo's hands. No, in the hands of Medina. In the threatening, stifling heat of the narrow alley he could feel the blind force that would solve everything, one way or another. He had been in this cave, locked in with his love for Kit and his sacrilege against the Church, for how long now? Too long. He remembered thinking, only this afternoon during her visit to the house, that there was no possible escape. But surely the trains of sparks crawling through the houses on either side of him would, this afternoon, rend the world in which he had locked himself? There would be no more doubts, no more conflicting impossibilities. And no more love?

She would be in the procession herself. He must prevent her. But she would insist. And why prevent her? If she was there, she would understand that the locked and barred room had fallen in upon them.

His head throbbed. He too was under excommunication, and he too could not sleep. It would be all right tomorrow. Evaristo would come, and in the dark of night they'd go into the cathedral and replace the Sacred Relic. Then it would be all right.

As Marcelino had said, it wouldn't be all right. Supposing Evaristo turned out to be wrong. Then his own life would be resting on a broken myth. There would be nothing left for him in this city, or this country. He'd have to find a new foundation, a new world. Why not Kit's?

'Who's there?'

The challenging voice was calm and cold.

He stopped, and saw the tall green figure under the gleam of the black winged hat, the rifle in its hands, and the yellow lamp burning beside the open gate.

He went close and the man said, 'Ah, it is *El Rondeño*. I have seen you in the ring, sir. This is a bad night to walk about.' He had a strong Extremaduran accent and César thought, What a night indeed, to cause a Guardia Civil to make light conversation.

'Have you heard about the water?' the Guardia asked, shifting his rifle to the other hand.

'Yes.'

'It is not true, of course, but these *baturros* will believe anything – saving your grace's presence.'

266

A dull whooshing rose in volume until it became very loud in the silent city. To the south over the roof-tops, a line of red fire trailed into the sky, and burst on a shower of red stars. Seconds later the explosion in the sky rattled the windows in the street.

'A rocket,' the Guardia Civil said softly. 'From the bank of the Milagro near the railroad yards. That's the City Police's responsibility . . . but they'll never catch him.'

Voices called to each other inside the houses, and from window to window. A child began screaming in hysterical terror.

'Tomorrow will be worse,' the Guardia said. 'Good night, *maestro*.'

'Good night.'

César went on quickly, going home now. Truly there was nothing else to do but go home, lie down, wake up, and wait for the inescapable.

CHAPTER 28

There was no shade where they were gathering, on the apron a hundred feet from the bulk of the main armaments hangar. A heat haze shimmered over the Llano Triste and silver mirage lakes turned the runway into standing water. The tall silver tails of the bombers stuck out above the haze, the silver bodies below quaked and seemed to move in the heat patterns. Wavering, almost human shapes moved around them, carrying out the pre-flight inspection.

Kit was wearing a black silk dress and short black gloves. Her arms were running with sweat in the long sleeves. Her mother waved a hand at the B-52s. 'Why are they flying off now, Ham? Shouldn't the officers be acting as pall-bearers, or something?'

Her father mopped his forehead. 'They don't have the choice. This is a SAC base, honey.'

Kit thought, Mother really has no idea what's happening. She knows it's hot, she knows there's a funeral, so she has to wear black with long sleeves; and that's all she knows.

Half a dozen other officers and wives had joined their group. Her father was speaking to Father Perreira – 'Have you heard the latest? All the saints in the cathedral were sweating last night. Couldn't you organize something more reassuring than that, father?' He laughed loudly, and slapped Father Perreira on the back.

Father Perreira said, 'When our saints sweat, Ham, it is sometimes a miracle, sometimes the temperature inside the church, and most often the temperature of the observer. It's no laughing matter.'

'Who's laughing?' Her father laughed again as he said it, but still without mirth.

Major Hurst said, 'That's not the latest. The fish are dying in the Milagro. They've been floating downstream, belly up ever since dawn.'

Her father said, 'Someone's dynamiting them upstream, then. Or poisoning the water up there.' He looked at his watch. 'Where in hell are the old couple? I'm going to pass out if they don't get here soon.'

Major Hurst said, 'It's not time yet, Ham. They didn't look to me like hurrying types.'

A hundred airmen marched on to the tarmac in formation, and stood easy beside two huge trailer trucks.

A captain said, 'They were letting off rockets all night. Red ones.'

'Who was?'

'God knows. The police never caught anyone.'

The Lindquists arrived in his official car, and all the men in the group turned. Lindquist returned the salutes gravely. Mrs Lindquist wandered off to speak to the senior nurse, and the colonel drew his exec aside. By straining her ears Kit could hear the low-voiced conversation between them.

The colonel said, 'General Guzmán telephoned, didn't he?'

'Yes, sir. He's got a battalion and a half standing by in their barracks. He wants to have them actually in the procession. He says he can get them there in time, if you ask him to.'

'No.'

'There's a lot of women going to be in the procession, colonel. About twenty of ours.'

'Including my wife. They've all been privately warned that there may be unpleasantness and danger?'

'Yes, sir.'

The colonel nodded in dismissal, and moved away to speak to others. Major Dant was talking to her father. 'And now they've got a Red plot on their hands, on top of everything else.'

Her father said, 'You mean Sarmiento?'

A captain asked, 'Who's he? I've never heard of him.'

Her father said, 'The big transportation man – Evaristo Sarmiento. He owns half the trucks in the province, and now he turns out to be a secret Red, and all set to start something – house full of bombs, pamphlets, tommy-guns. Christ knows what.'

Major Dant said, 'I find it hard to believe, Ham. I had lunch with him once, at one of the mayor's get-togethers.'

'Well, they came for him at three o'clock in the morning, and took him to Madrid.'

'Good-bye, Mr Sarmiento.'

Captain Janus said, 'What's this about our water being contaminated, major?'

Her father turned on the captain angrily. 'Nothing's wrong with our water, or the city's. If you go round spreading rumours you'll find yourself in trouble, Janus. Goddamn it, you ought to know better than that!'

'I didn't mean . . .' the Captain began.

'Cut it out, then,' her father said. He turned his back on him and muttered to Kit, 'Someone or other's been on the goddamn phone since eleven o'clock last night. Deny it, deny it, they don't believe a goddamn word.'

The Reverend Knight's car drew up beyond the group. Colonel Lindquist and Father Perreira leaned in to talk to the old couple in the back seat. Mrs Holmes was wearing a black cotton dress, short black cotton gloves, and a black straw hat with black and purple fruit on it, with no veil. She was holding a handkerchief to her face. The old man's coat was tight and high, like his collar. He sat upright in the car, nodding slowly to something the colonel was explaining to him.

Bill Lockman approached. She had not seen him since he had brought her home after her walk through the city. She thought, I should be embarrassed, but I'm not; to be honest, I'm glad to see him, because I'm frightened; I hope he walks close to me in the procession.

Bill said abruptly, 'Kit, I think you ought to stay back.'

She said, 'I can't.'

Bill burst out, 'I've a good mind to tell the Old Man he's got to order all the women to stay back. He's got no right to take them into what's waiting for us over there.'

She said, 'He must, Bill. That's what it's all about.' She had to speak louder over the stutter and throb of automobile engines starting up. The trailer trucks, full of enlisted men, began to grind out of the parking area. The haze was lifting, and the runway ran clear to the horizon, yellow striped and free of the mirage-lakes.

Lieutenant Jorgenson said, 'I just got back this morning, Bill. What's this I hear about the Spanish fighters flying a salute over the funeral?'

Bill said, 'After it, they're going to.'

'And the 52s are going out over the city during it?'

'Yes.'

'What's the Old Man trying to do? Show them we can wipe the dump off the map if they lay a finger on us?'

Her father said, 'Everyone for our car here? O.K. . . . Hop in.'

The De Soto glided off in its place in the long procession of trucks and cars, running down the straight streets between the concrete lamp standards towards the gate, the road, and the city. At the gate they turned left, and headed for the city. Kit peered out towards the north, straining her eyes for some glimpse of snow up there, praying that there would be, as a sign, coolness and light somewhere in the visible world. There was nothing, only the red earth and the rocks beyond, and the pale sky. Fear began to weigh more heavily on her.

She looked out of the back window, and saw the B-52s in the farthest distance, crawling down the taxi track, in line ahead like gorged vultures, slow and ungainly and heavy on the ground, huge wings flapping slowly. Faintly she heard the squeal of the motors. The first high tail was in position at the far end of the runway, two miles straight behind her, the long nose coming remorselessly round. The road dipped sharply into the Río Antiguo, and she turned forward.

The city rose slowly, close and harsh on its hill. From the bull-ring on the north to the humped remains of the Roman camp on the south, the afternoon sun pouring full on this western face, it blocked the horizon. From the flanks the grey and red and ochre stone climbed the central hill. Long flashes of sullen light glittered in the narrow windows, and the dome of the cathedral rode over all, red against the cloudless sky. At the summit of all, light glittered along the sword of Marco, Saint and Martyr.

The car rushed on. She tried to dry her hands, but the handkerchief was too small. The city waited, growing, climbing. The bridge opened before them. There stood the people, dark, massed, silent, waiting. They were in.

The centre of the Plaza de Mercado, where normally the stalls of fruit and vegetables and fish were set up, was being used as a parking area for the Americans' cars. On three sides the people waited, ten deep, in their dark clothes, their faded trousers and tattered and patched coats, all silent as scarecrows. On the fourth side, where the wasteland came to the edge of the Mercado, there were none of the people, only Americans and officials.

The hearse stood there beside the kerb. Four horses were harnessed to it. The horses wore tall black plumes, that nodded as they bowed and tossed their heads, and all their trappings were black and purple. The glass catafalque of the hearse contained two small wreaths, one of red and one of white carnations, but no casket or coffin.

Bill Lockman and Sergeant Olmbacher came up to her. Bill said, 'Pete and I are going to walk with you. Mike O'Leary's acting as pall-bearer in my place.'

She said, 'Thank you, Bill . . .' She added in a low voice, 'Don't forget my mother.'

Olmbacher said, 'I'll be right behind her. Don't worry.'

A narrow path opened among the people. Teetering on very high heels, her thin legs shining in cheap nylon stockings, her dress of black silk fitting tight across her stomach – Kit saw that she was pregnant – her face no more than a pale blur behind the thick veil, Dolores García, the mother of the dead boy, came slowly forward on the arm of her husband. A priest followed a step behind. Subdued blares and toots rose as bandsmen tested their instruments.

The priest said something to the Garcías. Even more slowly, with an obvious unwillingness, the Garcías came on towards the edge of the wasteland. Six people awaited them there: the Reverend Knight, Father Perriera, and a second Spanish priest; beyond these – Mr and Mrs Holmes, standing a foot apart, looking straight ahead; beyond them, alone – Colonel Lindquist. The second priest held a small oak casket in both hands, and the Reverend Knight a steel trowel.

Jacobo and Dolores García reached the group. Mr Holmes turned his head, spoke to his wife. Together they moved towards the Garcías.

Dolores García, holding tight to her husband's arm pushed

him round so that his body interposed between her and the Holmes, and their backs were turned. Mr Holmes took another pace towards the hostile backs, his face sad and one hand reaching out; but his wife touched him, and he stopped. He stood there a moment, looking at the backs of the Garcías, then patted his wife's hand and turned again to the wasteland.

The Spanish priest and the Reverend Knight paced slowly out together on to the wasteland, the priest carrying the casket and Knight the trowel. The two men knelt, and the priest opened the casket. The Reverend Knight took the trowel, and, digging firmly into the soil, put one scoop of earth into the casket and handed the trowel to the priest. The priest dug in his turn, poured the earth into the casket, and gently mixed it so that inside there was only one earth, indistinguishable. The Reverend Knight closed the casket, locked it, gave the key to the priest, and picked up the casket. The two men rose to their feet and paced back towards the Plaza. The Reverend Knight placed the casket inside the cafalque, between the wreaths.

The Medina Base brass band was forming up now in front of the statue of Luis Barrena, Mercado slum boy, like Pedro García, and famous nineteenth-century matador. Kit recognized familiar faces in the dress blues – the tall Negro who played a hot clarinet, the red-head who took the lead trumpet solos when most of these same men formed the Medina Cowboys, the man who had started the square dances going the Night of the Jota, now holding a pair of cymbals.

A deep roaring of jet engines grew in the west. The whining shriek neared and became louder. The shadow rushed across the Mercado and the silver shape, covering the sky, climbed slowly away to the east over the houses, eight thin black trails running back like rulers from the eight motors, sunlight sharp on metal tail and nose perspex and U.S.A.F. insignia, and the outline of the bomb bay doors clearly visible down the sides of the elongated belly.

Jacobo García and his wife and a priest took up position behind the hearse. The Holmeses and the Reverend Knight joined them, but the Garcías kept their heads averted. The four black horses nodded their black plumes and champed at their bits. Jacobo García's shiny blue suit was too small for him and his collar too tight, and the events of the past days and hours had passed beyond his capacities for observation, reaction, or grief. He was about twenty-eight, she thought, his face dark brown, his eyes blue. His big wrists and hands stuck out, hanging dumbly at his sides, as he stared in puzzlement at the crowd and the bands.

An acolyte bearing a tall crucifix, its lanyards held by two other boys, moved off at a stately pace up the right-hand roadway of the Paseo. The sycamore leaves were brown with dust, and the cathedral towered up at the top of the long rise. It would be so close by that wide direct route, and there would be room, and a sense of remoteness from the crowding, overhanging walls of the houses, and the crowding, surging people. She knew that that was why they were not going to go by that way.

The local band struck up with a loud clash of cymbals, and began to march in slow time. Clash ... clash ... clash ... and a heavy, ugly thudding from the brass drum. This was the same band that had assisted in degrading her at the '*fiesta*', the same men in the same cheap and ill-fitting uniforms of dark blue with yellow piping, caps still awry, still out of step, shambling forward ... and a single trumpet now, screaming a Moorish lament above the slow-paced brass harmonies.

César walked out of the crowd on the north side of the square. A policeman moved to stop him, then instead saluted. César reached her and said, 'I meant to be here earlier.'

Bill Lockman said, 'If you are a friend of the Garcías, the Spanish mourners are over there.' He pointed. 'If you're not, the procession's long enough already.'

César said, 'I do not know the Garcías, but I knew Lieutenant Holmes. I met him with you.'

'This group is Americans only,' Bill said.

'I know. But I will walk here.'

For a moment the two men faced each other in front of her. It was silly of them to fight, she thought. They both knew she was not an inanimate prize, to be carried off by the winner. Yet perhaps she was inanimate as far as they were concerned, for she could not imagine any action on her own part which would make her love for César practical, or turn the affection and reliance she felt for Bill into love. The Spanish band thudded and screamed in slow time up the Paseo. The U.S. Air Force Guard of Honour, that would fire the last salute, marched off with its two buglers on the flank.

César said 'I'm going to stay with her, at her side, the whole time.'

She said suddenly, 'Yes. Go on, Bill. You should be a pall-bearer. Please!'

273

Bill turned without a word and went to his position on the right side of the hearse. Twenty men of the Guild of San Fernando, Jacobo García's guild comrades and fellow labourers, began to move. The pall-bearers formed two single lines, six labourers in shiny suits on the left, three U.S. officers and three U.S. airmen on the right. The Holmeses and the Garcías were ready. Colonel Lindquist and Colonel Portuondo were ready, and behind them Lindquist's staff. Her father was there between Major Baun and Major Anstell. Here was her mother beside her, dabbing her nose. There were the mourners – a formless crowd of poorly dressed Spaniards, one hundred U.S. airmen in dress blue, summer-weight. Here around her were officers and sergeants and wives and daughters. Pete Olmbacher was at her heels, César at her right side, nearly touching her, looking as though he had not slept for many nights.

The slow thunder was again rising in the west, and again the unearthly scream rising under it. The crowd moved restlessly, where it stood thick along the fronts of the houses. The cathedral bells began to toll.

The tunnel-echoing roar faded. The coachman in black cocked-hat and faded black eighteenth-century frock-coat cracked his whip. The four horses leaned into the collars, their hoofs clattered, and the hearse began to move. The Holmeses and the Garcías began to move, then Colonel Linquist, then his staff . . . César touched her, and her feet moved – one, two . . . one, two . . . in time with the thud of the drum.

The crowd was moving, too. The wide sidewalks of the Paseo were already half full, and as the procession ground slowly forward it dragged all the people along with it. Thud – thud – thud – they shuffled along, crabbed little women in black, wearing bedroom slippers, young men, old men, middle-aged men, not many young women, no young children. A screaming jet noise filled the air; then the long, dying roar, and the eight black streaks barred the sky.

Thud – thud – thud – the procession entered the maw of the Calle Goya. The sweating police struggled to keep the crowd on the sidewalks, which had become narrow. They could not succeed, and the procession moved more slowly, no more than the central channel of a sluggish river hemmed between high stone banks. The fourth B-52 passed over.

Mrs Lindquist's small feet moved along just in front of her, step . . . step . . . step. Brassy music filled the canyon of the street from both directions now – behind, the Air Force band playing the 'Dead March' from *Saul*; in front the rough harmonies of the local band, the steady thud, and the single trumpet screaming in falling, quavering showers of notes. The music ran forward and back, and from side to side between the houses, the harmonies of one band, turned into discords by their union with the harmonies of the other, the tempo of the drums now falling together, now breaking into harsh syncopation, and that into momentary, lunatic dance rhythms by the added beat of the echoes. The fifth B-52 passed over.

She smelled flesh everywhere, and sweat, and skin, and the rankness of emotion. The insides of her thighs pressed stickily together as she took the endless slow steps, her gloves were wet, and the stones of the houses smelled of heat.

Her mother muttered, 'That Spanish band hasn't played a note in tune since it started – if you can call it a tune.'

Arenas now, the crowd denser, the sound louder and thicker, the smells hotter, more animal. The wall of an ugly building carried a brightly coloured *cartel* announcing an *enorme corrida de toros* for Friday, 22 August, starring the world-famed *diestros* Escobar, Miranda, and Aguirre. It would begin at five-thirty *en punto*. That was tomorrow. She glanced at César and saw him scanning the poster, a look of curious disbelief on his face. The sixth B-52 passed over, well to the north and behind them now, but still a man's voice rose from the crowd in a choking scream – 'Will it never end?'

Now Ibáñez, and the seventh and eighth B-52s. Now Alcalde, narrower still, climbing in cobbles between fifteenth-century tenements to the colonnaded bulk of the Ayuntamiento. The pace slowed still more as the horses leaned into the slope.

The ninth and last B-52 of SAC Mission Easy Fox tunnelled away into the sky. Above the conflict of the band a woman's voice, coming harsh and high and loud from a low balcony on the left of the street, ripped out a single phrase of tormented melody.

Woe, woe, woe, to humanity!

The sound struck like an arrow, the quavering notes splintering among the people and wounding all who heard. A barbed despair pierced Kit.

She reached for César's hand and gripped it fiercely. Another voice joined the first. The misery gouged more deeply in her, so that she could hardy understand what the wild, falling

275

voices cried. To right and left the crowd gasped as the arrows struck home.

'*Que se vayan!*' a man moaned. Away with them!

Woe woe to our children! The voices of the people rose in a soughing wave.

> *Woe to the pains of earth!*
> *A son has died, a mother dies, Spain dies!*

An old woman fell shrieking to her knees. The procession had stopped moving. The arrows of song fell thicker. The faces of the people became savage and fearful as they tried to escape. They blocked their ears, and pushed and shouted, but there was no escape.

The sounds turned into frenzy. All heads were turned in one direction, towards the back of the hearse. Between the people Kit saw Jacobo García vainly trying to hold his wife. Her veil hung round her face, ripped to tatters as she flung this way and that, and the bodice of her dress was torn. She shrieked, and threw out her arms, and tore again at her bodice, and seized her own hair and pulled her head wildly to and fro.

> *Life is a breath, pride is for ever!*

From both sides of the street the people surged forward. César held her tight, and Olmbacher moved up next to her mother.

> *Pray to the Virgin of Pilar,*
> *Pride of Aragon, Heart of Spain,*
> *Who stood unafraid before the invaders!*

César shouted across her at Olmbacher, 'Ready, Sergeant?'

Olmbacher said, 'Yes, sir.'

Mrs Holmes's straw hat seemed to rise above the heads of the crowd as she pushed Jacobo García aside, took both his wife's arms and held her tight. Mr Holmes's grey shock of hair was there, close to Jacobo García.

César's arm stiffened against Kit's chest, and threw her back. Something crashed to the cobbles just in front of Mrs Lindquist, and lay there, split in two, and raw. A brick.

César cried, 'Come on. Now!'

But there was no chance to move, for the people had formed

a tight wall, almost disciplined. They were packed, shoulder to shoulder, and now Kit saw the stones and the half bricks in their hands, and their eyes staring into her own. There was a man directly in front of César, on the left of the road. He was tall, thin, ragged. César's hand came up, level with the waist. 'You. Out of the way,' he said. She saw the blue barrel of the automatic in his hand, and the brick in the man's hand, the muscles in his neck, the sweat beaded in the stubble of his chin.

The toll of the cathedral bells rose to the surface as other sounds fell away, The man's head turned forward. So did Cesar's. Now her own.

Mr Holmes and Jacobo García and the priests and two or three policemen were standing huddled together at the tail of the hearse, like men who could not swim watching a sea rescue. They were watching Dolores García struggling in the arms of old Mrs Holmes.

Suddenly Dolores García's left hand broke free. It struck down, and her nails ripped a long triple gash down Mrs Holmes's face. The sigh of the crowd filled the street; then again the bells climbed out of silence. Dolores García stood, tensed, hand out like a claw to repeat what she had done. Mrs Holmes stepped forward, and again put her arms out. Dolores García struck again, but then she seemed to fall forward against Mrs Holmes, and Mrs Holmes's arm went round her, and Kit could see nothing more.

Out of the long silence, 'Forward!' a voice cried. 'Forward!'

Dolores García began to walk again, supported by the priest on one side and Mrs Holmes on the other. Jacobo walked, beside Mr Holmes. The whips cracked. The hearse began to move. The singers were firing their arrows again, again the trumpet blowing its tortured call.

> *Woe, woe, woe, to humanity!*
> *A son has died, a mother dies.*

To the right and left the people fell to their knees as the hearse reached them. The procession climbed the hill towards the cathedral, to the tolling of the bells and the discord of the bands, the tramp of feet and the stifled weeping of women.

> *Woe, woe, woe, for love is long,*
> *But life is short.*

277

Her heart lifted up in giant steps as sound and sights and emotion hammered into her that she belonged to a species that could reach this nobility. The intolerable, Castilian dignity of the Holmeses were hers. and the intolerable, universal agony of the young mother, all rising on a tide of love as the cymbals crashed before and behind. *Life is short, but love is long,* She turned to César, with eyes shining. His face was dead, and he stumbled like a sleepwalker beside her.

The voices of the *saeta* singers fell back as the procession passed out of Alcalde into the Plaza San Marco. The cathedral doors stood open all along the great south front. Armed police in grey and red flanked the steps and on the right stood a green and black row of the Guardia Civil. In the centre of the centre door the bishop waited in stole and mitre, shepherd's crook in hand. A pall-bearer was carrying the casket up the wide steps. The bishop raised his right hand in benediction. Dolores García's head was up as she slowly climbed the steps. Mrs Holmes at her side.

The bishop turned, and the white and purple went up into the blackness of the cathedral. All shape had gone from the procession now, and all difference between the procession and the people. It was a single mass of humanity that inched slowly up the steps, and she was part of it. Her mother was no longer with her, nor was César. Here and there she saw uniform caps and the taller heads of the American women above the black, but it was all one, all flowing uphill under the boom and crash of the bells. Down the Paseo, above the pruned trees and between the houses, the orange haze of evening lay like a flat sea across the plain to the west. The water towers of the base rose out of it, and the nearer edge of it bathed the stone feet of the city.

She entered the cathedral as the bells stoppd. The silence, and the act of passing under a high door, drew down a heavy velvet curtain between her senses and the events of which she was a part. It was a curtain of faded purple, on which, from time to time, certain images were projected in momentary clarity of emotion; as when Mr Holmes's halo of grey hair, passing up the centre of the nave, turned violet as the light from the rose window caught it; and the thousand candles whose tiny points of yellow light served to mark the dimensions of the darkness.

When the voices rose in antiphonal chant she moved back towards the doors. She had not been able to go far inside the

278

cathedral, and soon she was out again. She stood against a pillar near the corner of the south face, and leaned her head back against the cold stone. The fabric of the building shook as the organ played. For all its size, it had felt too small, so she had come out; and now the packed expanse of the Plaza San Marco was too small; even the city, even the encircling sea of the plain. Only the silent sky was big enough, and it hung distant and aloof from what was happening here.

The organ and the voices fell silent. Now they would be moving out, with the casket, to the cathedral plot on the north side. Now taking their places round the grave. Now lowering the casket into the opened earth. She heard the crackle of rifles firing blank, all volume and depth to the sound swallowed up by the stone and the mass of the cathedral and city. The bugles began the call of Taps.

Below the thin wail of the bugles she heard the rustle of air. It came from high, and all around. It grew in volume and deepened in pitch as the lamenting bugles cried. In the Plaza the people turned up their faces, until it was all white, all looking up to the sky. She looked up, and saw nine red darts, descending upon the earth in stepped-up echelon.

The first three flashed down, turning to silver as they came. For a second the needle noses and stubby wings pointed straight at her, then suddenly they pulled up and away and she saw the undersides as they passed over. The bugle call died.

A hollow boom rushed down from the sky. The air quaked, the cathedral lurched and settled back. The roaring echoes spread over the city and beyond.

The second flight of darts reached the foot of their dive, and pulled away.

No one moved in the Plaza, and no one made any sound but a deep sigh, each time, as three times the sonic crash boomed down from the sky.

The third flight of darts climbed red-tinted into the upper darkness, and vanished. Still the city stood silent, the only sound now the slow tinkling of broken glass falling out of a window across the street.

The people began to move. The voices rose. Already two men were ordering wine outside a bar opposite the Ayuntamiento. Near her a Guardia Civil shifted his position, and spoke to his comrade: 'They'll have to repair the rose window again if they do that very often.' They moved away, rifles slung.

Kit looked dazedly around. The street lamps were beginning

279

to glitter, and she was alone on the steps of the cathedral, soaked in sweat, shivering and exhausted. César, lonely and distraught, had vanished from her side nearly an hour ago. She hurried down the steps and ran as fast as she could up the Calle de los Obispos.

Book Three

PASODOBLE

CHAPTER 29

At the gate of the Casa Aguirre she slowed to a walk and tried to catch her breath. He would be in the library, if he was here. If not, she must find him, for he was lost.

A man was walking down the drive towards her, head bent and thin shoulders hunched. He looked up as she came close and she saw it was José the *apoderado,* the usual stub of dead black cigarette dangling from his lower lip. He looked tired and dispirited, a Times Square kid who'd failed to make a score. He muttered, 'Good evening, miss,' as he passed her.

A moment later she heard him call from behind her, 'Miss, wait!'

He came up quickly, took her arm and drew her round the corner of the house near the garage. The doors of the garage were open and the Hispano was in; César hadn't gone out in that, then.

José's face was again sharp as he threw down the stub of cigarette, lit another and began to draw it furiously as he talked. 'Miss, he's in trouble.'

'I know,' she said. 'I must get to him. What's happened? I don't understand.'

José said bitterly, 'He got shot in the credo.'

'But . . .' she began.

He waved the cigarette impatiently. 'Eh, how should you know? How old were you when Russia signed a pact with Hitler, in '39? He's in the first stage, for the moment. He won't do anything, yet. That's the trouble, because the Secret Police are going to come and get him.'

'What for? What's he done?'

'Plenty. But they'll charge him with what he didn't do – shooting at the bomber. And a lot more. I heard about it at four o'clock, and tried to get him to skip then . . . but he said he had to go to the funeral.'

281

She said, 'He came to walk beside me.'

'Yes,' José said. 'So you've lost him two hours, and the best chance he had. And now – he won't go, won't move, won't do anything. I waited here till he came back. For half an hour I've been trying to make him go . . . You love him, don't you?'

His small sharp eyes fixed on her with sudden intensity.

'Yes,' she said.

'Then make him go.'

She stood a moment, pulling her thoughts into focus. Time mattered; but not so much that she could afford to make a mistake through over-haste. José was speaking. 'It's going to be like what they did to Evaristo Sarmiento. He was in the same gang, the local leader. They're no more Communists than Franco is, but it's easy to pin that on a man, and they had a conspiracy all right.'

Kit walked out on to the drive. José hurried beside her. 'Do you want me to come with you?'

'No, thank you.'

'I'll wait here then . . . I'll give a warning if the police come, but I think we've got a few hours. I heard they'll come in the middle of the night . . .'

He faded back into the growing darkness against the side of the house. Kit reached the open french windows of the library and slipped in, closing them behind her.

César sat at his desk, upright, staring at the door. His head turned slowly as she entered, and slowly he rose to his feet. She went to him, and his arms came out with the same slowness and held her. Gradually his grip tightened, and she felt the increasing involvement of his muscles, and will. His head came down and he began to move across hers, weighing heavily on her as she turned her face up. He muttered in her ear, into her hair, '*Querida . . . querida mía . . . querida!*'

He broke free and stood a little distance from her. His face was flushed and unsteady. He pulled out a cigarette and lit it. He said, 'Fine funeral, wasn't it?'

She said 'I've seen José. Are you really in danger?'

He said, 'Yes . . . I seem to have made a small miscalculation about my own people.'

She said, 'Did you shoot at the B-52?'

'No. But of course I cannot prove it. They will probably give me a light sentence, perhaps only eighteen months. More as a lesson to the others than as a punishment. If I permit them to get me.'

282

He pulled the automatic from his pocket and looked at it. 'I could use this to good effect . . . all round,' he said.

She said, 'Put it away, César. Promise me you'll never use it. It isn't worth it.'

He put it back in his pocket. He said, 'On the other hand, why don't I let them get me? It will go against the grain, but why not? To fight would mean that there was something worth fighting for . . . I spit in the face of Spain. Do you know what I thought would happen at the funeral? That the people would reject all of you and everything you stood for – and that would include you personally, too, wouldn't it? So a part of me would have been destroyed anyway, because you're all I care for, humanly.'

She said, 'César, you can get away if you want to. There's time. We can find a way to do it.'

He went on speaking almost to himself, 'Do you remember coming here, so earnestly, determined to find out what was the root cause of the trouble between us? Well, you found it. Mission accomplished!'

'César . . .'

'What about you and me? How does the big answer fit us? . . . Do you love me? I love you more than I ever did.'

'Yes. César . . .'

'It's wonderful how quickly one can change. Evaristo became a Communist overnight. The same will happen to me. And do you know what the people will say, these people we've been trying to guide, these people whose spirit we thought we represented? They'll say, Aguirre a red? Well, I always suspected it.'

She said, 'Are you still a member of this – society?'

He said flatly, 'Me? I'm a member of nothing. Nothing at all.' He sat down.

She sat in the chair across the desk, opposite him, and laid her hand over his. 'César, do you really mean there's nothing to keep you here?'

He looked directly at her for the first time for some minutes. 'Nothing.'

She said, 'That's not true, but . . .'

She stopped, for her heart had begun to beat with a painful force. This was the moment of galvanic rebirth that she had expected and feared during the procession. Since she had carried out the penance he gave her, and they had immediately afterwards declared their love, love itself and the full aware-

283

ness of life had lain dormant under the force of the problems preventing fulfilment of them. Now the problems had been shattered by the explosion of this day's events.

She said, 'We'll go – you and I, together.'

His head was down, staring at a paper on his desk. It came up slowly. 'You and I?'

'Yes.'

'Where to?'

She spoke eagerly, 'France first. After that, wherever you want to go. America.'

He stood up. 'Why not?' He was speaking to himself. Again – 'Why not?' He seized her hand, 'And as soon as we are in France, we will be married?'

'Of course! ... Quick. We've got to go.' The need for action mounted; she could not stand still.

José slipped in, his eyes sharp. 'You've got to get a car. The Hispano won't do.'

She said, 'I'll get one.'

César said, 'But if you bring it here, the police will ...'

She said, 'I'll bring it to a rendezvous outside the city. Where?'

José said, 'Kilometre stone 3 on the Roldán road. Walking clothes. The only way out is by the smugglers' path to Roland's Breach.'

'When?'

'In an hour and a quarter. Nine o'clock, there ... The telephone will be tapped.'

'All right.' She hurried out of the room and along the passage. There was only one person to whom she could turn. She called the number and Bill came on at once. She said, 'Bill, I want to speak to Henry.'

After a moment he said, 'O.K. Shall I bring him in?'

'No. I must come out. I'll see him at the BOQ.'

'O.K.'

She hung up. Passport, money, papers were in the top right-hand drawer of the dressing-table in her bedroom at the base. Dad and Peggy were in town. She could leave a note for them. She lifted off the receiver once more and called a taxi. 'At once, please.'

'*Ahora mismo.* Five minutes, señora,' the voice answered.

César was at her elbow. He took her hand, crossed the hall and opened the door of the small drawing-room. Doña Teresa

284

was sewing in the corner, Bel reading on the sofa. César said, 'Mother . . , I'm leaving Spain, with Kit.'

*

She switched off the headlights and crawled forward more slowly for a quarter of a mile. The hump of the kilometre stone loomed up in the faint glow and she stopped the car. Instantly two dark shapes were there beside it. She slid across the seat and César got in. José's head appeared dimly silhouetted at the window. 'Good-bye, *maestro*.'

César said, 'Don't tell the management until tomorrow afternoon.'

José said. 'Of course not . . .'

'They're good bulls, aren't they?'

'Yes . . . Forget it, do you hear? They're nothing to do with you any more. I'll be all right. Of course I will. All of us.'

'Give my regards to Gordito and the rest . . .'

'You told me that, and about paying them off. Will you *go* now!

The Ford began to move.

César breathed out deeply. 'There! Look back, Kit look back at the lights of Medina. You won't see it again when we get round that hill ahead. Never again. I'm not going to look, not even in the mirror. I've done it . . . *You've* done it!'

'Not yet,' she said, and held his arm tight.

The exhaust burbled with a hollow jubilation against the stone parapets of a culvert. Then the sounds of motor and exhaust were lost in the empty plain. The Ford began to pick up speed. They came out of the broken ground and the lighted speedometer showed fifty miles an hour. The headlight beams flung ahead like arrows down the road, and the heat of the day's sun rose up to swirl about her in the wind of their passage.

Beside them the telegraph wires swooped and rose in the headlight beams. 'César,' she said suddenly, 'suppose they find out in Medina that you've gone – shouldn't we cut the telegraph wires?'

César hesitated. 'I suppose so. I don't know whether its really necessary.'

'We'd better,' she said. 'It would be awful to be stopped farther on. Besides, I must change. I didn't have time to at home.'

The car was slowing. César said, 'There's a place here some-where, where the wires are very low . . . Here.' The car stopped and César got out. She went into the back seat and struggled awkwardly out of girdle and stockings and dress and into the slacks and shirt. She heard the trunk opening, then a banging and twanging of wires, then the trunk closing. César returned, and glanced down at her in the door light. 'You look almost better in slacks,' he said. The Ford began to move again.

He seemed to be driving inordinately slowly, and she said, 'Shouldn't we go a little faster?'

The car accelerated and she said, 'What's at the end of the road?'

'Freedom!' he said lightly. Then – 'There's a carabinero post in a cave a little beyond the end of the road, past the last farmhouse. But we don't go that far. We leave the car in the woods about a mile short and go up a smugglers' path on to the plateau and over into France by Roland's Breach, the eastern one. The western's above the Ordesa.'

He was silent for a moment, then he said, 'Nothing behind us, everything in front. It is an extraordinary sensation. Like flying. Not in an aeroplane – free flight . . . I'm beginning to believe it. Do you love me?'

'You've asked me that before,' she said, turning to smile at him in the glow of the dash.

'I know,' he said. 'But if you should ever not love me, there'd be nothing in front either.'

She lit a cigarette nervously. She loved him, but there was no feeling of love now, only anxiety and determination. Over the frontier, it would be different.

Bill had been waiting outside the BOQ when she arrived in the taxi, to tell her the Ford was gassed up and the left blinker didn't work. She wanted to tell him that she thought more of him than she ever had, but impatience and worry kept pulling her away. It was likely that she would never see him again, but it had been impossible to tell him what she had learned about him, through what she had learned about herself. She could only say, 'I'm sorry. I'm so sorry,' and take the car and drive to the empty house to pick up some clothes. Sorry for what, she now thought painfully. That I can't have two men always, one to love and one to rely on? That seemed to be a common complaint of women. But while she had been talking to him for those few seconds, at the private acknowledgement that she would not see him again, a peculiar longing had possessed her. After all this time, and at that moment, with no diminution of her determination – her need – to escape with César . . . it was too much and she was ready to cry.

César said suddenly, 'Guardia Civil!'

At the farthest reach of the headlights the two men stood at the side of the road, the long green cloaks hanging straight from their shoulders and winged hats gleaming.

César said, 'They probably don't know me by sight, but . . .'

She flung herself across the seat against him, ripped open her shirt and put one arm around his neck. He understood at once, and as the car stopped his free hand slid round her and into the shirt, inside the bra. The Guardias were on her side, one coming forward, flashlight shining. She called out, in a blurred voice 'What's the matter, officer?'

Raising her head, she blocked the man's view of César's face and smiled blearily at him, her breasts half hanging over the top of the bra. 'Hi, there,' she mumbled. The Guardia's head snapped back, the flashlight flicked out, and the disgusted voice said *'Adelante!'*

César accelerated slowly. After a minute she slid away from him and did up her shirt. César said, 'I'm sorry . . .'

He began to drive noticeably faster. 'It's really going to happen,' he murmured.

A faint shimmer in the fender mirror caught her eye and she turned her head. Car headlights shone in the sky behind. 'There's a car back there,' she said.

César looked in his own mirror. 'I wonder. Is it the police . . . or just a traveller?'

She said, 'We can't afford to wait and find out. How far now?'

'Ten miles. We can make it.' His foot tramped down on the accelerator and the needle climbed steadily across round the dial. Sixty. Seventy.

'He's still there,' she said.

'Then it's the police. No one else would drive this speed on this road. I wish we had the Hispano . . .'

New lights flicked on the distance ahead, grew, separated, took shape as a truck behind dim sidelights, and slammed by with a hiccup of air and a jerk of the Ford's progress as the air slap pushed over the wheels. Nearly ninety miles an hour. She huddled down in the seat, willing herself not to be afraid. She had been faster than this with crazy boys, half drunk, once or twice. And they didn't have the muscles or reflexes or the

287

cold nerve of a matador. But César was no longer a matador, and didn't think like one. Her nails bit into her palms as the tyres screeched, the car flung to the left, some small animal flashed by on the right, César's wrist moving slightly, the car back on the track. Ninety-five. The headlights still followed, but she thought they had dropped back a little.

The engine screamed in frenzy. The wind howled, the metal rattled, the springs groaned, the tyres shrieked. Another light came out of the northern darkness, split in two, exploded past. The road began to climb with increasing steepness. The mountains rose black and steep on either side and the road surface deteriorated. The headlights followed remorselessly, falling back but following.

The smallest irregularities in the pavement sent the Ford hurtling back and forth. The straining tendons of César's hands stood out sharp in the dim light from the instruments.

'She can't hold the road much longer at this speed,' he shouted.

'Only three miles more!' she cried. 'Don't let them get us.'

A line of white posts screamed by in a single blur. A fan of light shone up over the prow of a hidden hill ahead. A car or truck was coming. The fan grew and spread, and the road rose. The arc of light burst over the brow of the hill and turned the windshield into a dusty blur. César's fierce application of the brakes threw her forward against the dash. The car bumped crazily as two wheels left the road and ran along the shoulder. The lights slammed by.

Looking back she saw them veer, swerve, and at last stop, pointed sideways across the narrow road. The headlights of the pursuers flung an arc in the sky a mile farther back. 'The truck's skidded across the road and stopped,' she cried exultantly.

Then they were plunging downhill, sharp right, left, right, in and out, climbing steep and hard with a torrent thundering among black pines under a black cliff to the right and pines to the left.

César braked sharply and the light switch clicked. The light went out and for a moment she could see nothing. The car bumped very slowly along a rough track between pine trees, in dense darkness.

Soon it stopped, and she jumped out. 'I'm ready,' she whispered. 'Which way?'

'That nice dress,' César said, peering over into the back seat.

'I suppose we've got to leave that behind as well as everything else. All right.'

He led into the forest, Kit followed the soft hiss of his footsteps over the pine needles. He said. 'The carabineros are to our right, about a mile and a half. Even if the police go straight to them, they're going to be over half an hour behind us –'

'If they follow us,' Kit said.

'They will,' he said positively. 'They can go faster than us – a little faster on the smugglers' path, quite a bit on the plateau. They'll gain on us.'

'Not on me,' she said defiantly. 'I'll keep my breath.'

The heat of the day still lingered in the forest, in the smell of the resin on the trunks; the sound of the river grew faint behind as the track steepened. She began to climb, moving one leg automatically past the other.

It was very dark, the crescent moon mostly hidden behind clouds and only occasionally riding out to cast a pale luminescence on the rock. The pines and the running water fell back, leaving nothing but the mental awareness of height and the knowledge that they were alone on the face of a vast perpendicular fall from darkness into darkness. There was no substance, except in that small piece immediately around them, which supported them. The invisible mass, as a whole, was far too steep to climb, but there were ledges on it, ten or fourteen inches wide, that climbed gradually across the face, turned and climbed again, slipped deep into the total darkness of a gully and emerged a hundred feet higher. The black wind moved slowly across the gulf and the rock, whispering in the grass and the clinging shrubs. She was glad it was not day, for now they came to a place where the path ended, and for fifty feet she was stepping only from iron bar to iron bar; but in the night there was nothing but darkness below and the same darkness above, and she thought, If I slip, I am likely to rush up as down. I might fall; or I might rush up in a breathless moment to the top of the cliff, and step off on to the short grass of the plateau.

Twice they stopped, listening but heard nothing of metal or of human movement; and that was the cliff. César silent in front of her, always ready with hand and weight when she needed him. They reached the plateau and rested a few minutes, without speaking, César's hand twined in hers, then went on again.

The frontier approached, the trackless way was hard, and

she was becoming tired. She set her mind to think, so that she would forget her weariness. Past that frontier ahead she would be César's wife. After all the dreaming about that state, and the yearning for it, now it was coming fast; and suddenly its shape was as dark and hidden as the shape of the peaks. The peaks at least were split by a gap for which they were heading, because César knew the way; but the other – she had no surety, for neither of them had been here before.

His back was broad and tall and vague just in front of her. It stopped moving and he said, 'There's the Breach.' Ahead a square gap showed in the blackness. A paler grey filled it, and rose on up to blend with the sky. A white blur ran along the lower line of the grey, and snow crunched under her shoes.

From behind metal clinked on stone. She seized César's hand and whispered fiercely, 'Run!' They ran up the last steep, over loose stones and patches of snow, her breath searing her lungs. The snow thickened imperceptibly into a carpet four inches deep where the winds had poured it evenly through the Breach, and a voice behind called *'Para!'* The black walls towered up on either side and a sharp crack split the air overhead. The sound of the shot boomed and echoed through the Breach, and under her feet the slope changed.

They began to move faster. Looking back once, she could see no one in the Breach, but it was dark up there. The wind blew stronger on this side, and warmer, and soon the brief snow fell back and they were again on stones and short grass.

César's voice rang out confidently now across the mountain. 'There's an open shelter about a thousand feet down. In a gully, at the top of a long pine wood. Our bridal suite!' Jubilantly he took her hand and began to run.

'It's all clear,' he cried. 'Nothing uneven, nothing to trip over!'

All her exhaustion had gone. Faster and faster they ran down the slope. The moon had set and it was again very dark. The wind blew scented out of France into her nostrils and soft on her cheek. They had left the uncompromising land behind them.

Breathless, they stopped, and she left the presence of small trees about her. César said, 'The shelter's there, across the clearing.' He called out, *'Hola! Qui est lá?'* . . . 'We've got it to ourselves.' He led her by the hand and said, 'Sit down there. I'll have a fire going in a minute.'

She listened to the hiss of pine needles, in the crack of dead twigs, and the pad of his feet as he moved to and fro in the black wood. A match scraped and the tiny bud of flame flared up in a blinding yellow aura of light, so that she shaded her eyes against it. The twigs began to crackle. The flames spread, and turned from orange to pale yellow.

He was crouched across the fire from her, looking at her with the smile etched into his ivory skin, now glowing and transparent. The pine trees clustered behind him and close over her head there was the ragged edge of the pine bough roof, and underneath her rows of cut branches, some green, some brown and sere from the days they had lain here. Beyond the stunted pines the darkness began.

César jumped up and went quickly about the wood, gathering bigger logs. He would disappear, and she would hear a heavy banging and sharp cracks, then he'd come slowly back, dragging logs and boughs, and then disappear again. She smoked a cigarette and waited calmly. It was done.

When the boughs were stacked high he threw himself down beside her. From his coat pocket he drew out a small silver flask, unscrewed the cap, and held it out to her. 'Cognac,' he said. 'Our wedding breakfast.'

She drank, then he in his turn. Carefully he rescrewed the cap, put the flask in his pocket, and lay on his back, his hands behind his head.

'Do you know what I was doing when that man shot at the B-52?' he said suddenly.

She shook her head.

'I was there, in the Río Antiguo, quite close to him. I was fighting with my pride – telling myself alternately that I couldn't live unless I went and apologized to you for what I'd said and done, and got you back ... and then that I was an Aguirre, and a man, and you'd have me on a string if I went to you.'

'I was feeling just the same,' she said gently. 'That sort of pride seems to be awfully dangerous.'

César said, 'I was born out of my place, or time. Father Francisco once told me that I could have been a jet pilot – or did he say I should have been? Of course he was right. Place or time was wrong for me, not both. I've spent my life trying to alter the time. Do you understand?'

'A little,' she said.

'Like Don Quixote, but very different. There I stood. like a lunatic, denying the movement of clocks and calendars – like

291

the English king Canute, ordering the tide to stop ... trying to live a life that was dead long before I was born, believing what every one else had stopped believing because it was stupid to believe it any more.'

'But the old things aren't dead,' she said carefully. 'I hope some of them never die.'

'The heart's dead,' César said eagerly. 'It's only the shell, the husk that you see – people wearing the *baturro* costume now and then, going to church at the proper time ... but the heart, what they *feel* like inside the costume, what they *feel* like inside the church – that's dead, because people have grown up, and become educated, and seen that what they were leaning on was nothing but superstitious nonsense, outworn tradition. Everyone except me and a few crackpots like me. Like the Gentlemen of Covadonga.'

'I know about them.'

'Crackpots, every one of them, and me the worst of all. But we could almost breathe life into the old way, when we were together ... until the funeral. Don Quixote Aguirre dropped dead there in the Calle del Alcalde, and I was left looking at the corpse, and wondering, Who is that, why in the name of common sense is he dressed up in that rig, in this century, and carrying that lance? ... No, I tried to change time, and couldn't. And now you've shown me the way to the only solution – change place.'

She said, 'I only wish we hadn't had to go like this ... running away.'

He said, 'But we did! Don't you see? The cage I've been in was so strong that it could only be broken by this kind of explosion, and you. Otherwise I'd still be there, waiting for them to build the cage round me again. Can't you see them, hammering the bars into place? Father Francisco saying. "You need this one to protect you from sin," and Ricardo, "This one's to protect you from licence," and my mother, "This one will guard your honour" ... and suddenly there I am, in a box, just as I was. No, dear, if we had left Spain slowly, reasonably, everything fixed and done in order, we wouldn't have left at all.'

She nodded. She understood, only too well.

Turning up her face, she invited him to kiss her and then, as a seal, opened her body to him, and fell asleep in the crook of his shoulder, but with her arm flung across him.

CHAPTER 30

Warmth was her first consciousness on awakening. Her eyes still closed, she wondered about it. The bedroom door was over there and the window there. No, she was at college, and the door was *there*.

She remembered that here there was no door, no college, no heavy toll of the cathedral bell. She was lying on a bed of pine boughs on the northern slope of the Pyrenees, a thousand feet below Roland's Breach, and she was warm. She had camped out many times as a child, and surely she should be cold and stiff. She remembered the love-making and the possessive warmth that had been her last memory. The warmth was still here. A miracle. She opened her eyes carefully.

The fire was enormous. Its flame stood five feet high and weaved like Oriental dancers in the centre of the clearing. The light jumped to the tops of the low pines, and she could see a long way into the wood, where it marched down the valley towards the farmed lands far below. Beyond the pines the firelight reddened the short grass, and above their conical tops the sky glowed. It was still night and she did not know how long she had slept.

César was bending over the fire, a stick in his hand. The end of the stick was alight, and he was poking at something in the heart of the fire. The depth of the bright red ash showed that the fire had been burning, as big as this for several hours. Something caught on the end of the stick and for a moment lifted up into full view higher in the flames. It was a heavy circlet of gold, sparkling with gems. It was a – The Armlet.

The effect of the fire and the physical reality of heat vanished. For a moment Kit lay paralysed with cold. Then she leaped up and ran to him. He heard her, and turned as she snatched the stick from his hand. The circlet glittered in a bed of ash under the flames. She scooped it out, scattering sparks and ash and pieces of burning wood, and threw it on to the grass ten feet off.

César methodically stamped out the blazes in the grass while she stood, the long stick burning in her hand, her breath coming in slow, terrified gasps.

César turned to her. 'I'm sorry you saw that. Otherwise, you'd never have known. Let me put it back in the fire now.'

He moved towards it and she cried, 'No!' and snatched it up. The pain leaped across her hand and she dropped it at once. 'Don't touch it!' she said. Her hand began to throb and she held it tight in the other, but the pain was nothing to the pulsing shock in her mind.

'*You* stole it?' she whispered.

'Evaristo and I,' he said. 'Stealing's not quite the right word. We didn't mean to keep it, or sell it.'

'But *why*?' she said.

He shrugged. 'The unknown soldier again. We thought people still cared. Let me melt it down.'

'No!' she said. 'How can you think of damaging it? It's ... a thousand years old!'

'Ah, my dearest, how American! Remember we're still in Europe. Spain's full of things a thousand years old, and all as useless as that Armlet.'

'We can't let it come to any harm,' she said.

'Why not? It's only an object of superstition. You don't believe in it, do you?'

'No,' she said. 'Not that it's holy or that it belonged to San Marco, but if it's valuable to a lot of people, we mustn't hurt it, or we'd be hurting them. It isn't as though they made human sacrifices to it.'

'They do,' César said. 'Sacrifices of liberty and free will.'

He sat down slowly beside the fire, staring into the leaping flames. She turned away and looked out beyond the clearing for guidance. A band of pale green ran along the eastern horizon, silhouetting the black slant of a far ridge. The peaks to the south stood out sharper against the faintest lightening, from black to purple, in the sky behind them over Spain.

She looked at the Armlet, and carefully touched it. It was almost cool. The fine edges were blurred where the gold had begun to melt round one half of the circle, and there were ugly black streaks on it; otherwise it was unharmed.

Now what? She could have understood if he had stolen it last night, after the funeral. But this was done over a year ago. How could the old César have done it? It was almost impossible to imagine the pressures that had made him, and the tortures he must have suffered since. These surely, and not any fear of arrest, were the true cause of his flight.

She thought slowly, Whatever way you looked, there was finally a perfectly clear Right, and only one.

'We must return it, darling,' she said when she was ready.

'How?' he said reasonably.

'We could mail it.'

'I suppose so. Packets are often lost or stolen in these parts.'

'We could give it to someone in France to take back to Medina. To the priest of a church.'

'The priest will have us arrested. He'll recognize it at once.'

She lifted her chin. 'I'll take it back.'

'Then you'll be arrested, and held as a hostage until I give myself up.'

'I wouldn't mind. They couldn't hold me for long, if you didn't come.'

'I cannot allow that. Spanish prisons are not like yours.'

She said, 'I don't really like any of those ideas. We'd still be branded as criminals.'

He said, 'Unless we destroy it. Abolish it for ever.'

'We can't do that . . . *Why* did you do it?'

'I've told you. Come, Kit, what's the matter with you? They've lost it, and it's a fraud, and you know it's a fraud and I know it's a fraud. If you won't let me melt it, let me bury it here. Then we'll see if another miracle will get it back to San Marco, the way it did in 1115.'

She moved her head impatiently. She said, 'What would happen if we went back to Spain?'

'I would be arrested and charged with the shooting at the bomber, probably a good deal more, too, and being a Red. And if I gave back the Armlet, with that too of course. You'd be deported.'

'They can't prove you shot at the B-52, can they?'

'No.'

'But you can prove that someone else did?'

'I doubt it. I know who did it. Rosario Lima's father.'

An irregular line of dim white fire was spreading along the top of the mountain wall to the south, and spilling down the slopes, where the snow lay. Colour had seeped into the world, so that the French grass was touched with green and Spain announced itself in the harsh red and black of its boundary cliffs.

She said, 'We can't live with this hanging over us. Nowhere. I mean, there's no *way* to live, either.'

295

He didn't answer and after a minute she insisted, 'Is there?'

Still he did not speak and she said, 'We've got to go back.'

She put out her hand to touch him, to show that she loved him and was his wife for better or for worse. And in truth now she did love him with all the old force, and the love spreading through her like daylight in the world.

He leaped to his feet, jerking her hand aside with the violence of his movement. 'Go back?' he cried passionately. 'You freed me, with your love, your determination that we should live free, and happy! Now you want me to go back. I can't! I won't. I'm free of Spain, free of superstition, free of the Church, free of the bulls and fear in the bull-ring, free of Europe, free of history . . . I'll do anything for you, except go back.'

'Then I'll go,' she said. 'Please let me!' She moved to snatch up the Armlet, but he was quicker, and it was in his hand, the golden glint coming from the firelight in the metal, for the sun had not risen.

'You're not going back alone,' he said.

Out of a deep and miserable conviction that there was no other course, she began again, 'Then we must go back together with the Armlet. Listen, dear . . . As soon as we get back I'll go to Colonel Lindquist, and tell him you didn't shoot at the B-52. I'll tell him who did –'

'No!' César interjected.

She rushed on, 'I'll tell him we're going to be married and you weren't Communists, and get him to speak to the bishop and the mayor and General Guzmán and whoever else can help. I know he'll do all he can for us, for me, because of the funeral.'

César's face was falling back into an exhausted calm, and she redoubled the urgency of her pleading.

'Nothing is as bad as it looks. Really it isn't. We've *got* to go back and get this done with. If you go to prison, I'll wait for you . . . I'll get lawyers, and you didn't steal, because you'll have returned it. That's not stealing, is it? Soon it'll all be over, and we can start again. We'll start this same way! Just like this, over the smugglers' path at night and through Roland's Breach and down to here, and make love just as we did last night, and wake up to this fire . . .'

He said, 'I'll never come back.'

She said, 'Of course you will! With me! Don't you want to marry me?'

'I have never wanted anything so much in my life, and never shall again,' he said. 'That's why I must ask you for the last time – don't make me go back.'

She said. 'There's absolutely no other way. For our name, for what we are going to be, and live as, we must . . .'

He said very gently, 'Very well, my love. You are as obstinate as a *baturra*, really, aren't you? Very well.'

'And you'll come back here with me?'

'If I'm free.'

'Promise.'

'I promise.'

Moving like a sleepwalker, he dug out earth with his hands and threw it on the fire. 'It might spread,' he said. 'But I don't think so. I have some biscuits. We can eat them as we go.'

'What's the hurry?' she asked. She twined her arms round his neck and kissed him on the lips, and whispered, 'I love you, I love you.'

'We must get on,' he said. 'So many things to do.'

They set out at once, and when they reached the Breach three quarters of an hour later, the sun rose. She stopped there and looked back over the slopes falling way into the generous bosom of France. César did not turn, and after a moment he said, 'Come on, Kit. The carabineros will be waiting for us.'

They crossed the plateau at a steady fast pace, and came to the edge of the cliffs. Kit held back and said, 'Let's rest a minute,' for the gulf of air flowed silently beneath, and the flat light cast long shadows from the toy pines across the miniature meadow, and at the doll's farmhouse down there. One wall of it was tinged pink by the sun, the other violet in the shade, and her head swam with the faint tremblings of the light. César said, still very gentle, 'It won't make it any better waiting here, my dearest. You can rest in the car.'

She started down the smuggler's path, on her right the wall of the cliff and on her left the three-thousand-foot fall to the valley floor, and dew shining in the yellow spikes of the clinging gorse tufts. The long path passed in a dream of fear, but the flat wood came at last and then quickly along the path, until César said, 'See. The loving arms are very long.'

She looked past him, and saw the Ford in a small clearing, and a man in a black habit sitting on the grass smoking a cigarette. Father Francisco got up as they approached and came forward with his arms outstretched. He embraced César warmly, and shook hands with Kit. 'It's nice to see you back,' he said. 'You look a little tired.'

César leaned wearily against the car, his head bowed. 'Where are the carabineros and the police? They were chasing us up here last night . . . They don't seem to have touched anything.'

'They were here when I came out a couple of hours ago,' Father Francisco said.

César said incuriously, 'How did you get out? Where's the Lambretta?'

The priest said, 'I came with Señor Aróstegui. Someone had cut the wires out here so he couldn't get hold of anyone to tell them to cancel the order for your arrest.'

'Why did they cancel it?' César asked uninterestedly.

'Pedro Lima confessed to shooting at the American bomber. I rather think that when Aróstegui told Madrid that, they decided not to press any of the other matters. Don Evaristo was enough, and, of course, you are a popular figure.'

'Well known, at least,' César said.

Kit shook his arm urgently. 'Then you're free, darling . . . of that.'

César nodded. He said, 'Why did Lima confess?'

Father Francisco said, 'An act of God. He was present at the funeral, with a brick in his pocket and in his heart the fixed intention of throwing it at the old Holmes couple. He didn't throw the brick, of course, but at midnight he did go to the police station and confess.'

Kit looked down at herself. The trousers were torn and soiled and the shirt rumpled and sweaty where she had slept in them. The voice of the torrent roared through the forest. She gathered her clothes from the back of the car and said, 'I'm going to wash and change.'

Across the motor road she climbed down the steep bank, and undressed quickly. Soon she must get back into those other clothes, the black funeral dress, the constricting girdle and the stockings, and return to Medina just as she had left it; but in the meantime she had been tired, and burned, and now naked. Kneeling by the stream she dashed water over her face and neck and breasts. Then she washed her feet, and sat until the numbness left her legs. She dressed quickly, her spirits rising as the tingling warmth spread through her face and body, and hurried back to the car.

No one spoke. She wondered whether César had said anything about the Armlet yet. Father Francisco waited till she had taken her place in front, then he climbed into the back. César got behind the wheel and backed the Ford down the forest path and on to the road.

They began to move faster. She leaned back. She must think. If César was not to be charged with shooting at the B-52 there was only the Armlet, and they were bringing it back. What kind of punishment would they give him for that? He'd have to pay to have it repaired ... a fine as well, perhaps ... a very big fine ... prison? It was possible, but ... but ...

She awoke with a start to see the cathedral dome towering out of the houses on the hill close ahead. There was an air of greeting in the Calle de los Obispos in the bright sun of mid-day, and now she could not sit still, in her anxiety to have it all done and finished with, so that they could turn again to the north, and freedom, and love.

At the front door of the Casa Aguirre the Lambretta was parked. Father Francisco hurried out and said, 'Thank you, César. Well, I must go. I shall be seeing you.'

César said, 'Wait, Father! I have something ...'

The priest was on the Lambretta, shouting above the racket of the little motor, 'Sorry, César. Urgent!' He roared off at high speed, kicking up gravel behind him.

César watched till he had disappeared, then turned and walked up the steps. Octavio was in the doorway. 'Good morning, señorita. Good morning, señorito. The lady your mother is in the small drawing-room, with your sister.'

Kit went slowly into the house, wondering. The strangeness of last night's departure was still here, and now they had returned from a honeymoon, or a week-end in San Sebastián, and Doña Teresa would hug her and say, Did you have a good time, how was the weather?

It was not quite like that in the drawing-room, for Doña Teresa and Bel were on their feet, both crying, and Pete Olmbacher was there.

Doña Teresa took out a handkerchief and carefully dried her eyes. Then she said, 'The police came quite soon after you left.'

'One lot rushed off and the rest searched everywhere!' Bel cried excitedly. 'They turned the whole house upside down!'

César was staring at Olmbacher. Doña Teresa said, 'The sergeant has ten days' leave, and I invited him to spend them here. If he is to marry Bel, it is time I made his acquaintance. And then, just after midnight, Father Francisco came. I told

him that you'd *said* you wouldn't be returning, but he said –
he was standing there looking out of the window – he said,
"Don't misjudge that young lady. She would call this absurd,
but she reminds me of another heretic, the greatest of all of
them, Martin Luther, who said, 'It is neither safe nor prudent
to do aught against conscience. Here stand I – I cannot do
otherwise. God help me. Amen.' . . . They will be back." Then
he left.'

After a long silence César said, 'Mother, I must go to the
cathedral.'

'Yes,' she said.

He said, 'Mother, I . . .'

She said, 'It is between you and Holy Church, who is also
your Mother. I will be here when you come back.'

César got up and walked out of the room, Kit following
close. She closed the drawing-room door behind them and said
urgently, 'Why do you have to go to the cathedral? You could
have given the Armlet to Father Francisco and just waited.
Now . . . let's find him and give it to him.'

César said, 'He will be in the cathedral for the Mass of
Intercession, the official beginning of the *fiesta* of San Marco.
. . . Should you not tell your parents you're back? Won't they
be worrying about you?'

For a moment she stared at him, then turned to the telephone. One thing at a time. And he was right about telling her
father and mother; she must not hurt anyone if she could help
it.

César stood beside her, staring out of the open front door
while she tried to get her father's house. There was no answer,
so she rang Colonel Lindquist's office. The even voice came
on – 'Lindquist.'

'Lindy, it's Kit . . . I'm back.'

'Oh. What happened?' His tone was non-committal.

She said, 'I can't tell you yet, but we had to come back. I'm
going to the cathedral now with César, but then we may be
leaving again –'

'You may?' he said. 'Haven't you made up your mind?'

'Oh, Lindy,' she cried, 'I have, but . . . you'll hear soon . . .
I can't get Dad or Peggy.'

'They've gone to France looking for you, to tell you all is
forgiven if you'll just come back and take a little more time to
decide.' She leaned her head against the wall miserably. His
voice was gentler when he spoke again, 'They're going to call

300

from Pau or Lourdes in an hour. I'll tell them, and they'll be back tonight. Anything I can do for you, Kit?'

'Not yet,' she said. 'Not now. Thank you.'

She hung up. César said, 'I think we'd better go to the cathedral now.'

José the *apoderado* walked in, pulling furiously at a cigarette. 'So it's true,' he said. His bloodshot eyes turned to Kit. 'Why did you let him come back?' Without waiting for an answer he whirled on César. 'You ... *sheep*! Well, your suit's in good condition, the swords are sharp, and I haven't told the management yet. Now I'll get the girl to make up your bed in the library where I can see you aren't disturbed. Even so you won't get more than two or three hours' sleep. Come along.'

César said ' I have a little job I must do first.'

José exploded, 'Little job! Now that you're back, you're back! You're a matador, damn you. This is the most important pairing of bulls you'll ever get. The first is a vicious, squinting mountain of a bastard, as high as a church and wide as a barn. They'll give you both ears and the tail if you just manage to walk out of the ring alive. The second is the most perfect animal I've ever seen – noble, brave, direct! With him, you can make an afternoon such as no one's seen since Manolete. But by God, if you don't match him they'll boo you from here to Ronda. By God, they'll kill you, and I'll be with them! And look at you – out on your feet! Come along and sleep now.'

César said gently, 'I am truly sorry, José, but I must go to the cathedral.'

CHAPTER 31

They climbed the cathedral steps, among the cooing pigeons, against a rising current of chanted music. As soon as they had passed from the sunlight of the Plaza into the gloom inside, he said, 'Stay here.'

He went forward into the darkness. The singing sounded fainter in here, somewhere high in the roof and a long way off. Her eyes pressed wide to catch the light, she saw his dim shape pause at the font, dip his fingers into the water, make the sign of the Cross on forehead and chest, and go forward again. Then

301

she lost sight of him as the cathedral and its occupants grew clearer and her vision spread to encompass it all.

The nave was full, and all the chairs occupied. The people seemed to be in blocks, rows of khaki here, rows of blue there, then a block of women, all in black, all the black mantillas lacing the pattern of their hair, rows of men in dark suits near the front, more uniforms, men in cutaways and striped trousers. . . . The mayor's four heralds in their tabards knelt on the stone behind the last row of chairs, among many women in plain dresses of black cotton, and there were a dozen U.S. airmen in uniform in a row near the back.

Her eye rose. Beyond the people the steps climbed in ordered sequence, red carpeted, to the high altar. Rows of candles flickered on it, and in the tall candelabra leading up to it. On the right a hundred candles burned in the shrine of San Marco, their light throwing a strong golden colour into the arched roof to the alcove, so that it made a shining semicircular halo of gold above the image of the Saint. On the left side of the altar steps there was a throne, and sitting in it a small old man wearing a scarlet skull cap and crimson robes. His hands rested on the arms of the throne, immobile, and the light from a ruby ring on his finger glowed steadily into her eye.

There was the focus of the cathedral – the high altar, flanked on one side by the lighted arch and the kneeling saint, on the other by the ornate throne and the crimson bishop, a single interlocked trinity of white and red and gold stretching across the far end of the view, above and beyond the people, who showed their backs to her in anonymity.

The singing stopped and subtly the focus changed, narrowing down from the far, wide brightness, and coming closer and concentrating on a man going slowly forward up the centre aisle towards the steps and the light. Now she saw nothing but César, and in the congregation the heads turned, by rows as he passed, until they too were concentrated on him, and the bishop's head had slowly turned, and the priest conducting the service was watching him.

At the foot of the altar steps he stopped. The bishop's ring flashed, and Father Francisco came towards César from a hidden place behind the bishop's throne. There was no sound at all in the cathedral as César held out both hands towards the young priest, his friend. Then César retreated a few paces, bowed to the High Altar, and knelt among the front row of worshippers. Father Francisco climbed steadily towards the

302

alcove of the saint, the golden circlet resting on his right palm, and that supported by his left.

When he reached the alcove he loosed the inner chain, and went in to fasten the Armlet in its place.

The bishop's ruby ring flashed again, and the officiating priest continued the service.

The cathedral began to stir. As yesterday in the streets of the Barrio, the people seemed to give emotion to the stone and the stone back to the people. A murmur of indistinguishable sound rose from the massed congregation in the nave, and climbed up the dusty beams of coloured light and out through the fretted windows, and hummed in the farthest, darkest corners of the chapels around the outer walls and in the purple-black vault of the roof. Like the bugles against the supersonic thunder the priest's voice shrank to a thin, small piping. The cathedral stones quaked to movement as people hurried past and out, to shout from the steps and make a confused roar in which she distinguished only the word *Brazalette* – Armlet. Now people began to hurry in, too. The stone became fragile as the walls of a tent, and only at the centre of the tent, where César knelt, was there stillness and silence. Around and in and out the people flowed, but among the movement black-dressed women of the Barrio knelt like rocks in the tide, their faces turned towards the beatitude.

She heard the same word over and over again, *Brazalete* ... *Brazalete* ... Then with it, the hissing syllables of *César*, and the curt roll of *Aguirre*. Looking back through the door between the people she saw that the Plaza was already half full, and more people were pouring into it. The sounds of voices, of shouts, of chanting, and whispers, and cries broke over her from both sides, gradually submerging her.

The service ended. The bishop rose from his throne and left the cathedral, followed by half a dozen priests. Everyone stood up in the nave, and for a moment began to surge in towards César; but Father Francisco come to him first, and César followed him, head raised, across the foot of the altar and out by the way that the bishop had taken..

The mayor's heralds passed her on their way out of the main doors, and the mayor with a heavy chain round his neck, and the corporation and deputy mayors in their cutaways, and Spanish generals and colonels with blue and red sashes, and Americans, and Spanish soldiers, and rich women, and the women of the Barrio.

The high bells were ringing, and from farther off came the boom of irregular, clustered explosions. All sound came from outside now. She closed her eyes, and leaned back against the stone.

'Kit – come with me please.'

She opened her eyes and followed Father Francisco, past the font where the reflection of the rose window hung in perfect miniature in the calm water, along the north wall, until Father Francisco stopped before a heavy, closed door. Opening it, he said gravely, 'Please go in.'

It was a small room, almost bare of furniture, lit by two windows on one side. Through the windows she could see the cloisters of the cathedral museum, a corner of the Plot with its clustered head stones, and the stone walk that ran towards the bishop's palace across the street. The bishop was standing near the middle of the room, César to one side, his back to the windows. Father Francisco had not entered with her, and when the heavy door closed behind her, they were alone.

The bishop said, 'Daughter, do you know the airman Sergeant Olmbacher, who wishes to marry Isabel de Aguirre?'

Kit stared at him dumbly. Olmbacher? Isabel? Who was Isabel? Had they stolen the Armlet?

She started, and whispered, 'Yes.'

'Father Perreira tells me that he is a good and upright man. Do you affirm this from your own knowledge?'

'Yes,' she said.

The bishop half turned towards César. 'My son, it is against the policy of Holy Church to put obstacles in the way of marriages, in the Faith, between persons who are old enough to know their own minds. Do you withdraw your objections to the marriage?'

César said in a low voice, 'I have already done so, my lord. I saw that they were in love with each other.'

The bishop said, 'That would have no meaning if the proposed marriage were not otherwise sanctioned by Holy Church.'

César bowed his head. Kit went close to him and took his hand, and held it tight so that they faced the bishop together.

The bishop's eyes flickered to hers, and held them. 'This man, César Aguirre, has told me that he wishes to marry you. Do you wish to marry him?'

She cleared her throat in order that she could answer very clearly. 'Yes.'

'Are you now willing to join the True Communion, with a

whole heart and mind? If not, do you think you might be willing to do so in the near future?'

For one moment the word would not come. The other hovered on her tongue, her heart beat loudly, and César's hand was cold in hers.

She said, 'No.'

The bishop turned to César. 'The Church will not countenance this marriage.'

César said, 'But, my lord, I have asked her to marry me, and she has accepted. I have promised.'

The bishop's old eyes wandered almost pityingly to her, and back again to César. 'You are well aware that an undertaking to marry a dissident has no canonical meaning. Nor has the so-called civil marriage which is permitted in some countries, since marriage is not an earthly contract but a divine sacrament. That is no more than concubinage, and mortal sin. Unless this young woman changes her views, you may not marry her inside the Church. That is, you may not marry her.'

Kit said heatedly, 'But . . .'

The bishop said, 'That is all, my son.'

César said in a low voice, 'Come on, dear . . .' Quickly dropping to one knee, he kissed the ring on the bishop's finger, as the bishop negligently raised his hand.

Outside the door Father Francisco had gone, but Pete Olmbacher was waiting for them.

'I've got my car outside, in Obispos . . .' he begun, but Kit turned quickly to César. 'What are they going to do? What happened?'

César said, 'I confessed to Father Francisco.' He stopped.

She said, 'Yes, yes, then –?'

'He gave me a religious penance.'

'And the bishop?'

'I told him, after confession.'

'But the police, what are they going to do?'

'Nothing.'

'Nothing! You mean . . . we're free? Nothing's going to happen at all? It's unbelievable . . . it's too wonderful for words, I told you nothing's as bad as it seems, didn't I? We can go right back at once . . .'

César said gently, 'We'd better go to the house now.'

'Yes,' she said, laughing. 'Get something to eat, and go!'

Outside, exploding rockets made a continuous barrage of cracks and thuds, The sky to the south, where they were being

F.R.–L

fired from the mounds of the Roman camp, prickled with small vivid flashes, and then little puffs of black smoke that quickly dissolved in the light wind. The street was full of people, but in a moment they were in the car, and the car was moving. The hubbub of voices went with them, and the frieze of faces peering into the car, and the thunder of the joyful explosions celebrating a long-past martyrdom.

As they turned into the drive she spoke quickly. 'Pete, stop outside the library, please. And ask them not to disturb us.'

In the opened french windows she stopped, confounded. The suit of lights lay in black and gold on the desk, the pink stockings on top, the black slippers on the floor below, on one side the false queue of the pigtail and on the other the black *montera*. The swords in their cases stood propped against the edge of the fireplace, the dress cape hung at full length from over the corner of the bookcase and three *muletas*, wrapped round their sticks, stood beside the swords.

She said, 'This – this is impossible, César. You're not really going to fight this afternoon, are you?'

He said, 'I must, now that I'm here, and able to.' He glanced at the clock on the mantel. 'It's only two hours.'

She said, 'You haven't had more than three hours' sleep in two days. You don't *want* to kill yourself, do you?'

'No,' he said quickly. 'I want to live.'

'Then don't be silly.'

'But I must, Kit.'

His eyes were dull with fatigue and he sat down suddenly on the edge of the desk, crushing the brocaded jacket of the suit of lights.

He said, 'It's not fair to the public, who have paid to see me.'

She said, 'The public? The people of Medina?' Her voice rose, in spite of herself. 'What do you think they're going to do to you now? We've got to get away.' He shook his head. She cried, 'I ... I'll have the authorities declare you're medically unfit! I'll call the doctor ...'

'Please,' he said. 'That won't help. No one will stop a matador going into the ring, even if he's dying. It's only the bull that has to have strength.'

She clenched her hands until the nails bit. She could hit him; she might take a sword and wound him so that he couldn't fight ...

She gave in suddenly. It would somehow be all right. It would have to be. She said 'All right ... I'll have the car and everything ready so that we can go immediately afterwards.'

'If I'm able,' he said.

'You *are* going to try to get yourself killed,' she cried. 'That
... that would be cowardly!'

'And sinful,' César said. 'No, I'm not going to try to.'

She began to cry. 'You, you w-were s-so happy to be free!'

He stepped forward and his arms went round her. She could
feel the agonized silent sobbing in his chest. She began to
break down totally under the wordless, overwhelming sincerity
of his pain.

There was a knock on the door-but she had neither the
strength nor the will to leave the circle of his arms. She heard
José's voice behind her. 'Come, little miss. He's got to rest. You
don't want him to be hurt, do you?'

His sharp voice was unexpectedly comforting and she let
him guide her out of the room. He was calling, 'Someone!
Come, please.' Then it was Juana's thin arms round her, and
Eloísa's voice murmuring. 'There, there, come along and lie
down in the drawing-room. Or would you like to go to your
old room? And I'll bring you some cognac? An aspirin?' And
then Bel the other side, 'The small drawing-room ... There.
There.' And Doña Teresa's hand cool against her forehead,
and she was lying on the sofa. Three aspirins, a sip of water.

'When do we leave for the *corrida*?' she asked, bracing herself to scream at them for they would say she mustn't go, she
was worn out, overwrought.

Doña Teresa's calm voice said, 'A quarter to five, punctually. We will come to you in good time. We will all be within
call if you want us.'

Then the door closed and she could open her eyes. The curtains were drawn and the light filtering through them was
tinged red. The ceiling was smooth, like the swept sand of
the arena, and the glow of blood was in it. Here and there
round the perimeter of vision bright colours sparkled in painting, ornament, and piece of furniture. Outside the house, and
the city, were full of people, tier to tier, all knowing, all watching. She was one of them, alone here in the front row, waiting.

CHAPTER 32

César took his place in the front row of the procession, between the other two matadors. He shook hands formally with them, in turn – Escobar on his left and Miranda on his right. It would depend on the bulls, as usual. Escobar who had been great half a dozen years ago, had announced his intention of retiring at the end of the season. Miranda was only a week senior to himself, but he could be very good too.

The trumpet sounded, the band began to play and the heralds urged their horses into a walk. The three matadors, without looking round or down, making no attempt to keep in step with each other or the band, strode slowly out on to the hot sand. César got the feel of it through the thin slippers in the first ten paces. It was a little softer than last time, but good, the footing firm everywhere, except a patch of something softer in front of Section 7, where the ring servants had spread too much fresh sand and not raked it absolutely even with the texture of the rest of the ring. It was rare for a bull to choose that section to fight out of, but it would have to be remembered. The crowd rose tier on tier, and round and round, and the band was playing. Above the president's box the upper row of the Moorish arches made the familiar pattern of cut-outs in brown-red paper against a backdrop of blue.

He knew he was too tired to fight but information kept trickling in through the senses that would not sleep. It was hot, the air light and dry, as it nearly always was in Aragon during the bull season. The flags of Spain and Medina flying over the main entrance showed a light breeze from the shady towards the sunny side; but that was up there. There was almost nothing at sand level. He could see no faintest stir of the grains behind the hoofs of the horses, and it was dry enough to rise an inch or two before settling, if there had been any wind. At waist level, also nothing – yet.

He felt the style of his stride subtly changing. He had been away from the bulls six weeks, and had started walking almost as he walked in the street. The mesmeric, interlocking circles of sand and stone and arch, like an endlessly repeated chant, had done their work. The voice of the crowd surged away to the borders of hearing, the dress cape bound and held him into the shape of a matador, and he moved like the others, with slow strides, stiff legged and insolent.

He stepped in front of the president's box and looked up, put his hand to his *montera*, and as he bowed slowly pressed it more firmly on to his head.

Now he was walking among his own men towards Section 3, letting the cape fall out of its careful folds, gathering it in his right hand. He saw her blonde head, and noticed that she was not wearing dark glasses. He would tell her, when he threw the cape up to her. Her eyes would be sore before the afternoon was out, and she'd have a headache tonight.

Several places beyond her, in the front row of Section 4, a movement caught his eye. Two people were standing up, looking at him and clapping loudly . . . a middle-aged man in a striped suit of the cheapest cloth, and a boy of about fifteen. Of course – Juan Cuervo of Saldavega, and his son, They'd guided him to a magnificent chamois above Benasque last fall, and he'd promised them the cape next time they came to a *corrida.*

He hesitated only a second; then walked on past Kit and, bowing slightly before the man and the boy, threw up his cape to them. The boy caught it with a cry of pleasure, shouting down, 'Thank you, sir, oh thank you!' The man turned in his place and beamed on all around him, his hands spread wide. A leather wine bottle hung from his shoulder and there was a basket of chickens at his feet. As César turned away he was offering his neighbours drinks from the bottle.

Duty, César thought. And correctitude. He could have loved her twice as much if that were possible, and still he would have had to do this. Well, she would understand, or she would not. If she did, she would understand much more, whatever decision finally flowered in the sand this afternoon.

José was beside him. 'Do you want a Benzedrine? It'll have time to take effect before your first comes in.'

He shook his head. He had fought before when almost as physically tired as he was now. Being a bullfighter on principle had meant living up to the traditions all the way, and pretending that was his real desire. Dully he remembered four successive *novilladas* with no more sleep than catnaps in a car jolting along intolerable roads, an assortment of drunken whores in and out of his bed, a fourteen-hour traditional drinking bout afterwards, and then an assignation with a duchess,

He would fight, because there was strength dormant somewhere in his muscles, and his nerves would draw on it. Meanwhile, the exhaustion served to deaden the usual fear. Even the Armlet had helped there, and he had not been expected to talk lightly with José, and crack cynical jokes with Gordito and García about the quality of the horses provided for them.

He looked up summoning a smile. They were sitting in their own places, the ones he owned as a member of the bull ring syndicate – front row, shade, Section 3. In a row they sat – his mother, Kit, Bel, and Olmbacher. Kit was looking at him, and he turned away. He had forgotten to tell her about the glasses. Marcia was there, in her usual place. There was Father Francisco, looking anxious under the wide black hat ... Plenty of Americans, just as different with their cameras and bright shirts, but somehow no longer isolated by the differences. Lockman would be here somewhere. He hated the spectacle and he hated him, César. Perhaps at this moment he thought he hated Kit, but he would be here.

The heralds were galloping round the arena, their black cloaks flying and the sand hurtling out from under their horses' hoofs. There were the keys, catching the sun as they arched down from the president's box ... caught cleanly and the people roaring. The people were the enemy of the matador. He looked curiously round at the ranked tiers of them. A full house, eight thousand of his fellow *baturros*, come to sit in judgement on him; and execute sentence?'

If she could know what was in his thoughts she would think that he had not made up his mind; but those words gave a wrong notion, for his personality was standing aside from the struggle, merely watching it, as the people would soon be watching him. The struggle was between spiritual forces that had their own life, and it was going on now, and would continue through the afternoon. Before the last bull died, some decision would surely be reached, and he could only pray that it would not be his own death. He needed to live – to make amends to her, or expiation to the Faith.

He was ready. He threw her a last look, then the trumpet sounded, and Escobar's first bull came out of the pen. His peons began the cape work. The animal was sluggish, and did not favour either horn. It should suit Escobar's purposeful, ugly determination well enough. Watching it from a *burladero* as Escobar gave it a few passes with the fighting cape, he thought, it is very sluggish but in its own way as determined as Escobar himself. Once it felt the mass of the picador's horse against its horn, it would not easily be drawn away in a *quite*.

The picador was in and giving the bull a severe punishment. The crowd was whistling. Third pic, his turn to make the *quite*. He'd have to get very close, and straight in front. The bull wouldn't charge until the picador shouted at it. The crowd heard the picador's shout, and the whistling rose to a frenzy of disapproval, but César noted only that the bull's sense of hearing was acute, and that it responded instantly to the human voice. Then he was there, by the horse's head, the cerise-and-yellow cape spread in his hands, as the bull momentarily broke away from the lance point. Now. He stepped forward, the cape thrown in a great fold before him, and called in a low voice, 'Ah, there!' The bull turned and charged him at once. He drew it away from the horse in a series of *verónicas*. Far enough now. He twined the cape round him in a *chicuelina*, turning the bull so sharply that it stopped in its tracks. He folded the cape over his arm and walked quietly towards the barrier.

There was something strange. Walking back to the barrier from a *quite* as good as that, executed with skill and knowledge and leaving the bull exactly where it should be by the rules, you walked into something that flowed warming over and past you. Noise, the applause of the people. Today, nothing. The judgement would be silent.

The *banderillas* went in, and Escobar made his dedication to the president. He was treating the animal with caution now, far more than it deserved, and the crowd was yelling at him. Well, he had saved up a lot of money, and he knew enough tricks to make it look passable, and the bull was not worthy of much better. He killed reasonably quickly and the trumpets sounded.

In the *callejón* César picked up a water jug and filled his mouth. The boy from Saldavega called down to him, 'Well done, sir! The best *quite* I've ever seen.' César spurted the water over the barrier on to the sand and nodded. How many *corridas* have you seen then, he wondered. Three? Five?

Miranda's bull now. César watched it and tried to be as intent as before; but his own was next, and he could feel Kit's presence more and more strongly. The afternoon light would be soft in her hair and if he turned he would meet the direct look

311

of her hazel eyes, unguarded by sun glasses, at only twenty feet range, and he would not be able to fight.

His own first bull . . . that was the monster José talked about on the way here in the Hispano. 'Don't worry about doing it right. That's all different now. These bastards want to see you killed, do you understand? They just want to see you twirling round on the horn with twelve inches of it in your guts. Spite them, *maestro*! Kill that first bastard any way you can, as quickly as you can . . .'

Miranda's *quite* was good. Now his own. Not so good this time, because the bull gave him no chance. It wanted to get away from the pic, and his *quite* amounted to only giving it an excuse to do so. Still no sound from the crowd whenever he was at work. A quick efficient kill, one ear for Miranda, a lot of shouting and clapping, a few leather bottles hurtling through the air, and the trumpet sounded.

The people hold their silence as the bull trots heavily into the ring and looks around. Very large, tall: wide horns, left one infinitesimally turned in. Gitano trails his cape from a *burladero* in Section 1 to one in Section 7. The animal attacks. Seems to favour right horn. Quicker turn and horn riposte than you'd expect from that size.

Now Ruiz from 8 to 2, the other direction. Still favours the right horn. Approaches slowly, commits itself to the actual charge from very close. Same quick turn and riposte. Now Modesto in Section 4. Forelegs probably not strong enough to last the fight without weakening. That will make him charge shorter still, and the horn ripostes will come lower because the legs won't have the power to lift the head, apart from the tiring of the tossing muscle. He has settled into Section 8, five yards out, his back to the barrier.

He walked slowly into the arena, the cape spread, and began a series of *verónicas*.

Now he fought by what he had learned and practised. He passed the bull closer on the left than on the right, because it hooked to the right and because its left horn was turned in, but the actual execution of the passes had become instinct, and the linking of them into a pattern was not a matter for thought. He was here, and the bull there. It came slow for a few paces, and suddenly heaved by. As it passed under his hands he could feel the change of its weight; and now it was there, and he here, and the cape had to be so, and it was.

312

The trumpet sounded and the picadors were in the ring. He walked back to a *burladero*, the crowd absolutely silent, even the man and boy from Saldavega. It was not fear of their neighbours that prevented them from cheering him he knew, but a feeling that he would rather they did not, because it would embarrass him to have allies. Perfectly correct. A matador must stand alone, and whatever was right for the occasion, that must be done.

The big bull faced García's pic bravely. García determined to break it so that it should not be dangerous when the time came for César to kill it, punished it without mercy. The crowd erupted into a frenzy of angry whistles and shouted abuse. Pleased, César nodded to himself: their silence was reserved for himself alone. That was correct. García began to break the rules, inciting the bull's charge, putting the pic in the previous wound, and turning it savagely when it was in. César watched quietly until the fourth pic had been given. Let them shriek that García's mother was a wide-legged spyhilitic whore. To kill this bull correctly, it had to have four pics.

The trumpet, and the *banderillas*. Ruiz nearly got caught in the armpit by the high horns. Gitano made a cowardly run and threw them at the bull, like darts. More catcalls and whistling from the people. Modesto approached from behind and a cushion sailed into the ring. César stirred impatiently. The animal wasn't as dangerous as that. The trumpet.

Gathering sword and *muleta* he left the *burladero* to the anxious whispering of José. 'Just give it three or four naturals to the left and then for God's sake kill it. You're not going to get an ear whatever you do, so murder it.'

Now he had to make the dedication. To whom? There had been no decision yet . . . He sighed with relief. The dedication of each matador's first bull was settled by custom – the *brindis* had to be made to the president of the *corrida*.

He began his *faena*. As he had expected, the bull was striking lower, especially on the ripostes. He gave it a series of low righthanded punishing passes to test its reactions, once turning it so sharply that its forelegs buckled. It got up quickly, and stood watching him from ten feet away. He had been too severe. He might have caused the animal to damage a tendon, with that great weight turning so suddenly. He would make some atonement by giving it four low, slow naturals on the dangerous side. . . . It was a pity the crowd could not acknowledge by their applause that they knew what he was doing, because of their vow of silence; but they did know. He must always remember that.

The horn ripped his jacket as the bull passed, momentarily upsetting his balance. He cursed silently, because his feet had been well placed but the twist imparted by the horn had dragged the bull's bloody shoulder across his stomach and chest, and it might look as though he had deliberately leaned in, after the horn had passed, to fake the effect. The crowd would know. They knew everything. He would do it again, giving the cloth another two inches of arm this time, to allow for the bull also having learned something.

Again; and the next float the hands high and present to the people in the sun one of the great emotions of the *corrida*, a moment when the bull's massive forepart struck upwards at the floating cloth, so that he seemed to be a lunging two-legged monster, brother to the matador so close beside him.

He fixed the bull, a little outside its favourite place, with another short series of naturals and a chest pass, and drew the sword from the shelter of the cloth, making ready to kill. He listened for the crowd's disapproval. Not yet, they would shout. They always did, however long and beautiful the *faena* had been. There was only silence. Very well.

He must give the bull plenty of room, for it hooked to the right and he must go in over the right horn. It stood in the edge of the crescent of sunlight, facing the sun. Perhaps it could not see too well. César moved slowly round it till it was he who faced the sun, the bull turning heavily with him. One of the *banderillas* had fallen out, the other five hung down and to the left, so the bull could not see them or be distracted by them even from the corner of his vision. The pic wounds gaped wide, and oozed blood in slow, thick pulses. Its left forefoot was six inches back from its right.

César raised the blade and sighted carefully along it. With his left hand he gently moved the *muleta* down and across his body. The bull brought its left foot forward to stand four square to the cloth, head down. César began to lean forward, bending the left knee, pointing the toe to take the weight, and then, just as his continued forward lean down the line of the sword blade would have overbalanced him, he plunged in high over the horns.

He felt a heavy crash and found himself in the air, his sword

314

hand empty, the *muleta* still tight held in his left. There was no sound. In a goring two things came almost together – from inside, the shock of the horn, soundless, painless, and incredibly heavy, like a locomotive or a brick wall, so that the whole body seemed to gasp; from outside, the gasp and roar of the people. This time there was no sound.

Another, lesser shock, and his hands and knees scrabbled in the sand. He fought for breath, and the bull was not on him. Bright capes dragged and turned somewhere to the right. José and another man were beside him, arms under his armpits.

He stood up unsteadily. The bull had not changed its position. The sword was in about half-way, a little too far back. In his determination to get over the high horns he had stretched too far.

'Did I get the point? Am I gored?' he asked José. His ribs had begun to hurt intolerably and his breath burned as he dragged it into his lungs.

'We don't know. Quick, *maestro*, to the infirmary . . .'

He looked down, felt his side, and looked at his hand. No blood, except what had passed from the bull to him in the earlier series of passes. José cried, 'Quick, César, you may have an internal injury.'

Perhaps, he thought. It felt like it. The bull must have raised its head suddenly as the sword entered, and tossed him with the round curve of the horn. It hurt badly now. Now he could get out of the ring and the city without more ado. Just fall again to the sand. Nothing difficult about that. If he let go of himself for an instant, for a moment relaxed the tension holding him together he would drop.

He pushed the men aside and walked to the barrier. Slowly José fetched another scabbard and held it out to him, cursing and pleading all the while. The crowd had made never a murmur.

César went back to the bull. Hooking the point of the new sword into the hilt of the one that was already in the bull's shoulders he jerked it out, sending it flying towards the centre of the ring. Then he lined up for another *estocada*, and this time, though he did not kill, he went in to the hilt, and in the right place. Two attempts with the *descabello* and the bull dropped.

Not a sound. It had probably been worth an ear, with that

315

animal; but the people were silent, though they knew everything. In the *callejón* José said, 'Now we will have that side of yours seen to . . .'

His family were on their feet, looking down at him with anxious faces. He said, 'It's nothing serious. Don't come.' He smiled at Kit, and before he turned away she had found a smile to answer him.

Escobar passed. 'Don't exert yourself to come back, César,' he said, 'I will be glad to take your second bull.'

César let José lead him away. He might faint if he stood about any more. It would be wrong to let the 'perfect' Martos go to Escobar when the people were waiting for the twenty minutes of judgement, to see what kind of man this was, who stole the Armlet and spat in the Saint's face. Also he would be running away from the dedication, and running away did not produce an answer. He'd found that out, at least.

The doctor in the infirmary was Juan Bolanos, an earnest young man whom César had known all his life. While the attendants stripped off the coat of César's suit of lights, and his shirt, José talked rapidly in an undertone to the doctor. César lay down on the operating table and the doctor came and peered at him, his glasses shining. The smell of ether was overpoweringly unpleasant and through the open door he could hear the surge and roar of the crowd. Escobar had luck today. He had only to avoid actually disgracing himself for the crowd to burst, now. The doctor's hands felt, tapped, kneaded.

'You have severe external contusion across the lower ribs on the right, here,' he said. 'One may be broken, perhaps two . . . Internal injuries are possible. We will not be able to make a prognosis on that for an hour or two yet, and after X-rays. No more fighting for you today, César.'

César looked up, smiling faintly. Juan was a *very* earnest young man, full of the honour of his profession. César said, 'Juan, you put some arnica on that bruise and bandage it tight.'

The doctor said, 'You shouldn't risk it.'

'You don't think there's anything wrong with me,' César said. 'Not really. Do you? Come on now.'

The doctor shrugged and did not answer. José burst out, 'For God's sake, man, stop acting like a tenth-rate Don Quixote – he's dead!'

'Get a move on, Juan,' César said.

The doctor bent to his work without another word. César lay

back and closed his eyes. He should be out there making the third *quite* for Escobar.

When he returned he must find a way to make the people respond. They were his people, and they should applaud him and shriek at him, and kill him if they wanted to, but not sit there holding in their emotion.

It was too cool and antiseptic in here. The sun had almost left the arena by now, but the colours would be bright still, and the harsh sand firm under his feet.

The doctor's voice was suddenly sharp – 'No visitors allowed in here, madame.'

'I must see him.'

César opened his eyes. Marcia Arocha was at the door, the attendants trying to bar her entry. 'Let her come,' he said, and lay back.

Marcia stepped quickly to his side and put her hand on his head. 'You are not going to fight the second, are you, *cariño mío?*'

Cariño mío. Their first year, the beach in the Galician cove, days in the salt wind and the perfume of her body at night, feats of sexual activity done between lust and laughter, going to sleep, knocked out, in her arms and her whispering and smiling over him. It was a word she had never used before where anyone else could hear it.

He said, 'The brute only bruised me.'

He noticed that she kept her voice warm and full of the past. 'Ah, don't be silly. I'll take you home . . . Escobar is anxious to fight to the last . . . It's all round the crowd.'

Marcia pleaded, the doctor went on working there a few inches away, José puffed furiously at a black cigarette in the corner, and they were all farther away than the crowd outside.

He shook his head and her voice became harsh. 'You mustn't! I . . . I had a dream. The second bull will kill you.'

'This is encouraging talk to give a matador, isn't it,' he said lightly.

'But it's true,' she said wildly. 'I did!'

José cut in. 'Go on. Tell him.'

Marcia said, 'Very well . . . That's true, but it isn't the only thing. Don't you realise that the people are waiting for you?'

'They don't make a sound when I'm in the ring,' he said.

'Because they're waiting for you. They're going to kill you.'

He thought about it slowly. It was possible. It was probable.

317

She hurried on. 'It's the funeral over again,' she said urgently. 'Then it was the Americans marching in to dare them. Now it's you. But you're not like the old American couple. Nothing will stop them this time.'

The bandaging was finished. He sat up and swung his legs over the edge of the table. 'My shirt, José.'

'Don't go back!' she cried. 'Leave now! I'll tell her to slip out and join you and you can be in France by nightfall.'

'I don't know,' César said. 'My jacket, José.'

'Are you going to stay then? I knew you would!'

'I don't know,' César said. 'I just don't know yet.'

He walked out, into the passage, into the *callejón* and the light and the roar of the arena.

Death on the horns of the perfect bull. *Muy español. Muy torero.* One could avoid it, if forewarned, by doing nothing that would bring death within striking distance. With a perfect bull, that distance could be measured to an inch. By the people, also. If he did not put himself within reach of death from the bull, which was the soul of the *fiesta brava*, they would themselves assume the part of the bull, and their response could not be measured to the inch.

The question was academic, because if the bull turned out to be as good as they said he would have no choice but to match its perfection, which meant living inside that inch for twenty minutes, and in that small space and time building a structure of such grace that no one who saw it would ever forget it.

A hush lay thick in the arena as the people waited for the fifth bull, Miranda's second, to come out of the pen. It charged out and Ruiz told him Escobar had been awarded two ears. César leaned over the barrier and watched the testing of Miranda's bull. He was impatient to get into the ring, for stiffness was setting in across his chest. It would be a disgraceful thing to fail his bull because of physical incapacity. He thought about taking a Benzedrine; but that would be wrong, too.

His turn came to make the *quite*, and he went out quickly. The bull was sharp to turn and follow, and with enough energy and lightness to take a series of *gaoneras*, when he had got it far enough away from the horse. They came off perfectly.

And absolute silence. Marcia was right. If this silence lasted to the end they would come over the barrier, still in silence, and kill him.

Miranda had decided to put in his *banderillas* himself, and time was running out. He stole a look at Kit. In five, six minutes he would not be able to look at her again. He remembered the first time he had seen her, in that same place. It would be romantic and pleasing to pretend to himself that he had fallen in love with her that moment – but it would be silly. All pretence was worthless. No, she had been a blonde American with innocent bedroom eyes and a good body. Where, exactly, he realized what she meant and could mean to him it was hard to say. But it was certain that now she meant everything that was embodied in their American aim, life, liberty, and the pursuit of happiness.

She was watching Miranda, who had finished the *banderillas* and was making his dedication to a woman in Section 2, at the end throwing his *montera* up to her with a graceful gesture.

César turned and watched Miranda's bull die, messily, and Miranda leaving the ring under a volley of whistles and cries and then the dead bull behind the galloping mules. Its right horn ploughed a deep furrow in the sand and one of the servants rushed along like Charlie Chaplin behind it, levelling it off with a rake.

He took his place behind a *burladero*, cape in hand, and stared intently at the low doors of the bull pen, and waited for the trumpet. The silence spread out from him, round the circle of the arena, and the tiers of stone, to the arches and the sky.

The trumpet sounded and the doors of the bull pen swung back.

The bull came out of the pen at half gallop, head carried straight and high, the hump of fighting muscle spread evenly across its shoulders. On the instant the arena slammed to its feet with a single gigantic gasp. The roar rose, passed like a squadron of jet bombers, and died. Silence again.

César ran out at once on to the sand and dropped to his knees. The bull gave immediate and full response. The head came up so that he could see better, and his horns were wide, bone-white with black tips, the last ten inches pointing straight forward. Like a tank suddenly accelerating, his hind parts sank under his effort and the powerful forelegs pulled at the sand. In two strides he reached full speed, running wide-legged yet light as a tiger on small hoofs, head high, tail streaming straight out and sand jerking up in clots behind. At six feet from César his head dropped and César began the *larga cambiada*, whirling the cerise and yellow round his head in a huge billow. The bull whirled with it, the cloth rippled over his back and down. He turned fast, and caught sight of Ruiz near the barrier. César gathered his cape and walked to the barrier, watching.

Ruiz runs on a diagonal across the arena, trailing his cape. The bull's head drops at six feet, and in a single movement he stabs at the flying cape with his left horn, leaping high in the air, an explosive snort of air forced out of his nostrils by the effort. Ruiz hurls himself headfirst over the barrier to safety. The bull turns like a cat and rams his right horn into the wood.

Gitano is in the ring now, running now, running on the opposite diagonal. The bull used the right horn for the stab at Ruiz; now with Gitano, on the other diagonal, he duplicates exactly the charge and thrust of the first time, but transposed, so that he strikes with the right horn in the preliminary attack and with the left at the barrier, where Gitano has reached shelter.

He turns in the direction of the horn he has used, both times; but that might be merely an accident of position.

Modesto cites head on from a few feet in front of the barrier, and the bull goes straight at him. Modesto drags the cape far to the left and the bull follows. Modesto takes cover quickly. Good, no more stabbing into the wood, or we might damage those wonderful horns that must be given a chance to kill me.

César walked into the ring, his cape folded. The second and third times, just now, the bull had broken into the full charge, at ten paces from the target. César estimated twelve paces. spread the cape, took two more steps, and anchored his feet. Fired from a cannon, the full shot forward. *Verónica* to the right. Another. Another. Half-*verónica*. Walk slowly to another section of the ring and begin again.

The bull fights in every section with the same fury, and in the middle, and near the barrier.

César twined cape and bull round him in a final *chicuelina*, unwound the cape, folded it over his arm, and made his way to a *burladero*. The bull watched him and the trumpets sounded. Time hurried on, in silence.

Gordito and García come in on their blindfolded quilt-swathed nags, lances high, Gordito for work, García in reserve. The crowd bursts into a crashing roar of anger.

It's all there, ready to explode, he thought. Exactly like the
320

funeral. He examined the bull carefully. Two pics, at least, he must have, though he could take more. He must come strong to death, yet he must feel the weight of the horse on his horns, and feel his strength rebuilding his pride.

The crowd whistles furiously, and everyone is on his feet.

César got behind Gordito and called over the barrier, 'By the rules!'

Gordito is in position, and Escobar on the flank ready to make the *quite*, and Ruiz is there, and the man with the switch is having no difficulty in keeping the horse steady. Gitano brings the bull slowly across the ring, making his move, but each time backing off before he charges, hiding horse and man from the bull behind the widespread cape. Gordito settles himself squarely in the saddle and pushes the lance out and ready across the horse's withers. The bull comes on behind the swirl of Gitano's cape. Twelve paces. Eight. Six. Gitano lets his cape fall into a slim line and stands aside.

The bull sees the horse. His hindquarters dig in, his head goes down and his forelegs lever out the sand, at full speed he pulls rather than pushes himself towards the horse and the thick point of the waiting lance. He charges on to the lance, forces remorselessly on until his heavy horns, both together, strike the horse in the quilted belly, low down. Gordito holds his position steadily, moving not an inch, giving the bull nothing, sparing nothing. It is not he who forces the lance point into the bull's shoulders, but the bull himself, by the obstinate fury of his perseverance against the horse. The bull tilts his head to the right and lifts horse and rider off the ground with his left horn, thrusting against the steady pressure of four inches of steel in his shoulders.

The bull backs off a moment, only to come in harder with the other horn. The hump of his fighting muscles rises in a huge knot. The horse rises in the air, all four legs out stiff as poles, Gordito in the saddle, the lance in the wound, the bull still pressing forward. Higher and higher, in slow motion, till Gordito and the horse's legs are parellel to the ground, the whole impossible tableau held together by the lance in the bull and the horns in the horse. Slowly the bull lifts higher and with a final heave throws horse and rider over his back. The tableau collapses in a clanging of leg armour and creak of saddlery and splintering of wood. Gordito falls far out on the sand, the horse across the bull's quarters, and the bull rises like a monster from the ruins, plunging down now on to Gordito. Escobar is

321

there, sweating fear, and at once the bull follows the cape. Two lightning hooks and he is in the centre of the ring.

Once more the whole process in another section of the ring, exactly by the rules. This time the bull rams his horn through Gordito's steel leg armour, breaking his shin-bone. He is carried off, grinning. 'By the rules, by God, we did it!'

The people are on their feet, stamping and roaring. The bull carries his head lower, but he is full of pride. Ruiz is at César's side screaming to make himself heard, 'Do you want to put them in yourself?'

César shook his head. Any other matador; himself, any other day; but the people were making a continuous thunder of noise and if he went out with the *banderillas* there would be a silence, twice as loud.

Ruiz takes the first pair. César has said nothing to him, but Ruiz knows. There are moments when anyone knows, and Ruiz has been in the ring for eighteen years. The first pair perfectly placed. Gitano's make two, and Modesto completed the fan.

The trumpet sounded. Like the black-and-white bull straining out of the *toril*, the decision came upon him, fully formed. Near the centre of the ring the good bull stood square to the president's box, head forward. The people waited, all standing in silence.

Life, liberty, the pursuit of happiness. Kit, her hands grasping the railing.

Death, discipline, the acceptance of sorrow. His people surrounding him.

He had hoped that the two would mate and from their union would come a compromise. But there could be no mating, for those ideas were not mare and stallion running free in an empty plain, but twins born at the same time from man's earliest consciousness, and ever since harnessed side by side as the lead horses of man's slow progress to his unknown destination, for ever separate, for ever pulling together.

From a little beyond the centre of the arena, where the bull waited, a man standing upright on his feet could see the sword-cross of San Marco on the top of the cathedral dome, rising out of the topmost arches of the *plaza de toros*. César walked steadily to the place, sword and *muleta* gathered in his left hand. Then he took off his *montera* and held it out at arm's length to the cross, arching his back and pressing forward his loins in the correct way. For a long moment he held out his arm

322

while the bull watched him, then he dropped his *montera* to the sand, and shook out the folds of the red cloth. The bull steadied himself for the fight. The sunlight had left the farthest reaches of the sand and only a small segment of the stands at the top of Sections 6 and 7 were bright. Everywhere else the colours were becoming dull, and César saw that the people were edging steadily downwards so that the forward places and the aisles between were packed with them. He began his *faena,* the ceremonial and virtuoso preparation for death, the matador's cadenza.

At the first punishing pass he turned the bull fast, as he had with his first, and, like that one, it fell to its knees, A tremendous roar of anger crashed over him. Whistles and shrieks dinned in his ears and volleys of cushions sailed out on the sand. The voices rose, screaming, 'No, no!'

César stepped back three paces slowly. The noise jerked at him with the sensation that the people were a single angry giant, viciously rubbing him in an ice-cold, rough towel. He felt strength surging into his legs, and stood a moment drawing deep breaths into his lungs. The dam had been broken.

He was now very conscious that he had long ago taken for himself the name of *El Rondeño.* To fight in the manner of Ronda meant to fight with absolute simplicity and no adornment; to keep the feet planted, but not stiffly; to bend the body low and slow; to make no exaggeration, flourish, or trickery; to kill honestly, in danger. He had tried, in a hundred *corridas* and by conscious effort, to live up to these ideals; now he must forget them, and be himself, and let the Ronda purity come if he possessed it. He approached the bull once more, and again began his *faena.*

The bull, and the cloth and the sword, and his body, began to move of their own accord. Soon he was lost in the centre of a fluid architecture of foam and silver and scarlet, its outlines prescribed by the circles of sand and people and stone. Naturals to right and left flowed into *molinetes,* to *afarolados,* and a series of *manoletinas,* and those into *arrucinas,* and those into six passes of death. He never dropped to his knees, or looked at the crowd, but worked within himself, and after five minutes wove the bull into tighter and tighter curves with his naturals, left it standing and exposed the sword.

He was wet with sweat and now for the first time since the second beginning of the *faena* heard the rolling thunder of the crowd. Since it seemed familiar in his ears, it must have been going on all the time. The band blared out his own favourite among all bullfight pasodobles, 'El Gato Montés.'

César approached the bull. The trumpets and drums became silent and the crowd with them. The distance from which the bull charged had shortened as it tired, until now it would not launch into the full charge from farther than five paces. César advanced slowly upon it, in full silence. At seven paces he shook out the *muleta* and held it in his left hand, well spread and as far down and to the right of his body as he could make it go. He raised the sword and sighted in profile over the horns. He began to pace forward, still in profile, the sword sighted, the bull's head sinking lower as he came. At the third pace he gave the *muleta* a single imperative jerk, without breaking his slow stride. The bull charged, and César broke into a swooping run, and plunged over the horn. Each took two paces, and met. César ran on, the sword gone, his hand rising of its own volition. He stopped and turned, hand raised. The bull lay on its nose on the sand, the hilt of the *estoque* starring its back, its head flat, the mouth that had never opened throughout the fight still tight shut, dead.

For a moment César stood while the voice of the people broke and came together, cracked like thunder, and rolled and reverberated around the arena. His *montera* lay at his feet. He picked it up, held it in his hand, and bowed automatically towards the distant cathedral and the invisible Saint to whom he had dedicated the bull.

They were running towards him across the sand and he must wait for them. The decisions came fast and firm upon him. This must be his last *corrida*. They were raising him up on their shoulders, but he must humble himself. Escobar was there with peons and ring servants. They were hacking off the bull's ears and tail and one hoof with blunt knives, and weeping. The breeder of the Martos bulls was being carried round, also weeping; then round and round the arena the mules dragged the dead bull at full gallop, whips cracking and the muleteers yelling, and all the while the voice of the crowd rolling in rhythmic thunder. The man from Saldavega was on his feet screaming, '*Al encuentro! Al encuentro!*'

For the first time since the *faena* César looked for his own family. They were not there. The weary smile was fixed on his face as he bounced along on the shoulders of the screaming mob, and he was hurling the ears and tail and the hoofs out to them; but Kit was not there, nor Bel, nor his mother. It was unbelievable that they should have left at such a moment. He shouted, 'Let me down!' but they rushed on, yelling, through a storm of leather bottles and flowers and purses of money. Then he saw his mother and Bel hurrying up an aisle among the crowd, and in front of them the broad back of Pete Olmbacher carrying a woman in his arms. Kit. The crowd closed up behind them then, and he saw a few people staring after the little procession hurrying towards the infirmary.

Minutes later he succeeded in struggling down from the shoulders, and ran to the infirmary.

She was sitting in a hard chair when he got there, his mother supporting her and the doctor standing aside with a half-full glass in his hand, and Pete and Bel watching anxiously. She began to cough and slowly raised her head.

'Sorry,' she whispered to Doña Teresa. 'I'm feeling much better now.'

'Lie down a moment,' the doctor said. They helped her on to the operating table, and she lay back and closed her eyes. She had not seen César yet. Doña Teresa took his arm and made a silent gesture towards the door. He nodded and followed her.

Her voice behind him called, 'César.'

He turned in the doorway. The doctor said, 'You must just lie quiet for a bit now, señorita.'

She said, 'Leave us alone, please . . .'

The doctor began to speak, but Doña Teresa said firmly, 'Come away, doctor. Pedro, Bel, you too. We'll be outside, my son.'

They were alone and he went to the edge of the bare table where she lay. Her hand rose and touched the brocaded jacket, thick with sweat and dust and blood. She whispered, 'Just after you killed . . . I knew I was going to faint. I tried so hard not to . . . And after it had begun . . . when I couldn't stop going and couldn't come back, I heard a voice, an American, saying, "If they can't stand the sight of blood, why do they come?"' She smiled weakly up at him and he ran his hand gently through her hair and laid it on her forehead. It was still cold and damp, but a little warmth was coming into it and the colour flowing back into her skin.

She took his hand in both her own and held it gently at her throat, where it rested. 'What are you going to do now, César?'

He hesitated, for in the moments after the bull died and before the crowd reached him, the primary choice had flowered into new decisions. He had known he must humble himself in penance for the past, and how he must do it; and he had known he must rededicate his life for the future, and how he must do it. But she was not Spanish, and she was exhausted. Perhaps he should wait till she was stronger to tell her.

But the hazel eyes were on his and warm and steady. He said, 'You walked through the city one night, alone . . . I shall pray the dean to allow me to guard the Armlet, alone, fasting in vigil, from tonight till Sunday night, and every Feast of San Marco the same, until I die, and after I die I shall leave money so that Holy Church can pay a man to do it in my memory, so that the people shall always remember who stole the Armlet and why.'

She nodded and he said, 'I shall encourage the *fiesta brava*, but I myself will not fight the bulls again, nor go with the Gentlemen of Covadonga. I think I can do more, in better ways, for what I believe in . . . My father's last wish was that I should become mayor of Medina . . . I am ready to serve.'

She slid carefully from the table, his arm supporting her. It was very wonderful to know that she would not do or say anything to debase what was between them. Nor was there any need to talk to her of renunciation, for it was not his strength but hers that had brought him finally to this place. The only thing that hurt now was that he would never be able to show her, in his life, how much he loved her. He bowed his head and kissed her hair, while her forehead rested against the soiled brocade of his jacket.

There was absolutely nothing to say, because it had been said in another way, older and stronger than language. He tilted up her chin and kissed her on the lips. They were warm and sweet, gently open, and strong. Then, as she stood alone in the middle of the antiseptic-smelling infirmary, her eyes closed and her head raised, he left her.

CHAPTER 33

Bill Lockman slowed his car and stuck his head out of the window. The white-helmeted traffic policeman who had stopped him, there at the end of the Puente Nuevo, saluted and spoke rapidly in Spanish. Seeing that Bill did not understand, he pointed south along the Calle García, and said in a loud voice, 'Zaragoza, Huesca, Lérida, Madrid, Barcelona, Paris, Nueva York ...' Then he waved his hand towards the Mercado, the Paseo, and the cathedral, and bawled, 'Midtown, no goddamn auto*mob*iles. Park!'

Bill grinned and said, 'O.K. I'm for midtown,' and parked the Ford among the hopeless tangle of a hundred other cars blocking the street ahead. Hatless, he began to walk slowly into the city, into a noise that seemed to have no centre, but, like an ocean, simply was, its waves battering themselves into final silence somewhere out on the Llano Triste behind him.

The mercado was full of noise, the people stirring it up and swimming in it rather than making it. A huge bonfire blazed in the middle, and rockets and fire crackers exploded with furious irregularity on the wasteland beyond. The six-foot bamboo sticks from which the rockets had been fired rained down impartially from the crackling sky, clattering on the roof-tops or falling with a sudden whistle and a whizz among the people like flaming spears.

One, two, three bands here alone. One local brass band playing pasodobles, tangos, and Sousa marches; a *jota* group with guitars and accordions; most of the Medina Cowboys in plain clothes, marching round and round. Kids dancing the jitterbug over there, others the *jota* here, older people foxtrotting, all among a mob simply yelling at the tops of their voices. A wine bottle was being thrust at him. He drank. Above them the statue of Luis Barrena, *muleta* extended, gave some shelter from the falling bamboo poles.

After a time he worked his way slowly across the Plaza and up the Calle de Jaca. The noise must surely lessen as he got away from the Mercado. But it didn't. Nearly thirty-six hours of it now, he thought, starting at noon on Saturday, and this was late Sunday evening. And before that they'd had the bullfight and then the four-hour religious procession. Their stamina and vitality were frightening. He was tired already, after a quarter of an hour.

In the Calle Goya shrieking voices descended on him, jerking him out of his reverie. He jumped to the sidewalk and six young men flashed by, running at full speed down the middle of the street. The one in front wore a wide red ribbon round his forehead, and the next a black ribbon. All the people were yelling, 'Negro! Negro!' or 'Rojo! Rojo!' Somewhere down the street the race ended and wine bottles were passed round. Six more young men thundered by.

Bill passed the dense group at the finish, and drank from two bottles. Flowers began to pelt him from both sides. He broke into a run, scurrying between rows of girls as they hurled the flowers at each other across the street. The flowers lay inches deep on the cobbles . . . He came upon young men wrestling. A flower had fallen down the front of his shirt. A red carnation. He pulled it out and stuck it behind his ear, and a pretty girl kissed him. The street was full of young men dancing, and the thud of drums.

He turned into the Calle Arenas. It was full of huge heads – of blackamoors, and monsters, and one-eyed ogres. They lurched down the street above human legs and torsos that were grotesquely small under them. A band of five men wove in and out among them, each man playing with one hand a drum strapped to his left side and with the other a piercing wooden pipe. The ogres were painted mainly black and red, and as they came bobbing and turning they were followed by a horde of shrieking dancing children. The ogres would turn suddenly and rush at the children, or at the crowds to the side, and the children hurled themselves away in paroxysms of genuine terror every time; and a moment later were again dancing and skipping forward in equally genuine joy.

Behind the grotesque heads came giants, and a brass band playing a slow march. There were ten giants, each twelve feet tall, two of them wearing crowns, the paint cracked and chipped on all their beatific wooden faces and the real cloth of their robes fluttering as they glided on, turned, bowed to each other, made a stately dance, and came on again.

He turned up Alcalde. Ham Fremantle was kneeling in the middle of the road, taking flash photos. Peggy stood on the edge of the sidewalk calling to him, 'Oh come on, Hamilton! Everyone's staring at you.'

Ham rose from his knee and hurried out of the way. 'Hi,

there!' he called, seeing Bill. 'What a spectacle!' He felt in his pockets for another bulb.

'Seen Kit?'

Bill said, 'No.'

Ham said, 'She's around. I think she's doing something for Doña Teresa at the Diputación.'

They parted. Bill wandered on past the Ayuntamiento into the Plaza San Marco. It was full of people, dancing, singing, and wandering around in groups. Half a dozen well-dressed ladies and two priests were gathered on the steps of the cathedral beside several big piles of clothing. Straggly lines of old men and women hobbled up to receive gifts – a shirt here, two pairs of socks there, a pullover to the next one. Doña Teresa and Bel de Aguirre were among the ladies distributing the gifts, and Bill watched, wondering and admiring.

He thought suddenly that he would go into the cathedral and stand or perhaps even kneel beside César for a time. That was a hell of a load to carry, entirely alone, and someone just being there might help, even though you hated the guy's guts. But he remembered hearing that César had left at sunset. It was too late; and in the strange atmosphere of Medina these days, it was quite possible that César would know his intention without any other word or action.

If Bel's up there on the steps, he thought, Pete Olmbacher won't be far away. Looking around, he soon saw him, leaning quietly against the plinth of the Bull, his eyes fixed on Bel where she worked with her mother. Bill went over and greeted him. Olmbacher stood upright with a grin. 'Good evening, Captain. How are your eardrums?'

'Shot.'

The sergeant said, 'Man, when are they going to run out of rockets?'

An extra sound was growing into existence behind and above the bands, the explosions, the rockets, the guitars and castanets and full-throated singing.

Bill looked up and Olmbacher said, 'Mission Dog Fox, coming in . . .'

'Through the rockets' red glare,' Bill said. 'They'll think the Spaniards don't really love us, after all.'

The landing lights of a B-52 suddenly shone out above the houses to the north-west over the bull-ring, and swept low and slow across the sky. In the city the noise increased as the mechanical scream of the jet motors blended into the man-made substance of sound below. In the Plaza some looked up, some took no notice.

Bill saw her then, coming down the Calle Zurbarán. She walked like the queen of the city, and as she came on the dancers and singers made way for her, and a young man gave a flower into her hand. There was a half smile on her face and she looked so tired, so lovely, and so rich in herself that Bill caught his breath in sudden leaping joy.

She would pass close. He moved forward to meet her.

Pete Olmbacher's hand fell on his arm and held him firmly back. 'Wait, Captain.'

Heart of War

by John Masters

January 1 1916: Europe is bleeding to death as the corpses rot from Poland to Gallipoli in the cruel grip of the Great War ...

HEART OF WAR
– follows the fate and fortunes of the Rowland family and those people bound up in their lives, the Cate squirearchy, the Strattons who manage the Rowland-owned factory, and the humble, multi-talented Gorse family.

HEART OF WAR
– during the years 1916 and 1917, the appalling slaughter of the Somme and Passchendaele cuts deep into the hearts of the British people as military conscription looms over Britain for the first time in a thousand years.

HEART OF WAR
– is the second self-contained volume in a trilogy entitled LOSS OF EDEN. It is probably the crowning achievement in the long and distinguished career of one of our leading contemporary novelists.

GENERAL FICTION   0 7221 0467 7   £1.95

And, also by John Masters in Sphere Books:
NOW, GOD BE THANKED
NIGHTRUNNERS OF BENGAL
THE FIELD-MARSHAL'S MEMOIRS
FANDANGO ROCK
THE HIMALAYAN CONCERTO

By the Green of the Spring

JOHN MASTERS

1918 dawns desolate over the fields of Flanders. Decimated by the worst war the world has ever seen, neither British nor German troops can break the deadlock of the trenches. After four years of murderous stalemate, peace seems buried for ever. But finally, one by one, the guns fall silent . . .

BY THE GREEN OF THE SPRING
relives the last terrible months of the Great War and the uneasy, exhausted peace which followed it.

BY THE GREEN OF THE SPRING
from the North-West Frontier to the war in France and the civil war in Ireland, John Masters follows the fortunes of four Kent families – the Cates, the Rowlands, the Strattons and the Gorses – through the cataclysm that ended the golden Edwardian dream for ever.

BY THE GREEN OF THE SPRING
is the third, self-contained volume of the **LOSS OF EDEN** trilogy, a magnificent conclusion to an enthralling epic of war and peace by a major contemporary novelist.

GENERAL FICTION   0 7221 0468 5   £2.50

The heroic and unforgettable saga of one man's rise to military glory

Man of War

JOHN MASTERS

Bestselling author of THE LOSS OF EDEN trilogy

Captain Bill Miller is a modern MAN OF WAR.

This is his story – a huge, enthralling adventure of a soldier of our times, living and fighting through most of the major battles of this century.

Miller's career spans both World Wars and half the globe; from the General Strike and Indian Independence, to the Spanish Civil War and Dunkirk . . . For over twenty years, the unorthodox son of a shopkeeper learns his craft against the explosive panorama of international history. And there are other hostilities to suffer too – two marriages lost to ambition and dedication; alienation from fellow soldiers for his tactical part in Franco's victory. Whatever the price, Miller paid in full, for those moments of glory on the beaches of Dunkirk . . .

A monumental epitaph to a bestselling, masterly genius, MAN OF WAR is the last great story from the major war writer, the novel that only John Masters could write.

'Brilliant . . . packed with pace and detail . . . a splendid storyteller and a master at describing battles and campaigns.' *Daily Telegraph.*

FICTION   0 7221 5877 7   £2.50

Don't miss other John Masters classics, also in Sphere paperback:

FANDANGO ROCK
THE DECEIVERS
BHOWANI JUNCTION
NIGHTRUNNERS OF BENGAL
THE HIMALAYAN CONCERTO

THE FIELD MARSHAL'S MEMOIRS
NOW, GOD BE THANKED
HEART OF WAR
BY THE GREEN OF THE SPRING

The explosive new thriller of World War II's most baffling enigma

THE JUDAS CODE
DEREK LAMBERT

Bestselling author of I, SAID THE SPY

A journalist advertises for information about the key to the Judas Code. An elderly gentleman turns up at his flat and threatens to kill him. But the journalist nevertheless manages to meet someone who tells him the story . . .

Hitler, Churchill and Stalin are all involved in a tale of intrigue and double-cross on an unrivalled scale. A young Czech in neutral Lisbon, a British intelligence agent operative of very divided loyalties and a beautiful Jewess are all manipulated by a master planner, in a breathtaking scheme to propel Russia and Germany into conflict, buying the Allies the most precious commodity of all: time.

'Mr. Lambert is ... . very informed about the known facts of the war into which he weaves his fantasy.' *Daily Telegraph*.

'Lambert certainly keeps the action moving.' *Liverpool Daily Post*.

FICTION/ADVENTURE THRILLER   0 7221 5350 3   £2.25

The Queen's Messenger

ROBERT L. DUNCAN

At Hong Kong airport, the unthinkable happens. A Queen's Messenger, a highly trusted diplomatic courier, goes missing – and with him, a key dispatch from a top-secret Western intelligence source, deep in the Communist-infested jungles of Thailand.

Only Gordon Clive of MI6 can track down the missing man and prevent fatal damage to Britain's South-East Asian network. But the stakes are appallingly high. For Clive's deadly quest for the Queen's Messenger will bring him face to face not only with the cold-blooded torturers and assassins of the KGB, but with the raging demons of his own tormented past . .

THE QUEEN'S MESSENGER
'Thrilling and chilling,
the properties of the best Ambler'
The Observer

ADVENTURE/THRILLER   0 7221 3108 9   £1.95

A selection of bestsellers from SPHERE

FICTION

CHANGES	Danielle Steel	£1.95 □
FEVRE DREAM	George R. R. Martin	£2.25 □
LADY OF FORTUNE	Graham Masterton	£2.75 □
THE JUDAS CODE	Derek Lambert	£2.25 □
FIREFOX DOWN	Craig Thomas	£2.25 □

FILM & TV TIE-INS

THE DUNE STORYBOOK	Joan Vinge	£2.50 □
ONCE UPON A TIME IN AMERICA	Lee Hays	£1.75 □
MORGAN'S BOY	Alick Rowe	£1.95 □
MINDER – BACK AGAIN	Anthony Masters	£1.50 □

NON-FICTION

BACHELOR BOYS – THE YOUNG ONES' BOOK	Rik Mayall, Ben Elton & Lise Mayer	£2.95 □
THE COMPLETE HANDBOOK OF PREGNANCY	Wendy Rose-Neil	£5.95 □
THE STORY OF THE SHADOWS	Mike Read	£2.95 □
THE HYPOCHONDRIAC'S HANDBOOK	Dr. Lee Schreiner and Dr. George Thomas	£1.50□

All Sphere books are available at your local bookshop or newsagent, or can be ordered direct from the publisher. Just tick the titles you want and fill in the form below.

Name_____

Address_____

_____

Write to Sphere Books, Cash Sales Department, P.O. Box 11, Falmouth, Cornwall TR10 9EN

Please enclose cheque or postal order to the value of the cover price plus:

UK: 55p for the first book, 22p for the second and 14p per copy for each additional book ordered to a maximum charge of £1.75.

OVERSEAS: £1.00 for the first book and 25p for each additional book.

BFPO & EIRE: 55p for the first book, 22p for the second book plus 14p per copy for the next 7 books, thereafter 8p per book.

Sphere Books reserve the right to show new retail prices on covers which may differ from those previously advertised in the text or elsewhere, and to increase postal rates in accordance with the PO.